UNCLE TOM'S
CHiLDREN

ALSO BY RICHARD WRIGHT

richard wright

UNCLE TOM'S CHILDREN

with an introduction by
RICHARD YARBOROUGH

THE RESTORED TEXT
ESTABLISHED BY THE LIBRARY OF AMERICA

HARPER**PERENNIAL** ● MODERN**CLASSICS**

NEW YORK ● LONDON ● TORONTO ● SYDNEY ● NEW DELHI ● AUCKLAND

HARPER**PERENNIAL** ● MODERN**CLASSICS**

A hardcover edition of *Uncle Tom's Children* was originally
published in 1940 by Harper & Brothers. A paperback edition
was published in 1965 by Perennial Library and reissued in 1989.
The text as restored by The Library of America was published in 1991
in a volume entitled *Richard Wright: Early Works*, which also included
Lawd Today! and *Native Son*.

P.S.™ is a trademark of HarperCollins Publishers.

HarperCollins books may be purchased for educational, business, or sales
promotional use. For information, please e-mail the Special Markets Depart-
ment at SPsales@harpercollins.com.

First HarperPerennial edition published 1993.

First Perennial edition published 2004.

First Harper Perennial Modern Classics edition published 2008.

Library of Congress Cataloging-in-Publication Data is available.

ISBN 978-0-06-145020-4

18 RRD 20 19 18 17 16 15 14 13

ARNOLD RAMPERSAD
WROTE THE NOTES FOR THIS VOLUME

Contents

Introduction to the Perennial Edition

> *I hold that, in the last analysis, the artist must bow to the monitor of his own imagination; must be led by the sovereignty of his own impressions and perceptions; must be guided by the tyranny of what troubles and concerns him personally; and that he must learn to trust the impulse, vague and compulsive as it may be, which moves him in the first instance toward expression. There is no other true path, and the artist owes it to himself and to those who live and breathe with him to render unto reality that which is reality's.*
>
> —*Richard Wright to Antonio Frasconi, 1944*

In a 1939 article entitled "The Negro: 'New' or Newer," the black critic Alain Locke hailed the publication of Richard Wright's *Uncle Tom's Children* the previous year as "a well-merited literary launching for what must be watched as a major literary career. . . . With this, our Negro fiction of social interpretation comes of age."[1] Roughly a decade and a half earlier, Locke had heralded the advent of another dramatic watershed in the Afro-American literary tradition: the New Negro Movement, also known as the Harlem Renaissance. But this latter phenomenon had involved many black artists working in a wide range of fields. Accordingly, one might suspect that Locke's grand characterization of

[1]Alain Locke, "The Negro: 'New' or Newer: A Retrospective Review of the Literature of the Negro for 1938." *Opportunity* 17 (1939): 8.

Wright's relatively thin collection of four novellas may
have been tinged with nostalgia on his part after he had
witnessed the precipitous subsidence of white interest in
things black that followed the heady 1920s when, as
Langston Hughes put it, "the Negro was in vogue." We
are left with the question: Did *Uncle Tom's Children*
truly merit Locke's rich praise?

With the hindsight of over half a century, we must
answer "yes." Indeed, the confidence with which one
would respond itself testifies to the tremendous impact
of Richard Wright's arrival on the American literary
landscape and the extent to which the aftershocks of his
work continue to be felt even today. His first published
book, *Uncle Tom's Children* marked the beginning of
what might be termed modern black "protest" litera-
ture; furthermore, at the time it constituted the most
unrelenting and rage-fueled critique of white racism
ever to surface in fiction written by blacks directed
toward a mainstream American readership. *Native Son*
aptly deserves acknowledgment as the most influential
African-American novel of the twentieth century. How-
ever, it was *Uncle Tom's Children* that brought Wright to
the attention of white critics and readers, many of
whom had never encountered a black text that so moved
and challenged them, thereby preparing the ground for
Native Son, the book that changed the course of Ameri-
can letters.

Born on September 4, 1908, to a schoolteacher and a
former sharecropper who soon deserted his family,
Rich rd Wright was raised by his mother and her rela-
tives in a South dominated at nearly every turn by racial
subordination. As his fellow author Margaret Walker
puts it, "The state of Mississippi, Adams County,
U.S.A., where Richard Wright was born, . . . was a

veritable hell."[2] The system of segregation known as Jim Crow had been in place since the late nineteenth century, and lynchings and other savage physical assaults on blacks were not uncommon in the decades before World War I. Although Wright was not above exaggerating the harshness of his life to make a political point, it is clear from his autobiography that his youth in the South was scarred by constant, brutal repression. In particular, Wright viewed the attempt by whites to break the spirits of Southern blacks, to make them complicitous in their own oppression, as perhaps the key racist imperative; and he resisted as doggedly as he could.

One form of both resistance and temporary escape for the young Wright was reading. Blessed with a vivid imagination, he found himself drawn early in life to books as well as to creative writing, in no small measure because both were forbidden to him. At home, his authoritarian maternal grandmother condemned fiction as sinful; and in his community, whites refused to permit blacks access to the public libraries. On the one hand, the story of how Wright as a young adult was able to borrow library books by pretending to be acting on behalf of a white employer demonstrates his ingenuity and stubbornness. On the other hand, it indicates the extent to which the Southern racist code consistently forced blacks to participate in a self-abnegating and degrading masquerade. If, as Wright felt quite strongly, many blacks were too often willing to accede to such humiliation, *he* would not do so if he could help it. For a young black man in the South with such a rebellious attitude, there were few viable options; flight was ultimately the one that Wright took.

[2]Margaret Walker, *Richard Wright: Daemonic Genius* (New York: Amistad-Warner, 1988), 13.

Wright left the South in late 1927 with a ninth-grade education and few marketable skills. To make matters worse, he had not been settled in Chicago long before the stock market crash of 1929 and the onset of the Great Depression. The low point for Wright during these years came when he was forced to apply to the Bureau of Public Welfare in order to take care of his mother and brother, who had joined him in the city. If such nightmarish experiences served to exacerbate Wright's growing disenchantment with the American economic system, his reading not only helped him to begin understanding his painful, confusing reality but also provided crucial models for meaningful self-expression.

One of the most significant of these early models was H. L. Mencken, whose books Wright had tracked down while living in Memphis in the mid-1920s after an editorial in a local white paper had vehemently attacked the iconoclastic and thorny social critic. Mencken's work had an immediate and galvanizing impact on Wright, who describes his response in this famous passage from his autobiography, *Black Boy*:

I was jarred and shocked by the style, the clear, clean, sweeping sentences. Why did he write like that? And how did one write like that? I pictured the man as a raging demon, slashing with his pen, consumed with hate, denouncing everything American, extolling everything European or German, laughing at the weaknesses of people, mocking God, authority. What was this? . . . Yes, this man was fighting, fighting with words. He was using words as a weapon, using them as one would use a club. Could words be weapons? Well, yes, for here they were.

Then, maybe, perhaps, I could use them as a weapon?[3]

What is so riveting about Wright's recollection here is the extent to which he was absolutely awestruck by the apparent capacity of literature to act, even to do violence, in the world. Desperately seeking a way to strike back at the oppressive forces dedicated to silencing him and to throttling his intellectual growth, the young Wright found in Mencken and, later, in American naturalists and realists such as Theodore Dreiser, Frank Norris, Stephen Crane, and Sinclair Lewis crucial literary paradigms for rendering social critique. It was not until he had moved to Chicago, however, that he was exposed to the systems of analysis that enabled him to more fully understand the bases for the oppression of blacks in the United States and then to feel capable of dramatizing it in fiction.

In "Blueprint for Negro Writing," Wright's earliest and most ambitious extended comment on black literature, he contends that, "anyone destitute of a theory about the meaning, structure and direction of modern society is a lost victim in a world he cannot understand or control."[4] In Chicago, Wright was deeply influenced by a number of major intellectual movements that together helped him to develop this all-important "theory." First, there was his ongoing exposure to the fiction of both American and European naturalists, whose work emphasized the power of external forces to shape personality. The scholar Michel Fabre notes that

[3]Richard Wright, *Black Boy*, res. ed. (New York: HarperPerennial, 1993), 293.
[4]Richard Wright, "Blueprint for Negro Writing." *New Challenge* 2.2 (1937): 61.

naturalistic fiction also "convinced Wright that his life, hemmed in by poverty and racism, was not the only life to be circumscribed."[5] That is, such texts showed Wright that although blacks may have suffered disproportionately under the exploitative social system in the United States, they were not its only victims. It would have been almost impossible for Wright to conceive of interracial efforts to bring about economic justice without first acknowledging the shared experience of oppression. The deterministic perspectives of the naturalists helped to provide him with this insight.

Wright encountered more systematic and rigorously analytical considerations of these same issues through his contact with the influential school of social science research headed by the well-known Robert E. Park at the University of Chicago. In his introduction to *Black Metropolis*, the landmark sociological study by St. Clair Drake and Horace R. Cayton, Wright acknowledges his debt to this scholarship:

> It was from the scientific findings of men like the late Robert E. Park, Robert Redfield, and Louis Wirth that I drew the meanings for my documentary book, *12,000,000 Black Voices*; for my novel, *Native Son*; it was from their scientific facts that I absorbed some of that quota of inspiration necessary for me to write *Uncle Tom's Children* and *Black Boy*.[6]

The impact of literary naturalism and the work of the "Chicago" sociologists on the development of Wright's

[5]Michel Fabre, "Beyond Naturalism?" in *Richard Wright*, ed. Harold Bloom (New York: Chelsea House, 1987), 41.

[6]Richard Wright, Introduction, in *Black Metropolis: A Study of Negro Life in a Northern City*, vol. 1, revised edition, St. Clair Drake and Horace R. Cayton (New York: Harbinger-Harcourt, 1970), xviii.

ideas during these years was considerable. Nonetheless, the single greatest intellectual force in his life at the time was communism.

Wright's introduction to communism came, appropriately enough, through his seeking out support for his burgeoning literary interests. Invited in 1933 to attend a meeting of the Chicago John Reed Club, the local affiliate of a nationwide organization of artists sponsored by the American Communist party, Wright found among the bright, ambitious young people there a commitment to both art and radical politics that encouraged him in his attempt to use literature to effect social change. In Ralph Ellison's words, Wright's discussions with these other aspiring artists "sharpened his conception of literary form and the relationship between fictional techniques and the world-view of Marxism."[7] Furthermore, the club's interracial membership provided Wright for the first time with a sense of community that had been lacking in his relations with both whites and, all too often, blacks before this point.

Wright also made invaluable literary contacts through his involvement in the Federal Writers' Project (FWP), a branch of the Works Project Administration established in 1935 to provide employment for professional writers during the Depression. Although the membership rosters of the various FWPs read like a who's who of American literature of the 1930s, the author Arna Bontemps singled out the Chicago branch as a hotbed of black artistic energy. In 1950, Bontemps recalled, "No other writers' project in the country produced comparable Negro talent during the depression. Chicago was

[7]Ralph Ellison, "Remembering Richard Wright," *Delta* 18 (1984): 6.

definitely the center of the second phase of Negro literary awakening."[8]

A decade earlier, the young writers of the New Negro Renaissance had boldly declared themselves artistic agents of change, bent on breaking old molds and discarding outworn paradigms. As their spokesperson Alain Locke put it in "The New Negro" in 1925, "The day of 'aunties,' 'uncles' and 'mammies' is . . . gone. Uncle Tom and Sambo have passed on. . . . The popular melodrama has about played itself out, and it is time to scrap the fictions, garret the bogeys and settle down to a realistic facing of facts."[9] In the 1930s, young writers such as Theodore Ward, William Attaway, Margaret Walker, Frank Yerby, and Willard Motley similarly sought to distinguish themselves from their immediate predecessors. In "Blueprint for Negro Writing," for instance, Wright, the most famous member of this group, criticizes earlier black authors for the way in which they chose to appeal to white readers:

> Generally speaking, Negro writing in the past has been confined to humble novels, poems, and plays, prim and decorous ambassadors who went a-begging to white America. They entered the Court of American Public Opinion dressed in the knee-pants of servility, curtsying to show that the Negro was not inferior, that he was human, and that he had a life comparable to that of other people.[10]

In contrast, the authorial stance of many of these new writers of the 1930s was confrontational and direct;

[8] Arna Bontemps, "Famous WPA Authors," *Negro Digest* 8.8 (1950): 46.

[9] Alain Locke, "The New Negro," in *The New Negro*, ed. Alain Locke (1925; reprint, New York: Antheneum, 1968), 5.

[10] Wright, "Blueprint for Negro Writing," 53.

their literary mode of choice, neonaturalism; their ideological orientation, Marxist; and their perspective, that of the proletariat—the Afro-American rural folk and urban working class. As Wright puts it in "Blueprint," the contemporary black author was "being called upon to do no less than create values by which his race is to struggle, live and die."[11] With this driving sense of mission and the ideological support of the white political left, Wright and his fellows set out to change the world with their pens.

Although his first publication appeared in the mid-1920s, Wright's artistic maturity dates from the early 1930s, when he began to publish poetry in radical periodicals such as *Left Front*, the literary magazine of the Chicago John Reed Club, and the American Communist party's *New Masses*. During this time, Wright also turned to journalism, with his first article (on the boxer Joe Louis) appearing in *New Masses* in October 1935. By May of 1937, when Wright left Chicago for New York City, he had established himself as one of the leading young writers of the American Communist party, which he had formally joined a few years earlier. Indeed, after arriving in New York, he was appointed head of the Harlem bureau of the *Daily Worker*, the Party's official paper; and he composed over two hundred articles in the last seven months of 1937 alone. In addition, he participated in the New York WPA Writers' Project, and he helped run *New Challenge*, a literary journal initially founded in 1934 as *Challenge* by the black writer Dorothy West.

During these productive years, Wright's creative energies also found outlet through fiction, with notably

[11]Ibid., 59.

mixed results. Throughout the mid-1930s, for example, he futilely attempted to find a publisher for the book that was to appear posthumously as *Lawd Today!* His proposal for another novel, tentatively entitled "Tarbaby's Dawn," met a similar fate. In contrast, Wright's short fiction received more encouraging responses. In early 1936, "Big Boy Leaves Home" was accepted for publication in *The New Caravan*; and in 1937, "Fire and Cloud" took second place in the O. Henry fiction competition and won five hundred dollars in a contest sponsored by *Story* magazine, which published it in March 1938. This award marked a real turning point in Wright's career, for it led directly to Harper's decision to bring out his collection of four novellas.

Uncle Tom's Children appeared in the spring of 1938 and created an immediate sensation. The majority of reviewers hailed Wright as a powerful, new black voice, dedicated, as Sterling Brown put it, to "revealing a people whose struggles and essential dignity have too long been unexpressed."[12] Even Eleanor Roosevelt favorably mentioned Wright's collection in her newspaper column, which boosted its sales considerably. The Book Union offered *Uncle Tom's Children* as one of its selections, and *The Nation* acclaimed it as among the ten best books of the year. In addition to the sudden celebrity that *Uncle Tom's Children* brought Wright, the money earned by the book, as well as a Guggenheim Fellowship that he received in 1939, allowed him to focus his energies over the next two years on the project that was to result in *Native Son*.

The success of *Uncle Tom's Children* was underscored by Harper's publication of an expanded edition of the

---

[12]Sterling A Brown, "From the Inside," review of *Uncle Tom's Children*, by Richard Wright, *Nation* 146 (1938): 448.

book in 1940. Besides the four original novellas, this new text included "The Ethics of Living Jim Crow," an autobiographical sketch that had been initially published in 1936 in *American Stuff*, an anthology of work by FWP writers, and "Bright and Morning Star," an award-winning story that had appeared in *New Masses* in May 1938. With these additions, the collection, as we now know it, was complete.*

In terms of subject matter, *Uncle Tom's Children* reflects the diversity of sources upon which Wright drew throughout his career in constructing his fiction. Not only did he mine his own firsthand knowledge of the South for material, but he also incorporated information gathered from his journalistic research. A series of interviews that he had conducted with black Communists in the mid-1930s proved especially helpful.

With regard to style, narrative strategies, and themes, *Uncle Tom's Children* demonstrates Wright's voracious assimilation of a wide range of literary influences. His reading of naturalists such as Dreiser and Norris, for instance, is quite evident, particularly in his depiction of human survival as often entailing struggle at the most immediate, physical level. Dramatic examples include Big Boy's battles with the snake and the dog in "Big Boy Leaves Home" and Mann's trials in the flood in "Down by the Riverside." Moreover, the psychological assumptions underlying naturalistic fiction prepared Wright for the economic determinism informing the Marxist literary aesthetic, which explains in part the readiness with which he adapted many of the tactics of what was termed proletarian fiction (or social realism) in the 1930s. Wright fully shared the social realists' commitment to focusing on the lives of working people vying desperately not just with the whims of a godless

world but also with the racism and economic exploita-
tion that, in their overwhelming insistence, themselves
become tantamount to natural forces. In addition, he
was mightily impressed with the sheer polemical vigor
of the leftist writings to which he was exposed through
his John Reed Club associates. In an essay entitled "I
Tried to Be a Communist," Wright describes his initial
reaction to reading this material: "The revolutionary
words leaped from the printed page and struck me with
tremendous force."[13] As he did in the case of Mencken's
work, Wright stresses the enormous power driving this
writing, a power exploding in the service of rigorous
social critique and energized by the liberatory hope that
Marxism could offer and that literary determinism alone
could not.

The extent to which Wright himself acknowledged
the impact on his artistic sensibility of the American nat-
uralists, of Russian realists such as Dostoevsky and Tol-
stoy, and of Marxist thought tends to obscure the
importance of other crucial literary sources. The first
consists of the popular fiction that Wright devoured in
his youth; Horatio Alger novels, detective stories, and
other "pulp" works—he read them all. The second is
that diverse body of literature broadly termed "Modern-
ist," produced by, among others, James Joyce, William
Faulkner, D. H. Lawrence, Joseph Conrad, and Marcel
Proust. Wright himself singled out Gertrude Stein,
whose "Melanctha" he describes in *I Wish I'd Written
That* as "the first realistic treatment of Negro life I'd
seen when I was trying to learn how to write. . . .
[T]his story made me see and accept for the first time in
my life the speech of Negroes, speech that fell all around

[13]Richard Wright, "I Tried to Be a Communist," *Atlantic Monthly*
174.2 (1944): 62.

me unheard."[14] (Echoes of Stein's experiments are especially evident in "Long Black Song.") Finally, like most of the young leftist authors of his generation, Wright was tremendously moved by the unadorned, straightforward prose style of Ernest Hemingway.

A third, often underestimated influence on *Uncle Tom's Children* is the literature produced by the New Negro Renaissance writers, a group with whom Wright, in some ways, did not want to be associated. In "Blueprint," for example, he contends that the contemporary black realist "requires a greater discipline and consciousness than was necessary for the so-called Harlem school of expression."[15] Yet he also urges black authors to acknowledge not just "the nationalist character of the Negro people" but also the extent to which "this nationalism is reflected in the whole of Negro culture, and especially in folklore."[16] The path that Wright and others took in seeking to tap the creative resistance and communal spirit informing the rich folklife of their people was one blazed a decade earlier by the very New Negro writers whose limitations Wright wished to transcend. In the case of Langston Hughes, the most influential Harlem Renaissance poet of the black folk, not only did Wright know of his work, but in the mid-1930s he delivered at least one public lecture on it.

It would be difficult to overestimate the impact of Hughes and other black authors on Wright's handling of folk materials, for *Uncle Tom's Children* represents one of the most ambitious and complex fictional uses of

[14]Richard Wright, Introduction to "Early Days of a Woman," in *I Wish I'd Written That: Selections Chosen by Favorite American Authors*, ed. Eugene J. Woods (New York: Whittlesey-McGraw Hill, 1946), 254.
[15]Wright, "Blueprint for Negro Writing," 63.
[16]Ibid., 56.

black folklore that had appeared to that time. The recurring motif of the train and the verbal jousting of the young men in "Big Boy Leaves Home," the biblical echoes underlying the role of the flood in "Down by the Riverside," and the depiction of Sue and her winding sheet in "Bright and Morning Star" all take on added resonance when one considers the rich black cultural freight that they carry. Indeed, much of the structural glue holding together the six pieces in this collection is provided by the pervasive and skillful manipulation of Afro-American folklore.

Although a few commentators have questioned the decision to open the expanded edition of *Uncle Tom's Children* with "The Ethics of Living Jim Crow," this autobiographical sketch constitutes one of the most potent firsthand indictments of the psychic costs of racial subordination to be found in American literature. In "Ethics" Wright dramatizes the arbitrary violence of whites, the explosive sexual component of racism, and the struggle of blacks to accommodate themselves to constant injustice and humiliation while maintaining a modicum of personal dignity—all of which serve as unifying themes for the entire volume.

But why, one might ask, did Wright feel the need to supplement the critically acknowledged power of his stories in this way? To answer this question, one must keep in mind Wright's commitment to literature as protest. As had scores of earlier black authors who sought to effect social change through their creative work, Wright probably experienced some ambivalence about using fiction as a political tool. On the one hand, it permitted a play of imagination that he must have found both deeply self-affirming and aptly suited for the assault on his white readers' sensibilities—on their hearts

as well as their heads—that he hoped would lead to a
new understanding of the horrors to which blacks were
so unfairly exposed. On the other hand, as several of the
reviews of *Uncle Tom's Children* demonstrated, readers
overly discomforted by the frankness of Wright's vigor-
ous critique could doubt the "reality" of the stories
themselves. By describing in his *own* voice instances of
racism not dissimilar to those experienced by his protag-
onists, Wright no doubt hoped that his authorial credi-
bility would prevent skeptical readers from questioning
the veracity of his fictional depiction of Southern race
relations. This authorial credibility is further reinforced
by his tightly controlled tone in "Ethics." Here, for in-
stance, Wright describes the fate of a black hotel worker
caught with a white prostitute:

> He was castrated and run out of town. Immediately
> after this all the bell-boys and hall-boys were called
> together and warned. We were given to understand
> that the boy who had been castrated was a "mighty,
> mighty lucky bastard." We were impressed with the
> fact that next time the management of the hotel
> would not be responsible for the lives of "trouble-
> makin' niggers." We were silent. (12)

We react with dismay to this passage not simply because
of the brutal events that Wright describes but more so
because his prose is so flat, so emotionally uninflected.
The effectiveness of this strategy is even clearer when we
then move to the more charged, at times poetic, lan-
guage of the stories themselves. This urge to take advan-
tage of both the potent appeal of fiction and the
documentary solidity of firsthand personal testimony in-
forms much of Wright's work.

The five stories that comprise the bulk of *Uncle Tom's
Children* fall into two sections. The first consists of "Big

Boy Leaves Home," "Down by the Riverside," and "Long Black Song"; the second, of "Fire and Cloud" and "Bright and Morning Star." And although these pieces were initially published independently, together they present the evolution of what might be called a black revolutionary consciousness.

In "Big Boy Leaves Home" and "Down by the River-side," nature, a fate given to cruelly absurd coincidence, and Southern whites all conspire in unrelenting assaults on the bodies and spirits of blacks whose only crime is to be black and in the wrong place at the wrong time. The names of Wright's protagonists—Big Boy and Mann—suggest the representative nature of their vic-timization and, especially in "Riverside," the extent to which the veritable erasure of black individuality is the ultimate goal of the racist white South. Even here, however, we see the beginnings of resistance. In "Big Boy Leaves Home," the black community, while dis-traught over the imminent explosion of white retalia-tion for Big Boy's act, nonetheless mobilizes to protect him with a practiced, nearly ritualistic set of strategies which eventually enable him to escape North. This flight from death manifests a survival instinct which, Wright would contend, can serve as the first step to-ward a more assertive and potentially successful form of self-defense.

If "Down by the Riverside" and "Long Black Song" both highlight the paucity of available options through which blacks can maintain their humanity in the face of racism, Wright also suggests in these stories that choos-ing the terms of one's own death in a world that refuses to let you live as a human being constitutes an existen-tial triumph of no small order. And where Mann's deci-sion in "Riverside" entails the simple act of running from the white troops who have him in custody, Silas in

"Long Black Song" actually engages in armed combat
with whites, determined to extract as dear a toll as pos-
sible before he is taken. Furthermore, Silas is far more
mature and self-aware than either Big Boy or Mann.
Thus, when confronting what he sees as the ultimate
violation of trust by his wife, Sarah, and the irreparable
damage done to his carefully constructed world by the
white traveling salesman, Silas knows the precise nature
of the alternatives before him:

> Ahm gonna be hard like they is! So hep me, Gawd,
> Ah'm gonna be *hard*! When they come fer me Ah'm
> gonna *be* here! N when they git me outta here
> theys gonna *know* Ahm gone! Ef Gawd lets me
> live Ahm gonna make em *feel* it! . . . But, Lawd, Ah
> don wanna be this way! It don mean nothin! Yuh die
> ef yuh fight! You die ef yuh don fight! Either way
> yuh die n it don mean nothin . . . (152–53)

Silas's militant resistance even in the face of apparently
empty options dramatizes Wright's belief that one must
finally impose his or her own meaning on reality. And
doing so in the face of death is, to Wright, heroic.

The remaining stories in *Uncle Tom's Children* elabo-
rate on these issues by presenting the protagonists—
Reverend Taylor in "Fire and Cloud" and Sue in
"Bright and Morning Star"—not as isolated individu-
als, but as social actors whose decisions have real conse-
quences for those for whom they care. This shift in
focus allows Wright to introduce for the first time in
the book the ideological alternative offered to Afro-
Americans by communism. "Fire and Cloud," the story
with which the original edition of *Uncle Tom's Children*
concluded, may be the one piece in the book that most
nearly approaches the Marxist paradigm for polemical

fiction. Yet Wright's commitment to taking seriously the cultural integrity of Afro-American religious beliefs prevents him from rejecting outright as ideologically backward and counterrevolutionary what he calls in "Blueprint" the "archaic morphology of Christian salvation."[17] Indeed, the figurative death that Taylor must endure on his way toward a stronger and more secular faith is couched in biblical terms even as his dilemma calls into question the efficacy of traditional Christian responses in combatting racial oppression.

"Bright and Morning Star," the final story in the collection, weaves together into a single fabric many of the major thematic and stylistic threads evident in the preceding pieces. In particular, we see even more vividly than in "Fire and Cloud" the complex psychological transition from a sensibility grounded in Christian ideology to a more activist perspective that engenders an empowering awareness of the revolutionary potential in *this* world of self-sacrifice, and even martyrdom. In further contrast to "Fire and Cloud," with its concluding image of interracial cooperation, "Bright and Morning Star" leaves unresolved the tension with which Wright himself struggled between the nationalist strain in black culture and the integrationist imperative underlying the Communist party's appeal to class solidarity. In Sue, Wright gives us a black character who can draw strength from both sources. However, that her mother-wit and well-justified suspicion of whites prove to be her most reliable tools in her attempt to safeguard an interracial group of local Communists demonstrates Wright's refusal to reduce the relationships between culture and ideology and between race and class to simple formulas.

[17]Ibid., 55.

In an oft-quoted statement from his 1940 essay "How 'Bigger' Was Born," Wright renders an extremely harsh judgment on *Uncle Tom's Children*: "When the reviews of that book began to appear, I realized that I had made an awfully naïve mistake. I found that I had written a book which even bankers' daughters could read and weep over and feel good about."[18] It is true that the testimony of commentators such as Eleanor Roosevelt, who described the book as "beautifully written and so vivid that I had a most unhappy time reading it," embodies the sentimental response to which Wright so vehemently objected.[19] Yet half a century later it appears that Wright was reacting less to particular flaws in *Uncle Tom's Children* and more to mainstream American culture's capacity to defuse the potency of harsh critique through the very act of commercial consumption and subsequent emotional release.

This is not to imply that Wright's first book is without weaknesses. Since its publication, critics have argued that the collection is uneven, with certain stories more finely constructed and effective than others. Particular attention has been paid to awkward coincidences in the plotting, especially in "Down by the Riverside." The success of Wright's attempt to yoke Marxist polemics to his powerful dramatizations of black Southern life has also been debated, as has what Michel Fabre calls his "compulsion to explain while describing."[20]

In her harsh 1938 review of *Uncle Tom's Children*, Zora Neale Hurston strongly objects to the violent male perspective that dominates the text. And although she does

[18]Richard Wright, "How 'Bigger' Was Born," in *Native Son*, res. ed. (New York: HarperPerennial, 1993), 531.
[19]Michel Fabre, *The Unfinished Quest of Richard Wright* (New York: Morrow, 1973), 162.
[20]Ibid., 84.

not specifically address Wright's depiction of black women, her comments anticipate reservations that many contemporary readers share on this issue.[21] Among other critics, Sherley Anne Williams argues that Wright consistently portrays black women in this collection (even the heroic Sue) as symbolic of "the reactionary aspects in Afro-American tradition."[22] Furthermore, she suggests that in focusing on the extent to which racism constitutes "an affront to the masculinity of black men," Wright reveals his inability to appreciate fully the pervasive nature of the sexism that is so deeply implicated in the oppressive patriarchal social order in the United States.[23]

Any thorough consideration of Wright's achievement in *Uncle Tom's Children* must take these problems into account, if only to remind us that he wrestled far more successfully with certain demons than he did with others. In the final analysis, much of the real strength of this book resides not in the verisimilitude with which he consistently represents the psychology of his black men and women but rather in the extent to which his fiction-making was propelled by a fierce determination to break the silence surrounding racism in the United States, a silence maintained in the interest of white supremacy and one to which too many blacks had acceded. As Saunders Redding puts it, "His talent was to smite the conscience—and to smite the conscience of both white

[21]Zora Neale Hurston, "Stories of Conflict," review of *Uncle Tom's Children*, by Richard Wright, *Saturday Review of Literature* 2 April 1938: 32.

[22]Sherley Anne Williams, "Papa Dick and Sister-Woman: Reflections on Women in the Fiction of Richard Wright," in *American Novelists Revisited: Essays in Feminist Criticism*, ed. Fritz Fleischmann (Boston: Hall, 1982), 398.

[23]Ibid., 406.

and black Americans."[24] In violating the unspoken agreement regarding what could or could not be uttered about race relations in this country, Wright brought to bear both the rhetorical force of leftist polemic and the imaginative energy and cultural richness of Afro-American folklore with a power and a coherence that he may never have again achieved in his later work.

As the title and epigraph of Wright's collection imply, *Uncle Tom's Children* constitutes a self-conscious rejection of the past, of roles and traditions that impoverished the spirit rather than nurtured it, that indirectly helped to perpetuate what sociologist Allison Davis terms "the age-old repressions formed under slavery and peonage."[25] Although he may have been ill-suited to the task of constructing the new roles and traditions that would mark the next phase of the black struggle for empowerment, with *Uncle Tom's Children*, Richard Wright, anticipating countless black authors who followed in his wake, could indeed proclaim, "Uncle Tom is dead!"

RICHARD YARBOROUGH
UNIVERSITY OF CALIFORNIA, LOS ANGELES

[24]Saunders Redding, "The Alien Land of Richard Wright," in *Five Black Writers*, ed. Donald B. Gibson (New York: New York University Press, 1970), 5.

[25]Allison Davis, *Leadership, Love, and Aggression* (New York: Harcourt, 1983), 179.

The post Civil War household word among Ne-groes—"He's an Uncle Tom!"—which denoted re-luctant toleration for the cringing type who knew his place before white folk, has been supplanted by a new word from another generation which says:—"Uncle Tom is dead!"

The Ethics of Living Jim Crow

AN AUTOBIOGRAPHICAL SKETCH

I

MY FIRST LESSON in how to live as a Negro came when I was quite small. We were living in Arkansas. Our house stood behind the railroad tracks. Its skimpy yard was paved with black cinders. Nothing green ever grew in that yard. The only touch of green we could see was far away, beyond the tracks, over where the white folks lived. But cinders were good enough for me and I never missed the green growing things. And anyhow, cinders were fine weapons. You could always have a nice hot war with huge black cinders. All you had to do was crouch behind the brick pillars of a house with your hands full of gritty ammunition. And the first woolly black head you saw pop out from behind another row of pillars was your target. You tried your very best to knock it off. It was great fun.

I never fully realized the appalling disadvantages of a cinder environment till one day the gang to which I belonged found itself engaged in a war with the white boys who lived beyond the tracks. As usual we laid down our cinder barrage, thinking that this would wipe the white boys out. But they replied with a steady bombardment of broken bottles. We doubled our cinder barrage, but they hid behind trees, hedges, and the sloping embankments of their lawns. Having no such fortifications, we retreated to the brick pillars of our homes. During the retreat a broken milk bottle caught me behind the ear, opening a deep gash which bled profusely. The sight of blood pouring over my face completely demoralized our ranks. My fellow-combatants left me standing paralyzed in the center of the yard, and scurried for their homes. A kind neighbor saw me and rushed me to a doctor, who took three stitches in my neck.

I sat brooding on my front steps, nursing my wound and waiting for my mother to come from work. I felt that a grave injustice had been done me. It was all right to throw cinders. The greatest harm a cinder could do was leave a bruise. But broken bottles were dangerous; they left you cut, bleeding, and helpless.

When night fell, my mother came from the white folks' kitchen. I raced down the street to meet her. I could just feel in my bones that she would understand. I knew she would tell me exactly what to do next time. I grabbed her hand and babbled out the whole story. She examined my wound, then slapped me.

"How come yuh didn't hide?" she asked me. "How come yuh awways fightin'?"

I was outraged, and bawled. Between sobs I told her that I didn't have any trees or hedges to hide behind. There wasn't a thing I could have used as a trench. And you couldn't throw very far when you were hiding behind the brick pillars of a house. She grabbed a barrel stave, dragged me home, stripped me naked, and beat me till I had a fever of one hundred and two. She would smack my rump with the stave, and, while the skin was still smarting, impart to me gems of Jim Crow wisdom. I was never to throw cinders any more. I was never to fight any more wars. I was never, never, under any conditions, to fight *white* folks again. And they were absolutely right in clouting me with the broken milk bottle. Didn't I know she was working hard every day in the hot kitchens of the white folks to make money to take care of me? When was I ever going to learn to be a good boy? She couldn't be bothered with my fights. She finished by telling me that I ought to be thankful to God as long as I lived that they didn't kill me.

All that night I was delirious and could not sleep. Each time I closed my eyes I saw monstrous white faces suspended from the ceiling, leering at me.

From that time on, the charm of my cinder yard was gone. The green trees, the trimmed hedges, the cropped lawns grew very meaningful, became a symbol. Even today when I think of white folks, the hard, sharp outlines of white houses surrounded by trees, lawns, and hedges are present somewhere in the background of my mind. Through the years they grew into an overreaching symbol of fear.

It was a long time before I came in close contact with white folks again. We moved from Arkansas to Mississippi. Here we had the good fortune not to live behind the railroad tracks, or close to white neighborhoods. We lived in the very heart of the local Black Belt. There were black churches and black preachers; there were black schools and black teachers; black groceries and black clerks. In fact, everything was so solidly black that for a long time I did not even think of white folks, save in remote and vague terms. But this could not last forever. As one grows older one eats more. One's clothing costs more. When I finished grammar school I had to go to work. My mother could no longer feed and clothe me on her cooking job.

There is but one place where a black boy who knows no trade can get a job, and that's where the houses and faces are white, where the trees, lawns, and hedges are green. My first job was with an optical company in Jackson, Mississippi. The morning I applied I stood straight and neat before the boss, answering all his questions with sharp yessirs and nosirs. I was very careful to pronounce my *sirs* distinctly, in order that he might know that I was polite, that I knew where I was, and that I knew he was a *white* man. I wanted that job badly.

He looked me over as though he were examining a prize poodle. He questioned me closely about my schooling, being particularly insistent about how much mathematics I had had. He seemed very pleased when I told him I had had two years of algebra.

"Boy, how would you like to try to learn something around here?" he asked me.

"I'd like it fine, sir," I said, happy. I had visions of "working my way up." Even Negroes have those visions.

"All right," he said. "Come on."

I followed him to the small factory.

"Pease," he said to a white man of about thirty-five, "this is Richard. He's going to work for us."

Pease looked at me and nodded.

I was then taken to a white boy of about seventeen.

"Morrie, this is Richard, who's going to work for us."

"Whut yuh sayin' there, boy!" Morrie boomed at me.

"Fine!" I answered.

The boss instructed these two to help me, teach me, give me jobs to do, and let me learn what I could in my spare time.

My wages were five dollars a week.

I worked hard, trying to please. For the first month I got along O.K. Both Pease and Morrie seemed to like me. But one thing was missing. And I kept thinking about it. I was not learning anything and nobody was volunteering to help me. Thinking they had forgotten that I was to learn something about the mechanics of grinding lenses, I asked Morrie one day to tell me about the work. He grew red.

"Whut yuh tryin' t' do, nigger, git smart?" he asked.

"Naw; I ain' tryin' t' git smart," I said.

"Well, don't, if yuh know whut's good for yuh!"

I was puzzled. Maybe he just doesn't want to help me, I thought. I went to Pease.

"Say, are you crazy, you black bastard?" Pease asked me, his gray eyes growing hard.

I spoke out, reminding him that the boss had said I was to be given a chance to learn something.

"Nigger, you think you're *white*, don't you?"

"Naw, sir!"

"Well, you're acting mighty like it!"

"But, Mr. Pease, the boss said . . ."

Pease shook his fist in my face.

"This is a *white* man's work around here, and you better watch yourself!"

From then on they changed toward me. They said good-morning no more. When I was just a bit slow in performing some duty, I was called a lazy black son-of-a-bitch.

Once I thought of reporting all this to the boss. But the mere idea of what would happen to me if Pease and Morrie should learn that I had "snitched" stopped me. And after all, the boss was a white man, too. What was the use?

The climax came at noon one summer day. Pease called me to his work-bench. To get to him I had to go between two narrow benches and stand with my back against a wall.

"Yes, sir," I said.

"Richard, I want to ask you something," Pease began pleasantly, not looking up from his work.

"Yes, sir," I said again.

Morrie came over, blocking the narrow passage between the benches. He folded his arms, staring at me solemnly.

I looked from one to the other, sensing that something was coming.

"Yes, sir," I said for the third time.

Pease looked up and spoke very slowly.

"Richard, *Mr.* Morrie here tells me you called me *Pease*."

I stiffened. A void seemed to open up in me. I knew this was the show-down.

He meant that I had failed to call him *Mr.* Pease. I looked at Morrie. He was gripping a steel bar in his hands. I opened my mouth to speak, to protest, to assure Pease that I had never called him simply *Pease*, and that I had never had any intentions of doing so, when Morrie grabbed me by the collar, ramming my head against the wall.

"Now, be careful, nigger!" snarled Morrie, baring his teeth. "*I* heard yuh call 'im *Pease*! 'N' if yuh say yuh didn't, yuh're callin' me a *lie*, see?" He waved the steel bar threateningly.

If I had said: No, sir, Mr. Pease, I never called you *Pease*, I would have been automatically calling Morrie a liar. And if I had said: Yes, sir, Mr. Pease, I called you *Pease*, I would have been pleading guilty to having uttered the worst insult that a Negro can utter to a southern white man. I stood hesitating, trying to frame a neutral reply.

"Richard, I asked you a question!" said Pease. Anger was creeping into his voice.

"I don't remember calling you *Pease*, Mr. Pease," I said cautiously. "And if I did, I sure didn't mean . . ."

"You black son-of-a-bitch! You called me *Pease*, then!" he spat, slapping me till I bent sideways over a bench. Morrie was on top of me, demanding:

"Didn't yuh call 'im *Pease*? If yuh say yuh didn't, I'll

rip yo' gut string loose with this bar, yuh black granny dodger! Yuh can't call a white man a lie 'n' git erway with it, you black son-of-a-bitch!"

I wilted. I begged them not to bother me. I knew what they wanted. They wanted me to leave.

"I'll leave," I promised. "I'll leave right *now*."

They gave me a minute to get out of the factory. I was warned not to show up again, or tell the boss.

I went.

When I told the folks at home what had happened, they called me a fool. They told me that I must never again attempt to exceed my boundaries. When you are working for white folks, they said, you got to "stay in your place" if you want to keep working.

II

My Jim Crow education continued on my next job, which was portering in a clothing store. One morning, while polishing brass out front, the boss and his twenty-year-old son got out of their car and half dragged and half kicked a Negro woman into the store. A policeman standing at the corner looked on, twirling his nightstick. I watched out of the corner of my eye, never slackening the strokes of my chamois upon the brass. After a few minutes, I heard shrill screams coming from the rear of the store. Later the woman stumbled out, bleeding, crying, and holding her stomach. When she reached the end of the block, the policeman grabbed her and accused her of being drunk. Silently, I watched him throw her into a patrol wagon.

When I went to the rear of the store, the boss and his son were washing their hands at the sink. They were chuckling. The floor was bloody and strewn with wisps of hair and clothing. No doubt I must have appeared pretty shocked, for the boss slapped me reassuringly on the back.

"Boy, that's what we do to niggers when they don't want to pay their bills," he said, laughing.

His son looked at me and grinned.

"Here, hava cigarette," he said.

Not knowing what to do, I took it. He lit his and held the match for me. This was a gesture of kindness, indicating that even if they had beaten the poor old woman, they would not beat me if I knew enough to keep my mouth shut.

"Yes, sir," I said, and asked no questions.

After they had gone, I sat on the edge of a packing box and stared at the bloody floor till the cigarette went out.

That day at noon, while eating in a hamburger joint, I told my fellow Negro porters what had happened. No one seemed surprised. One fellow, after swallowing a huge bite, turned to me and asked:

"Huh! Is tha' all they did t' her?"

"Yeah. Wasn't tha' enough?" I asked.

"Shucks! Man, she's a lucky bitch!" he said, burying his lips deep into a juicy hamburger. "Hell, it's a wonder they didn't lay her when they got through."

III

I was learning fast, but not quite fast enough. One day, while I was delivering packages in the suburbs, my bicycle tire was punctured. I walked along the hot, dusty road, sweating and leading my bicycle by the handle-bars.

A car slowed at my side.

"What's the matter, boy?" a white man called.

I told him my bicycle was broken and I was walking back to town.

"That's too bad," he said. "Hop on the running board."

He stopped the car. I clutched hard at my bicycle with one hand and clung to the side of the car with the other.

"All set?"

"Yes, sir," I answered. The car started.

It was full of young white men. They were drinking. I watched the flask pass from mouth to mouth.

"Wanna drink, boy?" one asked.

I laughed as the wind whipped my face. Instinctively obeying the freshly planted precepts of my mother, I said:

"Oh, no!"

The words were hardly out of my mouth before I felt something hard and cold smash me between the eyes. It was an empty whisky bottle. I saw stars, and fell backwards from the speeding car into the dust of the road, my feet becoming entangled in the steel spokes of my bicycle. The white men piled out and stood over me.

"Nigger, ain' yuh learned no better sense'n tha' yet?" asked the man who hit me. "Ain' yuh learned t' say *sir* t' a white man yet?"

Dazed, I pulled to my feet. My elbows and legs were bleeding. Fists doubled, the white man advanced, kicking my bicycle out of the way.

"Aw, leave the bastard alone. He's got enough," said one.

They stood looking at me. I rubbed my shins, trying to stop the flow of blood. No doubt they felt a sort of contemptuous pity, for one asked:

"Yuh wanna ride t' town now, nigger? Yuh reckon yuh know enough t' ride now?"

"I wanna walk," I said, simply.

Maybe it sounded funny. They laughed.

"Well, walk, yuh black son-of-a-bitch!"

When they left they comforted me with:

"Nigger, yuh sho better be damn glad it wuz us yuh talked t' tha' way. Yuh're a lucky bastard, 'cause if yuh'd said tha' t' somebody else, yuh might've been a dead nigger now."

IV

Negroes who have lived South know the dread of being caught alone upon the streets in white neighborhoods after the sun has set. In such a simple situation as this the plight of the Negro in America is graphically symbolized. While white strangers may be in these neighborhoods trying to get home, they can pass unmolested. But the color of a Negro's skin makes him easily recognizable, makes him suspect, converts him into a defenseless target.

Late one Saturday night I made some deliveries in a white neighborhood. I was pedaling my bicycle back to the store as fast as I could, when a police car, swerving toward me, jammed me into the curbing.

"Get down and put up your hands!" the policemen ordered.

I did. They climbed out of the car, guns drawn, faces set, and advanced slowly.

"Keep still!" they ordered.

I reached my hands higher. They searched my pockets and packages. They seemed dissatisfied when they could find nothing incriminating. Finally, one of them said:

"Boy, tell your boss not to send you out in white neighborhoods after sundown."

As usual, I said:

"Yes, sir."

V

My next job was as hall-boy in a hotel. Here my Jim Crow education broadened and deepened. When the bell-boys were busy, I was often called to assist them. As many of the rooms in the hotel were occupied by prostitutes, I was constantly called to carry them liquor and cigarettes. These women were nude most of the time. They did not bother about clothing, even for bell-boys. When you went into their rooms, you were supposed to take their nakedness for granted, as though it startled you no more than a blue vase or a red rug. Your presence awoke in them no sense of shame, for you were not regarded as human. If they were alone, you could steal sidelong glimpses at them. But if they were receiving men, not a flicker of your eyelids could show. I remember one incident vividly. A new woman, a huge, snowy-skinned blonde, took a room on my floor. I was sent to wait upon her. She was in bed with a thick-set man; both were nude and uncovered. She said she wanted some liquor and slid out of bed and waddled across the floor to get her money from a dresser drawer. I watched her.

"Nigger, what in hell you looking at?" the white man asked me, raising himself upon his elbows.

"Nothing," I answered, looking miles deep into the blank wall of the room.

"Keep your eyes where they belong, if you want to be healthy!" he said.

"Yes, sir."

VI

One of the bell-boys I knew in this hotel was keeping steady company with one of the Negro maids. Out of a clear sky the police descended upon his home and ar-

rested him, accusing him of bastardy. The poor boy
swore he had had no intimate relations with the girl.
Nevertheless, they forced him to marry her. When the
child arrived, it was found to be much lighter in com-
plexion than either of the two supposedly legal parents.
The white men around the hotel made a great joke of it.
They spread the rumor that some white cow must have
scared the poor girl while she was carrying the baby. If
you were in their presence when this explanation was
offered, you were supposed to laugh.

VII

One of the bell-boys was caught in bed with a white
prostitute. He was castrated and run out of town. Im-
mediately after this all the bell-boys and hall-boys were
called together and warned. We were given to under-
stand that the boy who had been castrated was a
"mighty, mighty lucky bastard." We were impressed
with the fact that next time the management of the hotel
would not be responsible for the lives of "trouble-
makin' niggers." We were silent.

VIII

One night, just as I was about to go home, I met one
of the Negro maids. She lived in my direction, and we
fell in to walk part of the way home together. As we
passed the white night-watchman, he slapped the maid
on her buttock. I turned around, amazed. The watch-
man looked at me with a long, hard, fixed-under stare.
Suddenly he pulled his gun and asked:

"Nigger, don't yuh like it?"

I hesitated.

"I asked yuh don't yuh like it?" he asked again, step-
ping forward.

"Yes, sir," I mumbled.

"Talk like it, then!"

"Oh, yes, sir!" I said with as much heartiness as I could muster.

Outside, I walked ahead of the girl, ashamed to face her. She caught up with me and said:

"Don't be a fool! Yuh couldn't help it!"

This watchman boasted of having killed two Negroes in self-defense.

Yet, in spite of all this, the life of the hotel ran with an amazing smoothness. It would have been impossible for a stranger to detect anything. The maids, the hall-boys, and the bell-boys were all smiles. They had to be.

IX

I had learned my Jim Crow lessons so thoroughly that I kept the hotel job till I left Jackson for Memphis. It so happened that while in Memphis I applied for a job at a branch of the optical company. I was hired. And for some reason, as long as I worked there, they never brought my past against me.

Here my Jim Crow education assumed quite a different form. It was no longer brutally cruel, but subtly cruel. Here I learned to lie, to steal, to dissemble. I learned to play that dual role which every Negro must play if he wants to eat and live.

For example, it was almost impossible to get a book to read. It was assumed that after a Negro had imbibed what scanty schooling the state furnished he had no further need for books. I was always borrowing books from men on the job. One day I mustered enough courage to ask one of the men to let me get books from the library in his name. Surprisingly, he consented. I cannot help but think that he consented because he was a Roman Catholic and felt a vague sympathy for Negroes, being himself an object of hatred. Armed with a library card, I obtained books in the following manner: I would write a note to the librarian, saying: "Please let this nigger boy have the following books." I would then sign it with the white man's name.

When I went to the library, I would stand at the desk, hat in hand, looking as unbookish as possible. When I received the books desired I would take them home. If the books listed in the note happened to be out, I would sneak into the lobby and forge a new one. I never took any chances guessing with the white librarian about what the fictitious white man would want to read. No doubt if any of the white patrons had suspected that some of the volumes they enjoyed had been in the home of a Negro, they would not have tolerated it for an instant.

The factory force of the optical company in Memphis was much larger than that in Jackson, and more urbanized. At least they liked to talk, and would engage the Negro help in conversation whenever possible. By this means I found that many subjects were taboo from the white man's point of view. Among the topics they did not like to discuss with Negroes were the following: American white women; the Ku Klux Klan; France, and how Negro soldiers fared while there; French women; Jack Johnson; the entire northern part of the United States; the Civil War; Abraham Lincoln; U. S. Grant; General Sherman; Catholics; the Pope; Jews; the Republican Party; slavery; social equality; Communism; Socialism; the 13th and 14th Amendments to the Constitution; or any topic calling for positive knowledge or manly self-assertion on the part of the Negro. The most accepted topics were sex and religion.

There were many times when I had to exercise a great

deal of ingenuity to keep out of trouble. It is a southern custom that all men must take off their hats when they enter an elevator. And especially did this apply to us blacks with rigid force. One day I stepped into an elevator with my arms full of packages. I was forced to ride with my hat on. Two white men stared at me coldly. Then one of them very kindly lifted my hat and placed it upon my armful of packages. Now the most accepted response for a Negro to make under such circumstances is to look at the white man out of the corner of his eye and grin. To have said: "Thank you!" would have made the white man *think* that you *thought* you were receiving from him a personal service. For such an act I have seen Negroes take a blow in the mouth. Finding the first alternative distasteful, and the second dangerous, I hit upon an acceptable course of action which fell safely between these two poles. I immediately—no sooner than my hat was lifted—pretended that my packages were about to spill, and appeared deeply distressed with keeping them in my arms. In this fashion I evaded having to acknowledge his service, and, in spite of adverse circumstances, salvaged a slender shred of personal pride.

How do Negroes feel about the way they have to live? How do they discuss it when alone among themselves? I think this question can be answered in a single sentence. A friend of mine who ran an elevator once told me:

"Lawd, man! Ef it wuzn't fer them polices 'n' them ol' lynch-mobs, there wouldn't be nothin' but uproar down here!"

Is it true what they say about Dixie?
Does the sun really shine all the time?
Do sweet magnolias blossom at everybody's door?
Do folks keep eating 'possum, till they can't eat no more?
Is it true what they say about Swanee?
Is a dream by that stream so sublime?
Do they laugh, do they love, like they say in ev'ry song? . . .
If it's true, that's where I belong.

—Popular Song.

I

Big Boy Leaves Home

I

***Y**O MAMA don wear no drawers* . . .
    Clearly, the voice rose out of the woods, and died away. Like an echo another voice caught it up:
Ah seena when she pulled em off . . .
Another, shrill, cracking, adolescent:
N she washed 'em in alcohol . . .
Then a quartet of voices, blending in harmony, floated high above the tree tops:
N she hung 'em out in the hall . . .
Laughing easily, four black boys came out of the woods into cleared pasture. They walked lollingly in bare feet, beating tangled vines and bushes with long sticks.

"Ah wished Ah knowed some mo lines t tha song."

"Me too."

"Yeah, when yuh gits t where she hangs em out in the hall yuh has t stop."

"Shucks, whut goes wid *hall*?"

"Call."

"Fall."

"Wall."

"Quall."

They threw themselves on the grass, laughing.

"Big Boy?"

"Huh?"

"Yuh know one thing?"

"Whut?"

"Yuh sho is crazy!"

"Crazy?"

"Yeah, yuh crazys a bed-bug!"

"Crazy bout whut?"

"Man, whoever hearda *quall*?"

"Yuh said yuh wanted something t go wid *hall*, didnt yuh?"

"Yeah, but whuts a *quall*?"

"Nigger, a *qualls* a *quall*."

They laughed easily, catching and pulling long green blades of grass with their toes.

"Waal, ef a *qualls* a *quall*, whut IS a *quall*?"

"Oh, Ah know."

"Whut?"

"Tha ol song goes something like this:

> *Yo mama don wear no drawers,*
>   *Ah seena when she pulled em off,*
> *N she washed em in alcohol,*
>   *N she hung em out in the hall,*
>   *N then she put em back on her QUALL!*"

They laughed again. Their shoulders were flat to the earth, their knees propped up, and their faces square to the sun.

"Big Boy, yuhs CRAZY!"

"Don ax me nothin else."

"Nigger, yuhs CRAZY!"

They fell silent, smiling, drooping the lids of their eyes softly against the sunlight.

"Man, don the groun feel warm?"

"Jus lika bed."

"Jeeesus, Ah could stay here ferever."

"Me too."

"Ah kin feel tha ol sun goin all thu me."

"Feels like mah bones is warm."

In the distance a train whistled mournfully.

"There goes number fo!"

"Hittin on all six!"

"Highballin it down the line!"

"Boun fer up Noth, Lawd, boun fer up Noth!"

They began to chant, pounding bare heels in the grass.

> *Dis train boun fo Glory*
> *Dis train, Oh Hallelujah*
> *Dis train boun fo Glory*
> *Dis train, Oh Hallelujah*
> *Dis train boun fo Glory*
> *Ef yuh ride no need fer fret er worry*
> *Dis train, Oh Hallelujah*
> *Dis train . . .*
>
> *Dis train don carry no gambler*
> *Dis train, Oh Hallelujah*
> *Dis train don carry no gambler*
> *Dis train, Oh Hallelujah*
> *Dis train don carry no gambler*
> *No fo day creeper er midnight rambler*
> *Dis train, Oh Hallelujah*
> *Dis train . . .*

When the song ended they burst out laughing, thinking of a train bound for Glory.

"Gee, thas a good ol song!"

"Huuuuummmmmmmmmman . . ."

"Whut?"

"Geeee whiiiiiiz . . ."

"Whut?"

"Somebody don let win! Das whut!"

Buck, Bobo and Lester jumped up. Big Boy stayed on the ground, feigning sleep.

"Jeeesus, tha sho stinks!"

"Big Boy!"

Big Boy feigned to snore.

"Big Boy!"

Big Boy stirred as though in sleep.

"Big Boy!"

"Hunh?"

"Yuh rotten inside!"

"Rotten?"

"Lawd, cant yuh smell it?"

"Smell whut?"

"Nigger, yuh mus gotta bad col!"

"Smell whut?"

"NIGGER, YUH BROKE WIN!"

Big Boy laughed and fell back on the grass, closing his eyes.

"The hen whut cackles is the hen whut laid the egg."

"We ain no hens."

"Yuh cackled, didnt yuh?"

The three moved off with noses turned up.

"C mon!"

"Where yuh-all goin?"

"T the creek fer a swim."

"Yeah, les swim."

"Naw buddy naw!" said Big Boy, slapping the air with a scornful palm.

"Aw, c mon! Don be a heel!"

"N git *lynched*? Hell naw!"

"He ain gonna see us."

"How yuh know?"

"Cause he ain."

"Yuh-all go on. Ahma stay right here," said Big Boy.

"Hell, let im stay! C mon, les go," said Buck.

The three walked off, swishing at grass and bushes with sticks. Big Boy looked lazily at their backs.

"Hey!"

Walking on, they glanced over their shoulders.

"Hey, niggers!"

"C mon!"

Big Boy grunted, picked up his stick, pulled to his feet, and stumbled off.

"Wait!"

"C mon!"

He ran, caught up with them, leaped upon their backs, bearing them to the ground.

"Quit, Big Boy!"

"Gawddam, nigger!"

"Git t hell offa me!"

Big Boy sprawled in the grass beside them, laughing and pounding his heels in the ground.

"Nigger, whut yuh think we is, hosses?"

"How come yuh awways hoppin on us?"

"Lissen, wes gonna double-team on yuh one of these days n beat yo ol ass good."

Big Boy smiled.

"Sho nough?"

"Yeah, don yuh like it?"

"We gonna beat yuh sos yuh cant walk!"

"N dare yuh t do nothin erbout it!"

Big Boy bared his teeth.

"C mon! Try it now!"

The three circled around him.

"Say, Buck, yuh grab his feets!"

"N yuh git his head, Lester!"

"N Bobo, yuh git berhin n grab his arms!"

Keeping more than arm's length, they circled round and round Big Boy.

"C mon!" said Big Boy, feinting at one and then the other.

Round and round they circled, but could not seem to get any closer. Big Boy stopped and braced his hands on his hips.

"Is all three of yuh-all scareda me?"

"Les git im some other time," said Bobo, grinning.

"Yeah, we kin ketch yuh when yuh ain thinkin," said Lester.

"We kin trick yuh," said Buck.

They laughed and walked together.

Big Boy belched.

"Ahm hongry," he said.

"Me too."

"Ah wished Ah hada big hot pota belly-busters!"

"Cooked wid some good ol salty ribs . . ."

"N some good ol egg cornbread . . ."

"N some buttermilk . . ."

"N some hot peach cobbler swimmin in juice . . ."

"Nigger, hush!"

They began to chant, emphasizing the rhythm by cutting at grass with sticks.

> *Bye n bye*
> *Ah wanna piece of pie*
> *Pies too sweet*
> *Ah wanna piece of meat*
> *Meats too red*
> *Ah wanna piece of bread*
> *Breads too brown*
> *Ah wanna go t town*
> *Towns too far*
> *Ah wanna ketch a car*
> *Cars too fas*
> *Ah fall n break mah ass*
> *Ahll understan it better bye n bye . . .*

They climbed over a barbed-wire fence and entered a stretch of thick woods. Big Boy was whistling softly, his eyes half-closed.

"LES GIT IM!"

Buck, Lester, and Bobo whirled, grabbed Big Boy about the neck, arms, and legs, bearing him to the ground. He grunted and kicked wildly as he went back into weeds.

"Hol im tight!"

"Git his arms! Git his arms!"

"Set on his legs so he cant kick!"

Big Boy puffed heavily, trying to get loose.

"WE GOT YUH NOW, GAWDDAMMIT, WE GOT YUH NOW!"

"Thas a Gawddam lie!" said Big Boy. He kicked, twisted, and clutched for a hold on one and then the other.

"Say, yuh-all hep me hol his arms!" said Bobo.

"Aw, we got this bastard now!" said Lester.

"Thas a Gawddam lie!" said Big Boy again.

"Say, yuh-all hep me hol his arms!" called Bobo.

Big Boy managed to encircle the neck of Bobo with his left arm. He tightened his elbow scissors-like and hissed through his teeth:

"Yuh got me, ain yuh?"

"Hol im!"

"Les beat this bastard's ass!"

"Say, hep me hol his *arms*! Hes got aholda mah *neck*!" cried Bobo.

Big Boy squeezed Bobo's neck and twisted his head to the ground.

"Yuh got me, ain yuh?"

"Quit, Big Boy, yuh chokin me; yuh hurtin mah neck!" cried Bobo.

"Turn me loose!" said Big Boy.

"Ah ain got yuh! Its the others whut got yuh!" pleaded Bobo.

"Tell them others t git t hell offa me or Ahma break yo neck," said Big Boy.

"Ssssay, yyyuh-all gggit ooooffa Bbig Boy. Hhhes got me," gurgled Bobo.

"Cant yuh hol im?"

"Nnaw, hhes ggot mmah nneck . . ."

Big Boy squeezed tighter.

"N Ahma break it too less yuh tell em t git t hell offa me!"

"Ttturn mmmeee lllloose," panted Bobo, tears gushing.

"Cant yuh hol im, Bobo?" asked Buck.

"Nnaw, yuh-all tturn im lloose; hhhes got mah nn-neck . . ."

"Grab his neck, Bobo . . ."

"Ah cant; yugurgur . . ."

To save Bobo, Lester and Buck got up and ran to a safe distance. Big Boy released Bobo, who staggered to his feet, slobbering and trying to stretch a crick out of his neck.

"Shucks, nigger, yuh almos broke mah neck," whimpered Bobo.

"Ahm gonna break yo ass nex time," said Big Boy.

"Ef Bobo coulda hel yuh we woulda had yuh," yelled Lester.

"Ah wuznt gonna let im do that," said Big Boy.

They walked together again, swishing sticks.

"Yuh see," began Big Boy, "when a ganga guys jump on yuh, all yuh gotta do is jus put the heat on one of them n make im tell the others t let up, see?"

"Gee, thas a good idee!"

"Yeah, thas a good idee!"

"But yuh almos broke mah neck, man," said Bobo.

"Ahma smart nigger," said Big Boy, thrusting out his chest.

II

They came to the swimming hole.

"Ah ain goin in," said Bobo.

"Done got scared?" asked Big Boy.

"Naw, Ah ain scared . . ."

"How come yuh ain goin in?"

"Yuh know ol man Harvey don erllow no niggers t swim in this hole."

"N jus las year he took a shot at Bob fer swimmin in here," said Lester.

"Shucks, ol man Harvey ain studyin bout us niggers," said Big Boy.

"Hes at home thinkin about his jelly-roll," said Buck. They laughed.

"Buck, yo mins lowern a snakes belly," said Lester.

"Ol man Harveys too doggone ol t think erbout jelly-roll," said Big Boy.

"Hes dried up; all the saps done lef im," said Bobo.

"C mon, les go!" said Big Boy.

Bobo pointed.

"See tha sign over yonder?"

"Yeah."

"Whut it say?"

"NO TRESPASSIN," read Lester.

"Know whut tha mean?"

"Mean ain no dogs n niggers erllowed," said Buck.

"Waal, wes here now," said Big Boy. "Ef he ketched us even like this thered be trouble, so we just as waal go on in . . ."

"Ahm wid the nex one!"

"Ahll go ef anybody else goes!"

Big Boy looked carefully in all directions. Seeing nobody, he began jerking off his overalls.

"LAS ONE INS A OL DEAD DOG!"

"THAS YO MA!"

"THAS YO PA!"

"THAS BOTH YO MA N YO PA!"

They jerked off their clothes and threw them in a pile under a tree. Thirty seconds later they stood, black and naked, on the edge of the hole under a sloping embankment. Gingerly Big Boy touched the water with his foot.

"Man, this waters col," he said.

"Ahm gonna put mah cloes back on," said Bobo, withdrawing his foot.

Big Boy grabbed him about the waist.

"Like hell yuh is!"

"Git outta the way, nigger!" Bobo yelled.

"Throw im in!" said Lester.

"Duck im!"

Bobo crouched, spread his legs, and braced himself against Big Boy's body. Locked in each other's arms, they tussled on the edge of the hole, neither able to throw the other.

"C mon, les me n yuh push em in."

"O.K."

Laughing, Lester and Buck gave the two locked bodies a running push. Big Boy and Bobo splashed, sending up silver spray in the sunlight. When Big Boy's head came up he yelled:

"Yuh bastard!"

"Tha wuz yo ma yuh pushed!" said Bobo, shaking his head to clear the water from his eyes.

They did a surface dive, came up and struck out across the creek. The muddy water foamed. They swam back, waded into shallow water, breathing heavily and blinking eyes.

"C mon in!"

"Man, the waters fine!"

Lester and Buck hesitated.

"Les wet em," Big Boy whispered to Bobo.

Before Lester and Buck could back away, they were dripping wet from handsful of scooped water.

"Hey, quit!"

"Gawddam, nigger! Tha waters col!"

"C mon in!" called Big Boy.

"We jus as waal go on in now," said Buck.

"Look n see ef anybodys comin."

Kneeling, they squinted among the trees.

"Ain nobody."

"C mon, les go."

They waded in slowly, pausing each few steps to catch their breath. A desperate water battle began. Closing eyes and backing away, they shunted water into one another's faces with the flat palms of hands.

"Hey, cut it out!"

"Yeah, Ahm bout drownin!"

They came together in water up to their navels, blowing and blinking. Big Boy ducked, upsetting Bobo.

"Look out, nigger!"

"Don holler so loud!"

"Yeah, they kin hear yo ol big mouth a mile erway."

"This waters too col fer me."

"Thas cause it rained yistiddy."

They swam across and back again.

"Ah wish we hada bigger place t swim in."

"The white folks got plenty swimmin pools n we ain got none."

"Ah useta swim in the ol Missippi when we lived in Vicksburg."

Big Boy put his head under the water and blew his breath. A sound came like that of a hippopotamus.

"C mon, les be hippos."

Each went to a corner of the creek and put his mouth just below the surface and blew like a hippopotamus. Tiring, they came and sat under the embankment.

"Look like Ah gotta chill."

"Me too."

"Les stay here n dry off."

"Jeeesus, Ahm col!"

They kept still in the sun, suppressing shivers. After some of the water had dried off their bodies they began to talk through clattering teeth.

"Whut would yuh do ef ol man Harveyd come erlong right now?"

"Run like hell!"

"Man, Ahd run so fas hed thinka black streaka lightnin shot pass im."

"But spose he hada gun?"

"Aw, nigger, shut up!"

They were silent. They ran their hands over wet, trembling legs, brushing water away. Then their eyes watched the sun sparkling on the restless creek.

Far away a train whistled.

"There goes number seven!"

"Headin fer up Noth!"

"Blazin it down the line!"

"Lawd, Ahm goin Noth some day."

"Me too, man."

"They say colored folks up Noth is got ekual rights."

They grew pensive. A black winged butterfly hovered at the water's edge. A bee droned. From somewhere came the sweet scent of honeysuckles. Dimly they could hear sparrows twittering in the woods. They rolled from side to side, letting sunshine dry their skins and warm their blood. They plucked blades of grass and chewed them.

"Oh!"

They looked up, their lips parting.

"Oh!"

A white woman, poised on the edge of the opposite embankment, stood directly in front of them, her hat in her hand and her hair lit by the sun.

"Its a woman!" whispered Big Boy in an underbreath. "A *white* woman!"

They stared, their hands instinctively covering their groins. Then they scrambled to their feet. The white woman backed slowly out of sight. They stood for a moment, looking at one another.

"Les git outta here!" Big Boy whispered.

"Wait till she goes erway."

"Les run, theyll ketch us here naked like this!"

"Mabbe theres a man wid her."

"C mon, les git our cloes," said Big Boy.

They waited a moment longer, listening.

"Whut t hell! Ahma git mah cloes," said Big Boy.

Grabbing at short tufts of grass, he climbed the embankment.

"Don run out there now!"

"C mon back, fool!"

Bobo hesitated. He looked at Big Boy, and then at Buck and Lester.

"Ahm goin wid Big Boy n git mah cloes," he said.

"Don run out there naked like tha, fool!" said Buck. "Yuh don know whos out there!"

Big Boy was climbing over the edge of the embankment.

"C mon," he whispered.

Bobo climbed after. Twenty-five feet away the woman

stood. She had one hand over her mouth. Hanging by fingers, Buck and Lester peeped over the edge.

"C mon back; that womans scared," said Lester.

Big Boy stopped, puzzled. He looked at the woman. He looked at the bundle of clothes. Then he looked at Buck and Lester.

"C mon, les git our cloes!"

He made a step.

"Jim!" the woman screamed.

Big Boy stopped and looked around. His hands hung loosely at his sides. The woman, her eyes wide, her hand over her mouth, backed away to the tree where their clothes lay in a heap.

"Big Boy, come back n wait till shes gone!"

Bobo ran to Big Boy's side.

"Les go home! Theyll ketch us here," he urged.

Big Boy's throat felt tight.

"Lady, we wanna git our cloes," he said.

Buck and Lester climbed the embankment and stood indecisively. Big Boy ran toward the tree.

"Jim!" the woman screamed. "Jim! Jim!"

Black and naked, Big Boy stopped three feet from her.

"We wanna git our cloes," he said again, his words coming mechanically.

He made a motion.

"You go away! You go away! I tell you, you go away!"

Big Boy stopped again, afraid. Bobo ran and snatched the clothes. Buck and Lester tried to grab theirs out of his hands.

"You go away! You go away! You go away!" the woman screamed.

"Les go!" said Bobo, running toward the woods.

CRACK!

Lester grunted, stiffened, and pitched forward. His forehead struck a toe of the woman's shoes.

Bobo stopped, clutching the clothes. Buck whirled. Big Boy stared at Lester, his lips moving.

"Hes gotta gun; hes gotta gun!" yelled Buck, running wildly.

CRACK!

Buck stopped at the edge of the embankment, his head jerked backward, his body arched stiffly to one side; he toppled headlong, sending up a shower of bright spray to the sunlight. The creek bubbled.

Big Boy and Bobo backed away, their eyes fastened fearfully on a white man who was running toward them. He had a rifle and wore an army officer's uniform. He ran to the woman's side and grabbed her hand.

"You hurt, Bertha, you hurt?"

She stared at him and did not answer.

The man turned quickly. His face was red. He raised the rifle and pointed it at Bobo. Bobo ran back, holding the clothes in front of his chest.

"Don shoot me, Mistah, don shoot me . . ."

Big Boy lunged for the rifle, grabbing the barrel.

"You black sonofabitch!"

Big Boy clung desperately.

"Let go, you black bastard!"

The barrel pointed skyward.

CRACK!

The white man, taller and heavier, flung Big Boy to the ground. Bobo dropped the clothes, ran up, and jumped onto the white man's back.

"You black sonsofbitches!"

The white man released the rifle, jerked Bobo to the ground, and began to batter the naked boy with his fists. Then Big Boy swung, striking the man in the mouth with the barrel. His teeth caved in, and he fell, dazed. Bobo was on his feet.

"C mon, Big Boy, les go!"

Breathing hard, the white man got up and faced Big Boy. His lips were trembling, his neck and chin wet with blood. He spoke quietly.

"Give me that gun, boy!"

Big Boy leveled the rifle and backed away.

The white man advanced.

"Boy, I say give me that gun!"

Bobo had the clothes in his arms.

"Run, Big Boy, run!"

The man came at Big Boy.

"Ahll kill yuh; Ahll kill yuh!" said Big Boy.

His fingers fumbled for the trigger.

The man stopped, blinked, spat blood. His eyes were bewildered. His face whitened. Suddenly, he lunged for the rifle, his hands outstretched.

CRACK!

He fell forward on his face.

"Jim!"

Big Boy and Bobo turned in surprise to look at the woman.

"Jim!" she screamed again, and fell weakly at the foot of the tree.

Big Boy dropped the rifle, his eyes wide. He looked around. Bobo was crying and clutching the clothes.

"Big Boy, Big Boy . . ."

Big Boy looked at the rifle, started to pick it up, but didn't. He seemed at a loss. He looked at Lester, then at the white man; his eyes followed a thin stream of blood that seeped to the ground.

"Yuh done killed im," mumbled Bobo.

"Les go home!"

Naked, they turned and ran toward the woods. When they reached the barbed-wire fence they stopped.

"Les git our cloes on," said Big Boy.

They slipped quickly into overalls. Bobo held Lester's and Buck's clothes.

"Whut we gonna do wid these?"

Big Boy stared. His hands twitched.

"Leave em."

They climbed the fence and ran through the woods. Vines and leaves switched their faces. Once Bobo tripped and fell.

"C mon!" said Big Boy.

Bobo started crying, blood streaming from his scratches.

"Ahm scared!"

"C mon! Don cry! We wanna git home fo they ketches us!"

"Ahm scared!" said Bobo again, his eyes full of tears.

Big Boy grabbed his hand and dragged him along.

"C mon!"

III

They stopped when they got to the end of the woods. They could see the open road leading home, home to ma and pa. But they hung back, afraid. The thick shadows cast from the trees were friendly and sheltering. But the wide glare of sun stretching out over the fields was pitiless. They crouched behind an old log.

"We gotta git home," said Big Boy.

"Theys gonna lynch us," said Bobo, half-questioningly.

Big Boy did not answer.

"Theys gonna lynch us," said Bobo again.

Big Boy shuddered.

"Hush!" he said. He did not want to think of it. He could not think of it; there was but one thought, and he clung to that one blindly. He had to get home, home to ma and pa.

Their heads jerked up. Their ears had caught the rhythmic jingle of a wagon. They fell to the ground and clung flat to the side of a log. Over the crest of the hill came the top of a hat. A white face. Then shoulders in a blue shirt. A wagon drawn by two horses pulled into full view.

Big Boy and Bobo held their breath, waiting. Their eyes followed the wagon till it was lost in dust around a bend of the road.

"We gotta git home," said Big Boy.

"Ahm scared," said Bobo.

"C mon! Les keep t the fields."

They ran till they came to the cornfields. Then they went slower, for last year's corn stubbles bruised their feet.

They came in sight of a brickyard.

"Wait a minute," gasped Big Boy.

They stopped.

"Ahm goin on t mah home n yuh better go on t yos."

Bobo's eyes grew round.

"Ahm scared!"

"Yuh better go on!"

"Lemme go wid yuh; theyll ketch me . . ."

"Ef yuh kin git home mabbe yo folks kin hep yuh t git erway."

Big Boy started off. Bobo grabbed him.

"Lemme go wid yuh!"

Big Boy shook free.

"Ef yuh stay here theys gonna lynch yuh!" he yelled, running.

After he had gone about twenty-five yards he turned and looked; Bobo was flying through the woods like the wind.

Big Boy slowed when he came to the railroad. He wondered if he ought to go through the streets or down the track. He decided on the tracks. He could dodge a train better than a mob.

He trotted along the ties, looking ahead and back. His cheek itched, and he felt it. His hand came away smeared with blood. He wiped it nervously on his overalls.

When he came to his back fence he heaved himself over. He landed among a flock of startled chickens. A bantam rooster tried to spur him. He slipped and fell in front of the kitchen steps, grunting heavily. The ground was slick with greasy dishwater.

Panting, he stumbled through the doorway.

"Lawd, Big Boy, whuts wrong wid yuh?"

His mother stood gaping in the middle of the floor. Big Boy flopped wordlessly onto a stool, almost toppling over. Pots simmered on the stove. The kitchen smelled of food cooking.

"Whuts the matter, Big Boy?"

Mutely, he looked at her. Then he burst into tears. She came and felt the scratches on his face.

"Whut happened t yuh, Big Boy? Somebody been botherin yuh?"

"They after me, Ma! They after me . . ."

"Who!"

"Ah . . . Ah . . . We . . ."

"Big Boy, whuts wrong wid yuh?"

"He killed Lester n Buck," he muttered simply.

"Killed!"

"Yessum."

"Lester n Buck!"

"Yessum, Ma!"

"How killed?"

"He shot em, Ma!"

"Lawd Gawd in Heaven, have mercy on us all! This is mo trouble, mo trouble," she moaned, wringing her hands.

"N Ah killed im, Ma . . ."

She stared, trying to understand.

"Whut happened, Big Boy?"

"We tried t git our cloes from the tree . . ."

"Whut tree?"

"We wuz swimmin, Ma. N the white woman . . ."

"*White* woman? . . ."

"Yessum. She wuz at the swimmin hole . . ."

"Lawd have mercy! Ah knowed yuh boys wuz gonna keep on till yuh got into somethin like this!"

She ran into the hall.

"Lucy!"

"Mam?"

"C mere!"

"Mam?"

"C mere, Ah say!"

"Whutcha wan, Ma? Ahm sewin."

"Chile, will yuh c mere like Ah ast yuh?"

Lucy came to the door holding an unfinished apron in her hands. When she saw Big Boy's face she looked wildly at her mother.

"Whuts the matter?"

"Wheres Pa?"

"Hes out front, Ah reckon."

"Git im, quick!"

"Whuts the matter, Ma?"

"Go git yo Pa, Ah say!"

Lucy ran out. The mother sank into a chair, holding a dish rag. Suddenly, she sat up.

"Big Boy, Ah thought yuh wuz at school?"

Big Boy looked at the floor.

"How come yuh didnt go t school?"

"We went t the woods."

She sighed.

"Ah done done all Ah kin fer yuh, Big Boy. Only Gawd kin hep yuh now."

"Ma, don let em git me; don let em git me . . ."

His father came into the doorway. He stared at Big Boy, then at his wife.

"Whuts Big Boy inter now?" he asked sternly.

"Saul, Big Boys done gone n got inter trouble wid the white folks."

The old man's mouth dropped, and he looked from one to the other.

"Saul, we gotta git im erway from here."

"Open yo mouth n talk! Whut yuh been doin?" The old man gripped Big Boy's shoulders and peered at the scratches on his face.

"Me n Lester n Buck n Bobo wuz out on ol man Harveys place swimmin . . ."

"Saul, its a *white* woman!"

Big Boy winced. The old man compressed his lips and stared at his wife. Lucy gaped at her brother as though she had never seen him before.

"Whut happened? Cant yuh-all talk?" the old man thundered, with a certain helplessness in his voice.

"We wuz swimmin," Big Boy began, "n then a white woman comes up t the hole. We got up right erway t git our cloes sos we could git erway, n she started screamin. Our cloes wuz right by the tree where she wuz standin, n when we started t git em she jus screamed. We tol her we wanted our cloes . . . Yuh see, Pa, she wuz standin right *by* our cloes; n when we went t git em she jus screamed . . . Bobo got the cloes, n then he shot Lester . . ."

"*Who* shot Lester?"

"The white man."

"Whut white man?"

"Ah dunno, Pa. He wuz a soljer, n he had a rifle."

"A soljer?"

"Yessuh."

"A *soljer*?"

"Yessuh, Pa. A soljer."

The old man frowned.

"N then whut yuh-all do?"

"Waal, Buck said, 'Hes gotta gun!' N we started runnin. N then he shot Buck, n he fell in the swimmin hole. We didn't see im no mo . . . He wuz close on us then. He looked at the white woman n then he started to shoot Bobo. Ah grabbed the gun, n we started fightin. Bobo jumped on his back. He started beatin Bobo. Then Ah hit im wid the gun. Then he started at me n Ah shot im. Then we run . . ."

"Who seen?"

"Nobody."

"Wheres Bobo?"

"He went home."

"Anybody run after yuh-all?"

"Nawsuh."

"Yuh see anybody?"

"Nawsuh. Nobody but a white man. But he didnt see us."

"How long fo yuh-all lef the swimmin hole?"

"Little while ergo."

The old man nervously brushed his hand across his eyes and walked to the door. His lips moved, but no words came.

"Saul, whut we gonna do?"

"Lucy," began the old man, "go t Brother Sanders n tell im Ah said c mere; n go t Brother Jenkins n tell im

Ah said c mere; n go t Elder Peters n tell im Ah said c
mere. N don say nothin t nobody but whut Ah tol yuh.
N when yuh git thu come straight back. Now go!"

Lucy dropped her apron across the back of a chair
and ran down the steps. The mother bent over, crying
and praying. The old man walked slowly over to Big Boy.

"Big Boy?"

Big Boy swallowed.

"Ahm talkin t yuh!"

"Yessuh."

"How come yuh didnt go t school this mawnin?"

"We went t the woods."

"Didnt yo ma send yuh t school?"

"Yessuh."

"How come yuh didnt go?"

"We went t the woods."

"Don yuh know thas wrong?"

"Yessuh."

"How come yuh go?"

Big Boy looked at his fingers, knotted them, and
squirmed in his seat.

"AHM TALKIN T YUH!"

His wife straightened up and said reprovingly:

"Saul!"

The old man desisted, yanking nervously at the shoul-
der straps of his overalls.

"How long wuz the woman there?"

"Not long."

"Wuz she young?"

"Yessuh. Lika gal."

"Did yuh-all say anythin t her?"

"Nawsuh. We jus said we wanted our cloes."

"N whut she say?"

"Nothin, Pa. She jus backed erway t the tree n
screamed."

The old man stared, his lips trying to form a question.

"Big Boy, did yuh-all bother her?"

"Nawsuh, Pa. We didn't *touch* her."

"How long fo the white man come up?"

"Right erway."

"Whut he say?"

"Nothin. He jus cussed us."

Abruptly the old man left the kitchen.

"Ma, cant Ah go fo they ketches me?"

"Sauls doin whut he kin."

"Ma, Ma, Ah don wan em t ketch me . . ."

"Sauls doin whut he kin. Nobody but the good Lawd kin hep us now."

The old man came back with a shotgun and leaned it in a corner. Fascinatedly, Big Boy looked at it.

There was a knock at the front door.

"Liza, see whos there."

She went. They were silent, listening. They could hear her talking.

"Whos there?"

"Me."

"Who?"

"Me, Brother Sanders."

"C mon in. Sauls waitin fer yuh."

Sanders paused in the doorway, smiling.

"Yuh sent fer me, Brother Morrison?"

"Brother Sanders, wes in deep trouble here."

Sanders came all the way into the kitchen.

"Yeah?"

"Big Boy done gone n killed a white man."

Sanders stopped short, then came forward, his face thrust out, his mouth open. His lips moved several times before he could speak.

"A *white* man?"

"They gonna kill me; they gonna kill me!" Big Boy cried, running to the old man.

"Saul, cant we git im erway somewhere?"

"Here now, take it easy; take it easy," said Sanders, holding Big Boy's wrists.

"They gonna kill me; they gonna lynch me!"

Big Boy slipped to the floor. They lifted him to a stool. His mother held him closely, pressing his head to her bosom.

"Whut we gonna do?" asked Sanders.

"Ah done sent fer Brother Jenkins n Elder Peters."

Sanders leaned his shoulders against the wall. Then, as the full meaning of it all came to him, he exclaimed:

"Theys gonna git a mob! . . ." His voice broke off and his eyes fell on the shotgun.

Feet came pounding on the steps. They turned toward the door. Lucy ran in crying. Jenkins followed. The old man met him in the middle of the room, taking his hand.

"Wes in bad trouble here, Brother Jenkins. Big Boy's done gone n killed a white man. Yuh-alls gotta hep me . . ."

Jenkins looked hard at Big Boy.

"Elder Peters says hes comin," said Lucy.

"When all this happen?" asked Jenkins.

"Near bout a hour ergo, now," said the old man.

"Whut we gonna do?" asked Jenkins.

"Ah wanna wait till Elder Peters come," said the old man helplessly.

"But we gotta work fas ef we gonna do anythin," said Sanders. "Well git in trouble jus standin here like this."

Big Boy pulled away from his mother.

"Pa, lemme go now! Lemme go now!"

"Be still, Big Boy!"

"Where kin yuh go?"

"Ah could ketch a freight!"

"Thas *sho* death!" said Jenkins. "Theyll be watchin em all!"

"Kin yuh-all hep me wid some money?" the old man asked.

They shook their heads.

"Saul, whut kin we do? Big Boy cant stay here."

There was another knock at the door.

The old man backed stealthily to the shotgun.

"Lucy go!"

Lucy looked at him, hesitating.

"Ah better go," said Jenkins.

It was Elder Peters. He came in hurriedly.

"Good evenin, everbody!"

"How yuh, Elder?"

"Good evenin."

"How yuh today?"

Peters looked around the crowded kitchen.

"Whuts the matter?"

"Elder, wes in deep trouble," began the old man. "Big Boy n some mo boys . . ."

" . . . Lester n Buck n Bobo . . ."

" . . . wuz over on ol man Harveys place swimmin . . ."

"N he don like us niggers *none*," said Peters emphatically. He widened his legs and put his thumbs in the armholes of his vest.

" . . . n some white woman . . ."

"Yeah?" said Peters, coming closer.

" . . . comes erlong n the boys tries t git their cloes where they done lef em under a tree. Waal, she started screamin n all, see? Reckon she thought the boys wuz after her. Then a white man in a soljers suit shoots two of em . . ."

" . . . Lester n Buck . . ."

"Huummm," said Peters. "Tha wuz ol man Harveys son."

"Harveys son?"

"Yuh mean the one tha wuz in the Army?"

"Yuh mean Jim?"

"Yeah," said Peters. "The papers said he wuz here fer a vacation from his regiment. N tha woman the boys saw wuz jus erbout his wife . . ."

They stared at Peters. Now that they knew what white person had been killed, their fears became definite.

"N whut else happened?"

"Big Boy shot the man . . ."

"Harveys *son?*"

"He had t, Elder. He wuz gonna shoot im ef he didnt . . ."

"Lawd!" said Peters. He looked around and put his hat back on.

"How long ergo wuz this?"

"Mighty near an hour, now, Ah reckon."

"Do the white folks know yit?"

"Don know, Elder."

"Yuh-all better git this boy outta here right now," said Peters. "Cause ef yuh don theres gonna be a lynchin . . ."

"Where kin Ah go, Elder?" Big Boy ran up to him.

They crowded around Peters. He stood with his legs wide apart, looking up at the ceiling.

"Mabbe we kin hide im in the church till he kin git erway," said Jenkins.

Peters' lips flexed.

"Naw, Brother, thall never do! Theyll git im there sho. N anyhow, ef they ketch im there itll ruin us all. We gotta git the boy outta town . . ."

Sanders went up to the old man.

"Lissen," he said in a whisper. "Mah son, Will, the one whut drives fer the Magnolia Express Comny, is taking a truck o goods t Chicawgo in the mawnin. If we kin hide Big Boy somewhere till then, we kin put im on the truck . . ."

"Pa, please, lemme go wid Will when he goes in the mawnin," Big Boy begged.

The old man stared at Sanders.

"Yuh reckon thas safe?"

"Its the only thing yuh *kin* do," said Peters.

"But where we gonna hide im till then?"

"Whut time yo boy leavin out in the mawnin?"

"At six."

They were quiet, thinking. The water kettle on the stove sang.

"Pa, Ah knows where Will passes erlong wid the truck out on Bullards Road. Ah kin hide in one of them ol kilns . . ."

"Where?"

"In one of them kilns we built . . ."

"But theyll git yuh there," wailed the mother.

"But there ain no place else fer im t go."

"Theres some holes big ernough fer me t git in n stay till Will comes erlong," said Big Boy. "Please, Pa, lemme go fo they ketches me . . ."

"Let im go!"

"Please, Pa . . ."

The old man breathed heavily.

"Lucy, git his things!"

"Saul, theyll git im out there!" wailed the mother, grabbing Big Boy.

Peters pulled her away.

"Sister Morrison, ef yuh don let im go n git erway from here hes gonna be caught shos theres a Gawd in Heaven!"

Lucy came running with Big Boy's shoes and pulled them on his feet. The old man thrust a battered hat on his head. The mother went to the stove and dumped the skillet of corn pone into her apron. She wrapped it, and unbuttoning Big Boy's overalls, pushed it into his bosom.

"Heres somethin fer yuh t eat; n pray, Big Boy, cause thas all anybody kin do now . . ."

Big Boy pulled to the door, his mother clinging to him.

"Let im go, Sister Morrison!"

"Run fas, Big Boy!"

Big Boy raced across the yard, scattering the chickens. He paused at the fence and hollered back:

"Tell Bobo where Ahm hidin n tell im t c mon!"

IV

He made for the railroad, running straight toward the sunset. He held his left hand tightly over his heart, holding the hot pone of corn bread there. At times he stumbled over the ties, for his shoes were tight and hurt his feet. His throat burned from thirst; he had had no water since noon.

He veered off the track and trotted over the crest of a hill, following Bullard's Road. His feet slipped and slid in the dust. He kept his eyes straight ahead, fearing every clump of shrubbery, every tree. He wished it were night. If he could only get to the kilns without meeting anyone. Suddenly a thought came to him like a blow. He recalled hearing the old folks tell tales of bloodhounds, and fear made him run slower. None of them had thought of that. Spose blood-houns wuz put on his trail? Lawd! Spose a whole pack of em, foamin n howlin, tore im t pieces? He went limp and his feet dragged.

Yeah, thas whut they wuz gonna send after im, blood-hounds! N then thered be no way fer im t dodge! Why hadnt Pa let im take tha shotgun? He stopped. He oughta go back n git tha shotgun. And then when the mob came he would take some with him.

In the distance he heard the approach of a train. It jarred him back to a sharp sense of danger. He ran again, his big shoes sopping up and down in the dust. He was tired and his lungs were bursting from running. He wet his lips, wanting water. As he turned from the road across a plowed field he heard the train roaring at his heels. He ran faster, gripped in terror.

He was nearly there now. He could see the black clay on the sloping hillside. Once inside a kiln he would be safe. For a little while, at least. He thought of the shotgun again. If he only had something! Someone to talk to . . . Thas right! Bobo! Bobod be wid im. Hed almost fergot Bobo. Bobod bringa gun; he knowed he would. N tergether they could kill the whole mob. Then in the mawning theyd git inter Will's truck n go far erway, t Chicawgo . . .

He slowed to a walk, looking back and ahead. A light wind skipped over the grass. A beetle lit on his cheek and he brushed it off. Behind the dark pines hung a red sun. Two bats flapped against that sun. He shivered, for he was growing cold; the sweat on his body was drying.

He stopped at the foot of the hill, trying to choose between two patches of black kilns high above him. He went to the left, for there lay the ones he, Bobo, Lester, and Buck had dug only last week. He looked around again; the landscape was bare. He climbed the embankment and stood before a row of black pits sinking four and five feet deep into the earth. He went to the largest and peered in. He stiffened when his ears caught the sound of a whir. He ran back a few steps and poised on his toes. Six foot of snake slid out of the pit and went into coil. Big Boy looked around wildly for a stick. He ran down the slope, peering into the grass. He stumbled over a tree limb. He picked it up and tested it by striking it against the ground.

Warily, he crept back up the slope, his stick poised. When about seven feet from the snake he stopped and waved the stick. The coil grew tighter, the whir sounded louder, and a flat head reared to strike. He went to the right, and the flat head followed him, the blue-black tongue darting forth; he went to the left, and the flat head followed him there too.

He stopped, teeth clenched. He had to kill this snake. Jus had t kill im! This wuz the safest pit on the hillside. He waved the stick again, looking at the snake before, thinking of a mob behind. The flat head reared higher. With stick over shoulder, he jumped in, swinging. The stick sang through the air, catching the snake on the side of the head, sweeping him out of coil. There was a brown writhing mass. Then Big Boy was upon him, pounding blows home, one on top of the other. He fought viciously, his eyes red, his teeth bared in a snarl. He beat till the snake lay still; then he stomped it with his heel, grinding its head into the dirt.

He stopped, limp, wet. The corners of his lips were white with spittle. He spat and shuddered.

Cautiously, he went to the hole and peered. He longed for a match. He imagined whole nests of them in there waiting. He put the stick into the hole and waved it around. Stooping, he peered again. It mus be awright. He looked over the hillside, his eyes coming back to the dead snake. Then he got to his knees and backed slowly into the hole.

When inside he felt there must be snakes all about him, ready to strike. It seemed he could see and feel them there, waiting tensely in coil. In the dark he imagined long white fangs ready to sink into his neck, his side, his legs. He wanted to come out, but kept still. Shucks, he told himself, ef there wuz any snakes in here they sho woulda done bit me by now. Some of his fear left, and he relaxed.

With elbows on ground and chin on palms, he settled. The clay was cold to his knees and thighs, but his bosom was kept warm by the hot pone of corn bread. His thirst returned and he longed for a drink. He was hungry, too. But he did not want to eat the corn pone. Naw, not now. Mabbe after erwhile, after Bobod came. Then theyd both eat the corn pone.

The view from his hole was fringed by the long tufts of grass. He could see all the way to Bullard's Road, and even beyond. The wind was blowing, and in the east the first touch of dusk was rising. Every now and then a bird floated past, a spot of wheeling black printed against the sky. Big Boy sighed, shifted his weight, and chewed at a blade of grass. A wasp droned. He heard number nine, far away and mournful.

The train made him remember how they had dug these kilns on long hot summer days, how they had made boilers out of big tin cans, filled them with water, fixed stoppers for steam, cemented them in holes with wet clay, and built fires under them. He recalled how they had danced and yelled when a stopper blew out of a boiler, letting out a big spout of steam and a shrill whistle. There were times when they had the whole hillside blazing and smoking. Yeah, yuh see, Big Boy wuz Casey Jones n wuz speedin it down the gleamin rails of the Southern Pacific. Bobo had number two on the Santa Fe. Buck wuz on the Illinoy Central. Lester the Nickel Plate. Lawd, how they shelved the wood in! The boiling water would almost jar the cans loose from

the clay. More and more pine-knots and dry leaves
would be piled under the cans. Flames would grow so
tall they would have to shield their eyes. Sweat would
pour off their faces. Then, suddenly, a peg would shoot
high into the air, and

Pssseeeezzzzzzzzzzzzzzzzzzzzz . . .

Big Boy sighed and stretched out his arm, quenching
the flames and scattering the smoke. Why didnt Bobo c
mon? He looked over the fields; there was nothing but
dying sunlight. His mind drifted back to the kilns. He
remembered the day when Buck, jealous of his winning,
had tried to smash his kiln. Yeah, that ol sonofabitch!
Naw, Lawd! He didnt go t say tha! Whut wuz he
thinkin erbout? Cussin the dead! Yeah, po ol Buck wuz
dead now. N Lester too. Yeah, it wuz awright fer Buck t
smash his kiln. Sho. N he wished he hadnt socked ol
Buck so hard tha day. He wuz sorry fer Buck now. N he
sho wished he hadnt cussed po ol Bucks ma, neither.
Tha wuz sinful! Mabbe Gawd would git im fer tha? But
he didnt go t do it! Po Buck! Po Lester! Hed never treat
anybody like tha ergin, never . . .

Dusk was slowly deepening. Somewhere, he could
not tell exactly where, a cricket took up a fitful song.
The air was growing soft and heavy. He looked over the
fields, longing for Bobo . . .

He shifted his body to ease the cold damp of the
ground, and thought back over the day. Yeah, hed been
dam right erbout not wantin t go swimmin. N ef hed
followed his right min hed neverve gone n got inter all
this trouble. At first hed said naw. But shucks, somehow
hed just went on wid the res. Yeah, he shoulda went on
t school tha mawnin, like Ma told im t do. But, hell,
who wouldnt git tireda awways drivin a guy t school!
Tha wuz the big trouble, awways drivin a guy t school.
He wouldnt be in all this trouble now ef it wuznt fer

that Gawddam school! Impatiently, he took the grass out of his mouth and threw it away, demolishing the little red school house . . .

Yeah, ef they had all kept still n quiet when tha ol white woman showed-up, mabbe shedve went on off. But yuh never kin tell erbout these white folks. Mabbe she wouldntve went. Mabbe tha white man woulda killed all of em! All *fo* of em! Yeah, yuh never kin tell erbout white folks. Then, ergin, mabbe tha white woman woulda went on off n laffed. Yeah, mabbe tha white man woulda said: *Yuh nigger bastards git t hell outta here! Yuh know Gawddam well yuh don berlong here!* N then they woulda grabbed their cloes n run like all hell . . . He blinked the white man away. Where wuz Bobo? Why didn't he hurry up n c mon?

He jerked another blade and chewed. Yeah, ef pa had only let im have tha shotgun! He could stan off a whole mob wid a shotgun. He looked at the ground as he turned a shotgun over in his hands. Then he leveled it at an advancing white man. *Boooom!* The man curled up. Another came. He reloaded quickly, and let him have what the other had got. He too curled up. Then another came. He got the same medicine. Then the whole mob swirled around him, and he blazed away, getting as many as he could. They closed in; but, by Gawd, he had done his part, hadnt he? N the newspapersd say: NIG-GER KILLS DOZEN OF MOB BEFO LYNCHED! Er mabbe theyd say: TRAPPED NIGGER SLAYS TWENTY BEFO KILLED! He smiled a little. Tha wouldnt be so bad, would it? Blinking the newspaper away, he looked over the fields. Where wuz Bobo? Why didnt he hurry up n c mon?

He shifted, trying to get a crick out of his legs. Shucks, he wuz gittin tireda this. N it wuz almos dark now. Yeah, there wuz a little bittie star way over yonder in the eas. Mabbe tha white man wuznt dead? Mabbe they wuznt even lookin fer im? Mabbe he could go back home now? Naw, better wait erwhile. Thad be bes. But, Lawd, ef he only had some water! He could hardly swallow, his throat was so dry. Gawddam them white folks! Thas all they wuz good fer, t run a nigger down lika rabbit! Yeah, they git yuh in a corner n then they let yuh have it. A thousan of em! He shivered, for the cold of the clay was chilling his bones. Lawd, spose they foun im here in this hole? N wid nobody t hep im? . . . But ain no use in thinkin erbout tha; wait till trouble come fo yuh start fightin it. But ef tha mob came one by one hed wipe em all out. Clean up the whole bunch. He caught one by the neck and choked him long and hard, choked him till his tongue and eyes popped out. Then he jumped upon his chest and stomped him like he had stomped that snake. When he had finished with one, another came. He choked him too. Choked till he sank slowly to the ground, gasping . . .

"Hoalo!"

Big Boy snatched his fingers from the white man's neck and looked over the fields. He saw nobody. Had someone spied him? He was sure that somebody had hollered. His heart pounded. But, shucks, nobody couldnt see im here in this hole . . . But mabbe theyd seen im when he wuz comin n had laid low n wuz now closin in on im! Praps they wuz signalin fer the others? Yeah, they wuz creepin up on im! Mabbe he oughta git up n run . . . Oh! Mabbe tha wuz Bobo! Yeah, Bobo! He oughta clim out n see ef Bobo wuz lookin fer im . . . He stiffened.

"Hoalo!"

"Hoalo!"

"Wheres yuh?"

"Over here on Bullards Road!"

"C mon over!"

"Awright!"

He heard footsteps. Then voices came again, low and far away this time.

"Seen anybody?"

"Naw. Yuh?"

"Naw."

"Yuh reckon they got erway?"

"Ah dunno. Its hard t tell."

"Gawddam them sonofabitchin niggers!"

"We oughta kill ever black bastard in this country!"

"Waal, Jim got two of em, anyhow."

"But Bertha said there wuz *fo*!"

"Where in hell they hidin?"

"She said one of em wuz named Big Boy, or somethin like tha."

"We went t his shack lookin fer im."

"Yeah?"

"But we didnt fin im."

"These niggers stick tergether; they don never tell on each other."

"We looked all thu the shack n couldnt fin hide ner hair of im. Then we drove the ol woman n man out n set the shack on fire . . ."

"Jeesus! Ah wished Ah coulda been there!"

"Yuh shoulda heard the ol nigger woman howl . . ."

"Hoalo!"

"C mon over!"

Big Boy eased to the edge and peeped. He saw a white man with a gun slung over his shoulder running down the slope. Wuz they gonna search the hill? Lawd, there wuz no way fer im t git erway now; he wuz caught! He shoulda knowed theyd git im here. N he didnt hava thing, notta thing t fight wid. Yeah, soon as the blood-houns came theyd fin im. Lawd, have mercy!

Theyd lynch im right here on the hill . . . Theyd git im n tie im t a stake n burn im erlive! Lawd! Nobody but the good Lawd could hep im now, nobody . . .

He heard more feet running. He nestled deeper. His chest ached. Nobody but the good Lawd could hep now. They wuz crowdin all round im n when they hada big crowd theyd close in on im. Then itd be over . . . The good Lawd would have t hep im, cause nobody could hep im now, nobody . . .

And then he went numb when he remembered Bobo. Spose Bobod come now? Hed be caught sho! Both of em would be caught! They'd make Bobo tell where he wuz! Bobo oughta not try to come now. Somebody oughta tell im . . . But there wuz nobody; there wuz no way . . .

He eased slowly back to the opening. There was a large group of men. More were coming. Many had guns. Some had coils of rope slung over shoulders.

"Ah tell yuh they still here, somewhere . . ."

"But we looked all over!"

"What t hell! Wouldnt do t let em git erway!"

"Naw. Ef they git erway notta woman in this town would be safe."

"Say, whuts tha yuh got?"

"Er pillar."

"Fer whut?"

"Feathers, fool!"

"Chris! Thisll be hot ef we kin ketch them niggers!"

"Ol Anderson said he wuz gonna bringa barrela tar!"

"Ah got some gasoline in mah car ef yuh need it."

Big Boy had no feelings now. He was waiting. He did not wonder if they were coming after him. He just waited. He did not wonder about Bobo. He rested his cheek against the cold clay, waiting.

A dog barked. He stiffened. It barked again. He

balled himself into a knot at the bottom of the hole, waiting. Then he heard the patter of dog feet.

"Look!"

"Whuts he got?"

"Its a snake!"

"Yeah, the dogs foun a snake!"

"Gee, its a big one!"

"Shucks, Ah wish he could fin one of them sonofabitchin niggers!"

The voices sank to low murmurs. Then he heard number twelve, its bell tolling and whistle crying as it slid along the rails. He flattened himself against the clay. Someone was singing:

"We'll hang ever nigger t a sour apple tree . . ."

When the song ended there was hard laughter. From the other side of the hill he heard the dog barking furiously. He listened. There was more than one dog now. There were many and they were barking their throats out.

"Hush, Ah hear them dogs!"

"When theys barkin like tha theys foun somethin!"

"Here they come over the hill!"

"WE GOT IM! WE GOT IM!"

There came a roar. Tha mus be Bobo; tha mus be Bobo . . . In spite of his fear, Big Boy looked. The road, and half of the hillside across the road, were covered with men. A few were at the top of the hill, stenciled against the sky. He could see dark forms moving up the slopes. They were yelling.

"By Gawd, we got im!"

"C mon!"

"Where is he?"

"Theyre bringing im over the hill!"

"Ah got a rope fer im!"

"Say, somebody go n git the others!"

"Where is he? Cant we see im, Mister?"

"They say Berthas comin, too."

"Jack! Jack! Don leave me! Ah wanna see im!"

"Theyre bringin im over the hill, sweetheart!"

"AH WANNA BE THE FIRS T PUT A ROPE ON THA BLACK BASTARDS NECK!"

"Les start the fire!"

"Heat the tar!"

"Ah got some chains t chain im."

"Bring im over this way!"

"Chris, Ah wished Ah hada drink . . ."

Big Boy saw men moving over the hill. Among them was a long dark spot. Tha mus be Bobo; tha mus be Bobo theys carryin . . . They'll git im here. He oughta git up n run. He clamped his teeth and ran his hand across his forehead, bringing it away wet. He tried to swallow, but could not; his throat was dry.

They had started the song again:

"We'll hang ever nigger t a sour apple tree . . ."

There were women singing now. Their voices made the song round and full. Song waves rolled over the top of pine trees. The sky sagged low, heavy with clouds. Wind was rising. Sometimes cricket cries cut surprisingly across the mob song. A dog had gone to the utmost top of the hill. At each lull of the song his howl floated full into the night.

Big Boy shrank when he saw the first tall flame light the hillside. Would they see im here? Then he remembered you could not see into the dark if you were standing in the light. As flames leaped higher he saw two men rolling a barrel up the slope.

"Say, gimme a han here, will yuh?"

"Awright, heave!"

"C mon! Straight up! Git t the other end!"

"Ah got the feathers here in this pillar!"

"BRING SOME MO WOOD!"

Big Boy could see the barrel surrounded by flames. The mob fell back, forming a dark circle. Theyd fin im here! He had a wild impulse to climb out and fly across the hills. But his legs would not move. He stared hard, trying to find Bobo. His eyes played over a long dark spot near the fire. Fanned by wind, flames leaped higher. He jumped. That dark spot had moved. Lawd, thas Bobo; thas Bobo . . .

He smelt the scent of tar, faint at first, then stronger. The wind brought it full into his face, then blew it away. His eyes burned and he rubbed them with his knuckles. He sneezed.

"LES GIT SOURVINEERS!"

He saw the mob close in around the fire. Their faces were hard and sharp in the light of the flames. More men and women were coming over the hill. The long dark spot was smudged out.

"Everbody git back!"

"Look! Hes gotta finger!"

"C MON! GIT THE GALS BACK FROM THE FIRE!"

"Hes got one of his ears, see?"

"Whuts the matter!"

"A woman fell out! Fainted, Ah reckon . . ."

The stench of tar permeated the hillside. The sky was black and the wind was blowing hard.

"HURRY UP N BURN THE NIGGER FO IT RAINS!"

Big Boy saw the mob fall back, leaving a small knot of men about the fire. Then, for the first time, he had a full glimpse of Bobo. A black body flashed in the light.

Bobo was struggling, twisting; they were binding his arms and legs.

When he saw them tilt the barrel he stiffened. A scream quivered. He knew the tar was on Bobo. The mob fell back. He saw a tar-drenched body glistening and turning.

"THE BASTARDS GOT IT!"

There was a sudden quiet. Then he shrank violently as the wind carried, like a flurry of snow, a widening spiral of white feathers into the night. The flames leaped tall as the trees. The scream came again. Big Boy trembled and looked. The mob was running down the slopes, leaving the fire clear. Then he saw a writhing white mass cradled in yellow flame, and heard screams, one on top of the other, each shriller and shorter than the last. The mob was quiet now, standing still, looking up the slopes at the writhing white mass gradually growing black, growing black in a cradle of yellow flame.

"PO ON MO GAS!"

"Gimme a lif, will yuh!"

Two men were struggling, carrying between them a heavy can. They set it down, tilted it, leaving it so that the gas would trickle down to the hollowed earth around the fire.

Big Boy slid back into the hole, his face buried in clay. He had no feelings now, no fears. He was numb, empty, as though all blood had been drawn from him. Then his muscles flexed taut when he heard a faint patter. A tiny stream of cold water seeped to his knees, making him push back to a drier spot. He looked up; rain was beating in the grass.

"Its rainin!"

"C mon, les git t town!"

" . . . don worry, when the fire git thu wid im hell be gone . . ."

"Wait, Charles! Don leave me; its slippery here . . ."

"Ahll take some of yuh ladies back in mah car . . ."

Big Boy heard the dogs barking again, this time closer. Running feet pounded past. Cold water chilled his ankles. He could hear raindrops steadily hissing.

Now a dog was barking at the mouth of the hole, barking furiously, sensing a presence there. He balled himself into a knot and clung to the bottom, his knees and shins buried in water. The bark came louder. He heard paws scraping and felt the hot scent of dog breath on his face. Green eyes glowed and drew nearer as the barking, muffled by the closeness of the hole, beat upon his eardrums. Backing till his shoulders pressed against the clay, he held his breath. He pushed out his hands, his fingers stiff. The dog yawped louder, advancing, his bark rising sharp and thin. Big Boy rose to his knees, his hands before him. Then he flattened out still more against the bottom, breathing lungsful of hot dog scent, breathing it slowly, hard, but evenly. The dog came closer, bringing hotter dog scent. Big Boy could go back no more. His knees were slipping and slopping in the water. He braced himself, ready. Then, he never exactly knew how—he never knew whether he had lunged or the dog had lunged—they were together, rolling in the water. The green eyes were beneath him, between his legs. Dognails bit into his arms. His knees slipped backward and he landed full on the dog; the dog's breath left in a heavy gasp. Instinctively, he fumbled for the throat as he felt the dog twisting between his knees. The dog snarled, long and low, as though gathering strength. Big Boy's hands traveled swiftly over the dog's back, groping for the throat. He felt dognails again and saw green eyes, but his fingers had found the throat. He choked, feeling his fingers sink; he choked, throwing back his head and stiffening his arms. He felt the dog's body heave, felt dognails digging into his loins. With strength flowing from fear, he closed his fingers, pushing his full weight on the dog's throat. The dog heaved again, and lay still . . . Big Boy heard the sound of his own breathing filling the hole, and heard shouts and footsteps above him going past.

For a long, long time he held the dog, held it long after the last footstep had died out, long after the rain had stopped.

V

Morning found him still on his knees in a puddle of rainwater, staring at the stiff body of a dog. As the air brightened he came to himself slowly. He held still for a long time, as though waking from a dream, as though trying to remember.

The chug of a truck came over the hill. He tried to crawl to the opening. His knees were stiff and a thousand needle-like pains shot from the bottom of his feet to the calves of his legs. Giddiness made his eyes blur. He pulled up and looked. Through brackish light he saw Will's truck standing some twenty-five yards away, the engine running. Will stood on the runningboard, looking over the slopes of the hill.

Big Boy scuffled out, falling weakly in the wet grass. He tried to call to Will, but his dry throat would make no sound. He tried again.

"Will!"

Will heard, answering:

"Big Boy, c mon!"

He tried to run, and fell. Will came, meeting him in the tall grass.

"C mon," Will said, catching his arm.

They struggled to the truck.

"Hurry up!" said Will, pushing him onto the runningboard.

Will pushed back a square trapdoor which swung above the back of the driver's seat. Big Boy pulled through, landing with a thud on the bottom. On hands and knees he looked around in the semi-darkness.

"Wheres Bobo?"

Big Boy stared.

"Wheres Bobo?"

"They got im."

"When?"

"Las night."

"The mob?"

Big Boy pointed in the direction of a charred sapling on the slope of the opposite hill. Will looked. The trapdoor fell. The engine purred, the gears whined, and the truck lurched forward over the muddy road, sending Big Boy on his side.

For a while he lay as he had fallen, on his side, too weak to move. As he felt the truck swing around a curve he straightened up and rested his back against a stack of wooden boxes. Slowly, he began to make out objects in the darkness. Through two long cracks fell thin blades of daylight. The floor was of smooth steel, and cold to his thighs. Splinters and bits of sawdust danced with the rumble of the truck. Each time they swung around a curve he was pulled over the floor; he grabbed at corners of boxes to steady himself. Once he heard the crow of a rooster. It made him think of home, of ma and pa. He thought he remembered hearing somewhere that the house had burned, but could not remember where . . . It all seemed unreal now.

He was tired. He dozed, swaying with the lurch.

Then he jumped awake. The truck was running smoothly, on gravel. Far away he heard two short blasts from the Buckeye Lumber Mill. Unconsciously, the thought sang through his mind: Its six erclock . . .

The trapdoor swung in. Will spoke through a corner of his mouth.

"How yuh comin?"

"Awright."

"How they git Bobo?"

"He wuz comin over the hill."

"Whut they do?"

"They burnt im . . . Will, Ah wan some water; mah throats like fire . . ."

"Well git some when we pass a fillin station."

Big Boy leaned back and dozed. He jerked awake when the truck stopped. He heard Will get out. He wanted to peep through the trapdoor, but was afraid. For a moment, the wild fear he had known in the hole came back. Spose theyd search n fin im? He quieted when he heard Will's footstep on the runningboard. The trapdoor pushed in. Will's hat came through, dripping.

"Take it, quick!"

Big Boy grabbed, spilling water into his face. The truck lurched. He drank. Hard cold lumps of brick rolled into his hot stomach. A dull pain made him bend over. His intestines seemed to be drawing into a tight knot. After a bit it eased, and he sat up, breathing softly.

The truck swerved. He blinked his eyes. The blades of daylight had turned brightly golden. The sun had risen.

The truck sped over the asphalt miles, sped northward, jolting him, shaking out of his bosom the crumbs of corn bread, making them dance with the splinters and sawdust in the golden blades of sunshine.

He turned on his side and slept.

II

Down by the Riverside

I

EACH STEP he took made the old house creak as though the earth beneath the foundations were soggy. He wondered how long the logs which supported the house could stand against the water. But what really worried him were the steps; they might wash away at any moment, and then they would be trapped. He had spent all that morning trying to make them secure with frayed rope, but he did not have much faith. He walked to the window and the half-rotten planks sagged under his feet. He had never realized they were that shaky. He pulled back a tattered curtain, wishing the dull ache would leave his head. Ah been feverish all day. Feels like Ah got the flu. Through a dingy pane he saw yellow water swirling around a corner of the barn. A steady drone filled his ears. In the morning the water was a deep brown. In the afternoon it was a clayey yellow. And at night it was black, like a restless tide of liquid tar. It was about six feet deep and still rising; it had risen two feet that day. He squinted at a tiny ridge of foam where the yellow current struck a side of the barn and veered sharply. For three days he had been watching that tiny ridge of foam. When it shortened he had hopes of seeing the ground soon; but when it lengthened he knew that the current was flowing strong again. All the seeds for spring planting were wet now. They gonna rot, he thought with despair. The morning before he had seen his only cow, Sally, lowing, wagging her head, rolling her eyes, and pushing

through three feet of water for the hills. It was then that
Sister Jeff had said that a man who would not follow a
cow was a fool. Well, he had not figured it that way.
This was his home. But now he would have to leave, for
the water was rising and there was no telling when or
where it would stop.

Two days ago he had told Bob to take the old mule
to Bowman's plantation and sell it, or swap it for a boat,
any kind of a boat. N Bob ain back here yit. Ef it ain
one thing its ernother. When it rains it pos. But, Lawd,
ef only tha old levee don break. Ef only tha ol levee don
break . . .

He turned away from the window, rubbing his fore-
head. A good dose of quinine would kill that fever. But
he had no quinine. Lawd, have mercy!

And worst of all there was Lulu flat on her back these
four days, sick with a child she could not deliver. His
lips parted in silent agony. It just did not seem fair that
one man should be hit so hard and on so many sides at
once. He shifted the weight of his body from his right
foot to his left, listening for sounds from the front
room, wondering how Lulu was. Ef she don have
tha baby soon Ahma have t git her outta here, some
way . . .

He leaned against a damp wall. Whut in the worls
keepin Bob so long? Well, in a way all of this was his
own fault. He had had a chance to get away and he had
acted like a fool and had not taken it. He had figured
that the water would soon go down. He had thought if
he stayed he would be the first to get back to the fields
and start spring plowing. But now even the mule was
gone. Yes, he should have cleared-out when the Govern-
ment offered him the boat. Now he had no money for a
boat, and Bob had said that he could not even get near
that Red Cross.

He took a gourd from the wall and dipped some muddy water out of a bucket. It tasted thick and bitter and he could not swallow it. He hung the gourd back and spat the water into a corner. He cocked his head, listening. It seemed he had heard the sound of a shot. There it was again. Something happenin in town, he thought. Over the yellow water he heard another shot, thin, dry, far away. Mus be trouble, mus be trouble somewhere. He had heard that the white folks were threatening to conscript all Negroes they could lay their hands on to pile sand- and cement-bags on the levee. And they were talking about bringing in soldiers, too. They were afraid of stores and homes being looted. Yes, it was hard to tell just what was happening in town. Shucks, in times like these theyll shoota nigger down jus lika dog n think nothin of it. Tha shootin might mean anything. But likely as not its jus some po black man gone . . .

He faced the window again, thinking, Ahma git mah pistol outta tha dresser drawer when Ah go inter Lulus room. He rolled the tattered curtain up as far as it would go; a brackish light seeped into the kitchen. He looked out; his house was about twelve feet above the water. And water was everywhere. Yellow water. Swirling water. Droning water. For four long days and nights it had been there, flowing past. For a moment he had the illusion that that water had always been there, and would always be there. Yes, it seemed that the water had always been there and this was just the first time he had noticed it. Mabbe somebody jus *dropped* them houses n trees down inter tha watah . . . He felt giddy and a nervous shudder went through him. He rubbed his eyes. Lawd, Ah got fever. His head ached and felt heavy; he wanted sleep and rest.

The view opposite his window was clear for half a mile. Most of the houses had already washed away. Nearby a few trees stood, casting black shadows into the yellow water. The sky was grey with the threat of rain. Suddenly every muscle in his body stretched taut as a low rumble of thunder rose and died away. He shook his head. Nothin could be worsen rain right now. A heavy rainll carry tha ol levee erway sho as hell . . .

"Brother Mann!"

He turned and saw Sister Jeff standing in the hall door.

"How Lulu?" he asked.

The old woman shook her head.

"She poly."

"Yuh reckon shell have it soon?"

"Cant say, Brother Mann. Mabbe she will n mabbe she wont. She havin the time of her life."

"Cant we do nothin fer her?"

"Naw. We jus have t wait, thas all. Lawd, Ahm scared shell never have tha baby widout a doctah. Her hips is jus too little."

"There ain no way t git a doctah now."

"But yuh gotta do something, Brother Mann."

"Ah don know whut t do," he sighed. "Where Peewee?"

"He sleep, in Lulus room."

She came close to him and looked hard into his face.

"Brother Mann, there ain nothin t eat in the house. Yuh gotta do something."

He turned from her, back to the window.

"Ah sent Bob wid the mule t try t git a boat," he said.

She sighed. He swallowed with effort, hearing the whisper of her soft shoes die away down the hall. No boat. No money. No doctah. Nothin t eat. N Bob ain back here yit. Lulu could not last much longer this way. If Bob came with a boat he would pile Lulu in and row her over to that Red Cross Hospital, no matter *what*. The white folks would take her in. They would *have* to take her in. They would not let a woman die just because she was black; they would not let a baby kill a woman. They would *not*. He grew rigid, looking out of the window, straining to listen. He thought he had heard another shot. But the only sound was the drone of swirling water. The water was darkening. In the open stretches it was a muddy yellow; but near the houses and trees it was growing black. *Its gittin night*, he thought. Then came the sound of shots, thin, dry, distant. Wun . . . Tuh . . . Three . . .

"Brother Mann! Its Bob!"

He hurried to the front door, walking heavily on the heels of his big shoes. He saw Bob standing far down on the long steps near the water, bending over and fumbling with a coil of rope. Behind him a white rowboat trembled in the current.

"How yuh come out, Bob?"

Bob looked up and flashed a white grin.

"See?" he said, pointing to the white boat.

Mann's whole body glowed. *Thank Gawd, we gotta boat! Now we kin git erway* . . .

"Who yuh git it from?"

Bob did not answer. He drew the rope tight and came up the steps.

"Ahm one tired soul," Bob said.

They went into the hall. Mann watched Bob pull out a pocket handkerchief and mop his black face. Peewee came in, rubbing his eyes and looking at Bob.

"Yuh git a boat, Uncle Bob?"

"Keep quiet, Peewee," said Mann.

Sister Jeff and Grannie came and stood behind Pee-wee. They looked from Bob to Mann. Bob tucked his handkerchief away, taking his time to do it, laughing a little.

"Lawd, Ahm one tired soul," he said again.

"Who bought the mule?" asked Mann.

"Ol man Bowman bought the mule, but he didnt wanna pay me much." Bob paused and pulled out a crumpled wad of one-dollar bills. "He gimme fifteen dollahs . . ."

"Is tha *all* he give yuh?"

"Ever penny, so hep me Gawd! N tha ol stingy white ape didnt wanna gimme tha, neither. Lawd, ol man Bowman hada pila dough on im big ernuff t choka cow! Ah swear t Gawd Ah never wanted t rob a man so much in all mah life . . ."

"Don yuh go thinkin sin, Bob!" said Grannie. "Wes got ernuff trouble here now widout yuh thinkin sin!"

Bob looked at her.

"Its a boat!" cried Peewee, running from the front door.

Mann stood fingering the bills.

"But how yuh git tha boat, Bob?" he asked.

"Is it our boat?" Peewee asked.

"Hush, Peewee!" Grannie said.

"Don worry! Yuhll git a chance t ride in tha boat, Peewee," said Bob. He laughed and caught Peewee up in his arms. He looked around, then dropped into a chair. "When Ah lef Bowmans place Ah caughta ride downtown in a motorboat wid Brother Hall. Ah went everwheres, lookin high n low fer a boat. Some wanted forty dollahs. Some fifty. Ah met one man whut wanted a hundred. Ah couldnt buy a boat nowheres, so Ah ups n steals a boat when nobody wuz lookin . . ."

"Yuh *stole* the boat?" asked Mann.

"There wouldnt be no boat out there now ef Ah hadnt."

"Son, yuh a fool t go stealin them white folks boats in times like these," said Grannie.

Bob slapped his thigh and laughed.

"Awright, Ma. Ahll take the boat back. Hows tha? Wan me t take it back?"

Grannie turned away.

"Ah ain gonna ride in it," she said.

"Awright. Stay here n drown in the watah," said Bob.

Mann sighed.

"Bob, Ah sho wished yuh hadnt stole it."

"Aw," said Bob with an impatient wave of his hand. "Whut yuh so scared fer? Ain nobody gonna see yuh wid it. All yuh gotta do is git in n make fer the hills n make fer em quick. Ef Ah hadnt stole tha boat yuh all woulda had t stay here till the watah washed yuh erway . . ." He pushed Peewee off his knee and looked up seriously. "How Lulu?"

"She poly," said Sister Jeff.

Grannie came forward.

"Whutcha gonna do, Mann? Yuh gonna take Lulu in the boat Bob done stole? Yuh know them white folks is gonna be lookin fer tha boat. Sistah James boy got killed in a flood jus like this . . ."

"She cant stay here in the fix she in," said Mann.

"Is Ah goin, Pa?" asked Peewee.

"Shut up fo Ah slaps yuh!" said Grannie.

"Whutcha gonna do, Brother Mann?" asked Sister Jeff.

Mann hesitated.

"Wrap her up," he said. "Ahma row her over t the Red Cross Hospital . . ."

Bob stood up.

"Red Cross Hospital? Ah thought yuh said yuh wuz gonna make fer the hills?"

"We gotta git Lulu t a doctah," said Mann.

"Yuh mean t take her in the boat Ah *stole*?"

"There ain nothin else t do."

Bob scratched his head.

"Mann, Ahm mighty scared yuhll git in trouble takin tha boat thu town. Ah stole tha boat from the Pos Office. Its ol man Heartfiels, n yuh know how he hates niggers. Everbody knows his boat when they see it; its white n yuh couldnt git erway wid it. N lissen, theres trouble a-startin in town, too. Tha levees still overflowin in the Noth, n theys spectin the one by the cement plant t go any minute. They done put ever nigger they could fin on the levee by the railroad, pilin san n cement bags. They drivin em like slaves. Ah heard they done killed two-three awready whut tried t run erway. N ef anything happened t yuh, yuh just couldnt git erway, cause two mo bridges done washed erway this mawnin n ain no trains runnin. Things awful bad there in town. A lotta them white folks done took down wid typhoid, n tha Red Cross is vaxinatin everbody, black n white. Everwhere Ah looked wuznt nothin but white men wid guns. They wuz a-waiting fer the soljers when Ah lef, n yuh know whut tha means . . ."

Bob's voice died away and they could hear Lulu groaning in the front room.

"Is yuh gonna take her, Brother Mann?" asked Sister Jeff.

"There ain nothin else t do," said Mann. "Ahll try t take tha boat back t the white folks aftah Ah git Lulu t the hospital. But Ah sho wish yuh hadnt stole tha boat, Bob. But we gotta use it now. Ah don like t rile them white folks . . ."

"Ah ain goin in tha boat!" said Grannie. "Ah ain goin outta here t meet mah death today!"

"Stay here n drown, then!" said Mann. "Ahm takin Lulu t the hospital!"

Grannie cried and went into the front room. Sister Jeff followed.

"Pa, is Ah goin?" asked Peewee.

"Yeah. Git yo cloes. N tell Grannie t git hers ef she don wanna stay here, cause Ahm gittin ready t leave!"

Bob was restless. He pursed his lips and looked at the floor.

"Yuh gotta hard job, rowin tha boat from here t the hospital. Yuhll be rowin ergin the current ever inch, n wid a boat full itll be the Devil t pay. The watahs twelve foot deep n flowin strong n tricky."

"There ain nothin else t do," sighed Mann.

"Yuh bettah take something wid yuh. Tha ain nobodys plaything there in town."

"Ahma take mah gun," said Mann. "But Ahm sho sorry yuh had t steal them white folks boat . . ."

Like a far away echo a voice floated over the water.

"Brother Mann! Yuh there, Brother Mann!"

"Thas Elder Murray," said Bob.

Mann opened the door. It was pitch black outside. A tall man was standing in a rowboat, his hand holding onto a rope by the steps.

"Tha yuh, Brother Mann?"

"How yuh, Elder?"

"Yuh all ain gone yit?"

"We jus fixin t go. Won't yuh come up?"

"Jus fer a minute."

Murray came up the steps and stood in the doorway, rubbing his hands.

"How Sistah Lulu?"

"We aimin t take her t the Red Cross . . ."

"Yuh mean t say she ain had tha baby *yit*?"

"She too little t have it widout a doctah, Elder."

"Lawd, have mercy! Kin Ah see her?"

Mann led the way into Lulu's room where a smoking pine-knot made shadows blink on the walls. Bob, Peewee, Sister Jeff, Grannie, Murray and Mann stood about the bed. Lulu lay on top of the bed-covers, wrapped in a heavy quilt. Her hair was disordered and her face was wet. Her breath came fast.

"How yuh feelin, Sistah Lulu?" asked Murray.

Lulu looked at him weakly. She was a small woman with large shining eyes. Her arms were stretched out at her sides and her hands clutched the quilt.

"How yuh feelin?" asked Murray again.

"She awful weak," said Grannie.

Murray turned to Mann.

"Lissen, yuh bettah be mighty careful takin tha boat thu town. Them white folks is makin trouble n that currents strong."

Mann turned from the bed to the dresser, eased his pistol out of the top drawer and slipped it into his pocket.

"Pa, whuts that?" asked Peewee.

"Hush!" said Mann.

"Brothers n Sistahs, les all kneel n pray," said Murray.

They all got to their knees. Lulu groaned. For a split second a blue sheet of lightning lit up the room, then a hard clap of thunder seemed to rock the earth. No one spoke until the last rumble had rolled away.

"Lawd Gawd Awmighty in Heaven, wes a-bowin befo Yuh once ergin, humble in Yo sight, a-pleadin fer fergiveness n mercy! Hear us today, Lawd! Hear us today ef Yuh ain never heard us befo! We needs Yuh now t hep us n guide us! N hep these po folks, Lawd! Deys Yo chillun! Yuh made em n Yuh made em in Yo own image! Open up their hearts n hep em t have faith in Yo word! N hep this po woman, Lawd! Ease her labor, fer Yuh said, Lawd, she has t bring foth her chillun in pain . . ."

Mann closed his eyes and rested his hands on his hips. That slow dull ache had come back to his head. He wished with all his heart that Elder Murray would hurry up and get through with the prayer, for he wanted to be in that boat. He would not feel safe until he was in that boat. It was too bad Bob had to steal it. But there was no help for that now. The quicker wes in tha boat the bettah, he thought. Ef them white folks come by here n take it back well all be jus where we wuz befo. Yeah, Ahma take tha boat back t the white folks aftah Ah git Lulu t the hospital. Oh, yeah! Mabbe the Elderll take *mah* boat n lemme have *his* since hes on his way t the hills? Lawd, yeah! Thall be a good way t dodge them white folks! Ahma ast im . . .

" . . . Lawd, Yuh said call on Yo name n Yuhd answer! Yuh said seek n fin! Today wes callin on Yuh n wes seekin Yuh, Lawd! Yuh said blieve in the blooda Yo son Jesus, n today wes blievin n waitin fer Yuh t hep us! N soften the hard hearts of them white folks there in town, Lawd! Purify their hearts! Fer Yuh said, Lawd, only clean hearts kin come t Yuh fer mercy . . ."

Mann rubbed his eyes and cleared his throat. Naw, he thought, ain no use astin the Elder t take mah boat. Hell wanna know why n then Ahll have t tell im Bob stole it. N the Elder ain gonna hep nobody he thinks ain doin right. Mabbe ef Ah tol ol man Heartfiel jus why Bob stole his boat mabbe he wont hol it ergin me? Yeah, he oughta be glad ef Ah brings im his boat back. N yeah, mabbe the Elder kin take Sistah Jeff n Bob t the hills in his boat? Thad hep a lots . . .

" . . . n save our souls for Jesus sake! Ahmen!"

Murray stood up and began to sing. The others chimed in softly.

Ahm gonna lay down mah sword n shiel
Down by the riverside
Down by the riverside
Down by the riverside
Ahm gonna lay down mah sword n shiel
Down by the riverside
Ah ain gonna study war no mo . . .

Ah ain gonna study war no mo
Ah ain gonna study war no mo
Ah ain gonna study war no mo
Ah ain gonna study war no mo
Ah ain gonna study war no mo
Ah ain gonna study war no mo . . .

Murray wiped his mouth with the back of his hand and fumbled with his hat.

"Waal, Brothers n Sistahs. Ahm gittin on t the hills. Mah folks is there awready. Ah gotta boatloada stuff outside, but theres room fer two-three mo ef anybody wanna go."

"Kin yuh take Sistah Jeff n Bob erlong?" asked Mann. "Sho!"

Grannie was crying; she pulled on her coat and went into the hall. Bob came from the kitchen with a bundle. Mann lifted Lulu in his arms. Murray held the door for him. Peewee followed, holding a ragged teddy bear. Sister Jeff put out the pine-knot. They all paused in the front doorway.

"Bob, yuh bettah go down n steady tha boat," said Mann.

"Lemme go wid yuh!" said Peewee.

"Yuh c mere!" said Grannie, grabbing his arm.

Bob pulled the boat close to the steps. Mann went down sideways, slowly.

"Take it easy, Brother Mann!" called Murray.

Mann stepped into the boat and rested Lulu in the back seat. Bob held her by the shoulders.

"C mon, yuh all!" Mann called to Grannie and Peewee.

They came, stepping gingerly. Murray helped them down.

"Ahll see yuh all at the hills!" he said.

Bob and Sister Jeff got into Murray's boat. Murray was first to shove off.

"Ahm gone, folks! Good-bye n Gawd bless yuh!"

"Good-bye!"

Mann grasped the oars, wet the handles to prevent creaking, dipped, pulled, and the boat glided outward, over the darkening flood.

II

To all sides of Mann the flood rustled, gurgled, droned, glistening blackly like an ocean of bubbling oil. Above his head the sky was streaked with faint grey light. The air was warm, humid, blowing in fitful gusts. All around he was ringed in by walls of solid darkness. He knew that houses and trees were hidden by those walls and he knew he had to be careful. As he rowed he could feel the force of the current tugging at his left. With each sweep of the oars he weighed the bulk of the boat in his back, his neck, his shoulders. And fear flowed under everything. Lawd, ef only tha ol levee don break! An oak tree loomed ghostily, its leaves whispering. He remembered it had stood at the fork of a road. His mind weaved about the clue of the tree a quick image of cornfield in sunshine. He would have to turn here at a sharp angle and make for the railroad. With one oar resting, he turned by paddling with the other.

The boat struck the current full, and spun. He bent to with the oars, straining, sweeping hard, feeling that now he must fight. He would have to keep the boat moving at a steady pace if he wanted to row in a straight line. And the strokes of the oars would have to be timed, not a second apart. He bent to, lifting the oars; he leaned back, dipping them; then he pulled with tight fingers, feeling the glide of the boat over the water in darkness. Lawd, ef only tha ol levee don break!

He began to look for the cotton-seed mill that stood to the left of the railroad. He peered, longing to see black stack-pipes. They were along here somewhere. Mabbe Ah done passed it? He turned to the right, bending low, looking. Then he twisted about and squinted his eyes. He stopped the boat; the oars dangled. He felt a sudden swerve that tilted him.

"Peewee, keep still!" Grannie whispered.

Lulu groaned. Mann felt wild panic. Quickly he retraced in his mind the route over which he thought he had come, and wondered what could be on the ground, what landmarks the water hid. He looked again, to the right, to the left, and over his shoulder. Then he looked straight upward. Two tall, black stack-pipes loomed seemingly a foot from his eyes. Ah wuznt lookin high ernuff, he thought. Westward would be houses. And straight down would be Pikes' Road. That would be the shortest way.

"Pa, is we there?" asked Peewee.

"Hush!"

He rowed from the stack-pipes, rowed with the houses in his mind, yearning for something to come out of the darkness to match an inner vision. Every six or seven strokes he twisted around to look. The current became stiff and the darkness thickened. For awhile he had the feeling that the boat was not moving. He set his heels, bent to as far as he could go, and made his sweeps with the oars as long as his arms could reach. His back was getting tired. His fingers burned; he paused a second and dipped them into the cold black water. That helped some. But there was only darkness ahead of him each time he turned to look for the houses on Pikes' Road. He wondered if he were on the *wrong* side of the mill! Mabbe Ahm headin the wrong way? He could not tell. And with each yard forward the current grew stiffer. He thought of the levee. Suddenly the boat swerved and spun. He caught his breath and plied the oars, losing all sense of direction. Is tha ol levee done broke? He heard Grannie cry: "Mann!" The boat leaped: his head hit something: stars danced in the darkness: the boat crashed with a bang: he clung to the oars, one was loose: but the other was jammed and would not move. The boat was still save for a hollow banging against a wall he could not see. He dropped the oars and groped his hands ahead in the darkness. Wood. Ridged wood. Is these them houses? He sensed that he was drifting backwards and clutched with his fingers, wincing from the sharp entry of splinters. Then he grabbed something round, cold, smooth, wet . . . It was wood. He clung tightly and stopped the boat. He could feel the tugging and trembling of the current vibrating through his body as his heart gave soft, steady throbs. He breathed hard, trying to build in his mind something familiar around the cold, wet, smooth pieces of wood. A series of pictures flashed through his mind, but none fitted. He groped higher, thinking with his fingers. Then suddenly he saw the whole street: sunshine, wagons and buggies tied to a water trough. This is old man Toms sto. And these were the railings that went around the front porch he was holding in his hands. Pikes' Road was around the house, in front of him. He thought a moment before picking up the oars, wondering if he could make it in that wild current.

"Whuts the mattah, Mann?" Grannie asked.

"Its awright," he said.

He wanted to reassure them, but he did not know what to say. Instead he grabbed the oars and placed one of them against an invisible wall. He set himself, flexed his body, and gave a shove that sent the boat spinning into the middle of the current. He righted it, striving to keep away from the houses, seeking for the street. He strained his eyes till they ached; but all he could see were dark bulks threatening on either side. Yet, that was enough to steer him clear of them. And he rowed, giving his strength to the right oar and then to the left, trying to keep in the middle.

"Look, Pa!"

"Whut?"

"Hush, Peewee!" said Grannie.

"Theres lights, see?"

"Where?"

"See? Right there, over yonder!"

Mann looked, his chin over his shoulder. There were two squares of dim, yellow light. For a moment Mann was puzzled. He plied the oars and steadied the boat. Those lights seemed *too* high up. He could not associate them. But they were on Pikes' Road and they seemed about a hundred yards away. Wondah whut kin tha be? Maybe he could get some help there. He rowed again, his back to the lights; but their soft, yellow glow was in his mind. They helped him, those lights. For awhile he rowed without effort. Where there were lights there were people, and where there were people there was help. Wondah whose house is tha? Is they white folks?

Fear dimmed the lights for a moment; but he rowed on
and they glowed again, their soft sheen helping him to
sweep the oars.

"Pa, cant we go there?"

"Hush, Peewee!"

The closer the lights came the lower they were. His
mind groped frantically in the past, sought for other
times on Pikes' Road and for other nights to tell him
who lived where those yellow lights gleamed. But the
lights remained alone, and the past would tell him noth-
ing. Mabbe they kin phone t town n git a boat t come n
git Lulu? Mabbe she kin res some there. The lights were
close now. Square yellow lights framed in darkness. They
were windows. He steered for the lights, feeling hunger,
fatigue, thirst. The dull ache came back to his head: the
oars were heavy, almost too heavy to hold: the boat
glided beneath the windows: he looked up, sighing.

"Is this the hospital, Pa?" asked Peewee.

"We goin in there, Mann?" asked Grannie.

"Ahma call," said Mann.

He cupped his hands to his mouth.

"Hello!"

He waited and looked at the windows; he heard the
droning water swallow his voice.

"Hello!" he hollered again.

A window went up with a rasping noise. A white face
came into the light. Lawd! Its a white man . . .

"Whos there?"

"Mann!"

"Who?"

"Mann! Mah wifes sick! Shes in birth! Ahm takin her
t the hospital! Yuh gotta phone in there?"

"Wait a minute!"

The window was empty. There was silence; he
waited, his face turned upward. He plied the oars and

steadied the boat in the swift current. Again a white face
came through. A pencil of light shot out into the dark-
ness; a spot of yellow caught the boat. He blinked,
blinded.

"Yuh gotta phone there, Mistah?" he called again,
dodging the glare of the flash-light.

Silence.

"Mah wifes sick! Yuh gotta phone!"

A voice came, cold, angry.

"Nigger, where you steal that boat?"

The window became filled with white faces. Mann
saw a white woman with red hair. He fumbled for the
oars in fear. He blinked his eyes as the light jumped to
and fro over his face.

"Where you steal that boat, nigger! Thats *my* boat!"

Then Mann heard softer voices.

"Thats our boat, Father! Its *white*!"

"Thats our boat, Henry! Thats *our* boat . . ."

"Dont you hear me, nigger! Bring that boat back
here!"

There were two pistol shots. Grannie screamed.
Mann swept the oars blindly; the boat spun. Lawd, thas
Heartfiel! N hes gotta gun! Mann felt the water rocking
him away.

"Nigger, dont you take that boat! Ill kill you!"

He heard two more shots: loudly the boat banged
against wood: he was thrown flat on his back. He jerked
up and tried to keep the yellow windows in sight. For a
moment he thought the windows were dark, but only
the flash-light had gone out. He held his breath and felt
the boat skidding along a wall, shaking with the current.
Then it was still: it seemed it had become wedged be-
tween two walls: he touched a solid bulk and tried to
shove away: the boat lurched: a shower of cold water
sprayed him: the boat became wedged again: he looked

for the windows: a third square of light burst out: he watched a white man with a hard, red face come out onto a narrow second-story porch and stand framed in a light-flooded doorway. The man was wearing a white shirt and was playing the yellow flare over the black water. In his right hand a gun gleamed. The man walked slowly down an outside stairway and stopped, crouching, at the water's edge. A throaty voice bawled:

"Nigger, bring that boat here! You *nigger!*"

Mann held still, frozen. He stared at the gun in the white man's hand. A cold lump forced its way up out of his stomach into his throat. He saw the disc of yellow sweep over the side of a house. The white man stooped, aimed and shot. He thinks Ahm over there! Lawd! Mann's mouth hung open and his lips dried as he breathed.

"You sonofabitch! Bring my boat here!"

"Mann!" Grannie whispered.

Mann fumbled in his pocket for his gun and held it ready. His hand trembled. He watched the yellow disc jump fitfully over the black water some fifty feet from him. It zig-zagged, pausing for instants only, searching every inch of the water. As it crept closer Mann raised his gun. The flare flickered to and fro. His throat tightened and he aimed. Then the flare hovered some five feet from him. He fired, twice. The white man fell backwards on the steps and slipped with an abrupt splash into the water. The flash-light went with him, its one eye swooping downward, leaving a sudden darkness. There was a scream. Mann dropped the gun into the bottom of the boat, grabbed the oars, threw his weight desperately, shoved out from the wall and paddled against the current.

"Henry! Henry!"

Mann rowed: he heard Grannie crying: he felt weak

from fear: he had a choking impulse to stop: he felt he was lost because he had shot a white man: he felt there was no use in his rowing any longer: but the current fought the boat and he fought back with the oars.

"Henry! Henry!"

It was a woman's voice, pleading; then a younger voice, shrill, adolescent, insistent.

"The nigger killed im! The nigger killed father!"

Mann rowed on into the darkness, over the black water. He could not see the lights now; he was on the other side of the building. But the screams came clearly.

"Stop, nigger! *Stop!* You killed my father! You bastard! You nigger!"

"Henry! Henry!"

Mann heard Grannie and Peewee crying. But their weeping came to him from a long way off, as though it were as far away as the voices that were screaming. It was difficult for him to get his breath as he bent on the left oar, then the right, keeping the boat in the middle of the bulks of darkness. Then all at once he was limp, nerveless; he felt that getting the boat to the hospital now meant nothing. Two voices twined themselves in his ears: Stop, nigger! Stop, nigger! Henry! Henry! They echoed and re-echoed even after he was long out of earshot.

Then suddenly the rowing became a little easier. He was in the clear again, away from the houses. He did not worry about directions now, for he knew exactly where he was. Only one half mile across Barrett's Pasture, and he would strike streets and maybe lights. He rowed on, hearing Grannie's crying and seeing Heartfield coming down the narrow steps with the flash-light and the gun. But he shot at me fo Ah shot im . . . Another thought made him drop the oars. Spose Heartfiels folks phone to town n tel em Ah shot im? He

looked around hopelessly in the darkness. Lawd, Ah
don wanna ride mah folks right inter death! The boat
drifted sideways, shaking with the tug of the current.

"Lulu," Grannie was whispering.

"How Lulu?" Mann asked.

"She sleep, Ah reckon," sighed Grannie.

Naw, Ahm goin on, no mattah *whut*! He could not
turn back now for the hills, not with Lulu in this boat.
Not with Lulu in the fix she was in. He gritted his teeth,
caught the oars, and rowed. High over his head a plane
zoomed; he looked up and saw a triangle of red and
green lights winging through the darkness. His fingers
were hot and loose, as though all the feeling in his
hands had turned into fire. But his body was cool; a
listless wind was drying the sweat on him.

"There the lights o town, Mann!" Grannie spoke.

He twisted about. Sure enough, there they were.
Shining, barely shining. Dim specks of yellow buried in
a mass of blackness. Lawd only knows whut wes ridin
inter . . . If he could only get Lulu to the hospital, if he
could only get Grannie and Peewee safely out of this
water, then he would take a chance on getting away. He
knew that that was what they would want him to do.
He swept the oars, remembering hearing tales of whole
black families being killed because some relative had
done something wrong.

A quick, blue fork of lightning lit up the waste of
desolate and tumbling waters. Then thunder exploded,
loud and long, like the sound of a mountain falling. It
began to rain. A sudden, sharp rain. Water trickled
down the back of his neck. He felt Grannie moving; she
was covering Lulu with her coat. He rowed faster, peer-
ing into the rain, wanting to reach safety before the boat
caught too much water. Another fifty yards or so and he
would be among the houses. Yeah, ef they ast me erbout

Heartfiel Ahma tell em the truth . . . But he knew he did not want to do that. He knew that that would not help him. But what else was there for him to do? Yes, he would have to tell the truth and trust God. Nobody but God could see him through this. Bob shouldna stole this boat . . . But here Ah am in it now . . . He sighed, rowing. N this rain! Tha ol levee might go wid this rain . . . Lawd, have mercy! He lowered his chin and determined not to think. He would have to trust God and keep on and go through with it, that was all. His feet and clothes were wet. The current stiffened and brought the boat almost to a standstill. Yeah, he thought, theres Rose Street. He headed the boat between two rows of houses.

"Halt! Who goes there?"

He pulled the oars. A glare of light shot from a second-story porch and made him blink. Two white soldiers in khaki uniforms leaned over the bannisters. Their faces were like square blocks of red and he could see the dull glint of steel on the tips of their rifles. Well, he would know now. Mabbe they done foun out erbout Heartfiel?

"Where you going, nigger?"

"Ahm takin mah wife t the hospital, suh. Shes in birth, suh!"

"What?"

"Mah wifes in birth, suh! Ahm takin her t the Red Cross!"

"Pull up to the steps!"

"Yessuh!"

He turned the boat and paddled toward steps that led down to the water. The two soldiers loomed over him.

"Whats your name?"

"Mann, suh."

"You got a pass?"

"Nawsuh."

"Don't you know youre violating curfew?"

"Nawsuh."

"What was all that shooting back there a little while ago?"

"Ah don know, suh."

"Didnt you hear it?"

"Nawsuh."

"Frisk im, Mac," said one of the soldiers.

"O.K. Stand up, nigger!"

One of the soldiers patted Mann's hips. Lawd, Ah hope they don see tha gun in the boat . . .

"Hes awright."

"What you say your name was?"

"Mann, suh."

"Where you from?"

"The South En, suh."

"I mean where you bring that boat from?"

"The South En, suh."

"You *rowed* here?"

"Yessuh."

"In *that* boat?"

"Yessuh."

The soldiers looked at each other.

"You aint lying, are you, nigger?"

"Oh, nawsuh," said Mann.

"What wrong with your woman?"

"She's in birth, suh."

One of the soldiers laughed.

"Well, Ill be Goddamned! Nigger, you take the prize! I always heard that a niggerd do anything, but I never thought anybody was fool enough to row a boat against that current . . ."

"But Mistah, mah wifes sick! She been sick fo days!"

"O.K. Stay here. Ill phone for a boat to take you in."

"Yessuh."

One of the soldiers ran up the steps and the other hooked Mann's boat to a rope.

"Nigger, you dont know how lucky you are," he said. "Six men were drowned today trying to make it to town in rowboats. And here you come, rowing *three* people . . ."

The soldier who had gone to telephone came back.

"Mistah, please!" said Mann. "Kin Ah take mah wife in there, outta the rain?"

The soldier shook his head.

"Im sorry, boy. Orders is that nobody but soldiers can be in these houses. Youll have to wait for the boat. Its just around the corner; it wont be long. But I dont see how in hell you rowed that boat between those houses without drowning! It mustve been tough, hunh?"

"Yessuh."

Mann saw a motorboat swing around a curve, its head-light sweeping a wide arc, its motor yammering. It glided up swiftly in a churn of foam. It was manned by two soldiers whose slickers gleamed with rain.

"Whats the rush?"

"Boy," said one of the soldiers, "I got a nigger here who beat everybody. He rowed in from the South End, against the current. Can you beat that?"

The soldiers in the boat looked at Mann.

"Says you!" said one, with a scornful wave of his white palm.

"Im telling the truth!" said the soldier. "Didn't you, boy?"

"Yessuh."

"Well, what you want us to do about it? Give im a medal?"

"Naw; his bitch is sick. Having a picaninny. Shoot em over to the Red Cross Hospital."

The soldiers in the boat looked at Mann again.

"They crowded out over there, boy . . ."

"Lawd, have mercy!" Grannie cried, holding Lulu's head on her lap.

"Mistah, please! Mah wife cant las much longer like this," said Mann.

"Awright! Hitch your boat, nigger, and lets ride!"

Mann grabbed the rope that was thrown at him and looped it to a hook on the end of his boat. He was standing when one of the soldiers yelled:

"Watch yourself, nigger!"

The motor roared and the boat shot forward; he fell back against Grannie, Lulu and Peewee. He straightened just as they made the turn. His boat leaned, scooping water, wetting him; then it righted itself. The rest of the drive was straight ahead, into darkness. He had hardly wiped the water out of his eyes before they slowed to a stop. His fingers groped nervously in the bottom of the boat for the gun; he found it and slipped it into his pocket.

"Awright, nigger, unload!"

He stood up and fronted a row of wide steps.

"Is this the hospital, suh?"

"Yeah; straight up!"

He lifted Lulu and stepped out. Grannie followed, leading Peewee by the hand. When he reached the top of the steps the door was opened by another white soldier.

"Where you going?"

"Ah got mah wife, suh. She sick . . ."

"Straight on to the back, till you see the sign."

"Yessuh."

He walked down a dim-lit hall. Grannie and Peewee shuffled behind. He smelled the warm scent of ether and disinfectant and it made him dizzy. Finally, he saw the sign:

FOR COLORED

He pushed open a door with his shoulder and stood blinking in a blaze of bright lights. A white nurse came.

"What you want?"

"Please, Mam . . . Mah wife . . . She sick!"

The nurse threw back the quilt and felt Lulu's pulse. She looked searchingly at Mann, then turned quickly, calling:

"Doctor Burrows!"

A white doctor came. He looked at Lulu's face. Her eyes were closed and her mouth was open.

"Bring her here, to the table," said the doctor.

Mann stretched Lulu out. Her face, her hair, and her clothes were soaking wet. Her left arm fell from the table and hung limp. The doctor bent over and pushed back the lids of her eyes.

"This your woman?"

"Yessuh."

"How long was she in birth?"

"Bout fo days, suh."

"Why didnt you bring her sooner?"

"Ah didnt hava boat n the watah had me trapped, suh."

The doctor lifted his eyes, rubbed his chin, and looked at Mann quizzically.

"Well, boy, shes dead."

"Suh?"

Grannie screamed and grabbed Peewee. The doctor straightened and laid the stethoscope on a white, marble-topped table. Lightning flicked through the room and thunder rolled rumblingly away, leaving a silence filled with the drone of hard, driving rain.

"*Suh!*" said Mann.

III

"Well, boy, its all over," said the doctor. "Maybe if you could have gotten her here a little sooner we could have saved her. The baby, anyway. But its all over now, and the best thing for you to do is get your folks to the hills."

Mann stared at the thin, black face; at the wet clothes; at the arm hanging still and limp. His lips moved, but he could not speak. Two more white nurses and another white doctor came and stood. Grannie ran to the table.

"Lulu!"

"Its awright, Aunty," said the doctor, pulling her away.

Grannie sank to the floor, her head on her knees.

"Lawd . . ."

Mann stood like stone now. Lulu dead? He seemed not to see the white doctors and nurses gathering around, looking at him. He sighed and the lids of his eyes drooped half-way down over the pupils.

"Poor nigger," said a white nurse.

Blankly, Mann stared at her. He wet his lips and swallowed. Something pressed against his knee and he looked down. Peewee was clinging to him, his little black face tense with fear. He caught Peewee by the hand, went over to the wall and stood above Grannie, hesitating. His fingers touched her shoulders.

"Awright," said the doctor. "Roll her out."

Mann turned and saw two white nurses rolling Lulu through a door. His throat tightened. Grannie struggled up and tried to follow the body. Mann pulled her back and she dropped to the floor again, crying.

"Its awright, Grannie," said Mann.

"You got a boat, boy?" asked the doctor.

"Yessuh," said Mann.

"Youre lucky. You ought to start out right now for the hills, before that current gets stronger."

".Yessuh."

Again Mann looked at Grannie and twice his hands moved toward her and stopped. It seemed that he wanted ever so much to say something, to do something, but he did not know what.

"C mon, Grannie," he said.

She did not move. A white nurse giggled, nervously. Mann stood squeezing his blistered palms, taking out of the intense pain a sort of consolation, a sort of forgetfulness. A clock began to tick. He could hear Grannie's breath catching softly in her throat; he could hear the doctors and nurses breathing; and beyond the walls of the room was the beat of sweeping rain. Somewhere a bell tolled, faint and far off.

Crash!

Everybody jumped. One of the nurses gave a short scream.

"Whats that?"

"Aw, just a chair fell over. Thats all . . ."

"Oh!"

The doctors looked at the nurses and the nurses looked at the doctors. Then all of them laughed, uneasily. There was another silence. The doctor spoke.

"Is that your mother there, boy?"

"Yessuh. Mah ma-in-law."

"Youll have to get her out of here."

"C mon, Grannie," he said again.

She did not move. He stooped and picked her up.

"C mon, Peewee."

He went through the door and down the hall with Peewee pulling at the tail of his coat.

"Hey, you!"

He stopped. A white soldier came up.

"Where you going?"

"Ahm gittin mah boat t take mah family t the hills . . ."

"Your boat was commandeered. Come over here and wait awhile."

"Comman . . ."

"We were short of boats and the boys had to take yours. But Ill get a motorboat to take you and your family to the hills. Wait right here a minute . . ."

"Yessuh."

He waited with Grannie in his arms. Lawd, they got me now! They knowed that was Heartfiel's boat! Mabbe they fixin t take me erway? What would they do to a black man who had killed a white man in a flood? He did not know. But whatever it was must be something far more terrible than at other times. He shifted his weight from foot to foot. He was more tired than he could ever remember having been. He saw Lulu lying on the table; he heard the doctor say: Well, boy, shes dead. His eyes burned. Lawd, Ah don care whut they do t me! Ah don care . . .

"Pa, where ma?"

"She gone, Peewee."

"Ain she comin wid us?"

"Naw, Peewee."

"How come, Pa?"

"She gonna stay wid Gawd now, Peewee."

"Awways?"

"Awways, Peewee."

Peewee cried.

"Hush, Peewee! Be a good boy, now! Don cry! Ahm here! N Grannies here . . ."

The white soldier came back with the colonel.

"Is this the nigger?"

"Thats him."

"Was that your rowboat outside?"

Mann hesitated.

"Yessuh, Capm."

"A white boat?"

"Yessuh."

"Are you sure it was yours?"

Mann swallowed and hesitated again.

"Yessuh."

"What was it worth?"

"Ah don know, Capm."

"What did you pay for it?"

"Bout f-fifty dollahs, Ah reckon."

"Here, sign this," said the colonel, extending a piece of paper and a pencil. "We can give you thirty-five dollars as soon as things are straightened out. We had to take your boat. We were short of boats. But Ive phoned for a motorboat to take you and your family to the hills. Youll be safer in that anyway."

"Yessuh."

He sat Grannie on the floor and sighed.

"Is that your mother there?"

"Yessuh. Mah ma-in-law."

"Whats wrong with her?"

"She jus ol, Capm. Her gal jus died n she takes it hard."

"When did she die?"

"Jus now, suh."

"Oh, I see . . . But whats wrong with you? Are you sick?"

"Nawsuh."

"Well, you dont have to go to the hills. Your folksll go on to the hills and you can stay here and help on the levee . . ."

"Capm, please! Ahm tired!"

"This is martial law," said the colonel, turning to the white soldier. "Put this woman and boy into a boat and ship them to the hills. Give this nigger some boots and a raincoat and ship him to the levee!"

The soldier saluted.

"Yessir, Colonel!"

"CAPM, PLEASE! HAVE MERCY ON ME, CAPM!"

The colonel turned on his heels and walked away.

"AHM TIRED! LEMME GO WID MAH FOLKS, PLEASE!"

The soldier glared at Mann.

"Aw, c mon, nigger! What in hells wrong with you? All the rest of the niggers are out there, how come you dont want to go?"

Mann watched the soldier go to the door, open it and look out into the rain.

"Mann!" Grannie whispered.

He leaned to her, his hands on his knees.

"Yuh go on t the levee! Mabbe them Heartfiel folks is out t the hills by now. Git over t where our folks is n mabbe yuh kin git erway . . ."

"C mon!" called the soldier. "Heres your boat!"

"*Here*, Grannie," whispered Mann. He slipped the fifteen dollars he had gotten from Bob into her hands.

"Naw," she said. "*Yuh* keep it!"

"Naw, *take* it!" said Mann. He pushed the money into the pocket of her coat.

"C MON, NIGGER! THIS BOAT CANT WAIT ALL NIGHT FOR YOU!"

He picked Grannie up again and carried her down the

steps. Peewee followed, crying. It was raining hard. After he had helped them into the boat he stood on the steps. Lawd, Ah wished Ah could go!

"All set?"

"All set!"

The motor droned and the boat shot out over the water, its spotlight cutting ahead into the rain.

"Good-bye!" Peewee called.

"Good-bye!" Mann was not sure that Peewee had heard and he called again. "Good-bye!"

"C mon, boy! Lets get your boots and raincoat. Youre going to the levee."

"Yessuh."

He followed the soldier into the office.

"Jack, get some hip-boots and a raincoat for this nigger and call for a boat to take him to the levee," the soldier spoke to another soldier sitting behind a desk.

"O.K. Heres some boots. And heres a raincoat."

The first soldier went out. Mann hoisted the boots high on his legs and put on the raincoat.

"Tired, nigger?" asked the soldier.

"Yessuh."

"Well, youve got a hard night ahead of you, and thats no lie."

"Yessuh."

Mann sat down, rested his head against a wall, and closed his eyes. Lawd . . . He heard the soldier talking over the telephone.

"Yeah. Yeah."

" . . . "

"The Red Cross Hospital."

" . . . "

"The niggers here now, waiting."

" . . . "

"O.K."

Mann heard the receiver click.

"The boatll be along any minute," said the soldier. "And while youre resting, unpack those boxes and lay the stuff on the floor."

"Yessuh."

Mann stood up and shook his head. A sharp pain stabbed at the front of his eyes and would not leave. He went to the back of the room where a pile of wooden boxes was stacked and got a crowbar. He pried open the top of a box and began to pull out raincoats and rubber boots. He worked mechanically, slowly, leaning against boxes, smelling fresh rubber and stale tobacco smoke. He felt the pistol in his pocket and remembered Heartfield. Ah got t git outta here some way. Go where they cant fin me. Lawd, take care Grannie! Take care Peewee, Lawd! Take care Bob! N hep me, Lawd. He thought of Lulu lying stretched out on the marble table with her arm hanging limp. He dropped the bundle of raincoats he was holding and bent over, sobbing.

"Whats the matter, nigger?"

"Ahm tired, Capm! Gawd knows Ahm tired!"

He slipped to the floor.

"What you crying about?"

"Capm, mah wifes dead! *Dead!*"

"Shucks, nigger! You ought to be glad youre not dead in a flood like this," said the soldier.

Mann stared at the blurred boots and raincoats. Naw, Lawd! Ah cant break down now! Theyll know somethings wrong ef Ah keep acting like this . . . Ah cant cry bout Lulu now . . . He wiped tears from his eyes with his fingers.

"Kin Ah have some watah, Capm?"

"Theres no water anywhere. You hungry?"

He was not hungry, but he wanted to reassure the soldier.

"Yessuh."

"Heres a sandwich you can have."

"Thank yuh, suh."

He took the sandwich and bit it. The dry bread balled in his mouth. He chewed and tried to wet it. Ef only that ol soljerd quit lookin at me . . . He swallowed and the hard lump went down slowly, choking him.

"Thatll make you feel better," said the soldier.

"Yessuh."

The door swung in.

"Awright, boy! Heres your boat! Lets go!"

"Yessuh."

He put the sandwich in his pocket and followed the soldier to the steps.

"Is this the nigger?"

"Yeah!"

"O.K. Pile in, boy!"

He got in; the boat turned; rain whipped his face. He bent low, holding onto the sides of the boat as it sped through water. He closed his eyes and again saw Heartfield come out on the narrow porch and down the steps. He heard again the two shots of his gun. But he shot at me fo Ah shot im! Then again he saw Lulu lying on the table with her arm hanging limp. Then he heard Peewee calling. Good-bye! Hate welled up in him; he saw the two soldiers in the front seat. Their heads were bent low. They might fin out any minute now . . . His gun nestled close to his thigh. Spose Ah shot em n took the boat? Naw! Naw! It would be better to wait till he got to the levee. He would know somebody there. And they would help him. He knew they would. N them white folks might be too busy botherin wid tha levee t think erbout jus one po black man . . . Mabbe Ah kin slip thu . . .

The boat slowed. Ahead loomed the dark stack-pipe

of the cement plant. Above his head a hundred spotlights etched a wide fan of yellow against the rain. As the boat swerved through a gate entrance and pulled to a platform, he saw lights and soldiers, heard voices calling. Black men stood on the edges of the platforms and loaded bags of sand and cement into boats. Long lines of boats were running to and fro between the levee and the cement plant. He felt giddy; the boat rocked. Soldiers yelled commands. An officer stepped forward and bawled:

"You get im!"

"Yeah!"

"O.K.! We got another one here! C mon, boy, hop in!"

A black boy moved forward.

"Mistah, kin Ah hava drinka watah?" asked the boy.

"Hell, naw! Theres no water anywhere! Get in the boat!"

"Yessuh."

Mann moved over to make room. He felt better already. He was with his people now. Maybe he could get away yet. He heard the officer talking to the soldiers.

"Hows things?"

"Pretty bad!"

"Hows it going?"

"Still overflowing from the North!"

"You think itll hold?"

"Im scared it wont!"

"Any cracks yet?"

"Shes cracking in two places!"

One of the soldiers whistled.

"Awright, let her go!"

"O.K.!"

The boat started out, churning water.

"Yuh gotta cigarette, Mistah?"

Mann turned and looked at the boy sitting at his side. "Naw; Ah don smoke."

"Shucks, Ah sho wish theyd lemme handle one of these boats," said the boy.

As they neared the levee Mann could see long, black lines of men weaving snake-fashion about the levee-top. In front of him he could feel the river as though it were a live, cold hand touching his face. The levee was a ridge of dry land between two stretches of black water. The men on the levee-top moved slowly, like dim shadows. They were carrying heavy bags on their shoulders and when they reached a certain point the bags were dumped down. Then they turned around, slowly, with bent backs, going to get more bags. Yellow lanterns swung jerkily, blinking out and then coming back on when someone passed in front of them. At the water's edge men unloaded boats; behind them stood soldiers with rifles. Mann held still, looking; the boat stopped and waited for its turn to dock at the levee.

Suddenly a wild commotion broke out. A siren screamed. On the levee-top the long lines of men merged into one whirling black mass. Shouts rose in a mighty roar. There came a vague, sonorous drone, like the far away buzzing in a sea-shell. Each second it grew louder. Lawd! thought Mann. That levees gone! He saw boats filling with men. There was a thunder-like clatter as their motors started up. The soldiers in the front seat were yelling at each other.

"You better turn around, Jim!"

The boat turned and started back.

"Wait for that boat and see whats happened!"

They slowed and a boat caught up with them.

"Whats happened?"

"The levees gone!"

"Step on it, Jim!"

Mann held his breath; behind him were shouts, and over the shouts was the siren's scream, and under the siren's scream was the loud roar of loosened waters.

IV

The boat shot back. The siren shrieked at needle-pitch, high, thin, shrill, quivering in his ears; and yellow flares turned restlessly in the sky. The boat slowed for the platform. There was a loud clamor and men rushed about. An officer bawled:

"Line up the boats for rescue work!"

"Its risin! Cant yuh *see* it risin?" The boy at Mann's side was nudging him. Mann looked at the water; a series of slow, heaving swells was rocking the boat. He remembered that the water had been some inches below the level of the platform when he had first come; now it was rising above it. As the men worked their boots splashed in the water.

"Who can handle a boat?" the officer asked.

"Ah kin, Mistah!" yelled the boy.

"Get a partner and come on!"

The boy turned to Mann.

"Yuh wanna go?"

Mann hesitated.

"Yeah. Ahll go."

"C mon!"

He climbed out and followed the boy to the end of the platform.

"Where are we sending em, General?" the officer asked.

"Shoot the first twenty to the Red Cross Hospital!"

"O.K.!" said the officer. "Whos the driver here?"

"Ahm the driver!" said the boy.

"Can you really handle a boat?"

"Yessuh!"

"Is he all right?" asked the general.

"Ah works fer Mistah Bridges," said the boy.

"We dont want too many niggers handling these boats," said the general.

"We havent enough drivers," said the officer.

"All right; let him go! Whos next?"

"Yours is the Red Cross Hospital, boy! Get there as fast as you can and get as many people out as you can and take em to the hills, see?"

"Yessuh!"

"You know the way?"

"Yessuh!"

"Whats your name?"

"Brinkley, suh!"

"All right! Get going!"

They ran to a boat and scrambled in. Brinkley fussed over the motor a minute, then raced it.

"All set!"

"O.K.!"

The boat swung out of the wide gate entrance; they were the first to go. They went fast, against the current, fronting the rain. They were back among the houses before Mann realized it. As they neared the hospital Mann wondered about the boy at his side. Would he help him to get away? Could he trust him enough to tell? If he could only stay in the boat until they carried the first load to the hills, he could slip off. He tried to see Brinkley's face, but the rain and darkness would not let him. Behind him the siren still screamed and it seemed that a thousand bells were tolling. Then the boat stopped short; Mann looked around, tense, puzzled.

"This ain the hospital," he said.

"Yeah, tis," said Brinkley.

Then he understood. He had been watching for the

steps up which he had carried Lulu. But the water had already covered the steps and was making for the first floor. He looked up. The same white soldier who had let him in before was standing guard.

"C mon in!"

They went in. The hospital was in an uproar. Down the hall a line of soldiers pushed the crowds back, using their rifles long-wise. The colonel came running out; he carried an axe in his hand.

"How many boats are coming?"

"Bout twenty, suh," said Brinkley.

"Are they on the way?"

"Yessuh."

"Theyll have to hurry. That water is rising at the rate of five feet an hour!"

The colonel turned to Mann.

"Come here, boy!"

"Yessuh!"

Mann followed the colonel up a flight of stairs. They stopped in a hall.

"Listen," began the colonel. "I want you . . ."

The lights went out, plunging them in darkness.

"Goddamn!"

Mann could hear the colonel breathing in heavy gasps. Then a circle of yellow light played over a wall. The colonel was standing in front of him with a flashlight.

"Get two of those tables from back there and pile one on top of the other, right here," said the colonel, indicating a spot just left of the stairway.

"Yessuh!"

When the tables were up the colonel gave Mann the axe.

"Get up there and knock a hole through that ceiling!"

"Yessuh!"

He scampered up and fumbled for a hold on the rickety tables. When he was on top the colonel set the beam of the flash-light on the ceiling.

"Work fast, boy! Youve got to cut a hole through there so we can take people out if that water beats the boats!"

"Yessuh!"

He whacked upward; with each blow the axe stuck in the wood; he set his feet wide apart on the tables and jerked downward to pull it out. He forgot everything but that he must cut a hole through this ceiling to save people. Even the memory of Lulu and Heartfield was gone from him. Then the lights came back just as suddenly as they had gone. He knew that that meant that the electric plant at the South End was threatened by water. As he swung the axe he felt sweat breaking out all over his body. He heard the colonel below him, fidgeting. The lights dimmed and flared again.

"Keep tha light on me, Capm!"

"Awright; but hurry!"

He had six planks out of the ceiling now. He used his hands and broke them off; his fingers caught splinters. He heard someone running up the steps. He looked down; a soldier was talking to the colonel.

"Its above the steps, Colonel! Its traveling for the first floor!"

"Any boats here yet?"

"Just three, sir!"

"Order everybody to this floor, and keep them quiet even if you have to shoot!"

"Yessir!"

Mann heard the soldier running down the steps.

"C mon, boy! Get that hole bigger than that! Youve got to cut a hole through that roof yet!"

"Yessuh!"

When the hole was big enough he pushed the axe

through and pulled himself into the loft. It was dark and he could hear the rain pounding. Suddenly the siren stopped. He had been hearing it all along and had grown used to it; but now that he could hear it no longer the silence it left in his mind was terrifying.

"Ah need some light up here, Capm!"

"Keep cutting! Ill get somebody to bring the flash-light up!"

The roof was easier to cut than the ceiling. He heard someone climbing up behind him. It was a white soldier with a flash-light.

"Where you want it, boy?"

"Right here, suh!"

Quickly he tore a wide hole: he felt a rush of air: rain came into his face: droning water filled his ears: he climbed onto the roof and looked below. Opposite the hospital a bunch of motorboats danced in the current. He stiffened. There was a loud cracking noise, as of timber breaking. He stretched flat on the roof and clung to the wet shingles. Moving into one of the paths of yellow light was a small house, turning like a spool in the wild waters. Unblinkingly he watched it whirl out of sight. *Mabbe Ah'll never git outta here* . . . More boats were roaring up, rocking. Then he stared at the water rising; he could *see* it rising. Across from him the roofs of one-story houses were barely visible.

"Here, give a lift!"

Mann caught hold of a white hand and helped to pull a soldier through. He heard the colonel hollering.

"All set?"

"Yessuh!"

"Send the boats to the side of the hospital! We are taking em from the roof!"

Boats roared and came slowly to the wall of the hospital.

"Awright! Coming through!"

On all fours Mann helped a white woman struggle through. She was wrapped in sheets and blankets. The soldier whipped the rope around the woman's body, high under her arms. She whimpered. Lawd, Lulu down there somewhere, Mann thought. Dead! She gonna be lef here in the flood . . .

"C mon, nigger, n give me a hand!"

"Yessuh!"

Mann caught hold of the woman and they took her to the edge of the roof. She screamed and pulled back.

"Let her go!"

They shoved her over and eased her down with the rope. She screamed again and hung limp. They took another, tied the rope, and eased her over. One woman's face was bleeding; she had scratched herself climbing through the hole. Mann could hear the soldier's breath coming in short gasps as he worked. When six had been let down a motor roared. A boat, loaded to capacity, crawled slowly away. The water was full of floating things now. Objects swirled past, were sucked out of sight. The second boat was filled. The third. Then the fourth. The fifth. Sixth. When the women and children were gone they began to ease the men over. The work went easier and faster with the men. Mann heard them cursing grimly. Now and then he remembered Lulu and Heartfield and he felt dizzy; but he would urge himself and it would pass.

"How many more, Colonel?" asked a soldier.

"About twelve! You got enough boats?"

"Just enough!"

Mann knew they had gotten them all out safely when he saw the colonel climb through. Brinkley came through last.

"Heres one more boat, without a driver!" a soldier called.

"Thas mah boat!" said Brinkley.

"Then you go next!" said the colonel.

Mann looped one end of the rope around a chimney and tied it. Brinkley caught hold and slid down, monkey-like. The colonel crawled over to Mann and caught his shoulder.

"You did well! I wont forget you! If you get out of this, come and see me, hear?"

"Yessuh!"

"Here, take this!"

Mann felt a piece of wet paper in his fingers. He tried to read it, but it was too dark.

"Thats the address of a woman with two children who called in for help," said the colonel. "If you and that boy think you can save em, then do what you can. If you cant, then try to make it to the hills . . ."

"Yessuh!"

The colonel went down. Mann was alone. For a moment a sense of what he would have to face if he was saved from the flood came to him. Would it not be better to stay here alone like this and go down into the flood with Lulu? Would not that be better than having to answer for killing a white man?

"Yuh comin?" Brinkley called.

Mann fumbled over the roof for the axe, found it, and stuck it in his belt. He put the piece of paper in his pocket, caught hold of the rope, and crawled to the edge. Rain peppered his face as he braced his feet against the walls of the house. He held still for a second and tried to see the boat.

"C mon!"

He slumped into the seat; the boat lurched. He sighed

and shed a tension which had gripped him for hours. The boat was sailing against the current.

"Heres somebody callin fer hep," said Mann, holding the piece of paper in front of Brinkley.

"Take the flash-light! Switch it on n lemme see ef Ah kin read it!"

Mann held the flash-light.

"Its Pikes Road!" said Brinkley. "Its the Pos Office! Its Miz Heartfiel . . ."

Mann stared at Brinkley, open-mouthed; the flash-light dropped into the bottom of the boat. His fingers trembled and the wind blew the piece of paper away.

"Heartfiel?"

"Ahma try t make it!" said Brinkley.

The boat slowed, turned; they shot in the opposite direction, with the current. Mann watched the head-light cut a path through the rain. Heartfiel?

V

"Watch it!"

Mann threw his hands before his eyes as though to ward off a blow. Brinkley jerked the boat to the right and shut off the motor. The current swept them backwards. In front the head-light lit a yellow circle of wet wood, showing the side of a house. The house was floating down the middle of the street. The motor raced, the boat turned and sailed down the street, going back over the route they had come. Behind them the house followed, revolving slowly, looming large. They stopped at a telegraph pole and Mann stood up and held the boat steady by clinging to a strand of cable wire that stretched above his head in the dark. All about him the torrent tumbled, droned, surged. Then

the spot of light caught the house full; it seemed like a
living thing, spinning slowly with a long, indrawn,
sucking noise; its doors, its windows, its porch turning
to the light and then going into the darkness. It
passed. Brinkley swung the boat around and they went
back down the street, cautiously this time, keeping in
the middle of the current. Something struck. They
looked. A chair veered, spinning, and was sucked away.
An uprooted tree loomed. They dodged it. They heard
noises, but could not tell the direction from which
they came. When they reached Barrett's Pasture they
went slower. The rain had slackened and they could see
better.

"Reckon we kin make it?" asked Brinkley.

"Ah don know," whispered Mann.

They swung a curve and headed for Pikes' Road.
Mann thought of Heartfield. He saw the woman with
red hair standing in the lighted window. He heard her
scream, Thats our boat, Henry! Thats our boat! The
boat slowed, swerving for Pikes' Road. Mann had the
feeling that he was in a dream. Spose Ah tol the boy?
The boat rushed on into the darkness. Ef we take tha
woman t the hills Ahm caught! Ahead he saw a box bob
up out of water and shoot under again. But mabbe they
didn't see me good? He could not be sure of that. The
light had been on him a long time while he was under
that window. And they knew his name; he had called it
out to them, twice. He ought to tell Brinkley. Ahm
black like he is. He oughta be willin t hep me fo he
would them . . . He tried to look into Brinkley's face;
the boy was bent forward, straining his eyes, searching
the surface of the black water. Lawd, Ah *got* t tell im!
The boat lurched and dodged something. Its mah life
ergin theirs! The boat slid on over the water. Mann
swallowed; then he felt that there would not be any use

in his telling; he had waited too long. Even if he spoke now Brinkley would not turn back; they had come too far. Wild-eyed, he gazed around in the watery darkness, hearing the white boy yell, You nigger! You bastard! Naw, Lawd! *Ah got t tell im!* He leaned forward to speak and touched Brinkley's arm. The boat veered again, dodging an object that spun away. Mann held tense, waiting, looking; the boat slid on over the black water. Then he sighed and wished with all his life that he had thrown that piece of paper away.

"Yuh know the place?" asked Brinkley.

"Ah reckon so," whispered Mann.

Mann looked at the houses, feeling that he did not want to look, but looking anyway. All he could see of the one-story houses were their roofs. There were wide gaps between them; some had washed away. But most of the two-story houses were still standing. Mann craned his neck, looking for Mrs. Heartfield's house, yet dreading to see it.

"Its erlong here somewhere," said Brinkley.

Brinkley turned the boat sideways and let the spotlight play over the fronts of the two-story houses. Mann wanted to tell him to turn around, to go back, to make for the hills. But he looked, his throat tight; he looked, gripping the sides of the boat; he looked for Mrs. Heartfield's house, seeing her hair framed in the lighted window.

"There it is!" yelled Brinkley.

At first Mann did not believe it was Mrs. Heartfield's house. It was dark. And he had been watching for two squares of yellow light, two lighted windows. And now, there it was, all dark. Mabbe they ain there? A hot wish rose in his blood, a wish that they were gone. Just gone anywhere, as long as they were not there to see him. He wished that their white bodies were at the bottom of the black waters. They were now ten feet from the house; the boat slowed.

"Mabbe they ain there," whispered Mann.

"We bettah call," said Brinkley.

Brinkley cupped his hand to his mouth and hollered: "Miz Heartfiel!"

They waited, listening, looking at the dark, shut windows. Brinkley must have thought that his voice had not carried, for he hollered again:

"Miz Heartfiel!"

"They ain there," whispered Mann.

"Look! Somebody's there! See?" breathed Brinkley. "Look!"

The window was opening; Brinkley centered the spot of light on it; a red head came through. Mann sat with parted lips, looking. He leaned over the side of the boat and waited for Mrs. Heartfield to call, Henry! Henry!

"Miz Heartfiel!" Brinkley called again.

"Can you get us? Can you get us?" she was calling.

"We comin! Wait a . . ."

A deafening noise cut out his voice. It was long, vibrant, like the sound of trees falling in storm. A tide of water swept the boat backwards. Mann heard Mrs. Heartfield scream. He could not see the house now; the spot-light lit a path of swirling black water. Brinkley raced the motor and jerked the boat around, playing the light again on the window. It was empty. There was another scream, but it was muffled.

"The watahs got em!" said Brinkley.

Again the boat headed into the middle of the current. The light was on the empty window. The house was moving down the street. Mann held his breath, feeling himself suspended over a black void. The house reached the center of the street and turned violently. It floated away from them, amid a sucking rush of water and the sound of splitting timber. It floundered; it shook in a trembling grip; then it whirled sharply to the left and crashed, jamming itself between two smaller houses. Mann heard the motor race; he was gliding slowly over the water, going toward the house.

"Yuh reckon yuh kin make it? Reckon we kin save em?" asked Brinkley.

Mann did not answer. Again they were ten feet from the house. The current speeding between the cracks emitted a thunderous roar. The outside walls tilted at an angle of thirty degrees. Brinkley carried the boat directly under the window and held it steady by clinging to a piece of jutting timber. Mann sat frozen, staring: in his mind he saw Mrs. Heartfield: something tickled his throat: he saw her red hair: he saw her white face: then he heard Brinkley speaking:

"Ahll hol the boat! Try t git in the windah!"

As though he were outside of himself watching himself, Mann felt himself stand up. He saw his hands reaching for the window ledge.

"Kin yuh make it? Here . . . Take the flash-light!"

Mann put the flash-light in his pocket and reached again. He could not make it. He tip-toed, standing on the top of the boat, hearing the rush of water below. His legs trembled; he stretched his arms higher.

"Kin yuh make it?"

"Naw . . ."

He rested a moment, looking at the window, wondering how he could reach it. Then he took the axe from his belt and thrust it into the window; he twisted the handle sideways and jerked. The blade caught. He leaned his weight against it. It held. He pulled up into the window and sat poised for a moment on his toes. He eased his feet to the floor. He stood a second in the droning darkness and something traveled over the entire surface of his body; it was cold, like the touch of wet feathers. He brought out the flash-light and focused it on the floor. He tried to call out Mrs. Heartfield's name, but could not. He swept the light: he saw a broken chair: a crumpled rug: strewn clothing: a smashed dresser: a tumbled bed: then a circle of red hair and a white face. Mrs. Heartfield sat against a wall, her arms about her two children. Her eyes were closed. Her little girl's head lay on her lap. Her little boy sat at her side on the floor, blinking in the light.

"Take my mother!" he whimpered.

The voice startled Mann; he stiffened. It was the same voice that had yelled, You nigger! You bastard! The same wild fear he had known when he was in the boat rowing against the current caught him. He wanted to run from the room and tell Brinkley that he could find no one; he wanted to leave them here for the black waters to swallow.

"Take my mother! Take my mother!"

Mann saw the boy's fingers fumbling; a match flared. The boy's eyes grew big. His jaw moved up and down. The flame flickered out.

"Its the nigger! Its the nigger!" the boy screamed.

Mann gripped the axe. He crouched, staring at the boy, holding the axe stiffly in his right fist. Something hard began to press against the back of his head and he saw it all in a flash while staring at the white boy and hearing him scream, "Its the nigger!" Yes, now, if he could swing that axe they would never tell on him and the black waters of the flood would cover them forever and he could tell Brinkley he had not been able to find them and the whites would never know he had killed a white man . . . His body grew taut with indecision. Yes, now, he would swing that axe and they would

never tell and he had his gun and if Brinkley found out
he would point the gun at Brinkley's head. He saw him-
self in the boat with Brinkley; he saw himself pointing
the gun at Brinkley's head; he saw himself in the boat
going away; he saw himself in the boat, alone, going
away . . . His muscles flexed and the axe was over his
head and he heard the white boy screaming, "Its the
nigger! Its the nigger!" Then he felt himself being lifted
violently up and swung around as though by gravity of
the earth itself and flung face downward into black
space. A loud commotion filled his ears: his body rolled
over and over and he saw the flash-light for an instant,
its one eye whirling: then he lay flat, stunned: he turned
over, pulled to his knees, dazed, surprised, shocked. He
crawled to the flash-light and picked it up with numbed
fingers. A voice whispered over and over in his ears, Ah
gotta git outta here . . . He sensed he was at an incline.
He swayed to his feet and held onto a wall. He heard
the sound of rushing water. He swept the spot of yel-
low. Mrs. Heartfield was lying face downward in a
V-trough to his right, where the floor joined the wall at
a slant. The boy was crawling in the dark, whimpering
"Mother! Mother!" Mann saw the axe, but seemed not
to realize that he had been about to use it. He knew
what had happened now; the house had tilted, had
tilted in the rushing black water. He saw himself as he
had stood a moment before, saw himself standing with
the axe raised high over Mrs. Heartfield and her two
children . . .

"Yuh fin em? Say, yuh fin em?"

Mann flinched, jerking his head around, trembling.
Brinkley was calling. A chill went over Mann. He turned
the spot on the window and saw a black face and beyond
the face a path of light shooting out over the water. *Naw*

. . . *Naw* . . . He could not kill now; he could not kill if someone were looking. He stood as though turned to steel. Then he sighed, heavily, as though giving up his last breath, as though giving up the world.

Brinkley was clinging to the window, still calling:

"C mon! Bring em out! The boats at the windah! C mon, Ah kin hep t take em out!"

Like a sleepwalker, Mann moved over to the white boy and grabbed his arm. The boy shrank and screamed:

"Leave me alone, you nigger!"

Mann stood over him, his shoulders slumped, his lips moving.

"Git in the boat," he mumbled.

The boy stared; then he seemed to understand.

"Get my mother . . ."

Like a little child, Mann obeyed and dragged Mrs. Heartfield to the window. He saw white hands helping.

"Get my sister!"

He brought the little girl next. Then the boy went. Mann climbed through last.

He was again in the boat, beside Brinkley. Mrs. Heartfield and her two children were in the back. The little girl was crying, sleepily. The boat rocked. Mann looked at the house; it was slanting down to the water; the window through which he had just crawled was about a foot from the level of the rushing current. The motor raced, but the roar came to him from a long ways off, from out of a deep silence, from out of a time long gone by. The boat slid over the water and he was in it; but it was a far away boat, and it was someone else sitting in that boat; not he. He saw the light plunging ahead into the darkness and felt the lurch of the boat as it plowed through water. But none of it really touched him; he was beyond it all now; it simply passed in front of his eyes like silent, moving shadows; like dim figures in a sick dream. He felt nothing; he sat, looking and seeing nothing.

"Yuh hardly made it," said Brinkley.

He looked at Brinkley as though surprised to see someone at his side.

"Ah thought yuh wuz gone when tha ol house went over," said Brinkley.

The boat was in the clear now, speeding against the current. It had stopped raining.

"Its gittin daylight," said Brinkley.

The darkness was thinning to a light haze.

"Mother? Mother . . ."

"Hush!" whispered Mrs. Heartfield.

Yes, Mann knew they were behind him. He felt them all over his body, and especially like something hard and cold weighing on top of his head; weighing so heavily that it seemed to blot out everything but one hard, tight thought: They got me now . . .

"Theres the hills!" said Brinkley.

Green slopes lay before him in the blurred dawn. The boat sped on and he saw jagged outlines of tents. Smoke drifted upward. Soldiers moved. Out of the depths of his tired body a prayer rose up in him, a silent prayer. Lawd, save me now! Save me now . . .

VI

It was broad daylight. The boat had stopped. The motor had stopped. And when Mann could no longer feel the lurch or hear the drone he grew hysterically tense.

"Waal, wes here," said Brinkley.

With fear Mann saw the soldiers running down the slopes. He felt the people in the seat behind him, felt their eyes on his back, his head. He knew that the white boy back there was hating him to death for having killed his father. He knew the white boy was waiting to scream, "You nigger! You bastard!" The soldiers closed in. Mann grabbed the side of the boat; Brinkley was climbing out.

"C mon," said Brinkley.

Mann stood up, swaying a little. They got me now, he thought. He stumbled on dry land. He took a step and a twig snapped. He looked around and tried to fight off a feeling of unreality. Mrs. Heartfield was crying.

"Here, take this blanket, Mrs. Heartfield," said one of the soldiers.

Mann walked right past them, waiting as he walked to hear the word that would make him stop. The landscape lay before his eyes with a surprising and fateful solidity. It was like a picture which might break. He walked on in blind faith. He reached level ground and went on past white people who stared sullenly. He wanted to look around, but could not turn his head. His body seemed encased in a tight vise, in a narrow black coffin that moved with him as he moved. He wondered if the white boy was telling the soldiers now. He was glad when he reached the tents. At least the tents would keep them from seeing him.

"Hey, you! Halt, there!"

He caught his breath, turning slowly. A white soldier walked toward him with a rifle. Lawd, this is it . . .

"Awright, you can take off that stuff now!"

"Suh?"

"You can take off that stuff, I say!"

"Suh? Suh?"

"Take off those boots and that raincoat, God-dammit!"

"Yessuh."

He pulled off the raincoat. He was trembling. He pushed the boots as far down his legs as they would go; then he stooped on his right knee while he pulled off the left boot, and on his left knee while he pulled off the right.

"Throw em over there in that tent!"

"Yessuh."

He walked on again, feeling the soldier's eyes on his back. Ahead, across a grassy square, were black people, his people. He quickened his pace. Mabbe Ah kin fin Bob. Er Elder Murray . . . Lawd, Ah wondah whuts become of Peewee? N Grannie? He thought of Lulu and his eyes blurred. He elbowed into a crowd of black men gathered around a kitchen tent. He sighed and a weight seemed to go from him. He looked into black faces, looked for hope. He had to get away from here before that white boy had the soldiers running him to the ground. He thought of the white boats he had seen tied down at the water's edge. Lawd, ef Ah kin git inter one of em . . .

"Yuh had some cawfee?"

A small black woman stood in front of him holding a tin cup. He smelt steam curling up from it.

"Yuh had yo cawfee yit?" the woman asked again. "There ain nothin here but cawfee."

"Nom."

"Here."

He took the extended cup and stood watching the steam curl. The woman turned to walk away.

"Mam, yuh seen a man by the name of Bob Cobb?"

"Lawd knows, Mistah. We don know whos here n who ain. Why don yuh ast over t the Red Cross Station? Thas where everybodys signin in at."

No, he could not go to the Red Cross. They would catch him there surely. He walked a few steps, sipping the coffee, watching for white faces over the brim of his cup. Then suddenly he felt confused, as though all that had happened a few hours ago was but a dream. He had no need to be afraid now, had he? Just to imagine that it was all a dream made him feel better. Lawd. Ahm sho tired! He finished the cup and looked over to the tent. Heat was expanding in his stomach. He looked around again. There were no white faces. Black men stood, eating, talking, Ahma ast some of em t hep me . . . He went over and extended his cup for another helping. The black woman stared, her eyes looking beyond him, wide with fear. He heard her give a short, stifled scream. Then he was jerked violently from behind; he heard the soft clink of tin as the cup bounded from his fingers. The back of his head hit the mud.

"Is this the nigger?"

"Yeah; thats the one! Thats the nigger!"

He was on his back and he looked up into the faces of four white soldiers. Muzzles of rifles pointed at his chest. The white boy was standing, pointing into his face.

"Thats the nigger that killed father!"

They caught his arms and yanked him to his feet. Hunched, he looked up out of the corners of his eyes, his hands shielding his head.

"Get your hands up, nigger!"

He straightened.

"Move on!"

He walked slowly, vaguely, his hands high in the air. Two of the soldiers were in front of him, leading the way. He felt a hard prod on his backbone.

"Walk up, nigger, and dont turn rabbit!"

They led him among the tents. He marched, staring straight, hearing his shoes and the soldiers' shoes sucking in the mud. And he heard the quick steps of the white boy keeping pace. The black faces he passed were blurred and merged one into the other. And he heard tense talk, whispers. For a split second he was there among those blunt and hazy black faces looking silently and fearfully at the white folks take some poor black man away. Why don they hep me? Yet he knew that they would not and could not help him, even as he in times past had not helped other black men being taken by the white folks to their death . . . Then he was back among the soldiers again, feeling the sharp prod of the muzzle on his backbone. He was led across the grassy square that separated the white tents from the black. There were only white faces now. He could hardly breathe.

"Look! They caughta coon!"

"C mon, they gotta nigger!"

He was between the soldiers, being pushed along, stumbling. Each step he took he felt his pistol jostling gently against his thigh. A thought circled round and round in his mind, circled so tightly he could hardly think it! They goin t kill me . . . They goin t kill me . . .

"This way!"

He turned. Behind him were voices; he knew a crowd was gathering. He saw Mrs. Heartfield looking at him; he saw her red hair. The soldiers stopped him in front of her. He looked at the ground.

"Is this the nigger, Mrs. Heartfield?"

"Yes, hes the one."

More white faces gathered around. The crowd blurred

and wavered before his eyes. There was a rising mutter of talk. Then he could not move; they were pressing in.

"What did he do?"

"Did he bother a white woman?"

"She says he did something!"

He heard the soldiers protesting.

"Get back now and behave! Get back!"

The crowd closed in tightly; the soldiers stood next to him, between him and the yelling faces. He grabbed a soldier, clinging, surging with the crowd. They were screaming in his ears.

"Lynch im!"

"Kill the black bastard!"

The soldiers struggled.

"Get back! You cant do that!"

"Let us have im!"

He was lifted off his feet in a tight circle of livid faces. A blow came to his mouth. The crowd loosened a bit and he fell to all fours. He felt a dull pain in his thigh and he knew he had been kicked. Out of the corners of his eyes he saw a moving tangle of feet and legs.

"Kill the sonofabitch!"

"GET BACK! GET BACK OR WE WILL SHOOT!"

They were away from him now. Blood dripped from his mouth.

"The general says bring him in his tent!"

He was snatched up and pushed into a tent. Two soldiers held his arms. A red face behind a table looked at him. He saw Mrs. Heartfield, her boy, her little girl. He heard a clamor of voices.

"Keep those people back from this tent!"

"Yessir!"

It grew quiet. He felt faint and grabbed his knees to

keep from falling. The soldiers were shaking him. He felt warm blood splashing on his hands.

"Cant you talk, you black bastard! Cant you talk!"

"Yessuh."

"Whats your name?"

"Mann, suh."

"Whats the charge against this nigger?"

"Looting and murder, General."

"Whom did he kill?"

"Heartfield, the Post Master, sir."

"*Heart*field?"

"Yessir."

"He stole our boat and killed father!" said the boy.

"Do you confess that, nigger?"

"Capm, he shot at me fo Ah shot im! He shot at me . . ."

"He stole our boat!" yelled the boy. "He stole our boat and killed father when he told him to bring it back!"

"Are you sure this is the man?"

"Hes the one, General! His name is Mann and I saw him under our window!"

"When was this?"

"Last night, at the Post Office."

"Who saw this?"

"I did," said Mrs. Heartfield.

"I saw im!" said the boy.

"Ah didnt steal that boat, Capm! Ah swear fo Gawd, Ah didnt!"

"You did! You stole our boat and killed father and left us in the flood . . ."

The boy ran at Mann. The soldiers pulled him back.

"Ralph, come here!" called Mrs. Heartfield.

"Keep still, sonny," said a soldier. "We can handle this!"

"Did you have that boat, nigger?" asked the general.

"Yessuh, but . . ."

"Where did you get it?"

He did not answer.

"What did you do with the boat?"

"The man at the hospital took it. But Ah didnt steal it, Capm . . ."

"Get Colonel Davis!" the general ordered.

"Yessir!"

"Nigger, do you know the meaning of this?"

Mann opened his mouth, but no words came.

"Do you know this means your life?"

"Ah didnt mean t kill im! Ah wuz takin mah wife t the hospital . . ."

"What did you do with the gun?"

Again he did not answer. He had a wild impulse to pull it out and shoot, blindly; to shoot and be killed while shooting. But before he could act a voice stopped him.

"Search im!"

They found the gun and laid it on the table. There was an excited buzz of conversation. He saw white hands pick up the gun and break it. Four cartridges spilled out.

"He shot daddy twice! He shot im twice!" said the boy.

"Did he *bother* you, Mrs. Heartfield?"

"No; not *that* way."

"The little girl?"

"No; but he came back to the house and got us out. Ralph says he had an axe . . ."

"When was *this*?"

"Early this morning."

"What did you go back there for, nigger?"

He did not answer.

"Did he *bother* you *then*, Mrs. Heartfield?"

"He was going to kill us!" said the boy. "He was holding the axe over us and then the house went over in the flood . . ."

There was another buzz of conversation.

"Heres Colonel Davis, General!"

"You know this nigger, Colonel?"

Mann looked at the ground. A soldier knocked his head up.

"He was at the hospital."

"What did he do there?"

"He helped us on the roof."

"Did he have a boat?"

"Yes; but we took it and sent him to the levee. Here, he signed for it . . ."

"What kind of a boat was it?"

"A white rowboat."

"That was *our* boat!" said the boy.

The piece of paper Mann had signed in the hospital was shoved under his eyes.

"Did you sign this, nigger?"

He swallowed and did not answer.

A pen scratched on paper.

"Take im out!"

"White folks, have mercy! Ah didnt mean t kill im! Ah swear fo Awmighty Gawd, Ah didnt . . . He shot at me! Ah wuz takin mah wife t the hospital . . ."

"Take im out!"

He fell to the ground, crying.

"Ah didnt mean t kill im! Ah didnt . . ."

"When shall it be, General?"

"Take im out *now*! Whos next?"

They dragged him from the tent. He rolled in the mud. A soldier kicked him.

"Git up and walk, nigger! You aint dead yet!"

He walked blindly with bent back, his mouth dripping blood, his arms dangling loose. There were four of them and he was walking in between. Tears clogged his eyes. Down the slope to his right was a wobbly sea of brown water stretching away to a trembling sky. And there were boats, white boats, free boats, leaping and jumping like fish. There were boats and they were going to kill him. The sun was shining, pouring showers of yellow into his eyes. Two soldiers floated in front of him, and he heard two walking in back. He was between, walking, and the sun dropped spangles of yellow into his eyes. They goin t kill me! They goin . . . His knees buckled and he went forward on his face. For a moment he seemed not to breathe. Then with each heave of his chest he cried:

"Gawd, don let em kill me! Stop em from killin black folks!"

"Get up and walk, nigger!"

"Ah didnt mean t do it! Ah swear fo Gawd, Ah didnt!"

They jerked him up; he slipped limply to the mud again.

"What we going to do with this black bastard?"

"We will have to carry 'im."

"Ill be Goddamn if *I* carry 'im."

One of them grabbed Mann's right arm and twisted it up the center of his back.

"Gawd!" he screamed. "Gawd, have mercy!"

"You reckon you can walk now, nigger?"

He pulled up and stumbled off, rigid with pain. They were among trees now, going up a slope. Through tears he saw the hazy tents of the soldiers' camp. Lawd, have mercy! Once there and he would be dead. There and then the end. Gawd Awmighty . . .

"Gotta cigarette, Charley?"

"Yeah."

A tiny flame glowed through spangles of yellow sunshine. A smoking match flicked past his eyes and hit waves of green, wet grass. His fear subsided into a cold numbness. Yes, now! Yes, through the trees! Right thu them trees! Gawd! They were going to kill him. Yes, now, he would die! He would die before he would let them kill him. Ahll die fo they kill me! Ahll *die* . . . He ran straight to the right, through the trees, in the direction of the water. He heard a shout.

"You sonofabitch!"

He ran among the trees, over the wet ground, listening as he ran for the crack of rifles. His shoes slipped over waves of green grass. Then came a shot. He heard it hit somewhere. Another sang by his head. He felt he was not running fast enough; he held his breath and ran, ran. He left the hazy trees and ran in the open over waves of green. He veered, hearing rifles cracking. His right knee folded; he fell, rolling over. He scrambled up, limping. His eyes caught a whirling glimpse of brown water and shouting white boats. Then he was hit again, in the shoulder. He was on all fours, crawling to the edge of the slope. Bullets hit his side, his back, his head. He fell, his face buried in the wet, blurred green. He heard the sound of pounding feet growing fainter and felt something hot bubbling in his throat; he coughed and then suddenly he could feel and hear no more.

The soldiers stood above him.

"You shouldntve run, nigger!" said one of the soldiers. "You shouldntve run, Goddammit! You shouldntve run . . ."

One of the soldiers stooped and pushed the butt of

his rifle under the body and lifted it over. It rolled heavily down the wet slope and stopped about a foot from the water's edge; one black palm sprawled limply outward and upward, trailing in the brown current . . .

III

Long Black Song

I

Go t sleep, baby
Papas gone t town
Go t sleep, baby
The suns goin down
Go t sleep, baby
Yo candys in the sack
Go t sleep, baby
Papas comin back . . .

OVER AND OVER she crooned, and at each lull of her voice she rocked the wooden cradle with a bare black foot. But the baby squalled louder, its wail drowning out the song. She stopped and stood over the cradle, wondering what was bothering it, if its stomach hurt. She felt the diaper; it was dry. She lifted it up and patted its back. Still it cried, longer and louder. She put it back into the cradle and dangled a string of red beads before its eyes. The little black fingers clawed them away. She bent over, frowning, murmuring: "Whut's the mattah, chile? Yuh wan some watah?" She held a dripping gourd to the black lips, but the baby turned its head and kicked its legs. She stood a moment, perplexed. Whuts wrong wid tha chile? She ain never carried on like this this tima day. She picked it up and went to the open door. "See the sun, baby?" she asked, pointing to a big ball of red dying between the branches of trees. The baby pulled back and strained its round black arms and legs against her stomach and shoulders. She knew it was tired; she could tell by the halting way it opened its mouth to draw in air. She sat on a wooden stool, unbuttoned the front of her dress, brought the baby closer and offered it a black teat. "Don baby wan suppah?" It pulled away and went limp, crying softly, piteously, as though it would never stop. Then it pushed its fingers against her breasts and wailed. Lawd, chile, whut yuh wan? Yo ma cant hep yuh less she knows whut yuh wan. Tears gushed; four white teeth flashed in red gums; the little chest heaved up and down and round black fingers stretched floorward. Lawd, chile, whuts wrong wid yuh? She stooped slowly, allowing her body to be guided by the downward tug. As soon as the little fingers touched the floor the wail quieted into a broken sniffle. She turned the baby loose and watched it crawl toward a corner. She followed and saw the little fingers reach for the tail-end of an old eight-day clock. "Yuh wan tha ol clock?" She dragged the clock into the center of the floor. The baby crawled after it, calling, "Ahh!" Then it raised its hands and beat on top of the clock Bink! Bink! Bink! "Naw, yuhll hurt yo hans!" She held the baby and looked around. It cried and struggled. "Wait, baby!" She fetched a small stick from the top of a rickety dresser. "Here," she said, closing the little fingers about it. "Beat wid this, see?" She heard each blow landing squarely on top of the clock Bang! Bang! Bang! And with each bang the baby smiled and said, "Ahh!" Mabbe thall keep yuh quiet erwhile. Mabbe Ah kin git some res now. She stood in the doorway. Lawd, tha chiles a pain! She mus be teethin. Er something . . .

She wiped sweat from her forehead with the bottom of her dress and looked out over the green fields rolling up the hillsides. She sighed, fighting a feeling of loneliness. Lawd, its sho hard t pass the days wid Silas gone. Been mos a week now since he took the wagon outta here. Hope ain nothin wrong. He mus be buyin a heapa stuff there in Colwatah t be stayin all this time. Yes; maybe Silas would remember and bring that five-yard piece of red calico she wanted. Oh, Lawd! Ah *hope* he don fergit it!

She saw green fields wrapped in the thickening gloam. It was as if they had left the earth, those fields, and were floating slowly skyward. The afterglow lingered, red, dying, somehow tenderly sad. And far away, in front of her, earth and sky met in a soft swoon of shadow. A cricket chirped, sharp and lonely; and it seemed she could hear it chirping long after it had stopped. Silas oughta c mon soon. Ahm tireda staying here by mahsef.

Loneliness ached in her. She swallowed, hearing Bang! Bang! Bang! Tom been gone t war mos a year now. N tha ol wars over n we ain heard nothin yit. Lawd, don let Tom be dead! She frowned into the gloam and wondered about that awful war so far away. They said it was over now. Yeah, Gawd had t stop em fo they killed everbody. She felt that merely to go so far away from home was a kind of death in itself. Just to go that far away was to be killed. Nothing good could come from men going miles across the seas to fight. N how come they wanna kill each other? How come they wanna make blood? Killing was not what men ought to do. Shucks! she thought.

She sighed, thinking of Tom, hearing Bang! Bang! Bang! She saw Tom, saw his big black smiling face; her eyes went dreamily blank, drinking in the red afterglow. Yes, God; it could have been Tom instead of Silas who was having her now. Yes; it could have been Tom she was loving. She smiled and asked herself, Lawd, Ah wondah how would it been wid Tom? Against the plush sky she saw a white bright day and a green cornfield and

she saw Tom walking in his overalls and she was with
Tom and he had his arm about her waist. She remem-
bered how weak she had felt feeling his fingers sinking
into the flesh of her hips. Her knees had trembled and
she had had a hard time trying to stand up and not just
sink right there to the ground. Yes; that was what Tom
had wanted her to do. But she had held Tom up and he
had held her up; they had held each other up to keep
from slipping to the ground there in the green cornfield.
Lawd! Her breath went and she passed her tongue over
her lips. But that was not as exciting as that winter
evening when the grey skies were sleeping and she and
Tom were coming home from church down dark Lov-
er's Lane. She felt the tips of her teats tingling and
touching the front of her dress as she remembered how
he had crushed her against him and hurt her. She had
closed her eyes and was smelling the acrid scent of dry
October leaves and had gone weak in his arms and had
felt she could not breathe any more and had torn away
and run, run home. And that sweet ache which had
frightened her then was stealing back to her loins now
with the silence and the cricket calls and the red after-
glow and Bang! Bang! Bang! Lawd, Ah wondah how
would it been wid Tom?

She stepped out on the porch and leaned against the
wall of the house. Sky sang a red song. Fields whispered
a green prayer. And song and prayer were dying in si-
lence and shadow. Never in all her life had she been so
much alone as she was now. Days were never so long as
these days; and nights were never so empty as these
nights. She jerked her head impatiently, hearing Bang!
Bang! Bang! Shucks! she thought. When Silas had gone
something had ebbed so slowly that at first she had not
noticed it. Now she felt all of it as though the feeling
had no bottom. She tried to think just how it had hap-

pened. Yes; there had been all her life the long hope of white bright days and the deep desire of dark black nights and then Silas had gone. Bang! Bang! Bang! There had been laughter and eating and singing and the long gladness of green cornfields in summer. There had been cooking and sewing and sweeping and the deep dream of sleeping grey skies in winter. Always it had been like that and she had been happy. But no more. The happiness of those days and nights, of those green cornfields and grey skies had started to go from her when Tom had gone to war. His leaving had left an empty black hole in her heart, a black hole that Silas had come in and filled. But not quite. Silas had not quite filled that hole. No; days and nights were not as they were before.

She lifted her chin, listening. She had heard something, a dull throb like she had heard that day Silas had called her outdoors to look at the airplane. Her eyes swept the sky. But there was no plane. Mabbe its behin the house? She stepped into the yard and looked upward through paling light. There were only a few big wet stars trembling in the east. Then she heard the throb again. She turned, looking up and down the road. The throb grew louder, droning; and she heard Bang! Bang! Bang! There! A car! Wondah whuts a car doin comin out here? A black car was winding over a dusty road, coming toward her. Mabbe some white mans bringing Silas home wida loada goods? But, Lawd, Ah *hope* its no trouble! The car stopped in front of the house and a white man got out. Wondah whut he wans? She looked at the car, but could not see Silas. The white man was young; he wore a straw hat and had no coat. He walked toward her with a huge black package under his arm.

"Well, howre yuh today, Aunty?"

"Ahm well. How yuh?"

"Oh, so-so. Its sure hot today, hunh?"

She brushed her hand across her forehead and sighed.

"Yeah; it is kinda warm."

"You busy?"

"Naw, Ah ain doin nothin."

"Ive got something to show you. Can I sit here, on your porch?"

"Ah reckon so. But, Mistah, Ah ain got no money."

"Havent you sold your cotton yet?"

"Silas gone t town wid it now."

"Whens he coming back?"

"Ah don know. Ahm waitin fer im."

She saw the white man take out a handkerchief and mop his face. Bang! Bang! Bang! He turned his head and looked through the open doorway, into the front room.

"Whats all that going on in there?"

She laughed.

"Aw, thas jus Ruth."

"Whats she doing?"

"She beatin tha ol clock."

"Beating a *clock*?"

She laughed again.

"She wouldnt go t sleep so Ah give her tha ol clock t play wid."

The white man got up and went to the front door; he stood a moment looking at the black baby hammering on the clock. Bang! Bang! Bang!

"But why let her tear your clock up?"

"It ain no good."

"You could have it fixed."

"We ain got no money t be fixin no clocks."

"Havent you got a clock?"

"Naw."

"But how do you keep time?"

"We git erlong widout time."

"But how do you know when to get up in the morning?"

"We jus git up, thas all."

"But how do you know what time it is when you get up?"

"We git up wid the sun."

"And at night, how do you tell when its night?"

"It gits dark when the sun goes down."

"Havent you ever had a clock?"

She laughed and turned her face toward the silent fields.

"Mistah, we don need no clock."

"Well, this beats everything! I dont see how in the world anybody can live without time."

"We jus don need no time, Mistah."

The white man laughed and shook his head; she laughed and looked at him. The white man was funny. Jus lika lil boy. Astin how do Ah know when t git up in the mawnin! She laughed again and mused on the baby, hearing Bang! Bang! Bang! She could hear the white man breathing at her side; she felt his eyes on her face. She looked at him; she saw he was looking at her breasts. Hes jus lika lil boy. Acks like he cant understan *nothin*!

"But you need a clock," the white man insisted. "Thats what Im out here for. Im selling clocks and gra- phophones. The clocks are made right into the grapho- phones, a nice sort of combination, hunh? You can have music and time all at once. Ill show you . . ."

"Mistah, we don need no clock!"

"You dont have to buy it. It wont cost you anything just to look."

He unpacked the big black box. She saw the strands

of his auburn hair glinting in the afterglow. His back bulged against his white shirt as he stooped. He pulled out a square brown graphophone. She bent forward, looking. Lawd, but its pretty! She saw the face of a clock under the horn of the graphophone. The gilt on the corners sparkled. The color in the wood glowed softly. It reminded her of the light she saw sometimes in the baby's eyes. Slowly she slid a finger over a beveled edge; she wanted to take the box into her arms and kiss it.

"Its eight o'clock," he said.

"Yeah?"

"It only costs fifty dollars. And you dont have to pay for it all at once. Just five dollars down and five dollars a month."

She smiled. The white man was just like a little boy. Jus lika chile. She saw him grinding the handle of the box.

"Just listen to this," he said.

There was a sharp, scratching noise; then she moved nervously, her body caught in the ringing coils of music.

When the trumpet of the Lord shall sound . . .

She rose on circling waves of white bright days and dark black nights.

. . . *and time shall be no more* . . .

Higher and higher she mounted.

And the morning breaks . . .

Earth fell far behind, forgotten.

. . . *eternal, bright and fair* . . .

Echo after echo sounded.

When the saved of the earth shall gather . . .

Her blood surged like the long gladness of summer.

. . . over on the other shore . . .

Her blood ebbed like the deep dream of sleep in winter.

And when the roll is called up yonder . . .

She gave up, holding her breath.

I'll be there . . .

A lump filled her throat. She leaned her back against a post, trembling, feeling the rise and fall of days and nights, of summer and winter; surging, ebbing, leaping about her, beyond her, far out over the fields to where earth and sky lay folded in darkness. She wanted to lie down and sleep, or else leap up and shout. When the music stopped she felt herself coming back, being let down slowly. She sighed. It was dark now. She looked into the doorway. The baby was sleeping on the floor. Ah gotta git up n put tha chile t bed, she thought.

"Wasnt that pretty?"

"It wuz pretty, awright."

"When do you think your husbands coming back?"

"Ah don know, Mistah."

She went into the room and put the baby into the cradle. She stood again in the doorway and looked at the shadowy box that had lifted her up and carried her away. Crickets called. The dark sky had swallowed up the earth, and more stars were hanging, clustered, burning. She heard the white man sigh. His face was lost in shadow. She saw him rub his palms over his forehead. Hes jus lika lil boy.

"Id like to see your husband tonight," he said. "I've got to be in Lilydale at six o'clock in the morning and I wont be back through here soon. I got to pick up my buddy over there and we're heading North."

She smiled into the darkness. He was just like a little boy. A little boy selling clocks.

"Yuh sell them things alla time?" she asked.

"Just for the summer," he said. "I go to school in winter. If I can make enough money out of this Ill go to Chicago to school this fall . . ."

"Whut yuh gonna be?"

"*Be?* What do you mean?"

"Whut yuh goin t school fer?"

"Im studying science."

"Whuts tha?"

"Oh, er . . ." He looked at her. "Its about why things are as they are."

"Why things is as they *is?*"

"Well, its something like that."

"How come yuh wanna study tha?"

"Oh, you wouldnt understand."

She sighed.

"Naw, Ah guess Ah wouldnt."

"Well, I reckon Ill be getting along," said the white man. "Can I have a drink of water?"

"Sho. But we ain got nothin but well-watah, n yuhll have t come n git."

"Thats all right."

She slid off the porch and walked over the ground with bare feet. She heard the shoes of the white man behind her, falling to the earth in soft whispers. It was black dark now. She led him to the well, groped her way, caught the bucket and let it down with a rope; she heard a splash and the bucket grew heavy. She drew it up, pulling against its weight, throwing one hand over the other, feeling the cool wet of the rope on her palms.

"Ah don git watah outta here much," she said, a little out of breath. "Silas gits the watah mos of the time. This buckets too heavy fer me."

"Oh, wait! Ill help!"

His shoulder touched hers. In the darkness she felt his warm hands fumbling for the rope.

"Where is it?"

"Here."

She extended the rope through the darkness. His fingers touched her breasts.

"Oh!"

She said it in spite of herself. He would think she was thinking about that. And he was a white man. She was sorry she had said that.

"Wheres the gourd?" he asked. "Gee, its dark!"

She stepped back and tried to see him.

"Here."

"I cant see!" he said, laughing.

Again she felt his fingers on the tips of her breasts. She backed away, saying nothing this time. She thrust the gourd out from her. Warm fingers met her cold hands. He had the gourd. She heard him drink; it was the faint, soft music of water going down a dry throat, the music of water in a silent night. He sighed and drank again.

"I was thirsty," he said. "I hadnt had any water since noon."

She knew he was standing in front of her; she could not see him, but she felt him. She heard the gourd rest against the wall of the well. She turned, then felt his hands full on her breasts. She struggled back.

"Naw, Mistah!"

"Im not going to hurt you!"

White arms were about her, tightly. She was still. But hes a *white* man. A *white* man. She felt his breath com-

ing hot on her neck and where his hands held her
breasts the flesh seemed to knot. She was rigid, poised;
she swayed backward, then forward. She caught his
shoulders and pushed.

"Naw, naw . . . Mistah, Ah cant do that!"

She jerked away. He caught her hand.

"Please . . ."

"Lemme go!"

She tried to pull her hand out of his and felt his fin-
gers tighten. She pulled harder, and for a moment they
were balanced, one against the other. Then he was at
her side again, his arms about her.

"I wont hurt you! I wont hurt you . . ."

She leaned backward and tried to dodge his face. Her
breasts were full against him; she gasped, feeling the full
length of his body. She held her head far to one side;
she knew he was seeking her mouth. His hands were on
her breasts again. A wave of warm blood swept into her
stomach and loins. She felt his lips touching her throat
and where he kissed it burned.

"Naw, naw . . ."

Her eyes were full of the wet stars and they blurred,
silver and blue. Her knees were loose and she heard her
own breathing; she was trying to keep from falling. But
hes a *white* man! A *white* man! Naw! Naw! And still she
would not let him have her lips; she kept her face
away. Her breasts hurt where they were crushed
against him and each time she caught her breath she
held it and while she held it it seemed that if she would
let it go it would kill her. Her knees were pressed hard
against his and she clutched the upper parts of his arms,
trying to hold on. Her loins ached. She felt her body
sliding.

"Gawd . . ."

He helped her up. She could not see the stars now; her eyes were full of the feeling that surged over her body each time she caught her breath. He held her close, breathing into her ear; she straightened, rigidly, feeling that she had to straighten or die. And then her lips felt his and she held her breath and dreaded ever to breathe again for fear of the feeling that would sweep down over her limbs. She held tightly, hearing a mounting tide of blood beating against her throat and temples. Then she gripped him, tore her face away, emptied her lungs in one long despairing gasp and went limp. She felt his hand; she was still, taut, feeling his hand, then his fingers. The muscles in her legs flexed and she bit her lips and pushed her toes deep into the wet dust by the side of the well and tried to wait and tried to wait until she could wait no longer. She whirled away from him and a streak of silver and blue swept across her blood. The wet ground cooled her palms and knee-caps. She stumbled up and ran, blindly, her toes flicking warm, dry dust. Her numbed fingers grabbed at a rusty nail in the post at the porch and she pushed ahead of hands that held her breasts. Her fingers found the door-facing; she moved into the darkened room, her hands before her. She touched the cradle and turned till her knees hit the bed. She went over, face down, her fingers trembling in the crumpled folds of his shirt. She moved and moved again and again, trying to keep ahead of the warm flood of blood that sought to catch her. A liquid metal covered her and she rode on the curve of white bright days and dark black nights and the surge of the long gladness of summer and the ebb of the deep dream of sleep in winter till a high red wave of hotness drowned her in a deluge of silver and blue that boiled her blood and blistered her flesh *bangbangbang* . . .

II

"Yuh bettah go," she said.

She felt him standing by the side of the bed, in the dark. She heard him clear his throat. His belt-buckle tinkled.

"Im leaving that clock and graphophone," he said.

She said nothing. In her mind she saw the box glowing softly, like the light in the baby's eyes. She stretched out her legs and relaxed.

"You can have it for forty instead of fifty. Ill be by early in the morning to see if your husbands in."

She said nothing. She felt the hot skin of her body growing steadily cooler.

"Do you think hell pay ten on it? Hell only owe thirty then."

She pushed her toes deep into the quilt, feeling a night wind blowing through the door. Her palms rested lightly on top of her breasts.

"Do you think hell pay ten on it?"

"Hunh?"

"Hell pay ten, wont he?"

"Ah don know," she whispered.

She heard his shoe hit against a wall; footsteps echoed on the wooden porch. She started nervously when she heard the roar of his car; she followed the throb of the motor till she heard it when she could hear it no more, followed it till she heard it roaring faintly in her ears in the dark and silent room. Her hands moved on her breasts and she was conscious of herself, all over; she felt the weight of her body resting heavily on shucks. She felt the presence of fields lying out there covered with night. She turned over slowly and lay on her stomach, her hands tucked under her. From somewhere came a creaking noise. She sat upright, feeling fear. The wind sighed. Crickets called. She lay down again, hearing shucks rustle. Her eyes looked straight up in the darkness and her blood sogged. She had lain a long time, full of a vast peace, when a far away tinkle made her feel the bed again. The tinkle came through the night; she listened, knowing that soon she would hear the rattle of Silas' wagon. Even then she tried to fight off the sound of Silas' coming, even then she wanted to feel the peace of night filling her again; but the tinkle grew louder and she heard the jangle of a wagon and the quick trot of horses. Thas Silas! She gave up and waited. She heard horses neighing. Out of the window bare feet whispered in the dust, then crossed the porch, echoing in soft booms. She closed her eyes and saw Silas come into the room in his dirty overalls as she had seen him come in a thousand times before.

"Yuh sleep, Sarah?"

She did not answer. Feet walked across the floor and a match scratched. She opened her eyes and saw Silas standing over her with a lighted lamp. His hat was pushed far back on his head and he was laughing.

"Ah reckon yuh thought Ah wuznt never comin back, hunh? Cant yuh wake up? See, Ah got that red cloth yuh wanted . . ." He laughed again and threw the red cloth on the mantel.

"Yuh hongry?" she asked.

"Naw, Ah kin make out till mawnin." Shucks rustled as he sat on the edge of the bed. "Ah got two hundred n fifty fer mah cotton."

"Two hundred n fifty?"

"Nothin different! N guess whut Ah done?"

"Whut?"

"Ah bought ten mo acres o lan. Got em from ol man Burgess. Paid im a hundred n fifty dollahs down. Ahll pay the res next year ef things go erlong awright. Ahma have t git a man t hep me nex spring . . ."

"Yuh mean hire somebody?"

"Sho, hire somebody! Whut yuh think? Ain tha the way the white folks do? Ef yuhs gonna git anywheres yuhs gotta do just like they do." He paused. "Whut yuh been doin since Ah been gone?"

"Nothin. Cookin, cleanin, n . . ."

"How Ruth?"

"She awright." She lifted her head. "Silas, yuh git any lettahs?"

"Naw. But Ah heard Tom wuz in town."

"In *town*?"

She sat straight up.

"Yeah, thas whut the folks wuz sayin at the sto."

"Back from the war?"

"Ah ast erroun t see ef Ah could fin im. But Ah couldnt."

"Lawd, Ah wish hed c mon home."

"Them white folks sho's glad the wars over. But things wuz kinda bad there in town. Everwhere Ah looked wuznt nothin but black n white soljers. N them white folks beat up a black soljer yistiddy. He wuz jus in from France. Wuz still wearin his soljers suit. They claimed he sassed a white woman . . ."

"Who wuz he?"

"Ah don know. Never saw im befo."

"Yuh see An Peel?"

"Naw."

"Silas!" she said reprovingly.

"Aw, Sarah, Ah jus couldnt git out there."

"Whut else yuh bring sides the cloth?"

"Ah got yuh some high-top shoes." He turned and looked at her in the dim light of the lamp. "Woman, ain yuh glad Ah bought yuh some shoes n cloth?" He laughed and lifted his feet to the bed. "Lawd, Sarah, yuhs sho sleepy, ain yuh?"

"Bettah put tha lamp out, Silas . . ."

"Aw . . ." He swung out of the bed and stood still for a moment. She watched him, then turned her face to the wall.

"Whuts that by the windah?" he asked.

She saw him bending over and touching the graphophone with his fingers.

"Thasa graphophone."

"Where yuh git it from?"

"A man lef it here."

"When he bring it?"

"Today."

"But how come he t leave it?"

"He says hell be out here in the mawnin t see ef yuh wans t buy it."

He was on his knees, feeling the wood and looking at the gilt on the edges of the box. He stood up and looked at her.

"Yuh ain never said yuh wanted one of these things."

She said nothing.

"Where wuz the man from?"

"Ah don know."

"He white?"

"Yeah."

He put the lamp back on the mantel. As he lifted the globe to blow out the flame, his hand paused.

"Whos hats this?"

She raised herself and looked. A straw hat lay bottom upwards on the edge of the mantel. Silas picked it up and looked back to the bed, to Sarah.

"Ah guess its the white mans. He must a lef it . . ."

"Whut he doin *in our room?*"

"He wuz talkin t me bout tha graphophone."

She watched him go to the window and stoop again to the box. He picked it up, fumbled with the price-tag and took the box to the light.

"Whut this thing cos?"

"Forty dollahs."

"But its marked fifty here."

"Oh, Ah means he said fifty . . ."

He took a step toward the bed.

"Yuh lyin t me!"

"Silas!"

He heaved the box out of the front door; there was a smashing, tinkling noise as it bounded off the front porch and hit the ground.

"Whut in hell yuh lie t me fer?"

"Yuh broke the box!"

"Ahma break yo Gawddam neck ef yuh don stop lyin t me!"

"Silas, Ah ain lied t yuh!"

"Shut up, Gawddammit! Yuh did!"

He was standing by the bed with the lamp trembling in his hand. She stood on the other side, between the bed and the wall.

"How come yuh tell me tha thing cos *forty* dollahs when it cos *fifty*?"

"Thas whut he tol me."

"How come he take *ten* dollahs off fer yuh?"

"He ain took nothin off fer me, Silas!"

"Yuh lyin t me! N yuh lied t me bout Tom, too!"

She stood with her back to the wall, her lips parted, looking at him silently, steadily. Their eyes held for a moment. Silas looked down, as though he were about to believe her. Then he stiffened.

"Whos this?" he asked, picking up a short yellow pencil from the crumpled quilt.

She said nothing. He started toward her.

"Yuh wan me t take mah raw-hide whip n make yuh talk?"

"Naw, naw, Silas! Yuh wrong! He wuz figgerin wid tha pencil!"

He was silent a moment, his eyes searching her face.

"Gawddam yo black soul t hell, don yuh try lyin t me! Ef yuh start layin wid white men Ahll hoss-whip yuh t a incha yo life. Shos theres a Gawd in Heaven Ah will! From sunup t sundown Ah works mah guts out t pay them white trash bastards whut Ah owe em, n then Ah comes n fins they been in mah house! Ah cant go into their houses, n yuh know Gawddam well Ah cant! They don have no mercy on no black folks; wes just like dirt under their feet! Fer ten years Ah slaves lika dog t git mah farm free, givin ever penny Ah kin t em, n then Ah comes n fins they been in mah house . . ." He was speechless with outrage. "Ef yuh wans t eat at mah table yuhs gonna keep them white trash bastards out, yuh hear? Tha white ape kin come n git tha damn box n Ah ain gonna pay im a cent! He had no bisness leavin it here, n yuh had no bisness lettin im! Ahma tell tha sonofabitch something when he comes out here in the mawnin, so hep me Gawd! Now git back in tha bed!"

She slipped beneath the quilt and lay still, her face turned to the wall. Her heart thumped slowly and heavily. She heard him walk across the floor in his bare feet. She heard the bottom of the lamp as it rested on the mantel. She stiffened when the room darkened. Feet whispered across the floor again. The shucks rustled from Silas' weight as he sat on the edge of the bed. She was still, breathing softly. Silas was mumbling. She felt sorry for him. In the darkness it seemed that she could see the hurt look on his black face. The crow of a rooster came from far away, came so faintly that it seemed she had not heard it. The bed sank and the shucks cried out in dry whispers; she knew Silas had stretched out. She heard him sigh. Then she jumped because he jumped. She could feel the tenseness of his body; she knew he was sitting bolt upright. She felt his hands fumbling jerkily under the quilt. Then the bed heaved amid a wild shout of shucks and Silas' feet hit the floor with a loud boom. She snatched herself to her elbows, straining her eyes in the dark, wondering what was wrong now. Silas was moving about, cursing under his breath.

"Don wake Ruth up!" she whispered.

"Ef yuh say one mo word t me Ahma slap yuh inter a black spasm!"

She grabbed her dress, got up and stood by the bed, the tips of her fingers touching the wall behind her. A match flared in yellow flame; Silas' face was caught in a circle of light. He was looking downward, staring intently at a white wad of cloth balled in his hand. His black cheeks were hard, set; his lips were tightly pursed. She looked closer; she saw that the white cloth was a man's handkerchief. Silas' fingers loosened; she heard the handkerchief hit the floor softly, damply. The match went out.

"Yuh little bitch!"

Her knees gave. Fear oozed from her throat to her stomach. She moved in the dark toward the door, struggling with the dress, jamming it over her head. She heard the thick skin of Silas' feet swish across the wooden planks.

"Ah got mah raw-hide whip n Ahm takin yuh t the barn!"

She ran on tiptoe to the porch and paused, thinking of the baby. She shrank as something whined through air. A red streak of pain cut across the small of her back and burned its way into her body, deeply.

"Silas!" she screamed.

She grabbed for the post and fell in dust. She screamed again and crawled out of reach.

"Git t the barn, Gawddammit!"

She scrambled up and ran through the dark, hearing the baby cry. Behind her leather thongs hummed and feet whispered swiftly over the dusty ground.

"Cmere, yuh bitch! Cmere, Ah say!"

She ran to the road and stopped. She wanted to go back and get the baby, but she dared not. Not as long as Silas had that whip. She stiffened, feeling that he was near.

"Yuh jus as well c mon back n git yo beatin!"

She ran again, slowing now and then to listen. If she only knew where he was she would slip back into the house and get the baby and walk all the way to Aunt Peel's.

"Yuh ain comin back in mah house till Ah beat yuh!"

She was sorry for the anger she knew he had out there in the field. She had a bewildering impulse to go to him and ask him not to be angry; she wanted to tell him that there was nothing to be angry about; that what she had done did not matter; that she was sorry; that after all she was his wife and still loved him. But there was no way she could do that now; if she went to him he would whip her as she had seen him whip a horse.

"Sarah! Sarah!"

His voice came from far away. Ahm goin git Ruth. Back through dust she sped, going on her toes, holding her breath.

"Saaaarah!"

From far off his voice floated over the fields. She ran into the house and caught the baby in her arms. Again she sped through dust on her toes. She did not stop till she was so far away that his voice sounded like a faint echo falling from the sky. She looked up; the stars were paling a little. Mus be gittin near mawnin. She walked now, letting her feet sink softly into the cool dust. The baby was sleeping; she could feel the little chest swelling against her arm. She looked up again; the sky was solid black. Its gittin near mawnin. Ahma take Ruth t An Peels. N mabbe Ahll fin Tom . . . But she could not walk all that distance in the dark. Not now. Her legs were tired. For a moment a memory of surge and ebb rose in her blood; she felt her legs straining, upward. She sighed. Yes, she would go to the sloping hillside back of the garden and wait until morning. Then she would slip away. She stopped, listening. She heard a faint, rattling noise. She imagined Silas' kicking or throwing the smashed graphophone. Hes mad! Hes sho mad! Aw, Lawd! . . . She stopped stock still, squeezing the baby till it whimpered. What would happen when that white man came out in the morning? She had forgotten him. She would have to head him off and tell him. Yeah, cause Silas jus mad ernuff t kill! Lawd, hes mad ernuff t kill!

III

She circled the house widely, climbing a slope, groping her way, holding the baby high in her arms. After awhile she stopped and wondered where on the slope she was. She remembered there was an elm tree near the edge; if she could find it she would know. She groped farther, feeling with her feet. Ahm gittin los! And she did not want to fall with the baby. Ahma stop here, she thought. When morning came she would see the car of the white man from this hill and she would run down the road and tell him to go back; and then there would be no killing. Dimly she saw in her mind a picture of

men killing and being killed. White men killed the black
and black men killed the white. White men killed the
black men because they could, and the black men killed
the white men to keep from being killed. And killing
was blood. Lawd, Ah wish Tom wuz here. She shud-
dered, sat on the ground and watched the sky for signs
of morning. Mabbe Ah oughta walk on down the road?
Naw . . . Her legs were tired. Again she felt her body
straining. Then she saw Silas holding the white man's
handkerchief. She heard it hit the floor, softly, damply.
She was sorry for what she had done. Silas was as good
to her as any black man could be to a black woman.
Most of the black women worked in the fields as crop-
pers. But Silas had given her her own home, and that
was more than many others had done for their women.
Yes, she knew how Silas felt. Always he had said he was
as good as any white man. He had worked hard and
saved his money and bought a farm so he could grow
his own crops like white men. Silas hates white folks!
Lawd, he sho hates em!

The baby whimpered. She unbuttoned her dress and
nursed her in the dark. She looked toward the east.
There! A tinge of grey hovered. It wont be long now.
She could see ghostly outlines of trees. Soon she would
see the elm, and by the elm she would sit till it was light
enough to see the road.

The baby slept. Far off a rooster crowed. Sky deep-
ened. She rose and walked slowly down a narrow, curv-
ing path and came to the elm tree. Standing on the edge
of a slope, she saw a dark smudge in a sea of shifting
shadows. That was her home. Wondah how come Silas
didnt light the lamp? She shifted the baby from her
right hip to her left, sighed, struggled against sleep. She
sat on the ground again, caught the baby close and
leaned against the trunk of a tree. Her eye-lids drooped

and it seemed that a hard cold hand caught hold of her right leg—or was it her left leg? she did not know which—and began to drag her over a rough litter of shucks and when she strained to see who it was that was pulling her no one was in sight but far ahead was darkness and it seemed that out of the darkness some force came and pulled her like a magnet and she went sliding along over a rough bed of screeching shucks and it seemed that a wild fear made her want to scream but when she opened her mouth to scream she could not scream and she felt she was coming to a wide black hole and again she made ready to scream and then it was too late for she was already over the wide black hole falling falling falling . . .

She awakened with a start and blinked her eyes in the sunshine. She found she was clutching the baby so hard that it had begun to cry. She got to her feet, trembling from fright of the dream, remembering Silas and the white man and Silas' running her out of the house and the white man's coming. Silas was standing in the front yard; she caught her breath. Yes, she had to go and head that white man off! Naw! She could not do that, not with Silas standing there with that whip in his hand. If she tried to climb any of those slopes he would see her surely. And Silas would never forgive her for something like that. If it were anybody but a white man it would be different.

Then, while standing there on the edge of the slope looking wonderingly at Silas striking the whip against his overall-leg—and then, while standing there looking—she froze. There came from the hills a distant throb. Lawd! The baby whimpered. She loosened her arms. The throb grew louder, droning. Hes comin fas! She wanted to run to Silas and beg him not to bother the white man. But he had that whip in his hand. She

should not have done what she had done last night.
This was all her fault. Lawd, ef anything happens t im
its mah blame . . . Her eyes watched a black car speed
over the crest of a hill. She should have been out there
on the road instead of sleeping here by the tree. But it
was too late now. Silas was standing in the yard; she
saw him turn with a nervous jerk and sit on the edge of
the porch. He was holding the whip stiffly. The car
came to a stop. A door swung open. A white man got
out. Thas im! She saw another white man in the front
seat of the car. N thats his buddy . . . The white man
who had gotten out walked over the ground, going to
Silas. They faced each other, the white man standing up
and Silas sitting down; like two toy men they faced each
other. She saw Silas point the whip to the smashed gra-
phophone. The white man looked down and took a
quick step backward. The white man's shoulders were
bent and he shook his head from left to right. Then
Silas got up and they faced each other again; like two
dolls, a white doll and a black doll, they faced each other
in the valley below. The white man pointed his finger
into Silas' face. Then Silas' right arm went up; the whip
flashed. The white man turned, bending, flinging his
hands to shield his head. Silas' arm rose and fell, rose
and fell. She saw the white man crawling in dust, trying
to get out of reach. She screamed when she saw the
other white man get out of the car and run to Silas.
Then all three were on the ground, rolling in dust, grap-
pling for the whip. She clutched the baby and ran.
Lawd! Then she stopped, her mouth hanging open. Si-
las had broken loose and was running toward the house.
She knew he was going for his gun.

"Silas!"

Running, she stumbled and fell. The baby rolled in
the dust and bawled. She grabbed it up and ran again.

The white men were scrambling for their car. She reached level ground, running. Hell be killed! Then again she stopped. Silas was on the front porch, aiming a rifle. One of the white men was climbing into the car. The other was standing, waving his arms, shouting at Silas. She tried to scream, but choked; and she could not scream till she heard a shot ring out.

"Silas!"

One of the white men was on the ground. The other was in the car. Silas was aiming again. The car started, running in a cloud of dust. She fell to her knees and hugged the baby close. She heard another shot, but the car was roaring over the top of the southern hill. Fear was gone now. Down the slope she ran. Silas was standing on the porch, holding his gun and looking at the fleeing car. Then she saw him go to the white man lying in dust and stoop over him. He caught one of the man's legs and dragged the body into the middle of the road. Then he turned and came slowly back to the house. She ran, holding the baby, and fell at his feet.

"Siiilas!"

IV

"Git up, Sarah!"

His voice was hard and cold. She lifted her eyes and saw blurred black feet. She wiped tears away with dusty fingers and pulled up. Something took speech from her and she stood with bowed shoulders. Silas was standing still, mute; the look on his face condemned her. It was as though he had gone far off and had stayed a long time and had come back changed even while she was standing there in the sunshine before him. She wanted to say something, to give herself. She cried.

"Git the chile up, Sarah!"

She lifted the baby and stood waiting for him to speak, to tell her something to change all this. But he said nothing. He walked toward the house. She followed. As she attempted to go in, he blocked the way. She jumped to one side as he threw the red cloth outdoors to the ground. The new shoes came next. Then Silas heaved the baby's cradle. It hit the porch and a rocker splintered; the cradle swayed for a second, then fell to the ground, lifting a cloud of brown dust against the sun. All of her clothes and the baby's clothes were thrown out.

"Silas!"

She cried, seeing blurred objects sailing through the air and hearing them hit softly in the dust.

"Git yo things n go!"

"Silas."

"Ain no use yuh sayin *nothin* now!"

"But theyll kill yuh!"

"There ain nothin Ah kin do. N there ain nothin yuh kin do. Yuh done done too Gawddam much awready. Git yo things n go!"

"Theyll kill yuh, Silas!"

He pushed her off the porch.

"GIT YO THINGS N GO T AN PEELS!"

"Les *both* go, Silas!"

"Ahm stayin here till they come back!"

She grabbed his arm and he slapped her hand away. She dropped to the edge of the porch and sat looking at the ground.

"Go way," she said quietly. "Go way fo they comes. Ah didnt mean no harm . . ."

"Go way fer whut?"

"Theyll *kill* yuh . . ."

"It don make no difference." He looked out over the sun-filled fields. "Fer ten years Ah slaved mah life out t git mah farm free . . ." His voice broke off. His lips moved as though a thousand words were spilling silently out of his mouth, as though he did not have breath enough to give them sound. He looked to the sky, and then back to the dust. "Now, its all gone. *Gone* . . . Ef Ah run erway, Ah ain got nothin. Ef Ah stay n fight, Ah ain got nothin. It don make no difference which way Ah go. Gawd! Gawd, Ah wish alla them white folks wuz dead! *Dead*, Ah tell yuh! Ah wish Gawd would kill em *all*!"

She watched him run a few steps and stop. His throat swelled. He lifted his hands to his face; his fingers trembled. Then he bent to the ground and cried. She touched his shoulders.

"Silas!"

He stood up. She saw he was staring at the white man's body lying in the dust in the middle of the road. She watched him walk over to it. He began to talk to no one in particular; he simply stood over the dead white man and talked out of his life, out of a deep and final sense that now it was all over and nothing could make any difference.

"The white folks ain never gimme a chance! They ain never give no black man a chance! There ain nothin in yo whole life yuh kin keep from em! They take yo lan! They take yo freedom! They take yo women! N then they take yo life!" He turned to her, screaming. "N then Ah gits stabbed in the back by mah own blood! When mah eyes is on the white folks to keep em from killin me, mah own blood trips me up!" He knelt in the dust again and sobbed; after a bit he looked to the sky, his face wet with tears. "Ahm gonna be hard like they is! So hep me, Gawd, Ah'm gonna be *hard*! When they come fer me Ah'm gonna *be* here! N when they git me outta here theys gonna *know* Ahm gone! Ef Gawd lets me live

Ahm gonna make em *feel* it!" He stopped and tried to get his breath. "But, Lawd, Ah don wanna be this way! It don mean nothin! Yuh die ef yuh fight! Yuh die ef yuh don fight! Either way yuh die n it don mean nothin . . ."

He was lying flat on the ground, the side of his face deep in dust. Sarah stood nursing the baby with eyes black and stony. Silas pulled up slowly and stood again on the porch.

"Git on t An Peels, Sarah!"

A dull roar came from the south. They both turned. A long streak of brown dust was weaving down the hillside.

"Silas!"

"Go on cross the fiels, Sarah!"

"We kin *both* go! Git the hosses!"

He pushed her off the porch, grabbed her hand, and led her to the rear of the house, past the well, to where a path led up a slope to the elm tree.

"Silas!"

"Yuh git on fo they ketch yuh too!"

Blind from tears, she went across the swaying fields, stumbling over blurred grass. It ain no use! She knew it was now too late to make him change his mind. The calves of her legs knotted. Suddenly her throat tightened, aching. She stopped, closed her eyes and tried to stem a flood of sorrow that drenched her. Yes, killing of white men by black men and killing of black men by white men went on in spite of the hope of white bright days and the desire of dark black nights and the long gladness of green cornfields in summer and the deep dream of sleeping grey skies in winter. And when killing started it went on, like a red river flowing. Oh, she felt sorry for Silas! Silas . . . He was following that long river of blood. Lawd, how come he wans t stay there

like tha? And he did not want to die; she knew he hated
dying by the way he talked of it. Yet he followed the old
river of blood, knowing that it meant nothing. He fol-
lowed it, cursing and whimpering. But he followed it.
She stared before her at the dry, dusty grass. Somehow,
men, black men and white men, land and houses, green
cornfields and grey skies, gladness and dreams, were all a
part of that which made life good. Yes, somehow, they
were linked, like the spokes in a spinning wagon wheel.
She felt they were. She knew they were. She felt it when
she breathed and knew it when she looked. But she
could not say how; she could not put her finger on it
and when she thought hard about it it became all mixed
up, like milk spilling suddenly. Or else it knotted in her
throat and chest in a hard aching lump, like the one she
felt now. She touched her face to the baby's face and
cried again.

There was a loud blare of auto horns. The growing
roar made her turn round. Silas was standing, seemingly
unafraid, leaning against a post of the porch. The long
line of cars came speeding in clouds of dust. Silas moved
toward the door and went in. Sarah ran down the slope
a piece, coming again to the elm tree. Her breath was
slow and hard. The cars stopped in front of the house.
There was a steady drone of motors and drifting clouds
of dust. For a moment she could not see what was hap-
pening. Then on all sides white men with pistols and
rifles swarmed over the fields. She dropped to her knees,
unable to take her eyes away, unable it seemed to
breathe. A shot rang out. A white man fell, rolling over,
face downward.

"Hes gotta gun!"

"Git back!"

"Lay down!"

The white men ran back and crouched behind cars.

Three more shots came from the house. She looked, her head and eyes aching. She rested the baby in her lap and shut her eyes. Her knees sank into the dust. More shots came, but it was no use looking now. She knew it all by heart. She could feel it happening even before it happened. There were men killing and being killed. Then she jerked up, being compelled to look.

"Burn the bastard out!"

"Set the sonofabitch on fire!"

"Cook the coon!"

"Smoke im out!"

She saw two white men on all fours creeping past the well. One carried a gun and the other a red tin can. When they reached the back steps the one with the tin can crept under the house and crept out again. Then both rose and ran. Shots. One fell. A yell went up. A yellow tongue of fire licked out from under the back steps.

"Burn the nigger!"

"C mon out, nigger, n git yos!"

She watched from the hill-slope; the back steps blazed. The white men fired a steady stream of bullets. Black smoke spiraled upward in the sunshine. Shots came from the house. The white men crouched out of sight, behind their cars.

"Make up yo mind, nigger!"

"C mon out er burn, yuh black bastard!"

"Yuh think yuhre white now, nigger?"

The shack blazed, flanked on all sides by whirling smoke filled with flying sparks. She heard the distant hiss of flames. White men were crawling on their stomachs. Now and then they stopped, aimed, and fired into the bulging smoke. She looked with a tense numbness; she looked, waiting for Silas to scream, or run out. But the house crackled and blazed, spouting yellow plumes to the blue sky. The white men shot again, sending a hail of bullets into the furious pillars of smoke. And still she could not see Silas running out, or hear his voice calling. Then she jumped, standing. There was a loud crash; the roof caved in. A black chimney loomed amid crumbling wood. Flames roared and black smoke billowed, hiding the house. The white men stood up, no longer afraid. Again she waited for Silas, waited to see him fight his way out, waited to hear his call. Then she breathed a long, slow breath, emptying her lungs. She knew now. Silas had killed as many as he could and had stayed on to burn, had stayed without a murmur. She filled her lungs with a quick gasp as the walls fell in; the house was hidden by eager plumes of red. She turned and ran with the baby in her arms, ran blindly across the fields, crying, "Naw, Gawd!"

IV

Fire and Cloud

I

"A NAUGHTS *a naught*. . . ."

As he walked his eyes looked vacantly on the dusty road, and the words rolled without movement from his lips, each syllable floating softly up out of the depths of his body.

"*N fives a figger*. . . ."

He pulled out his pocket handkerchief and mopped his brow without lessening his pace.

"*All fer the white man*. . . ."

He reached the top of the slope and paused, head down.

"*N none fer the nigger*. . . ."

His shoulders shook in half-laugh and half-shudder. He finished mopping his brow and spat, as though to rid himself of some bitter thing. He thought, Thas the way its awways been! Wistfully he turned and looked back at the dim buildings of the town lying sprawled mistily on the crest of a far hill. Seems like the white folks jus erbout owns this whole worl! Looks like they done conquered *everthing*. We black folks is jus los in one big white fog. . . . With his eyes still on the hazy buildings, he flexed his lips slowly and spoke under his breath:

"They could do something! They could do *something*, awright! Mabbe ef five er six thousan of us marched downtown we could *scare* em inter doin something! Lawd knows, mabbe them Reds *is* right!"

He walked again and tucked his handkerchief back into his pocket. He could feel the heat of the evening over all his body, not strongly, but closely and persistently, as though he were holding his face over a tub of steaming suds. Far below him, at the bottom of the valley, lay a cluster of bleak huts with window panes red-lit from dying sunlight. Those huts were as familiar to his eyes as a nest is to the eyes of a bird, for he had lived among them all his life. He knew by sight or sound every black man, woman and child living within those huddled walls. For a moment an array of soft black faces hovered before his eyes. N whut kin Ah tell em? Whut kin Ah say t em? He stopped, looked at the ground and sighed. And then he saw himself as he had stood but a few minutes ago, facing the white woman who sat behind the brown, gleaming desk: her arms had been round, slender, snow-white, like cold marble; her hair had been the color of flowing gold and had glinted in the sunlight; her eyes had been wide and grey behind icily white spectacles. It seemed he could hear her saying in her dry, metallic voice: I'm sorry, Taylor. You'll just have to do the best you can. Explain it to them, make them understand that we cant do anything. Everybodys hongry, and after all, it's no harder on your people than it is on ours. Tell them they'll just have to wait. . . .

He wagged his head and his lips broke in a slow sick smile. Whut she know erbout bein hongry? Whut she know erbout it? He walked again, thinking, Here Ah is a man called by Gawd t preach n whut kin Ah do? Hongry folks lookin t me fer hep n whut kin Ah do? Ah done tried everthing n cant do *nuthin*! Shucks, mabbe Hadley n Greens right? They *might* be right. Gawd knows, they *might* be right.

He lifted his head and saw the wide fields plunging before him, down the hillside. The grass was dark and green. All this! he thought. All *this* n folks hongry! Good Gawd, whuts *wrong*! He saw the road running before him, winding, vanishing, the soft yellow dust filled with the ruts of wagon wheels and tiny threads of auto tires. He threw back his head and spoke out loud:

"The good Lawds gonna clean up this ol worl some day! Hes gonna make a new Heaven n a new Earth! N Hes gonna do it in a eye-twinkle change! Hes gotta do it! Things cant go on like this ferever! Gawd knows they cant!" He pulled off his coat and slung it under his left arm. "Waal, there ain nothin t do but go back n tell em. . . . Tell em the white folks wont let em eat. . . ."

The road curved, descending among the green fields that tumbled to a red sky. This was the land on which the Great God Almighty had first let him see the light of His blessed day. This was the land on which he had first taken unto himself a wife, leaving his mother and father to cleave to her. And it was on the green slopes of these struggling hills that his first-born son, Jimmy, had romped and played, growing to a strong, upright manhood. He wagged his head, musing: Lawd, them wuz the good ol days. . . . There had been plenty to eat; the blessings of God had been overflowing. He had toiled from sunup to sundown, and in the cool of the evenings his wife, May, had taught him to read and write. Then God had spoken to him, a quiet, deep voice coming out of the black night; God had called him to preach His word, to spread it to the four corners of the earth, to save His black people. And he had obeyed God and had built a church on a rock which the very gates of Hell could not prevail against. Yes, he had been like Moses, leading his people out of the wilderness into the Promised Land. He sighed, walking and taking his coat from his left arm and tucking it under his right. Yes, things had been clear-cut then. In those days there had stretched before his eyes a straight and narrow path and he had walked in it, with the help of a Gracious God.

On Sundays he had preached God's Word, and on Mondays and Tuesdays and Wednesdays and Thursdays and Fridays and Saturdays he had taken old Bess, his mule, and his plow and had broke God's ground. For a moment while walking through the dust and remembering his hopes of those early years he seemed to feel again the plow handles trembling in his calloused hands and hear the earth cracking and breaking open, black, rich and damp; it seemed he could see old Bess straining forward with the plow, swishing her tail and tossing her head and snorting now and then. Yes, there had been something in those good old days when he had walked behind his plow, between the broad green earth and a blue sweep of sunlit sky; there had been in it all a surge of will, clean, full, joyful; the earth was his and he was the earth's; they were one; and it was that joy and will and oneness in him that God had spoken to when He had called him to preach His Word, to save His black people, to lead them, to guide them, to be a shepherd to His flock. But now the whole thing was giving way, crumbling in his hands, right before his eyes. And every time he tried to think of some way out, of some way to stop it, he saw wide grey eyes behind icily white spectacles. He mopped his brow again. Mabbe Hadley n Greens right. . . . Lawd, Ah don know whut t do! Ef Ah fight fer things the white folk say Ahma bad nigger stirrin up trouble. N ef Ah don do nothin, we starve. . . . But somethings *gotta* be done! Mabbe ef we hada demonstration like Hadley n Green said, we could *scare* them white folks inter doin something. . . .

He looked at the fields again, half-wistfully, half-curiously. Lawd, we could make them ol fiels bloom ergin. We could make em feed us. Thas whut Gawd put em there fer. Plows could break and hoes could chop and hands could pick and arms could carry. . . . On and on that could happen and people could eat and feel as he had felt with the plow handles trembling in his hands, following old Bess, hearing the earth cracking and breaking because he wanted it to crack and break; because he willed it, because the earth was his. And they could sing as he had sung when he and May were first married; sing about picking cotton, fishing, hunting, about sun and rain. They could. . . . But whuts the usa thinkin erbout stuff like this? Its all gone now. . . . And he had to go and tell his congregation, the folks the Great God Almighty had called him to lead to the Promised Land—he had to tell them that the relief would give them no food.

That morning he had sent a committee of ten men and women from his congregation to see the mayor. Wondah how they come out? The mayor tol em something, sho! So fer hes been pretty wid me even ef he is a white man. As his feet sank softly into the dust he saw Mayor Bolton; he saw the red chin that always had a short, black stubble of beard; he saw the cigar glowing red in front of a pink, fat face. But he needs something t scare im now, he thought. Hes been runnin over us too long. . . .

He reached the bottom of the slope, turned into a cinder path, and approached the huts. N Lawd, when Ah do try t do somethin mah own folks wont stan by me, wont stick wid me. Theres ol Deacon Smith a-schemin n a-plottin, jus a-watchin me lika hawk, jus a-waitin fer me t take mah eyes off the groun sos he kin trip me up, sos he kin run t the white folks n tell em Ahm doin somethin wrong! A black snake in the grass! A black Judas! Thas all he is! Lawd, the Devils sho busy in this worl. . . .

He was walking among the crowded huts now.
hello reveren

"How yuh tonight, sonny!" Let ol Deacon Smith tell it, no matter whut Ah *do*, Ahm wrong. . . .

good evenin reveren

"Good evenin, Sistah!" Hes been a-tryin t cheat me outta mah church ever since hes been erroun here. . . .

how yuh tonight reveren taylor

"Jus fine. N how yuh tonight, Brother?" Hes awways a-whisperin berhin mah back, a-tryin t take mah congregation erway from me. . . . N when he ain doin that hes a-tryin his bes t give me wrong advice, jus like the Devil a-tryin t tempt Jesus. But Ahma gonna march on wida hepa Gawd. . . . Yeah, Ah might preach a sermon erbout tha nex Sunday.

As he turned into the street leading to his home and church, he saw a tall brown-skinned boy hurrying towards him. Here comes Jimmy! Ah bet hes lookin fer me. . . . Lawd, Ah hope ain nothin wrong. . . .

II

"Pa!" said Jimmy breathlessly when he was some twenty feet away.

Taylor stopped.

"Whuts the mattah, son?"

Jimmy came close.

"The mayors at home, waitin t see yuh," he whispered.

"The *mayor*?"

"Yeah, n two mo white men. One of em is the Chiefa Police."

"They there *now*?"

"Yeah; in the parlor."

"How long they been there?"

"Bout two-three minutes, Ah reckon. N lissen, Pa . . . Sam wuz by jus now. He say the white folks is ridin up n down the streets in their cars warnin all the black folks t stay off the streets cause theres gonna be trouble. . . ."

"Sam say tha?"

"Thas whut he tol me. N lissen, Pa . . . Ahma git Sam n Pete n Bob n Jack n some mo boys together sos ef anything happens. . . ."

Taylor gripped Jimmy's shoulders.

"Naw, son! Yuh fixin t git us *all* inter trouble now! Yuh cant do nothing like tha! Yuh gotta be careful! Ef them white folks jus *thought* we wuz doin something like that theyd crack down on us! Wed hava riot!"

"But we cant let em ride erroun n talk big n we do nothin!"

"Lissen here, son! Yuh do whut Ah tell yuh t do!" He shook Jimmy's shoulders and his voice was husky. "Yuh go tell them boys t do *nothin* till Ah see em, yuh hear me? Yuh young fools fixin t git us *all* murdered!"

"We jus as waal git killed fightin as t git killed doin nothin," said Jimmy sullenly.

"Yuh go n do whut Ah tol yuh, *hear* me? Ah gotta go n see tha mayor. . . ."

"Hes here t see yuh erbout tha demonstration," said Jimmy.

"How yuh know?"

"Cause thas whut everybodys sayin."

"Who yuh hear say tha?"

"Deacon Smiths spreadin the word."

Taylor winced as though struck by a blow and looked at the dust.

"Hes tellin alla deacons n the church membahs tha the mayors here t stop yuh," said Jimmy. "Hes tellin em yuhs mixed up wid the Reds."

"Deacon Smith there now, *too?*"

"Yeah; hes in the basement wida other deacons. Theys waitin t see yuh."

"How long they been there?"

"Bout hafa hour. N Hadley n Greens in the Bible Room, waitin t talk wid yuh, too. . . ."

Fear gripped Taylor and he stammered:

"Ddddid the mmmmayor ssssee em?"

"Naw, ain nobody seen em yit. Ah brought em in thu the back do and tol em t wait fer yuh. Ahm mighty scared wid them Reds waitin fer yuh in the Bible Room and tha Chiefa Police waitin fer yuh in the parlor. Ef ol Deacon Smith knowed tha he sho would make a lotta trouble. . . ."

"Where yo ma?"

"She upstairs, sewin."

"She know whuts happenin?"

"Naw, Pa."

Taylor stood still, barely breathing.

"Whut yuh gonna do, Pa?" asked Jimmy.

"Yuh go n tell them boys not t do nothin wrong, son. Go on n tell em now! Ah got too much on mah hans now widout yuh boys stirrin up mo trouble!"

"Yessuh."

"Yuh bettah go n do it *now!*"

"Yessuh."

He watched Jimmy hurry down the street. Lawd, Ah hope tha boy don go n git inter trouble. . . .

"Yuh do whut Ah tol yuh, Jimmy!" he yelled.

"Yessuh!" Jimmy hollered back.

He saw Jimmy turn a dusty corner, and go out of sight. Hadley n Greens there in the Bible Room n the Chiefa Police is waitin in the parlor! Ah cant let them white folks see them Reds! N ef Deacon Smith tells on me theyll lynch me. . . . Ah gotta git em

out of tha church widout em seein each other. . . .
Good Gawd, whut a mess!

III

No sooner had he opened the door of his church than
he heard a crescendo of voices. They back awready! Tha
committees back! Aw, Ah bet the mayor followed em
here. . . . He walked down the hall, turned into the
church's waiting room, and saw a roomful of black faces.

"Reveren Taylor! The mayor run us out!"

"He put the police on us!"

The black brothers and sisters ran to Taylor and sur-
rounded him.

"The mayor tol us t git out n don come back no mo!"

A thin black woman swung onto Taylor's arm,
crying:

"Whut Ahm gonna do? Ah ain gotta mouthful of
bread at home!"

"Sistahs n Brothers, jusa minute," said Taylor. "Firs,
tell me whut the mayor said. . . ."

"He say he cant do *nothin*! N say fer us not t come
back t his office no *mo*! N say ef we do hes gonna put us
in jail!"

"In *jail*?" asked Taylor.

"Thas whut he said."

"N he tol us not t march, Reveren. He said ef we
demonstrated hed put us *all* in jail."

"Who tol em yuh wuz gonna march?" asked Taylor.

"Ah bet it wuz tha ol Deacon Smith," said Sister
Harris.

"The Bible says testify whut yuh see n speak whut
yuh know," said Sister Davis to Sister Harris.

"Ah knows whut Ahm talkin erbout!" blazed Sister
Harris.

"Sistahs n Brothers, les don start no fuss," said Taylor, sighing and dropping his shoulders.

"Whut they tell yuh at the relief station, Reveren Taylor?" asked Sister James.

"They say they cant do nothin," said Taylor.

The thin black woman came and knelt at Taylor's feet, her face in her hands.

"Reveren Taylor, it ain fer me Ahm astin! Its fer mah chillun! Theys hongry! It ain fer me, its fer them! Gawd, have mercy, theys hongry. . . ."

Taylor stepped back, ran his hand into his pocket and pulled out a palmful of loose coins.

"Here, Sistahs n Brothers, split this up between yuh all. Its ever cent Ah got in this worl, so hep me Gawd!"

He laid the coins on a small table. Brother Booker divided them as far as they would go. Then they swarmed around him again.

"Reveren, whut we gonna do?"

"Cant we make the white folks do something fer us?"

"Ahm tireda bein hongry!"

"Reveren, mah babys sick n Ah cant git her no milk!"

"Reveren, whut kin Ah tell mah wife?"

"Lawd knows, Ahm jus erbout sick of this!"

"Whut kin we do, Reveren?"

Taylor looked at them and was ashamed of his own helplessness and theirs.

"Sistahs n Brothers, les call on the great Gawd who made us n put us in this worl. . . ."

He clasped his hands in front of him, closed his eyes, and bowed his head. The room grew still and silent.

"Lawd Gawd Awmighty, Yuh made the sun n the moon n the stars n the earth n the seas n mankind n the beasts of the fiels!"

yes jesus

"Yuh made em all, Lawd, n Yuh tol em whut t do!"

yuh made em lawd

"Yuhs strong n powerful n Yo will rules this worl!"

yuh rules it lawd

"Yuh brought the chillun of Israel outta the lan of Egypt!"

yuh sho did

"Yuh made the dry bones rise up outta the valley of death n live!"

yuh made em live lawd

"Yuh saved the Hebrew chillun in the fiery furnace!"

yes jesus

"Yuh stopped the storm n yuh made the sun stan still!"

yuh stopped it lawd

"Yuh knocked down the walls of Jericho n Yuh kept Jona in the belly of the whale!"

yuh kept im lawd

"Yuh let Yo son Jesus walk on watah n Yuh brought Im back from the dead!"

have mercy jesus

"Yuh made the lame walk!"

yuh did it lawd

"Yuh made the blin see!"

hep us now lawd

"Yuh made the deaf hear!"

glory t the mos high

"Lawd, Yuhs a rock in the tima trouble n Yuhs a shelter in the tima storm!"

he is he is

"Lawd, Yuh said Yuhd strike down the wicked men who plagued Yo chillun!"

glory t gawd

"Yuh said Yuhd destroy this ol worl n create a new Heaven n a new Earth!"

wes waitin on yuh jesus

"Lawd, Yuh said call on Yo name n Yuhd answer!"
yuh said it lawd n now wes callin
"Yuh made us n put the breatha life in us!"
yuh did lawd
"Now look down on us, Lawd! Speak t our hearts n let us know whut Yo will is! Speak t us like Yuh spoke t Jacob!"
speak lawd n our souls will be clay in yo hans
"Lawd, ack in us n well obey! Try us, Lawd, try us n watch us move t Yo will! Wes helpless at Yo feet, a-waitin fer Yo sign!"
send it lawd
"The white folks say we cant raise nothin on Yo earth! They done put the lans of the worl in their pockets! They done fenced em off n nailed em down! Theys a-tryin t take Yo place, Lawd!"
speak t em lawd
"Yuh put us in this worl n said we could live in it! Yuh said this worl wuz Yo own! Now show us the sign like Yuh showed Saul! Show us the sign n well ack! We ast this in the name of Yo son Jesus who died tha we might live! Amen!"
amen amen
Taylor stopped and opened his eyes. The room was quiet; he could hear the clock ticking softly above his head, and from the rear came the sound of children playing back of the church. The sisters and brothers rose from their knees and began talking in subdued tones.

"But, Reveren, whut kin we *do*?"

"The issues wid Gawd now, Sistahs n Brothers."

"Is we gonna march?"

"Is yuh goin wid us t the mayor?"

"Have faith, Sistahs n Brothers. Gawd takes care of His own."

"But Ahm hongry, Reveren. . . ."

"Now, Sistahs n Brothers, Ah got t go. Ah got business t tend t. . . ."

He pushed ahead of the black hands that clung to his sleeve.

"Reveren Taylor. . . ."

The thin black woman wailed, kneeling:

"Please, Reveren, cant yuh do *somethin*. . . ."

He pushed through the door, closed it, and stood for a moment with his eyes shut and his fingers slowly loosening on the knob, his ears filled with the sound of wailing voices.

IV

How come all this gotta happen at *once*? Folks a-beggin fer bread n the mayor here t see me n them Reds a-waitin in the Bible Room. . . . Ef Deacon Smith knowed tha hed ruin me sho! Ah cant let the mayor see them Reds. . . . Naw, Gawd! He looked at a door at the far end of the room, then hurried to it and opened it softly.

"May!" he called in a hoarse whisper.

"Hunh?"

"C mere, quick!"

"Whutcha wan, Dan?"

"C mon in the *room*, May!"

She edged through the half-opened door and stood in front of him, wide-eyed.

"Whutcha wan, Dan?"

"Now, lissen. . . ."

"Ain nothin wrong, is it, Dan? Ain nothin happened, is it?"

He grabbed her arm.

"Naw, n don git scared!"

"Ah ain scared!"

"Yuh cant do whut Ah wan yuh t do ef yuhs scared!"

"Ah *ain* scared, Dan!"

"Lissen. . . ."

"Yeah?"

"The mayors here, in the parlor. N the Chiefa Police. . . ."

She stood stock still and seemed not to breathe.

"The *mayor?*"

"Yeah. . . ."

"*Ain* nothin wrong, is it, Dan?"

"There wont be ef yuh lissen n try t do right."

"Be careful, Dan!"

"Yeah," he said, his voice low and husky. "Go in and tell them white folks Ahm sick, hear?"

She stepped back from him and shook her head.

"Gawd *ain* wid yuh when yuh lie, Dan!"

"We *gotta* lie t white folks! Theys on our necks! They *make* us lie t them! Whut kin we do but lie?"

"*Dan!*"

"Lissen t whut Ahm tellin yuh, May! Tell the mayor Ahm gittin outta bed t see im. Tell im Ahm dressin, see? Tell im t wait a few minutes."

"Yeah?"

"Then go t the basement n tell Deacon Smith Ahm wid the mayor. Tell im n the other deacons t wait."

"Now?"

"Yeah; but Ah ain thu yit. Yuh know Hadley n Green?"

"Them *Reds?*"

"Yeah. . . ."

"Dan!" said May, her lungs suspiring in one gasp of amazed helplessness.

"May, fer Chrissakes!"

She began to cry.

"Don do nothin wrong, Dan, please! Don fergit

Jimmy! Hes jus a young boy n hes gotta grow up in this town wid these white folks. Don go n do nothin n fix it so he wont hava chance. . . . Me n yuh don mattah, but thinka him, Dan, please. . . ."

Taylor swallowed and looked hard at her.

"May, yuh do whut *Ah* tell yuh t do! Ah know whut Ahm doin. Hadley n Greens downstairs, in the Bible Room. Tell em so nobody kin hear yuh, hear?—tell em aftah yuh don tol the others—tell em t come in here. Let em in thu *yo* room. . . ."

"Naw!"

She tried to get through the door. He ran to her and caught her hand again.

"Yuh do whut Ah tell yuh, May!"

"Ah ain gonna have them Reds in *here* wid tha mayor n Chiefa Police out *there*! Ah *ain*!"

"Go on n do whut Ah tell yuh, May!"

"Dan!"

"Go *erhead*, May!"

He pushed her. She went through the door, slowly, looking back at him. When the door was closed he rammed his hands deep into his pants' pockets, turned to the open window, and looked out into the street. It was profoundly quiet, save for the silvery sound of children's voices back of the church. The air was soft, warm, and full of the scent of magnolias and violets. Window panes across the street were blood-red from dying sunlight. A car sped past, lifting a great cloud of yellow-brown dust. He went to the center of the room and stood over a table littered with papers. He cocked his head, listening. He heard a door slam; footsteps echoed and ceased. A big eight-day clock above his head boomed six times; he looked and his eyes strayed up and rested on a gleaming, brass cross. Gawd, hep me now! Jus hep me t go thu wid this! Again he heard a door

slam. Lawd, Ah hope May do right now. . . . N Ah
hope Jimmy don go n ack a fool. . . . He crossed the
floor on tiptoe, opened the door, and peeped into
May's room. It was empty. A slender prism of dust-
filled sunlight cut across the air. He closed the door,
turned, pulled off his coat and threw it across the table.
Then he loosened his collar and tie. He went to the
window again and leaned with his back against the
ledge, watching the door of May's room. He heard a
hoarse voice rise and die. Footsteps again sounded and
ceased. He frowned, listening. How come its takin May
so long? He started when a timid knock came. He hur-
ried to the door and cracked it.

V

"Hello, Reverend Taylor!" said Hadley, a white
man.

"How yuh, Brother Hadley?"

"N how yuh, Reveren?" asked Green, a black man.

"Ahm fine, Brother Green. C mon in, yuh all."

Hadley and Green edged through the door.

"Say, whuts alla mystery?" asked Green.

"Ssssh! Don talk so loud," cautioned Taylor. "The
mayor n the Chiefa Police is out there."

The Negro and the white man stood stone still.

"Do they know wes here?" asked Green.

"Naw, n don git scared. They done come t see me
erbout tha demonstration. . . ."

Hadley and Green looked at each other.

"Pull down tha shade," whispered Green, pointing a
shaking, black finger.

Quickly, Hadley moved to one side, out of range of
the window. His cheeks flushed pink. Taylor lowered
the shade and faced them in the semi-darkness. The eyes

of the white man and the black man were upon him steadily.

"Waal?" said Green.

"Ah spose yuh know whuts up," said Taylor.

"Theyre here to scare you," said Hadley.

"Ahm trustin Gawd," sighed Taylor.

"Whut yuh gonna tell em?" asked Green.

"Thas whut Ah wanna see yuh all erbout," said Taylor.

"O.K. Whut kin we do?" asked Green.

Taylor looked around and motioned toward two chairs.

"Set down, Brothers."

"Naw, this is awright," said Green, still standing.

"Come on," said Hadley. "What's on your mind?"

Taylor folded his arms and half-sat and half-leaned on the edge of the table.

"Yuh all think wes gonna have many folks out in the mawnin fer the demonstration?"

"Whut yuh mean?" asked Green.

"When Ahm talkin wid the mayor and Chiefa Police Ah wanna know how many folks Ahm talkin fer. There ain no use in us havin a demonstration ef ain but a few of us is gonna be out there. The police will try t kill us then. . . ."

"How many folks we can get out tomorrow depends a great deal on you, Reverend," said Hadley.

"Hows that?" asked Taylor.

"If you had let us use your name on those handbills, we could say five thousand easily. . . ."

Taylor turned sharply to Hadley.

"Lissen, Brother, Ah done tol yuh Ah cant do tha! N there ain no use in us talkin erbout it no mo! Ah done told yuh Ah cant let them white folks know Ahm callin folks t demonstrate. Aftah all, Ahma preacher. . . ."

"Its yo duty, Reveren," said Green. "We owes it our black folks."

"Ahm doin mah duty as Gawd lets me see it," said Taylor.

"All right, Reverend," said Hadley. "Heres what happened: Weve covered the city with fifteen thousand leaflets. Weve contacted every organization we could think of, black and white. In other words, weve done all *we* could. The rest depends on the leaders of each group. If we had their active endorsement, none of us would have to worry about a crowd tomorrow. And if we had a crowd we would not have to worry about the police. If they see the whole town turning out, theyll not start any trouble. Now, youre known. White and black in this town respect you. If you let us send out another leaflet with your name on it calling for. . . ."

Taylor turned from them and drew his hand nervously across his face. Hadley and Green were silent, watching him. Taylor went to the window and pulled back the curtain slightly and peeped out. Without turning he said softly:

"Ah done tol yuh all Ah ain scareda lettin yuh use mah name."

"We don mean *tha*," said Green hastily.

"Ef it wuz jus me who wuz takin the chance," said Taylor, "Ah wouldnt care none. But Gawd knows it ain right fer me to send them po folks out inter the streets in fronta police. Gawd knows, Ah cant do tha!"

"Honest, Reveren," said Green, touching Taylor's arm. "Ah don understan. Yuh done been thu harder things than this befo."

"N Ahll go thu wid em ergin," said Taylor proudly.

"All right!" said Hadley. "You can say the word that can make this thing a success. If you dont and we have no crowd, then youre to blame. . . ."

Taylor's eyes narrowed and when he spoke there was a note of anger in his voice.

"Gawd hep yuh ef yuhs a-tryin t say yuh gonna blame me ef things don go right!"

"Naw, Reveren!" said Green, coming hurriedly forward and spreading his black hands softly upon the air. "Don feel that way! Wes all jus in a jam. We got t do either two things: Call off this demonstration and let the folks stay hongry, er git as many as we kin together n go downtown in the mawnin. Ef we git five thousan down there the police wont bother us. Ef yuh let us send out yo name tellin the black folks. . . ."

"Naw, Brother!" said Taylor emphatically.

"Then the demonstrations going to be smashed," said Hadley. "*You* can stop it! You have the responsibility and the blame!"

Taylor sighed.

"Gawd knows Ah ain t blame. Ahm doin whut mah heart tells me t do. . . ."

"Then whats keeping you from working with us?" asked Hadley. "Im a white man and Im here willing to fight for your peoples rights!"

"Ahm wid yuh, Brother!" said Taylor in a voice which carried a deep note of pleading. "Ahm wid yuh no mattah whut yuh *think*! But yuh *cant* use mah name! Ef them white folks knowed Ah wuz callin mah folks in the streets t demonstrate, they wouldnt never gimme a chance t git something fer mah folks ergin. . . ."

"Thats just it, Reverend," said Hadley. "Dont be afraid of their turning you down because youre fighting for your people. If they knew youd really fight, theyd dislike you; yes? But you can *make* them give something to *all* of your people, not just to *you*. Dont you see, Taylor, youre standing *between* your people and the white folks. You can make them give something to *all* of them. And the poor, hungry white folks will be with you."

"Ah cant lead mah folks t go ergin them white folks like tha," said Taylor. "Thas *war!*"

Hadley came close to Taylor.

"Reverend, cant you see thats just the way the white folks *want* you to feel? Are you leading your folks just because the white folks *say* you should, or are you leading them because you *want* to? Dont you believe in what youre doing? What kind of leaders are black people to have if the white folks pick them and tell them what to do?"

"Brothers, Ahma Christian, n whut yuhs astin fer is something tha makes blood!" thundered Taylor.

Hadley and Green looked at each other.

"Waal, whut yuh gonna tell the mayor?" asked Green.

Taylor stood in the center of the room with his hands in his pockets, looking down at his feet. His voice came low, as though he were talking to himself, trying to convince himself.

"Ahma tell em mah folks is hongry. Ahma tell em they wanna march. Ahma tell em ef they march Ahma march wid em. Ahma tell em they wan bread. . . ."

"Reverend," asked Hadley, "why do you feel that this is so different from all the other times youve gone straight to the white folks and *demanded* things for your people?"

"It is different!" said Taylor.

"You didnt say that when you saved Scott from that *mob!*"

"Tha wuz different, Brother Hadley."

"I dont see it."

Taylor's voice came low.

"Ah feels differently erbout it, Brothers."

"You saved Scotts life. All right, youre saving the

lives of your congregation now. Scott was one man, but there are five hundred starving people in your church."

"We ain facin no mob now, Brother Hadley."

"Then what in Gods name are we facing, Reverend? If those police wholl be out there in the morning with their guns and clubs arent a *legal* mob, then what. . . ."

"Its more than a mob, Brother Hadley."

Hadley and Green shook their heads.

"Ah don understan yuh, Reveren," said Green.

"When Ah saved Scott from tha mob, Ah wuz goin ergin *some* of the white folks. But this thing is going ergin em *all*! This is too much like war!"

"You mean youre going against the ones with *money* now!" said Hadley. "Over three thousand of the poor white folks will be with *us*. . . ."

"But, Brother Hadley, the white folks whos got moneys got *everthing*! This is jus like civil war!"

"Reverend," said Hadley, "cant you see that if they were not afraid they wouldnt be here asking to *talk* with you? Go in and talk with them, speak to them in the name of five thousand hungry people. Tell the mayor and the Chief of Police that if they dont give the relief back we will demonstrate."

"Ah cant do tha, Brothers. Ah cant let these white folks think Ahm leadin mah folks tha way. Ah tol yuh brothers when Ah ergreed t work wid yuh Ahd go as fer as Ah could. Waal, Ah done done tha. Now, yuh here astin me t threaten this whole town n Ah ain gonna do tha!" said Taylor.

"Yuh astin fer bread, Reveren," said Green.

"Its threatenin, Brothers," said Taylor. "N tha ain Gawds way!"

"So youll let your folks starve before youll stand up and talk to those white folks?" asked Hadley.

"Ahm ackin as Gawd gives me the light t see," said Taylor.

There was silence. Then Hadley laughed, noiselessly.

"Well," he said. "I didn't know you felt this way, Reverend. I thought we could count on you. You know the Party will stand behind you no matter what happens."

"Ahm sorry, Brother Hadley," said Taylor.

"When kin we see yuh t fin out whut the mayor n Chiefa Police say?" asked Green.

Taylor looked at his watch.

"Its a little aftah six now. Make it half-pas six. Thall gimme time t see the Deacon Board."

Green sighed.

"O.K."

"O.K."

Taylor held the door for them. Then he stood in the center of the room and looked miles through the floor. Lawd, Ah hope Ahm doin right. N they think Ahm scared. . . . He flushed hot with shame and anger. He sat in a chair for a moment, then got right up. He drummed his fingers on the corner of the table. Shucks, Ah jus as waal see them white folks now n git it over wid. Ah knowed this wuz comin up! Ah knowed it! He went through May's room, walking slowly, softly, seeing in his mind the picture of the fat, pink face of Mayor Bolton and the lean, red face of Chief of Police Bruden. As he turned into the narrow hall that led to the parlor he heard children yelling in the playground. He went down a stairway, opened a door, and walked through his hushed, dim-lit church. Pale rose light fell slantwise through stained windows and glinted on mahogany pews. He lifted his eyes and saw the figure of Christ on a huge snow-white cross. Gawd, hep me now! Lemme do the right thing! He followed a red carpet to a door that opened into the parlor. He paused and

passed his tongue over his dry lips. He could feel his
heart beating. Ahll let them do all the talkin. Ahll jus tell
em mah folks is hongry. Thas all Ah kin do. Slowly, he
turned the knob, his lips half-parted in dread.

VI

"Why, hello, Dan!"

"Good evenin, Mistah Mayor."

"Howve you been, Dan?"

"Fairly well, wid the hepa Gawd, suh."

Taylor shook hands with a tall, fat white man in a
blue serge suit.

"Its been a long time since Ive seen you, Dan."

"Yessuh. It sho has, yo Honah."

"Hows Jimmy?"

"Jus fine, suh."

"Thats a fine boy youve got, Dan."

"Ahm sho glad yuh think so, suh."

"If you raise that boy right he will be a leader of his
people some day, Dan."

"Thas the one hope of mah life, suh," said Taylor
with deep emotion.

"May was tellin me youre sick," said the mayor.

"Aw, it ain nothin, suh. Jusa summer col, suh."

"I didnt mean to bother you if youre sick, Dan."

"Thas awright, suh. Ahm feelin much bettah now,
suh."

"Oh, youll pull through all right; itll take a lot more
than a summer cold to kill old war-horses like you and
me, eh, Dan?"

The mayor laughed and winked.

"Ahm hopin Gawd spares me a few mo years, suh,"
said Taylor.

"But at least you look all right now," said the mayor.

"Say, Dan, I want you to meet Chief Bruden. This is Dan, Chief, the boy I was telling you about."

"How yuh, Mistah Chief?" asked Taylor.

A black cigar burned red in Bruden's mouth. He shifted his thin body and growled:

"Hello, boy."

"And, Dan, this is Mr. Lowe, head of our fine Industrial Squad."

"How yuh, suh?" asked Taylor.

Lowe nodded with half-closed eyes.

"Sit down, Dan," said the mayor.

"Yessuh."

Taylor sat on the edge of a chair and rested his palms lightly on his knees.

"Maybe our little visit is a surprise, hunh?" asked the mayor.

"Yessuh. It is. But Ahm glad to be of any hep Ah kin, suh."

"Good! I knew youd talk that way. Now, Dan, we want you to help us. Youre a responsible man in this community; thats why we are here."

"Ah tries t do mah duty as Gawd shows it t me, suh."

"Thats the spirit, Dan!" The mayor patted Taylor's knee. "Now, Im going to be perfectly frank with you, Dan." The mayor peeled a wrapper from a black cigar. "Here, have one."

"Thank yuh, suh." Taylor put the cigar into his vest pocket. "Ahll smoke it aftah dinner, suh."

There was a silence during which the three white men looked at Taylor.

"Dan," began the mayor, "its not every nigger Id come to and talk this way. Its not every nigger Id trust as Im about to trust you." The mayor looked straight at Taylor. "Im doing this because Ive faith in you. Ive known you for twenty-five years, Dan. During that time I think Ive played pretty fair with you, havent I?"

Taylor swallowed.

"Ahll have t say yuh have, yo Honah."

"Mister Lowe and the Chief here had another plan," said the mayor. "But I wouldnt hear of it. I told them Id work this thing *my* way. I thought *my* way would be much better. After all, Dan, you and I have worked together in the past and I dont see why we cant work together now. Ive backed you up in a lot of things, Dan. Ive backed you even when other white folks said you were wrong. But I believe in doing the right thing. After all, we are human beings, arent we?"

"Yessuh."

"What Ive done for you in the past Im willing to do again. You remember Scott, dont you?"

"Yessuh. Yuhs been a big hep t me n mah folks, suh."

"Well, Dan, my office is always open to you when you want to see me about any of your problems or the problems of your people," said the mayor.

"N Gawd knows Ah sho thanks yuh, suh!"

The mayor bit off the tip of his cigar and spat it into a brass spittoon.

"I'm not going to beat about the bush, Dan."

The mayor paused again. There was silence. Taylor felt called upon to say something.

"Yessuh. Ah sho preciates tha, suh."

"You know these Goddam Reds are organizing a demonstration for to-morrow, dont you?" asked the mayor.

Taylor licked his lips before he answered.

"Yessuh. Ah done heard a lotta folks talkin erbout it, suh."

"Thats too bad, Dan," said the mayor.

"Folks is talking erbout it everwhere. . . ." began Taylor.

"What *folks?*" interjected Bruden.

"Waal, mos everbody, suh."

Bruden leaned forward and shook his finger in Taylor's face.

"Listen, boy! I want you to get this straight! Reds aint *folks!* Theyre Goddam sonofabitching lousy bastard rats trying to wreck our country, see? Theyre stirring up race hate! Youre old enough to understand that!"

"Hes telling you straight, boy," said Lowe. "And furthermore. . . ."

"Say, whats all this?" demanded the mayor, turning to Lowe and Bruden. "Wait a minute! Whats the big idea of talking to Dan like that? Hes not mixed up in anything like that. Save that kind of talk for bad niggers. . . ."

"The quicker all you niggers get sense enough in your Goddam thick skulls to keep away from them Reds the better off youll be!" said Bruden, ignoring the mayor.

"Aw, c mon," said the mayor. "Dans all right. Aint that right, Dan?"

Taylor looked down and saw at his feet a sharp jutting angle of sunshine falling obliquely through a window. His neck felt hot. This is the show-down, he thought. Theys tryin t trap me. . . . He cleared his throat and looked up slowly and saw the mayor gazing at him with cold grey eyes. He shifted his body slightly and saw the glint of Chief Bruden's police star; he saw Lowe's red lips twisted in half-smile and half-leer.

"Isnt that right, Dan?" the mayor asked again.

"Yessuh. Whut yuh white folks say is right. N Ah ergrees wid yuh. But Ah ain foolin wid nobody thas tryin t stir up race hate; naw, *suh!* Ah ain never done nothin

like tha n Ah never will, so hep me Gawd! Now, erbout
this demonstration: Yessuh, Ah heard erbout it. Thas all
everbodys been talking erbout erroun here fer a week,
yo Honah. Waal, suh, Ahll tell yuh. Theys jus hongry.
Theys marchin cause they don know whut else t do, n
thas the truth from here t Heaven! Mistah Mayor, theys
hongry! Jus plain *hongry*! Ah give mah las dime today t a
woman wid eight chillun. . . ."

"We know all about that, Dan," said the mayor.

"Everybodys hungry," said Bruden.

"Boy, cant you see we are all in the *same* boat?" asked
Lowe.

"Waal. . . ." drawled Taylor.

"Thingsll be straightened out soon, Dan," interjected
the mayor soothingly. "We will see that nobody
starves."

"Ah beg yo pardon, suh. A man died jus the other
day from starvation. . . ."

Taylor's voice died in his throat and he looked at the
floor. He knew that he had said too much.

"I reckon that makes you out a liar, don't it?" Bruden
asked the mayor.

"Aw, naw, suh!" said Taylor eagerly. "Ah ain disputin
nobodys word, suh. Ah jus thought yuh hadnt heard
erbout it. . . ."

"We know all about it," said Bruden, turning his head
away and looking out of the window; as though he was
through with the conversation, as though his mind was
made up.

"What do they think theyre going to get by march-
ing?" asked Lowe.

"They think they kin git some bread," said Taylor.

"It wont get em a Goddam crumb!" said Lowe.

There was silence. Taylor looked again at the jutting
angle of sunshine and heard the mayor's shoes shifting

uneasily on the brown carpet. A match struck; he heard it drop with an angry hiss into the spittoon.

"I dont see why we cant get along, Dan," drawled the mayor.

"Ahm willin t git erlong, Mistah Mayor!" protested Taylor.

"Dan, here we all are, living in good old Dixie. There are twenty-five thousand people in this town. Ten thousand of those people are black, Dan. Theyre your people. Now, its our job to keep order among the whites, and we would like to think of you as being a responsible man to keep order among the blacks. Lets get together, Dan. You know these black people better than we do. We want to feel we can depend on you. Why dont you look at this thing the right way? You know Ill never turn you down if you do the right thing. . . ."

"Mistah Mayor, as Gawds mah judge, Ahm doin right when Ah tell yuh mah folks is hongry. . . ."

"Youre not doing right when you act like a Goddam Red!" said Lowe.

"These niggers around here trust you, Dan," said the mayor. "Theyll do what you tell them to do."

"Speak to them," urged Lowe. "Tell them whats right."

"Mistah Mayor, Gawd in Heaven knows mah people is hongry," said Taylor humbly.

The mayor threw his body forward in the chair and rested his hands on his knees.

"Listen, Dan. I know just how you feel. We *all* feel that way. White people are hungry, too. But weve got to be prudent and do this thing right. Dan, youre a leader and youve got great influence over your congregation here." The mayor paused to let the weight of his words sink in. "Dan, I helped you to get that influence by doing your people a lot of favors through *you* when you came into my office a number of times." The mayor looked at Taylor solemnly. "Im asking you now to use that influence and tell your people to stay *off* the streets tomorrow!"

When Taylor spoke he seemed to be outside of himself, listening to his own words, aghast and fearful.

"Ahm sho thankful as Gawd knows fer all yuh done done fer me n mah people, suh. But mah word don go so fer in times like these, yo Honah. These folks is lookin t me fer bread n Ah cant give it t em. They hongry n Ah cant tell em where t eat. Theys gonna march no mattah whut Ah say. . . ."

"Youve got influence here, Dan, and you can use it!"

"They wouldnt be marchin ef they wuznt hongry, yo Honah!"

"Thats Red talk, nigger!" said Lowe, standing.

"Aw, thas all right, Lowe," said the mayor, placatingly.

"Im not going to sit here and let this Goddam nigger insult me to my face!" said Lowe.

Taylor stood up.

"Ahm sorry, suh!"

"You *will* be sorry when you find a Goddam rope around your neck!" said Lowe.

"Now, now," said the mayor, laying his hand on Lowe's arm. He turned to Taylor. "You dont mean you wont speak to em, do you, Dan?"

"There ain nothin Ah kin say t em, Mistah Mayor. . . ."

"Youre doing the wrong thing, Dan!"

"Ahm lettin Gawd be mah judge, suh!"

"If you dont do the right thing *we* will be your judges!" said Lowe.

"Ahm trustin Gawd, suh."

"Well, Goddammit, you better let Him guide you right!" said Bruden, jumping to his feet.

"But white folks!" pleaded Taylor. "Mah folks cant plant nothin! Its ergin the law! They cant git no work! Whut they gonna do? They don wan no trouble. . . ."

"Youre heading for a plenty right now!" said Bruden.

The mayor spoke and his voice was low and resigned.

"Ive done all I could, Dan. You wouldnt follow my advice, now the rest is up to Mister Lowe and Chief Bruden here."

Bruden's voice came with a shout:

"A niggers a nigger! I was against coming here talking to this nigger like he was a white man in the first place. He needs his teeth kicked down his throat!" Bruden poked the red tip of his cigar at Taylor's face. "Im the Chief of Police of this town, and Im here to see that orders kept! The Chamber of Commerce says therell be no demonstration tomorrow. Therell be three hundred police downtown in the morning to see that thats done. If you send them niggers down there, or if you let these Goddam Reds fool you into it, Ill not be responsible for whatll happen! Weve never had a riot in this town, but youre plotting one right now when you act like this! And you know wholl get the worst of it!"

"Can't yuh do something, Mistah Mayor? Can't yuh fix it sos we kin git some relief?"

The mayor did not answer; Lowe came close to him.

"We know youve been seeing Hadley and Green! We know whats going on! So watch yourself, nigger!"

"Suh?"

They went out. Taylor stood at the window and saw them get into their car and disappear in a cloud of dust around a corner. He sat down, feeling sweat over all his body. Gawd knows whut t do. . . . He brought Lowe n Bruden here t threaten me. . . . N they know erbout Hadley and Green. . . . Somebody tol. . . . He looked up, hearing the soft boom of a clock. Hadley n

Greens comin back here at six-thirty. . . . He went down the hall thinking, Lawd, ef Ah only knowed whut t do. . . .

VII

May met him in the hall.

"Whut they say, Dan?" she asked with suppressed hysteria.

"Don bother me now, May!"

"There wont be no trouble, will it, Dan?"

"Naw, May! Now, please! Yuh worryin me!"

"Yuhll spoil things fer Jimmy, Dan! Don do nothin wrong! Its fer Jimmy Ahm astin!"

"Itll be awright! Now, lemme go!"

He hurried down the hallway, leaving her crying. Good Gawd! How come she wont leave me erlone. Firs, its Jimmy; then its her. . . . Ef it ain one its the other. . . . He went to the end of the hall, down the steps, turned, and came to the door of the Deacon Room. He heard subdued voices. He knew that the deacons were waiting for him, waiting for some definite word. Shucks, Ahm willin t go thu wid tha march ef they is. Them white folks cant kill us *all*. . . . He pushed the door in. The voices ceased. He saw a dense cloud of tobacco smoke and a circle of black faces. He forced a wan smile.

"Good evenin, Brothers!" he said.

"How yuh, Reveren?" asked Deacon Bonds.

"Ahm sorry Ahm late," said Taylor.

"Wuz tha the mayor out there?" asked Deacon Williams.

Taylor paused and pulled out his handkerchief.

"Yeah, Brothers, it wuz the mayor. N the Chiefa Police n tha man Lowe from the Red Squad. . . ."

"RED SQUAD!" shouted Deacon Smith, jumping to his feet with an outraged look.

"Whut they say, Reveren?" asked Deacon Williams quietly, ignoring Deacon Smith.

Taylor sighed and looked at the floor. For a moment he loathed them because he knew they were expecting an answer to their questions. They were expecting him to speak now as he had always spoken, to the point, confidently, and finally. He had wanted them to do the talking, and now they were silent, waiting for him to speak. Lawd, Ah hope Ahm doin right. Ah don wanna lead these folks wrong. . . .

"They know all erbout tha demonstration," he said.

"But whut they *say*?" asked Deacon Bonds.

"Shucks, man! Yuh *know* whut they said!" said Deacon Smith. "Yuh *know* how them white folks feel erbout this thing!"

"They don wan us t march," said Taylor. "They said ef we march theyll put the police on us. . . ."

Deacon Smith leveled his forefinger at Taylor and intoned:

"AH TOL YUH SO!"

"They said therell be a riot," Taylor went on stubbornly.

"Yessuh! Brothers, wes gotta do *right*!" said Deacon Smith, banging his open palm down on the table. "Ah awways said wes gotta do *right*, Reveren!"

"Ahm prayin t Gawd t guide us right," said Taylor.

"Yuh sho don ack like it!" said Deacon Smith.

"Let the Reveren finish, will yuh?" asked Deacon Bonds.

"Wes gotta do right!" said Deacon Smith again, sitting down, folding his arms, crossing his legs and turning his face sternly away.

"Whut else they say, Reveren?" asked Deacon Bonds.

Taylor sighed.

"They say wes mixed up wid the Reds. . . ."

"N by Gawd we *is*!" bawled Deacon Smith. "At least *yuh* is! Ah tol yuh t leave them Reds erlone! They don mean *no*body *no* good! When men starts t deny Gawd, nothin good kin come from em!"

"Brother Smith, let the Reveren talk, will yuh?" asked Deacon Williams.

"He ain talkin *sense*!" said Deacon Smith.

"They say therell be three hundred police downtown in the mawnin," said Taylor, ignoring Smith. "They say only Washington kin do something erbout relief, n tha we mus wait. . . ."

"N Gawd Awmighty knows thas all we kin do: wait!" said Deacon Smith.

"Fer Chrissakes, Brother Smith, let im talk!" said Deacon Williams. "We all know *yuhs* scared!"

"Ah ain scared! Ah got *sense*! Ah. . . ."

"Yuh sho don ack like it, the way yuh shoot off yo mouth!" said Deacon Williams.

Deacon Smith stood up.

"Yuh cant talk tha way t me!"

"Then keep yo big mouth shut!" said Deacon Williams.

"Whos gonna make me?"

"Brothers, please!" begged Taylor.

"A fool kin see tha the white folks is scared!" said Deacon Williams.

"N jus cause theys *scared*, theyll kill *any*body whuts fool ernuff t go downtown in the mawnin," said Deacon Smith.

"Shucks, Ahm willin t taka chance," said Deacon Hilton.

"Me too!"

"We ain got nothin t lose!"

"Any *fool* kin git his head busted!" said Deacon Smith.

"Brothers, fer the lova Gawd, quit fussin!" said Taylor.

They were silent. Taylor looked at them, letting his eyes rove from face to face.

"Brothers, this is the case," he said finally. "They threatenin us not t march, but they ain sayin our folks kin git no relief. Now, Ah figgers ef we hada big crowd downtown in the mawnin they wont bother us. . . ."

"Thas whut *yuh* think," sneered Deacon Smith.

"N ef we don hava big crowd, theyll smash us. Now, its up t us. . . ."

"Reveren, do the *po* white folks say they gonna be *wid* us?" asked Deacon Jones.

"Brother Hadley tol me theys gonna be wid us," said Taylor.

"Tha Hadley is a lie n the trutha Gawd ain in im!" shouted Deacon Smith. "Tha white man is jus tryin t trick yuh, Ahm tellin yuh!"

"Waal, we kin never know less we try n see," said Deacon Bonds.

"Yeah, but they ain gonna let yuh try but *once*," said Deacon Smith.

"Waal, Ah ain got but *one* time t die!" said Deacon Bonds.

"Ah think the white folksll be there," said Taylor. "Theys hongry, too. . . ."

"Yuhll wake up *some* day!" said Deacon Smith.

"Whut yuh gonna do, Reveren?" asked Deacon Williams.

"Do the congregation wanna march?" asked Taylor.

"They say theys *gonna* march!"

"Waal, Ahll march wid em," said Taylor quietly. "They wont march erlone. . . ."

Deacon Smith waved his arms and screamed.

"Yeah yuhll march! But yuhs scared t let' em use yo name! Whut kinda leader *is* yuh? Ef yuhs gonna ack a fool n be a Red, then how come yuh wont come on out n say so sos we kin all hear it? Naw, yuh ain man ernuff t say whut yuh is! Yuh wanna stan in wid the white folks! Yuh wanna stan in wid the Reds! Yuh wanna stan in wid the congregation! Yuh wanna stan in wid the Deacon Board! Yuh wanna stan in wid *ever*body n yuh stan in wid *no*body!"

"Ahm ackin accordin t mah lights!" said Taylor.

"Waal, they ain lettin yuh see fer!" said Deacon Smith.

"Ef yuh gotta plan bettah than mine, Brother Smith, tell us erbout it!"

"AH SAY WE OUGHTNT MARCH!"

"Then, whut we gonna do?"

"Wait n see how things come out!"

"Ahm tireda waitin," said Taylor.

"How come yuh didnt send yo name out on them leaflets?" demanded Deacon Smith. Without waiting for Taylor to answer, he flared: "Ahll tell yuh why yuh didnt! Yuh *scared*! Yuh didnt wan them white folks t know yuhs mixed up in this demonstration. Yuh wanted em t think yuh wuz being pushed erlong by other folks n yuh couldnt help whut wuz happenin! But, Reveren, as sho as theres a Gawd in Heaven yuh ain foolin nobody!"

Taylor stood up.

"Brother Smith, Ah knows whut yuhs up t! Yuh tryin t run me outta mah church, but yuh cant! Gawd Awmighty Himself put me here n Ahm stayin till He says fer me t go! Yuh been schemin t git me out, but yuh cant do it this way! It ain right n Gawd knows it ain! Yeah; ef mah folks marches in the mawnin Ahm marchin wid em!"

"Thas the time, Reveren!"

"We kin show tha ol mayor something!"

"N therell be white folks wid us, too!"

"Ahll go wid the Reveren n the congregation!"

"Ahll go!"

"N me too!"

"Gawd ain wid yuh when yuh ain in the right!" said Deacon Smith.

"Gawd didnt mean fer folks t be hongry!" said Deacon Bonds.

"But He ain wid yuh when yuh stirrin up trouble, makin blood n riots!" said Deacon Smith. "N any man whut sets here n calls himself a leader called by Gawd t preach n leads his folks the wrong way is a fool n the spirita Gawd ain in im!"

"Now, wait a minute there, Brother Smith!" said Taylor. "Yuhs talkin *dangerous*!"

"Ah say any man whut leads his folks inter guns n police. . . ."

"Ain nobody leadin us *nowhere*!" said Deacon Bonds.

"We gwine *ourselves*!" said Deacon Williams.

"Ah ain in this!" said Deacon Smith, jumping again to his feet. "Ah ain in this n Ahm gonna do whut Ah kin t hep mah people!"

The room grew quiet.

"Whut yuh mean, Brother Smith?" asked Taylor.

"Ah say Ahm gonna hep mah people!" said Deacon Smith again.

Taylor walked over to him.

"Is yuh gonna tell the white folks on us?"

Deacon Smith did not answer.

"Talk, Brother Smith!" said Taylor. "Tell us whut yuh mean!"

"Ah means whut Ah means!" said Deacon Smith; and

he clamped his teeth tight, sat again, crossed his legs, folded his arms and stared at the blank wall.

Taylor swallowed and looked at the floor. Lawd, Ah don know whut t do! Ah wish this wuz over. . . . This niggers gonna tell on us! Hes gonna tell the white folks sos he kin stan in wid em. . . .

"Brother Smith. . . ." began Taylor.

The door opened and Jimmy stepped into the room. "Say, Pa!"

"Whut yuh wan, son?"

"Somebodys out front t see yuh. Theys in a car. Theys white folks."

"Scuse me, Brothers," said Taylor. "Ahll be right back."

"Wes gonna set right here till yuh git back," said Deacon Smith.

When outside the door, Taylor turned to Jimmy.

"Who is they, Jimmy? How come they wouldnt come in?"

"Ah dunno, Pa. The car drove up jus as Ah wuz comin thu the gate. They white men. They said fer yuh t come right out."

"Awright. N, son, yuh bettah go see bout yo ma."

"Whuts the mattah?"

"Shes jus upset erbout the demonstration."

"Is they gonna march, Pa?"

"Ah reckon so."

"Is many gonna be out?"

"Ah dunno, son. Ah hope so. Yuh bettah go see erbout yo ma now."

"Yessuh."

"Yuh tell them boys whut Ah tol yuh?"

"Yessuh."

Taylor paused at the front door and peeped out from behind a curtain. In front of his gate was a long black car. Who kin tha be? For a moment he thought the mayor had come back. But his cars grey. . . . He opened the door and walked slowly down the steps. Lawd, mabbe we oughtnt go thu wid this demonstration aftah all? We might all be sorry ef somebodys killed in the mawnin. . . . He walked along a flower-bordered path that smelt of violets and magnolias. Dust rested filmily on tree leaves. The sun was almost gone. As he came to the car a white face looked out.

"You Taylor?"

"Yessuh," answered Taylor, smiling.

The rear door of the car opened and the white man stepped to the ground.

"So youre Taylor, hunh?"

"Yessuh," said Taylor again, still smiling, but puzzled. "Kin Ah be of service t yuh, suh?"

Taylor saw it coming, but could do nothing. He remembered afterward that he had wanted to ask, Whut yuh doin? The blow caught him flush on the point of the jaw, sending him flying backward. His head struck the edge of the runningboard; a flash of red shot before his eyes. He rolled, face downward, into a bed of thick violets. Dazed, he turned his head, trying to speak. He felt a hand grab the back of his collar and jerk him up.

"Get in the car, nigger!"

"Say, whut yuh. . . ."

"Shut up and get in the car, Goddam you!"

A blow came to his right eye. There were three white men now. They lifted him and rammed him down on the floor in the back of the car.

"Say, yuh cant do this!"

"Get your Goddam mouth shut, you bastard!"

A hard palm slapped him straight across his face. He struggled up, protesting.

"You. . . ."

The heel of a shoe came hard into his solar plexus. He doubled up, like a jackknife. His breath left, and he was rigid, half-paralyzed.

"You think you can run this whole Goddam town, don't you? You think a nigger can run over white folks and get away with it?"

He lay still, barely breathing, looking at blurred white faces in the semi-darkness of the roaring car.

VIII

The moment he tried to tell the direction in which the car was moving he knew he had waited too long. He remembered dimly that they had turned corners at least three times. He lay with closed eyes and wondered what they were going to do with him. She gonna be worried t death, he thought, thinking of May. And then he thought of Jimmy and said to himself, Ah hope he don go n ack a fool now. . . . The numbness which had deadened most of his stomach and chest was leaving. He felt sweat on his back and forehead. The car slowed, turned; then it ran fast again. He knew by the way the rocks crunched beneath the humming rubber tires that they were speeding over gravel. Whut roads this? He could not tell. There were so many gravel roads leading out of town. He tried to recall how long he had lain there half-paralyzed from that kick in the solar plexus. He was confused; it might have been five minutes or it might have been an hour. The car slowed again, turning. He smelt the strong scent of a burning cigarette and heard the toll of a far off church bell. The car stopped; he heard the sound of other cars, gears shifting and motors throbbing. We mus be at some crossroads. But he could not guess which one. He had an impulse to call for help. But there would not be any use in his doing that now. Mabbe they white folks any-how. He would be better off as he was; even six white men were better than a mob of white men. The car was speeding again, lurching. He smelt dust, clay dust. Then he heard a hard, rasping voice:

"How is he?"

"O.K."

"Keep im quiet!"

"O.K."

He said nothing. He began to wonder how many of them were in the car. Yes, he should have been watching for something like this. *They been threatenin me fer a long time. Now this is it.* The car was gradually slowing with that long slow slowing preceding a final stop. He felt the rubber tires turning over rough ground; his head rocked from side to side, hitting against the lower back of the front seat. Then the car stopped; the motor stopped; for a moment there was complete silence. Then he heard wind sighing in trees. *Wes out in the country somewhere. In the woods,* he thought.

"O.K.?"

"O.K.!"

He heard a door open.

"C mon, nigger! Get up and watch yourself!"

He pulled up and caught a glimpse of starry sky. As his feet hit the ground his head began to ache. He had lain cramped so long the blood had left his limbs; he took a step, kicking out his legs to restore circulation. His arms were grabbed from behind and he felt the pressure of a kneecap in the center of his spine. He gasped and reeled backward.

"Where you think youre going?"

He rested on his knees, his body full of pain. He heard a car door slam.

"Awright, nigger! Lets go! Straight ahead!"

He got up and twisted his head about to see who had spoken. He saw four blurred white faces and then they were blotted out. He reeled backward again, his head striking the ground. A pain knotted in his temple.

"Get up, nigger! Keep your eyes in front, and walk, Goddammit!"

He pulled up and limped off, his head down. Mabbe they gonna shoot me? His feet and the feet behind him made a soft *cush-cush* in the dew-wet grass and leaves.

"Aw right, nigger!"

He stopped. Slowly he raised his eyes; he saw a tall white man holding a plaited leather whip in his hand, hitting it gently against his trousers' leg.

"You know what this is, nigger?"

He said nothing.

"Wont talk, hunh? Well, this is a nigger-lesson!"

The whip flashed in faint starlight. The blow numbed his lips. He tasted blood.

"You know what this is? Im asking you again, nigger?"

"Nawsuh," he whispered.

"This is a nigger-whip!"

The leather whacked across his shoulders.

"Mistah, Ah ain done nothin!"

"Aw, naw! You aint done nothing! You aint never done a Goddam thing, have you?" White men were standing close around him now. "All you ever do is play around with Reds, dont you? All you ever do is get crowds of niggers together to threaten white folks, dont you? When we get through with you tonight youll know how to stay in a niggers place! C mon! Get that Goddam vest off!"

He did not move. The whip wrapped itself around his neck, leaving a ring of fire.

"You want me to *beat* it off you?"

He pulled off the vest and held it in his hands.

"C mon! Get that shirt and undershirt off!"

He stripped to his waist and stood trembling. A night wind cooled his sweaty body; he was conscious of his back as he had never been before, conscious of every square inch of black skin there. One of the white men walked off a few paces and stopped.

"Bring im over here!"

"O.K.!"

They guided him with prods and kicks.

"On your knees, nigger!"

He did not move. Again his arms were caught from behind and a kneecap came into the center of his back. Breathless, he dropped, his hands and knees cooling in the wet grass. He lifted his fingers to feel his swelling lips; he felt his wrists being grabbed and carried around the trunk of a tree. He held stiffly and struggled against a rope.

"Let go!"

His arms went limp. He rested his face against a cold tree-trunk. A rope cut into his wrists. They tied his feet together, drawing the rope tight about his ankles. He looked around; they stood watching.

"Well, nigger, what do you know?"

"Nothin, suh."

"Youre a preacher, aint you?"

"Yessuh."

"Well, lets hear you pray some!"

He said nothing. The whip lashed across his bare back, *whick!* He flinched and struggled against the rope that cut his wrists to the bone. The leather thong hummed again, *whick!* and his spine arched inward, like a taut bow.

"Goddam your black soul, pray!"

He twisted his face around, pleading:

"Please, Mistah! Don whip me! Ah ain done nothin. . . ."

Another lash came across his half-turned cheek, *whick!* He jerked around and sheltered his face against the treetrunk. The lash hit his back, *whick!*

"*Hit* that black bastard, Bob!"

"Let me have that whip!"

"Naw, wait a minute!"

He said nothing. He clenched his teeth, his whole body quivering and waiting. A split second after each blow his body would lurch, as though absorbing the shock.

"You going to pray? You want me to beat you till you *cant* pray?"

He said nothing. He was expecting each blow now; he could almost feel them before they came, stinging, burning. Each flick came straight on his back and left a streak of fire, a streak that merged with the last streak, making his whole back a sheet of living flame. He felt his strength ebbing; he could not clench his teeth any more. His mouth hung open.

"Let me have it, Bob?"

"Naw, its my turn!"

There was a pause. Then the blows came again; the pain burned its way into his body, wave upon wave. It seemed that when he held his muscles taut the blows hurt less; but he could not hold taut long. Each blow weakened him; each blow told him that soon he would give out. Warm blood seeped into his trousers, ran down his thighs. He felt he could not stand it any longer; he held his breath, his lungs swelling. Then he sagged, his back a leaping agony of fire; leaping as of itself, as though it were his but he could not control it any longer. The weight of his body rested on his arms; his head dropped to one side.

"Ahhlll pppprray," he sobbed.

"Pray, then! Goddam you, pray!"

He tried to get his breath, tried to form words, hearing trees sighing somewhere. The thong flicked again, *whick!*

"Aint you going to pray!"

"Yyyyyessuh. . . ."

He struggled to draw enough air into his lungs to make his words sound.

"Ooour Fffather. . . ."

The whip cut hard, *whick!* pouring fire and fire again.

"Have mercy, Lawd!" he screamed.

"Pray, nigger! Pray like you *mean* it!"

". . . wwwhich aaaaart in hheaven . . . hhhallowed bbe Tttthy nname. . . ." The whip struck, *whick!* "Ahm prayin, Mmmmistah!"

"Goddam your black heart, *pray!*"

". . . Tttthine kkkindom ccome . . . Ttthy wwill bbe ddddone. . . ."

He sobbed, his breath leaving his lungs, going out from him, not wanting to stay to give sound to his words. The whip brought more fire and he could not stand it any longer; his heart seemed about to burst. He screamed, stretched his knees out and twisted his arms till he lay sideways, half on his stomach. The whip came into his stomach, *whick!* He turned over; it came on his back again, *whick!* He stopped struggling and hung limply, his weight suspended on arms he could not feel. Then fire flamed over all his body; he stiffened, glaring upward, wild-eyed.

"Whats the matter, nigger? You hurt?"

"Awright, kill me! Tie me n kill me! Yuh white trash cowards, kill me!"

"Youre tough, aint you? Just wait! We'll kill you, you black sonofabitch!"

"Lemme have that whip!"

"C mon, now! Its my turn!"

"Give me that whip, Ellis!"

He was taut, but not feeling the effort to be taut.

"We'll git yuh white trash some day! So hep me Gawd, we'll git yuh!"

The whip stopped.

"Say that again, Goddam you!"

The whip lashed, *whick!* but there was no streak of fire now; there was only one sheet of pain stretching all over his body, leaping, jumping, blazing in his flesh.

"Say it!"

He relaxed and closed his eyes. He stretched his legs out, slowly, not listening, not waiting for the whip to fall. *say it whick! say it whick! say it whick!* He groaned. Then he dropped his head and could not feel any more.

IX

Moonlight pained his eyeballs and the rustle of tree leaves thundered in his ears. He seemed to have only a head that hurt, a back that blazed, and eyes that ached. In him was a feeling that some power had sucked him deep down into the black earth, had drained all strength from him. He was waiting for that power to go away so he could come back to life, to light. His eyes were half-open, but his lids did not move. He was thirsty; he licked his lips, wanting water. Then the thunder in his ears died, rolling away. He moved his hand and touched his forehead; his arm fell limply in the wet grass and he lay waiting to feel that he wanted to move. As his blood began to flow swiftly again he felt sweat breaking out over his body. It seemed he could hear a tiny, faraway sound whispering over and over like a voice in an empty room: Ah got fever. . . . His back rested on a bed of fire, the imprint of leaves and grass searing him with a scalding persistence. He turned over on his stomach and groaned. Then he jerked up, half-sitting. He was fully conscious now, fighting for his strength, remembering the curses, the prayer and the whip. The voice whispered again, this time louder: Ah gotta git home. . . . With fumbling fingers he untied the rope from his ankles and wrists. They didnt kill me, he thought. He stood up and the dark earth swayed and the stars blurred. Lawd, have mercy! He found himself on his knees; he had not known when he had started falling; he just found himself on his knees. Lawd, Ahm weak! He stood up again, more slowly this time, holding onto a tree. He would have to get his shirt; he could not go through the streets with a naked and bleeding back. He put one foot in front of the other with conscious effort, holding his body stiffly. Each slight twist of his shoulders sent a wave of liquid metal over him. In the grass at his feet his shirt was smeared like a white blur. He touched it; it was wet. He held it, instinctively fearing to put it on. When it did touch, his whole back blazed with a pain so intense that it seemed to glow white hot. No, he could not put it on now. Stiffly, he went among the trees, holding the shirt in his hands, looking at the ground.

He stopped at the edge of a dirt road, conscious of the cool steady stars and the fire that smoldered in his back. Whut roads this? He could not tell. Then he heard a clock striking so faintly that it seemed to be tolling in his own mind. He counted, Wun, Tuh. . . . Its tuh erclock, he thought. He could not stay here all night; he had to go in one direction or another. He watched the brown dusty road winding away in the darkness, like a twisting ribbon. Then he ducked his head, being seared again with fire and feeling a slight rush of air brush across his face. A small bird wheeled past his eyes and fluttered dizzily in the starlight. He watched it veer and dip, then crash softly into a tree limb. It fell to the ground, flapping tiny wings blindly. Then the bird twittered in fright and sailed straight upward into the starlight, vanishing. He walked northward, not going anywhere in particular, but walked northward because the bird had darted in that direction.

The road curved, turned to gravel, crunching under his shoes. This mus be the way, he thought. There were fences along the sides of the road now. He went faster, holding his legs stiffly to avoid pulling the muscles in his back. A church steeple loomed in the starlight, slender and faint. Yeah, thas Houstons church. N Ah gotta go thu a white neighborhood, he thought with despair. He saw houses, white, serene and cool in the night. Spose Ah go to Houston? Naw, hes white. *White*. . . . Even tho he preaches the gospel Ah preaches, he might not take me in. . . . He passed a small graveyard surrounded by a high iron picket fence. A *white* graveyard, he thought and snickered bitterly. Lawd Gawd in Heaven, even the dead cant be together! He stopped and held his shirt in his hands. He dreaded trying to put it on, but he had to. Ah cant go thu the streets like this. Gingerly, he draped the shirt over his shoulders; the whole mass of bruised and mangled flesh flamed, glowed white. With a convulsive movement he rammed his arms into the sleeves, thinking that the faster he did it the less pain there would be. The fire raged so he had a wild impulse to run, feeling that he would have no time then to suffer. But he could not run in a white neighborhood. To run would mean to be shot, for a burglar, or anything. Stiff-legged, he went down a road that turned from brown dust to black asphalt. Ahead street lamps glowed in round, rosy hazes.

Far down the shadow-dappled pavement he heard the sound of feet. He walked past a white man, then he listened to the white man's footsteps dying away behind him. He stopped at a corner and held onto a telephone pole. It would be better to keep in the residential district than to go through town. He would be stopped and questioned in town surely. And jailed maybe. Three blocks later on a white boy came upon him so softly and suddenly that he started in panic. After the boy had gone he turned to look; he saw the boy turning, looking at him. He walked on hurriedly. A block later a white woman appeared. When she was some fifty feet away she crossed to the other side of the street. Hate tightened his throat, then he emptied his lungs in a short, silent, bitter laugh. Ah ain gonna bother yuh, white lady. Ah only wan t git home. . . .

Like a pillar of fire he went through the white neighborhood. Some day theys gonna burn! some day theys gonna burn in Gawd Awmightys fire! How come they make us suffer so? The worls got too mucha everthing! Yit they bleed us! They fatten on us like leeches! There ain no groun yuh kin walk on tha they don own! N Gawd knows tha ain right! He made the earth fer us all! He ain tol no lie when He put us in this worl n said be fruitful n multiply. . . . Fire fanned his hate; he stopped and looked at the burning stars. "Gawd, ef yuh gimme the strength Ahll tear this ol buildin down! Tear it down, Lawd! Tear it down like ol Samson tore the temple down!" He walked again, mumbling. "Lawd, tell me whut t do! Speak t me, Lawd!" He caught his breath; a dark figure came out of the shadows in front of him. He saw a glint of metal; it was a policeman. He held erect and walked rapidly. Ahll stop, he thought. He wont have t ast me t stop. . . . He saw the white face drawing closer. He stopped and waited.

"Put your hands up, nigger!"

"Yessuh."

He lifted his arms. The policeman patted his hips, his sides. His back blazed, but he bit his lips and held still.

"Who you work for?"

"Ahma preacher, suh."

"A *preacher*?"

"Yessuh."

"What you doing out here this time of night?"

"Ah wuz visitin a sick man, a janitah, suh, whut comes t mah church. He works fer Miz Harvey. . . ."

"Who?"

"Miz Harvey, suh."

"Never heard of her, and Ive been on this beat for ten years."

"She lives right back there, suh," he said, half-turning and pointing.

"Well, you look all right. You can go on. But keep out of here at night."

"Yessuh."

He was near his own people now. Across a grassy square he could see the top of the round-house glinting dully in the moonlight. The black asphalt turned to cinders and the houses were low, close together, squatting on the ground as though hiding in fear. He saw his church and relaxed. He came to the steps, caught hold of a bannister and rested a moment.

When inside he went quietly down a hall, mounted the stairs, and came to the door of his room. He groped in the dark and felt the bed. He tried to pull off the shirt. It had stuck. He peeled it. Then he eased onto the bed and lay on his stomach. In the darkness his back seemed to take new fire. He went to the kitchen and wet a cloth with cold water. He lay down again with the cloth spread over him. That helped some. Then he began to shake. He was crying.

X

The door creaked.

"Tha yuh, Pa?"

"Son?"

"Good Gawd, wes been lookin all over fer yuh! Where yuh been? Mas worried t death!"

"C mon in, son, n close the do."

"Don yuh wanna light?"

"Naw; close the do."

There was a short silence.

"Whuts the mattah, Pa? Yuh sick?"

"Close the do n set down, son!"

Taylor could hear Jimmy's breathing, then a chair scraping over the floor and the soft rustle of Jimmy's clothes as he sat.

"Whuts the mattah, Pa? Whut happened?"

Taylor stared in the darkness and slowly licked his swollen lips. He wanted to speak, but somehow could not. Then he stiffened, hearing Jimmy rise.

"Set *down*, son!"

"But, Pa. . . ."

Fire seethed not only in Taylor's back, but all over, inside and out. It was the fire of shame. The questions that fell from Jimmy's lips burned as much as the whip had. There rose in him a memory of all the times he had given advice, counsel, and guidance to Jimmy. And he wanted to talk to him now as he had in the past. But his impulses were deadlocked. Then suddenly he heard himself speaking, hoarsely, faintly. His voice was like a whisper rising from his whole body.

"They whipped me, son. . . ."

"Whipped yuh? Who?"

Jimmy ran to the bed and touched him.

"Son, set *down!*"

Taylor's voice was filled with a sort of tense despair. He felt Jimmy's fingers leaving him slowly. There was a silence in which he could hear only his own breath struggling in his throat.

"Yuh mean the *white* folks?"

Taylor buried his face in his pillow and tried to still the heaving in his chest.

"They beat me, son. . . ."

"Ahll git a doctah!"

"Naw!"

"But yuhs hurt!"

"Naw; lock the do! Don let May in here. . . ."

"Goddam them white bastards!"

"Set down, son!"

"Who wuz they, Pa?"

"Yuh cant do nothin, son. Yuhll have t wait. . . ."

"Wes been waitin too long! All we do is wait, *wait!*"

Jimmy's footsteps scuffed across the floor. Taylor sat up.

"Son?"

"Ahma git mah gun n git Pete n Bob n Joe n Sam! Theyll see they cant do this t us!"

Taylor groped in the darkness; he found Jimmy's shoulders.

"C mon, son! Ahm awright. . . ."

"Thas the reason why they kill us! We take everthing they put on us! We take everthing! *Everthing!*"

"Yuh cant do nothin *erlone*, Jimmy!"

Jimmy's voice was tense, almost hysterical.

"But we kin *make* em know they cant do this t us widout us doin *some*thing! Aw, hell, Pa! Is we gonna be dogs *all* the time?"

"But theyll kill yuh, son!"

"Somebody *has* t die!"

Taylor wanted to tell Jimmy something, but he could not find the words. What he wanted to say boiled in him, but it seemed too big to come out. He flinched from pain, pressing his fingers to his mouth, holding his breath.

"Pa?"

"Yeah, son?"

"Hadley n Green wuz here t see yuh three-fo times."

"Yeah?"

Jimmy said nothing. Taylor twisted around, trying to see his son's face in the darkness.

"Whut they say, son?"

"Aw, hell! It don mattah. . . ."

"Tell me whut they *said*!"

"Ttthey ssaid. . . . Aw, Pa, they didn't know!"

"Whut they *say*?"

"They said yuh had done run out on em. . . ."

"Run *out*?"

"Everbody wuz astin where yuh wuz," said Jimmy. "Nobody knowed. So they tol em yuh run out. N Brother Smith had the Deacon Board t vote yuh outta the church. . . ."

"Vote me *out*?"

"They said they didn't wan yuh fer pastah no mo. It wuz Smith who made em do it. He tol em yuh had planned a demonstration n lef em holdin the bag. He fussed n stormed at em. They thought they wuz doin right. . . ."

Taylor lay on his bed of fire in the darkness and cried. He felt Jimmy's fingers again on his face.

"Its awright, Pa. We'll git erlong somehow. . . ."

"Seems like Gawds done lef me! Ahd die fer mah people ef Ah only knowed how. . . ."

"Pa. . . ."

"How come Ah cant never do nothin? All mah life Ah done tried n cant do nothin! *Nothin!*"

"Its awright, Pa!"

"Ah done lived all mah life on mah knees, a-beggin n a-pleadin wid the white folks. N all they gimme wuz crumbs! All they did wuz kick me! N then they come wida gun n ast me t give mah own soul! N ef Ah so much as talk lika man they try t kill me. . . ."

He buried his face in the pillow, trying to sink himself into something so deeply that he could never feel again. He heard Jimmy turning the key in the lock.

"Son!"

Again he ran to Jimmy and held him.

"*Don* do tha, son!"

"Thingsll awways be like this less we *fight!*"

"Set down, son! Yo po ol pas a-*beggin* yuh t set down!"

He pulled Jimmy back to the bed. But even then it did not seem he could speak as he wanted to. He felt what he wanted to say, but it was elusive and hard to formulate.

"Son. . . ."

"Ah ain gonna live this way, Pa!"

He groped for Jimmy's shoulders in the darkness and squeezed them till the joints of his fingers cracked. And when words came they seemed to be tearing themselves from him, as though they were being pushed upward like hot lava out of a mountain from deep down.

"Don be a fool, son! Don thow you life erway! We cant do nothin erlone."

"But theys gonna treat us this way as long as we *let* em!"

He had to make Jimmy understand; for it seemed that

in making him understand, in telling him, he, too, would understand.

"We gotta git wid the *people*, son. Too long we done tried t do this thing our way n when we failed we wanted t run out n pay-off the white folks. Then they kill us up like flies. Its the *people*, son! Wes too much erlone this way! Wes los when wes erlone! Wes gotta be wid our folks. . . ."

"But theys killin us!"

"N theyll keep on killin us less we learn how t fight! Son, its the people we mus gid wid us! Wes empty n weak this way! The reason we cant do nothin is cause wes so much erlone. . . ."

"Them Reds wuz right," said Jimmy.

"Ah dunno," said Taylor. "But let nothin come tween yuh n *yo* people. Even the Reds cant do nothin ef yuh lose yo people. . . ." Fire burned him as he talked, and he talked as though trying to escape it. "Membah whut Ah tol yuh prayer wuz, son?"

There was silence, then Jimmy answered slowly:

"Yuh mean lettin Gawd be so real in yo life tha everthing yuh do is cause of Im?"

"Yeah, but its different now, son. Its the *people*! Theys the ones whut mus be real t us! Gawds wid the people! N the peoples gotta be real as Gawd t us! We cant hep ourselves er the people when wes erlone. Ah been wrong erbout a lotta things Ah tol yuh, son. Ah tol yuh them things cause Ah thought they wuz right. Ah tol yuh t work hard n climb t the top. Ah tol yuh folks would lissen t yuh then. But they wont, son! All the will, all the strength, all the power, all the numbahs is in the people! Yuh cant live by yoself! When they beat me tonight, they beat *me*. . . . There wuznt nothin Ah could do but lay there n hate n pray n cry. . . . Ah couldnt *feel* mah people, Ah couldn't *see* mah people, Ah couldn't *hear* mah people. . . . All Ah could feel wuz tha whip cuttin mah blood out. . . ."

In the darkness he imagined he could see Jimmy's face as he had seen it a thousand times, looking eagerly, his eyes staring before him, fashioning his words into images, into life. He hoped Jimmy was doing that now.

"Ahll awways hate them bastards! Ahll *aw*ways hate em!"

"Theres other ways, son."

"Yuhs sick, Pa. . . ."

"Wes all sick, son. Wes gotta think erbout the people, night n day, think erbout em so hard tha our po selves is fergotten. . . . Whut they suffer is whut Ah suffered las night when they whipped me. Wes gotta keep the people wid us."

Jimmy was silent. A soft knock came at the door.

XI

"Dan!"

"Thas ma," said Jimmy.

Taylor heard Jimmy rise to his feet; he gripped Jimmy's hands.

"Please, Pa! Let her come in n hep yuh!"

"Naw."

"Dan!"

Jimmy broke from him; he heard the key turn in the lock. The door opened.

"Dan! Fer Gawds sake, whuts the mattah?"

Jimmy switched on the light. Taylor lay blinking at May's anxious face. He felt shame again, knowing that he should not feel it, but feeling it anyway. He turned over and buried his face in his hands.

"Dan!"

She ran and knelt at the side of the bed.

"They tried t kill im, Ma! They beat im!" said Jimmy.

"Ah knowed them white folks wuz gonna do something like this! Ah knowed it," sobbed May.

Taylor sat up.

"Yuh be still! Lay down!" said May.

She pushed him back onto the bed.

"Cant yuh do something fer im, Ma? Hes sufferin tha way."

Taylor heard May leave the room and come back.

"Hol still, Dan. This ain gonna hurt yuh. . . ."

He felt warm water laving him, then something cool that smelled of oil. He heard Jimmy moving to and fro, getting things for May. When his back was dressed he felt the bed sink as May sat on the edge of it. The heavy odors of violets and magnolias came to him; he was slowly coming back to the world again. He was the same man, but he was coming back somehow changed. He wondered at the strange peace that seeped into his mind and body there in the room with May and Jimmy, with the white folks far off in the darkness.

"Feel bettah, Dan?"

"Ahm awright."

"Yuh hongry?"

"Naw."

He wanted to talk to Jimmy again, to tell him about the black people. But he could not think of words that would say what he wanted to say. He would tell it somehow later on. He began to toss, moving jerkily, more now from restlessness of mind than from the dying fire that still lingered in his body.

XII

Suddenly the doorbell pealed. Taylor turned and saw May and Jimmy looking at each other.

"Somebody at the do," said Jimmy in a tense voice.

"Yuh reckon they white folks?" asked May.

"Yuh bettah go down, Jimmy," said Taylor.

"Ef its any white folks tell em Dans out," said May.

Jimmy's footsteps died away on the stairs. A door slammed. There were faint sounds of voices. Footsteps echoed, came on the stairs, grew loud. Taylor knew that more than one person was coming up. He lifted himself and sat on the edge of the bed.

"Dan, yuh cant git up! Youhll make yoself sick!"

He ignored her. The door opened and Jimmy ran in.

"Its Brother Bonds, Pa!"

Bonds stood in the doorway with his head wrapped in blood-stained bandages. His face twitched and his eyes stared at something beyond the walls of the room, as though his attention had been riveted once and for always upon one fixed spot.

"Whut happened, Brother?" asked Taylor.

Bonds stared, dazed, with hunched and beaten shoulders. Then he sank to the floor, sobbing softly:

"They beat me! They beat mah chillun! They beat mah wife! They beat us all cause Ah tol em t git outta mah house! Lawd, how long Yuh gonna let em treat us this way? How long Yuh gonna let em make us suffer?"

May sobbed. Jimmy ran out of the room. Taylor caught him on the stairs.

"Don be a fool, boy! Yuh c mon back here, *now*!"

Jimmy flopped on the edge of a chair and mumbled to himself. The room was quiet save for the rustle of tree leaves that drifted in from the outside and the sound of Bonds sobbing on the floor. As Taylor stood his own suffering was drowned in a sense of widening horror. There was in his mind a vivid picture of all the little dingy huts where black men and women were crouched, afraid to stir out of doors. Bonds stopped crying and looked at Taylor; again that sense of shame spread over Taylor, inside and out. It stirred him to speech.

"Who else they beat, Brother?"

"Seem like everbody, Reveren! Them two Commoonists got beat something terrible n they put em in jail. N Ah heard they kilt one black man whut tried t fight back. They ketchin everbody they kin on the streets n lettin em have it. They ridin up n down in cars. . . ."

Jimmy cursed. The doorbell pealed again.

"Git me a shirt, May!"

"Dan, yuh ain able t do nothin!"

The doorbell pealed again, then again. Taylor started toward the dresser; but May got there before he did and gave him a shirt.

"Dan, be careful!"

"C mon downstairs, Brother Bonds. N yuh, too, Jimmy," said Taylor.

XIII

The church's waiting room was full. Black men and women sat and stood, saying nothing, waiting. Arms were in slings; necks were wrapped in white cloth; legs were bound in blood-stained rags.

"LOOK AT WHUT YUH DONE DONE!" a voice bawled.

It was Deacon Smith. Taylor's eyes went from face to face; he knew them all. Every Sunday they sat in the pews of his church, praying, singing, and trusting the God he gave them. The mute eyes and silent lips pinned him to a fiery spot of loneliness. He wanted to protest that loneliness, wanted to break it down; but he did not know how. No parables sprang to his lips now to give form and meaning to his words; alone and naked, he stood ashamed. Jimmy came through the door and placed his hand on his shoulder.

"Its daylight, Pa. The folks is gatherin in the playground! theys waitin fer yuh. . . ."

Taylor went into the yard with the crowd at his heels. It was broad daylight and the sun shone. The men in their overalls and the women with children stood about him on all sides, silent. A fat black woman elbowed her way in and faced him.

"Waal, Reveren, we done got beat up. Now, is we gonna march?"

"Yuh wanna march?" asked Taylor.

"It don make no difference wid me," she said. "Them white folks cant do no mo than theys awready done."

The crowd chimed in.

"N Gawd knows they cant!"

"Ahll go ef the nex one goes!"

"Ah gotta die sometime, so Ah jus as waal die now!"

"They cant kill us but once!"

"Ahm tired anyhow! Ah don care!"

"The white folks says theys gonna meet us at the park!"

Taylor turned to Jimmy.

"Son, git yo boys together n tell em t roun up everbody!"

"Yessuh!"

May was pulling at his sleeve.

"Dan, yuh *cant* do this. . . ."

Deacon Smith pushed his way in and faced him.

"Yuhll never set foot in a church ergin ef yuh lead them po black folks downtown t be killed!"

The crowd surged.

"Ain nobody leadin us nowhere!"

"We goin ourselves!"

"Is we gonna march, Reveren?"

"Yeah; soon as the crowd gits together," said Taylor.

"Ain nobody t blame but yuh ef yuh carry em t their *death*!" warned Deacon Smith.

"How come yuh don shut yo old big mouth n let the Reveren talk?" asked the fat woman.

"Sistah, Ah got as much right t speak as yuh!"

"Waal, don speak to me, yuh hear!"

"Somebody has t say something when ain *nobody* got no sense!"

"Man, don yuh tell me Ah ain got no sense!"

"Yuh sho don ack like it!"

"Ah got as much sense as yuh got!"

"How come yuh don use it?"

The fat sister slapped Deacon Smith straight across his face. Taylor ran between them and pried them apart. The crowd surged and screamed.

"Ef he touches Sistah Henry ergin Ahll kill im!"

"He ain got no bisness talkin tha way t a woman!"

Taylor dragged the fat woman toward the gate. The crowd followed, yelling. He stopped and faced them. They circled around, tightly, asking questions. May had hold of his sleeve. Jimmy came to him.

"Pa, theys comin!"

Taylor turned and walked across the yard with the crowd following. He took two planks and laid them upon the ends of two saw-horses and made a solid platform. He climbed up and stood in the quiet sunshine. He did not know exactly what it was he wanted to say, but whatever it was he would say it when they were quiet. He felt neither fear nor joy, just an humble confidence in himself, as though he were standing before his mirror in his room. Then he was conscious that they were quiet; he took one swift look over their heads, heads that stretched away to the street and beyond, a solid block of black, silent faces; then he looked down, not to the dust, but just a slight lowering of eyes, as though he were no longer looking at them, but at something within himself.

"Sistahs n Brothers, they tell me the Deacon Boards done voted me outta the church. Ef thas awright wid yuh, its awright wid me. The white folks says Ahma bad nigger n they don wanna have nothin else t do wid me. N thas awright, too. But theres one thing Ah wanna say. Ah knows how yuh feel erbout bein hongry. N how yuh feel is no different from how Ah feel. Yuh been waitin a week fer me t say whut yuh ought t do. Yuh been wonderin how come Ah didnt tell yuh whut yuh oughta do. Waal. . . ."

He paused and looked over the silent crowd; then again his eyes, his gaze, went inward.

"Sistahs n Brothers, the reason Ah didnt say nothin is cause Ah didnt know *whut* t say. N the only reason Ahm speakin now is cause Ah *do* know. Ah know whut t do. . . ."

He paused again, swallowing. The same feeling which had gripped him so hard last night when he had been talking to Jimmy seized him. He opened his mouth to continue; his lips moved several times before words came; and when they did come they fell with a light and hoarse whisper.

"Sistahs n Brothers, las night the white folks took me out t the woods. They took me out cause Ah tol em yuh wuz hongry. They ast me t tell yuh not t march, n Ah tol em Ah wouldnt. Then they beat me. They tied me t a tree n beat me till Ah couldnt feel no mo. They beat me cause Ah wouldnt tell yuh not t ast fer bread. They said yuhd blieve everthing Ah said. All the time they wuz hepin me, all the time they been givin me favors, they wuz doin it sos *they* could tell *me* t tell *yuh* how t ack! Sistahs n Brothers, as Gawds mah judge, Ah thought Ah wuz doin right when Ah did tha. Ah thought Ah wuz doin right when Ah tol yuh t do the things they said. N cause Ah wouldnt do it this time, they tied me t a tree n beat me till mah blood run. . . ."

Mist covered his eyes. He heard the crowd murmuring; but he did not care if they were murmuring for or against him; he wanted to finish, to say what he had been trying so hard to say for many long hours.

"Sistahs n Brothers, they whipped me n made me take the name of *Gawd* in vain! They made me say mah prayers n beat me n laughed! They beat me till Ah couldnt membah nothin! All last night Ah wuz lyin stretched out on the groun wid mah back burnin. . . . All this mawnin befo day Ah wuz limpin thu white folks streets. Sistahs n Brothers, Ah *know* now! Ah done seen the *sign*! Wes gotta git together. Ah know whut yo life is! Ah done felt it! Its *fire*! Its like the fire that burned me las night! Its sufferin! Its hell! Ah cant bear this fire erlone! Ah know now whut t do! Wes gotta git close t one ernother! Gawds done spoke! Gawds done sent His sign. Now its fer us t ack. . . ."

The crowd started yelling:

"We'll go ef yuh go!"

"Wes ready!"

"The white folks says theyll meet us at the park!"

The fat black woman started singing:

"So the sign of the fire by night
N the sign of the cloud by day
A-hoverin oer
Jus befo
As we journey on our way. . . ."

Taylor got down. He moved with the crowd slowly toward the street. May went with him, looking, wondering, saying nothing. Jimmy was at his side. They sang as they marched. More joined along the way.

When they reached the park that separated the white district from the black, the poor whites were waiting. Taylor trembled when he saw them join, swelling the mass that moved toward the town. He looked ahead and saw black and white marching; he looked behind and saw black and white marching. And still they sang:

"So the sign of the fire by night. . . ."

They turned into the street that led to town.

"N the sign of the cloud by day. . . ."

Taylor saw blue-coated policemen standing lined along the curb.

"A-hoverin o'er. . . ."

Taylor felt himself moving between the silent lines of blue-coated white men, moving with a sea of placards and banners, moving under the sun like a pregnant cloud. He said to himself, They ain gonna bother us! They bettah *not* bother us. . . .

"Jus befo. . . ."

Across a valley, in front of him, he could see the buildings of the town sprawled on a hill.

"As we journey on our way. . . ."

They were tramping on pavement now. And the blue-coated men stood still and silent. Taylor saw Deacon Smith standing on the curb, and Smith's face merged with the faces of the others, meaningless, lost. Ahead was the City Hall, white and clean in the sunshine. The autos stopped at the street corners while the crowd passed; and as they entered the downtown section people massed quietly on the sidewalks. Then the crowd began to slow, barely moving. Taylor looked ahead and wondered what was about to happen; he wondered without fear; as though whatever would or could happen could not hurt this many-limbed, many-legged, many-handed crowd that was he. He felt May clinging to his sleeve. Jimmy was peering ahead. A policeman came running up to him.

"You Taylor?"

"Yessuh," he said, quietly, his gaze straight and steady.

"The mayors down front; he wants to see you!"

"Tell im Ahm back here," said Taylor.

"But he wants to see the leader up front!"

"Tell im Ahm back here," said Taylor again.

The man hesitated, then left; they waited, quiet, still. Then the crowd parted. Taylor saw Mayor Bolton hurrying toward him, his face beet-red.

"Dan, tell your people not to make any trouble! We dont want any trouble, Dan. . . ."

"There ain gonna be no trouble, yo Honah!"

"Well, tell them they can get food if they go back home, peacefully. . . ."

"Yuh tell em, yo Honah!"

They looked at each other for a moment. Then the mayor turned and walked back. Taylor saw him mount the rear seat of an auto and lift his trembling hands high above the crowd, asking for silence, his face a pasty white.

A baptism of clean joy swept over Taylor. He kept his eyes on the sea of black and white faces. The song swelled louder and vibrated through him. This is the way! he thought. Gawd ain no lie! He ain no lie! His eyes grew wet with tears, blurring his vision: the sky trembled; the buildings wavered as if about to topple; and the earth shook. . . . He mumbled out loud, exultingly:

"Freedom belongs t the strong!"

V

Bright and Morning Star

I

S HE STOOD with her black face some six inches from the moist windowpane and wondered when on earth would it ever stop raining. It might keep up like this all week, she thought. She heard rain droning upon the roof and high up in the wet sky her eyes followed the silent rush of a bright shaft of yellow that swung from the airplane beacon in far off Memphis. Momently she could see it cutting through the rainy dark; it would hover a second like a gleaming sword above her head, then vanish. She sighed, troubling, Johnny-Boys been trampin in this slop all day wid no decent shoes on his feet. . . . Through the window she could see the rich black earth sprawling outside in the night. There was more rain than the clay could soak up; pools stood everywhere. She yawned and mumbled: "Rains good n bad. It kin make seeds bus up thu the groun, er it kin bog things down lika watah-soaked coffin." Her hands were folded loosely over her stomach and the hot air of the kitchen traced a filmy veil of sweat on her forehead. From the cook stove came the soft singing of burning wood and now and then a throaty bubble rose from a pot of simmering greens.

"Shucks, Johnny-Boy coulda let somebody else do all tha runnin in the rain. Theres others bettah fixed fer it than he is. But, naw! Johnny-Boy ain the one t trust nobody t do nothing. Hes gotta do it *all* hissef. . . ."

She glanced at a pile of damp clothes in a zinc tub. Waal, Ah bettah git t work. She turned, lifted a smoothing iron with a thick pad of cloth, touched a spit-wet finger to it with a quick, jerking motion: *smiiitz!* Yeah; its hot! Stooping, she took a blue work-shirt from the tub and shook it out. With a deft twist of her shoulder she caught the iron in her right hand; the fingers of her left hand took a piece of wax from a tin box and a frying sizzle came as she smeared the bottom. She was thinking of nothing now; her hands followed a lifelong ritual of toil. Spreading a sleeve, she ran the hot iron to and fro until the wet cloth became stiff. She was deep in the midst of her work when a song rose up out of the far off days of her childhood and broke through half-parted lips:

> *Hes the Lily of the Valley, the Bright n Mawnin Star*
> *Hes the Fairest of Ten Thousan t mah soul . . .*

A gust of wind dashed rain against the window. Johnny-Boy oughta c mon home n eat his suppah. Aw, Lawd! Itd be fine ef Sug could eat wid us tonight! Itd be like ol times! Mabbe aftah all it wont be long fo he comes back. Tha lettah Ah got from im las week said *Don give up hope.* . . . Yeah; we gotta live in hope. Then both of her sons, Sug and Johnny-Boy, would be back with her.

With an involuntary nervous gesture, she stopped and stood still, listening. But the only sound was the lulling fall of rain. Shucks, ain no usa me ackin this way, she thought. Ever time they gits ready to hol them meetings Ah gits jumpity. Ah been a lil scared ever since Sug went t jail. She heard the clock ticking and looked. Johnny-Boys a *hour* late! He sho mus be havin a time doin all tha trampin, trampin thu the mud. . . . But her fear was a quiet one; it was more like an intense brooding than a fear; it was a sort of hugging of hated facts so

closely that she could feel their grain, like letting cold
water run over her hand from a faucet on a winter
morning.

She ironed again, faster now, as if she felt the more
she engaged her body in work the less she would think.
But how could she forget Johnny-Boy out there on
those wet fields rounding up white and black Commu-
nists for a meeting tomorrow? And that was just what
Sug had been doing when the sheriff had caught him,
beat him, and tried to make him tell who and where his
comrades were. Po Sug! They sho musta beat the boy
somethin awful! But, thank Gawd, he didnt talk! He ain
no weaklin, Sug ain! Hes been lion-hearted all his life
long.

That had happened a year ago. And now each time
those meetings came around the old terror surged back.
While shoving the iron a cluster of toiling days re-
turned; days of washing and ironing to feed Johnny-Boy
and Sug so they could do party work; days of carrying a
hundred pounds of white folks' clothes upon her head
across fields sometimes wet and sometimes dry. But in
those days a hundred pounds was nothing to carry care-
fully balanced upon her head while stepping by instinct
over the corn and cotton rows. The only time it had
seemed heavy was when she had heard of Sug's arrest.
She had been coming home one morning with a bundle
upon her head, her hands swinging idly by her sides,
walking slowly with her eyes in front of her, when Bob,
Johnny-Boy's pal, had called from across the fields and
had come and told her that the sheriff had got Sug.
That morning the bundle had become heavier than she
could ever remember.

And with each passing week now, though she spoke
of it to no one, things were becoming heavier. The tubs
of water and the smoothing iron and the bundle of

clothes were becoming harder to lift, with her back aching so; and her work was taking longer, all because Sug was gone and she didn't know just when Johnny-Boy would be taken too. To ease the ache of anxiety that was swelling her heart, she hummed, then sang softly:

He walks wid me, He talks wid me
He tells me Ahm His own. . . .

Guiltily, she stopped and smiled. Looks like Ah jus cant seem t fergit them ol songs, no mattah how hard Ah tries. . . . She had learned them when she was a little girl living and working on a farm. Every Monday morning from the corn and cotton fields the slow strains had floated from her mother's lips, lonely and haunting; and later, as the years had filled with gall, she had learned their deep meaning. Long hours of scrubbing floors for a few cents a day had taught her who Jesus was, what a great boon it was to cling to Him, to be like Him and suffer without a mumbling word. She had poured the yearning of her life into the songs, feeling buoyed with a faith beyond this world. The figure of the Man nailed in agony to the Cross, His burial in a cold grave, His transfigured Resurrection, His being breath and clay, God and Man—all had focused her feelings upon an imagery which had swept her life into a wondrous vision.

But as she had grown older, a cold white mountain, the white folks and their laws, had swum into her vision and shattered her songs and their spell of peace. To her that white mountain was temptation, something to lure her from her Lord, a part of the world God had made in order that she might endure it and come through all the stronger, just as Christ had risen with greater glory from the tomb. The days crowded with trouble had enhanced her faith and she had grown to love hardship with a bitter pride; she had obeyed the laws of the white folks with a soft smile of secret knowing.

After her mother had been snatched up to heaven in a chariot of fire, the years had brought her a rough working-man and two black babies, Sug and Johnny-Boy, all three of whom she had wrapped in the charm and magic of her vision. Then she was tested by no less than God; her man died, a trial which she bore with the strength shed by the grace of her vision; finally even the memory of her man faded into the vision itself, leaving her with two black boys growing tall, slowly into manhood.

Then one day grief had come to her heart when Johnny-Boy and Sug had walked forth demanding their lives. She had sought to fill their eyes with her vision, but they would have none of it. And she had wept when they began to boast of the strength shed by a new and terrible vision.

But she had loved them, even as she loved them now; bleeding, her heart had followed them. She could have done no less, being an old woman in a strange world. And day by day her sons had ripped from her startled eyes her old vision, and image by image had given her a new one, different, but great and strong enough to fling her into the light of another grace. The wrongs and sufferings of black men had taken the place of Him nailed to the Cross; the meager beginnings of the party had become another Resurrection; and the hate of those who would destroy her new faith had quickened in her a hunger to feel how deeply her new strength went.

"Lawd, Johnny-Boy," she would sometimes say, "Ah just wan them white folks t try t make me tell *who* is *in* the party n who *ain*! Ah just wan em t try, n Ahll show em somethin they never thought a black woman could have!"

But sometimes like tonight, while lost in the forgetfulness of work, the past and the present would become mixed in her; while toiling under a strange star for a new freedom the old songs would slip from her lips with their beguiling sweetness.

The iron was getting cold. She put more wood into the fire, stood again at the window and watched the yellow blade of light cut through the wet darkness. Johnny-Boy ain here yit. . . . Then, before she was aware of it, she was still, listening for sounds. Under the drone of rain she heard the slosh of feet in mud. Tha ain Johnny-Boy. She knew his long, heavy footsteps in a million. She heard feet come on the porch. Some woman. . . . She heard bare knuckles knock three times, then once. Thas some of them comrades! She unbarred the door, cracked it a few inches, and flinched from the cold rush of damp wind.

"Whos tha?"

"Its me!"

"Who?"

"Me, Reva!"

She flung the door open.

"Lawd, chile, c mon in!"

She stepped to one side and a thin, blond-haired white girl ran through the door; as she slid the bolt she heard the girl gasping and shaking her wet clothes. Somethings wrong! Reva wouldna walked a mile t mah house in all this slop fer nothin! Tha gals stuck onto Johnny-Boy. Ah wondah ef anything happened t im?

"Git on inter the kitchen, Reva, where its warm."

"Lawd, Ah sho is wet!"

"How yuh reckon yuhd be, in all tha rain?"

"Johnny-Boy ain here *yit*?" asked Reva.

"Naw! N ain no usa yuh worryin bout im. Jus yuh git them shoes off! Yuh wanna ketch yo deatha col?" She stood looking absently. Yeah; its somethin about the party er Johnny-Boy thas gone wrong. Lawd, Ah wondah ef her pa knows how she feels bout Johnny-Boy? "Honey, yuh hadnt oughta come out in sloppy weather like this."

"Ah had t come, An Sue."

She led Reva to the kitchen.

"Git them shoes off n git close t the stove so yuhll git dry!"

"An Sue, Ah got somethin t tell yuh . . ."

The words made her hold her breath. Ah bet its somethin bout Johnny-Boy!

"Whut, honey?"

"The sheriff wuz by our house tonight. He come t see pa."

"Yeah?"

"He done got word from somewheres bout tha meetin tomorrow."

"Is it Johnny-Boy, Reva?"

"Aw, naw, An Sue! Ah ain hearda word bout im. Ain yuh seen im tonight?"

"He ain come home t eat yit."

"Where kin he be?"

"Lawd knows, chile."

"Somebodys gotta tell them comrades tha meetings off," said Reva. "The sheriffs got men watchin our house. Ah had t slip out t git here widout em followin me."

"Reva?"

"Hunh?"

"Ahma ol woman n Ah wans yuh t tell me the truth."

"Whut, An Sue?"

"Yuh ain tryin t fool me, is yuh?"

"*Fool* yuh?"

"Bout Johnny-Boy?"

"Lawd, naw, An Sue!"

"Ef theres anythin wrong jus tell me, chile. Ah kin stan it."

She stood by the ironing board, her hands as usual folded loosely over her stomach, watching Reva pull off her water-clogged shoes. She was feeling that Johnny-Boy was already lost to her; she was feeling the pain that would come when she knew it for certain; and she was feeling that she would have to be brave and bear it. She was like a person caught in a swift current of water and knew where the water was sweeping her and did not want to go on but had to go on to the end.

"It ain nothin bout Johnny-Boy, An Sue," said Reva. "But we gotta do somethin er we'll all git inter trouble."

"How the sheriff know about tha meetin?"

"Thas whut pa wans t know."

"Somebody done turned Judas."

"Sho looks like it."

"Ah bet it wuz some of them new ones," she said.

"Its hard t tell," said Reva.

"Lissen, Reva, yuh oughta stay here n git dry, but yuh bettah git back n tell yo pa Johnny-Boy ain here n Ah don know when hes gonna show up. *Some*bodys gotta tell them comrades t stay erway from yo pas house."

She stood with her back to the window, looking at Reva's wide, blue eyes. Po critter! Gotta go back thu all tha slop! Though she felt sorry for Reva, not once did she think that it would not have to be done. Being a woman, Reva was not suspect; she would *have* to go. It was just as natural for Reva to go back through the cold rain as it was for her to iron night and day, or for Sug to be in jail. Right now, Johnny-Boy was out there on those dark fields trying to get home. Lawd, don let em git im tonight! In spite of herself her feelings became torn. She loved her son and, loving him, she loved what he was trying to do. Johnny-Boy was happiest when he was working for the party, and her love for him was for his happiness. She frowned, trying hard to fit something together in her feelings: for her to try to stop Johnny-Boy was to admit that all the toil of years meant nothing; and to let him go meant that sometime or other he would be caught, like Sug. In facing it this way she felt a little stunned, as though she had come suddenly upon a blank wall in the dark. But outside in the rain were people, white and black, whom she had known all her life. Those people depended upon Johnny-Boy, loved him and looked to him as a man and leader. Yeah; hes gotta keep on; he cant stop now. . . . She looked at Reva; she was crying and pulling her shoes back on with reluctant fingers.

"Whut yuh carryin on tha way fer, chile?"

"Yuh done los Sug, now yuh sendin Johnny-Boy . . ."

"Ah got t, honey."

She was glad she could say that. Reva believed in black folks and not for anything in the world would she falter before her. In Reva's trust and acceptance of her she had found her first feelings of humanity; Reva's love was her refuge from shame and degradation. If in the early days of her life the white mountain had driven her back from the earth, then in her last days Reva's love was drawing her toward it, like the beacon that swung through the night outside. She heard Reva sobbing.

"Hush, honey!"

"Mah brothers in jail too! Ma cries ever day . . ."

"Ah know, honey."

She helped Reva with her coat; her fingers felt the scant flesh of the girl's shoulders. She don git ernuff t eat, she thought. She slipped her arms around Reva's waist and held her close for a moment.

"Now, yuh stop that cryin."

"A-a-ah c-c-cant hep it. . . ."

"Everythingll be awright; Johnny-Boyll be back."

"Yuh think so?"

"Sho, chile. Cos he will."

Neither of them spoke again until they stood in the doorway. Outside they could hear water washing through the ruts of the street.

"Be sho n send Johnny-Boy t tell the folks t stay erway from pas house," said Reva.

"Ahll tell im. Don yuh worry."

"Good-bye!"

"Good-bye!"

Leaning against the door jamb, she shook her head slowly and watched Reva vanish through the falling rain.

II

She was back at her board, ironing, when she heard feet sucking in the mud of the back yard; feet she knew from long years of listening were Johnny-Boy's. But tonight, with all the rain and fear, his coming was like a leaving, was almost more than she could bear. Tears welled to her eyes and she blinked them away. She felt that he was coming so that she could give him up; to see him now was to say good-bye. But it was a good-bye she knew she could never say; they were not that way toward each other. All day long they could sit in the same room and not speak; she was his mother and he was her son. Most of the time a nod or a grunt would carry all the meaning that she wanted to convey to him, or he to her. She did not even turn her head when she heard him come stomping into the kitchen. She heard him pull up a chair, sit, sigh, and draw off his muddy shoes; they fell to the floor with heavy thuds. Soon the kitchen was full of the scent of his drying socks and his burning pipe. Tha boys hongry! She paused and looked at him over her shoulder; he was puffing at his pipe with his head tilted back and his feet propped up on the edge of the stove; his eyelids drooped and his wet clothes steamed from the heat of the fire. Lawd, tha boy gits mo like his pa ever day he lives, she mused, her lips breaking in a slow faint smile. Hols tha pipe in his mouth just like his pa usta hol his. Wondah how they woulda got erlong ef his pa hada lived? They oughta liked each other, they so much alike. She wished there could have been other children besides Sug, so Johnny-Boy would not have to be so much alone. A man needs a woman by his side. . . . She thought of Reva; she liked Reva; the brightest glow her heart had ever known was when she had learned that Reva loved Johnny-Boy. But beyond Reva were cold white faces. Ef theys caught it means *death*. . . . She jerked around when she heard Johnny-Boy's pipe clatter to the floor. She saw him pick it up, smile sheepishly at her, and wag his head.

"Gawd, Ahm sleepy," he mumbled.

She got a pillow from her room and gave it to him.

"Here," she said.

"Hunh," he said, putting the pillow between his head and the back of the chair.

They were silent again. Yes, she would have to tell him to go back out into the cold rain and slop; maybe to get caught; maybe for the last time; she didn't know. But she would let him eat and get dry before telling him that the sheriff knew of the meeting to be held at Lem's tomorrow. And she would make him take a big dose of soda before he went out; soda always helped to stave off a cold. She looked at the clock. It was eleven. Theres time yit. Spreading a newspaper on the apron of the stove, she placed a heaping plate of greens upon it, a knife, a fork, a cup of coffee, a slab of cornbread, and a dish of peach cobbler.

"Yo suppahs ready," she said.

"Yeah," he said.

He did not move. She ironed again. Presently, she heard him eating. When she could no longer hear his knife tinkling against the edge of the plate, she knew he was through. It was almost twelve now. She would let him rest a little while longer before she told him. Till one er'clock, mabbe. Hes so tired. . . . She finished her ironing, put away the board, and stacked the clothes in her dresser drawer. She poured herself a cup of black coffee, drew up a chair, sat down and drank.

"Yuh almos dry," she said, not looking around.

"Yeah," he said, turning sharply to her.

The tone of voice in which she had spoken had let him know that more was coming. She drained her cup and waited a moment longer.

"Reva wuz here."

"Yeah?"

"She lef bout a hour ergo."

"Whut she say?"

"She said ol man Lem hada visit from the sheriff today."

"Bout the meetin?"

"Yeah."

She saw him stare at the coals glowing red through the crevices of the stove and run his fingers nervously through his hair. She knew he was wondering how the sheriff had found out. In the silence he would ask a wordless question and in the silence she would answer wordlessly. Johnny-Boys too trustin, she thought. Hes trying t make the party big n hes takin in folks fastern he kin git t know em. You cant trust ever white man yuh meet. . . .

"Yuh know, Johnny-Boy, yuh been takin in a lotta them white folks lately . . ."

"Aw, ma!"

"But, Johnny-Boy . . ."

"Please, don talk t me bout tha now, ma."

"Yuh ain t ol t lissen n learn, son," she said.

"Ah know whut yuh gonna say, ma. N yuh wrong. Yuh cant judge folks jus by how yuh feel bout em n by how long yuh done knowed em. Ef we start tha we wouldnt have *no*body in the party. When folks pledge they word t be with us, then we gotta take em in. Wes too weak t be choosy."

He rose abruptly, rammed his hands into his pockets, and stood facing the window; she looked at his back in a long silence. She knew his faith; it was deep. He had always said that black men could not fight the rich bosses alone; a man could not fight with every hand against him. But he believes so hard hes blind, she thought. At odd times they had had these arguments before; always she would be pitting her feelings against the hard necessity of his thinking, and always she would lose. She shook her head. Po Johnny-Boy; he don know . . .

"But ain nona our folks tol, Johnny-Boy," she said.

"How yuh know?" he asked. His voice came low and with a tinge of anger. He still faced the window and now and then the yellow blade of light flicked across the sharp outline of his black face.

"Cause Ah know em," she said.

"*Any*body mighta tol," he said.

"It wuznt nona *our* folks," she said again.

She saw his hand sweep in a swift arc of disgust.

"*Our* folks! Ma, who in Gawds name is *our* folks?"

"The folks we wuz born n raised wid, son. The folks we *know!*"

"We cant make the party grow tha way, ma."

"It mighta been Booker," she said.

"Yuh don know."

". . . er Blattberg . . ."

"Fer Chrissakes!"

". . . er any of the fo-five others whut joined las week."

"Ma, yuh jus don wan me t go out tonight," he said.

"Yo ol ma wans yuh t be careful, son."

"Ma, when yuh start doubtin folks in the party, then there ain no end."

"Son, Ah knows ever black man n woman in this parta the county," she said, standing too. "Ah watched em grow up; Ah even heped birth n nurse some of em; Ah knows em *all* from way back. There ain none of em that *coulda* tol! The folks Ah know jus don open they dos n ast death t walk in! Son, it wuz some of them *white* folks! Yuh jus mark mah word n wait n see!"

"Why is it gotta be *white* folks?" he asked. "Ef they tol, then theys jus Judases, thas all."

"Son, look at whuts befo yuh."

He shook his head and sighed.

"Ma, Ah done tol yuh a hundred times. Ah cant see white n Ah cant see black," he said. "Ah sees rich men n Ah sees po men."

She picked up his dirty dishes and piled them in a pan. Out of the corners of her eyes she saw him sit and pull on his wet shoes. Hes goin! When she put the last dish away he was standing fully dressed, warming his hands over the stove. Jus a few mo minutes now n he'll be gone, like Sug, mabbe. Her throat tightened. This black mans fight takes *ever*thin! Looks like Gawd put us in this worl jus t beat us down!

"Keep this, ma," he said.

She saw a crumpled wad of money in his outstretched fingers.

"Naw; yuh keep it. Yuh might need it."

"It ain mine, ma. It berlongs t the party."

"But, Johnny-Boy, yuh might hafta go erway!"

"Ah kin make out."

"Don fergit yosef too much, son."

"Ef Ah don come back theyll need it."

He was looking at her face and she was looking at the money.

"Yuh keep tha," she said slowly. "Ahll give em the money."

"From where?"

"Ah got some."

"Where yuh git it from?"

She sighed.

"Ah been savin a dollah a week fer Sug ever since hes been in jail."

"Lawd, ma!"

She saw the look of puzzled love and wonder in his eyes. Clumsily, he put the money back into his pocket.

"Ahm gone," he said.

"Here; drink this glass of soda watah."

She watched him drink, then put the glass away.

"Waal," he said.

"Take the stuff outta yo pockets!"

She lifted the lid of the stove and he dumped all the papers from his pocket into the fire. She followed him to the door and made him turn round.

"Lawd, yuh tryin to maka revolution n yuh cant even keep yo coat buttoned." Her nimble fingers fastened his collar high around his throat. "There!"

He pulled the brim of his hat low over his eyes. She opened the door and with the suddenness of the cold gust of wind that struck her face, he was gone. She watched the black fields and the rain take him, her eyes burning. When the last faint footstep could no longer be heard, she closed the door, went to her bed, lay down, and pulled the cover over her while fully dressed. Her feelings coursed with the rhythm of the rain: Hes gone! Lawd, Ah *know* hes gone! Her blood felt cold.

III

She was floating in a grey void somewhere between sleeping and dreaming and then suddenly she was wide awake, hearing and feeling in the same instant the thunder of the door crashing in and a cold wind filling the room. It was pitch black and she stared, resting on her elbows, her mouth open, not breathing, her ears full of the sound of tramping feet and booming voices. She knew at once: They lookin fer im! Then, filled with her will, she was on her feet, rigid, waiting, listening.

"The lamps burnin!"

"Yuh see her?"

"Naw!"

"Look in the kitchen!"

"Gee, this place smells like niggers!"

"Say, somebodys here er been here!"

"Yeah; theres fire in the stove!"

"Mabbe hes been here n gone?"

"Boy, look at these jars of jam!"

"Niggers make good jam!"

"Git some bread!"

"Heres some cornbread!"

"Say, lemme git some!"

"Take it easy! Theres plenty here!"

"Ahma take some of this stuff home!"

"Look, heres a pota greens!"

"N some hot cawffee!"

"Say, yuh guys! C mon! Cut it out! We didnt come here fer a feas!"

She walked slowly down the hall. They lookin fer im, but they ain got im yit! She stopped in the doorway, her gnarled, black hands as always folded over her stomach, but tight now, so tightly the veins bulged. The kitchen was crowded with white men in glistening raincoats. Though the lamp burned, their flashlights still glowed in red fists. Across her floor she saw the muddy tracks of their boots.

"Yuh white folks git outta mah house!"

There was quick silence; every face turned toward her. She saw a sudden movement, but did not know what it meant until something hot and wet slammed her squarely in the face. She gasped, but did not move. Calmly, she wiped the warm, greasy liquor of greens from her eyes with her left hand. One of the white men had thrown a handful of greens out of the pot at her.

"How they taste, ol bitch?"

"Ah ast yuh t git outta mah house!"

She saw the sheriff detach himself from the crowd and walk toward her.

"Now, Anty . . ."

"White man, don yuh *Anty* me!"

"Yuh ain got the right sperit!"

"Sperit hell! Yuh git these men outta mah house!"

"Yuh ack like yuh don like it!"

"Naw, Ah don like it, n yuh knows dam waal Ah don!"

"Whut yuh gonna do bout it?"

"Ahm tellin yuh t git outta mah house!"

"Gittin sassy?"

"Ef telling yuh t git outta mah house is sass, then Ahm sassy!"

Her words came in a tense whisper; but beyond, back of them, she was watching, thinking, judging the men.

"Listen, Anty," the sheriff's voice came soft and low. "Ahm here t hep yuh. How come yuh wanna ack this way?"

"Yuh ain never heped yo *own* sef since yuh been born," she flared. "How kin the likes of yuh hep me?"

One of the white men came forward and stood directly in front of her.

"Lissen, nigger woman, yuh talkin t *white* men!"

"Ah don care who Ahm talkin t!"

"Yuhll wish some day yuh did!"

"Not t the likes of yuh!"

"Yuh need somebody t teach yuh how t be a good nigger!"

"*Yuh* cant teach it t me!"

"Yuh gonna change yo tune."

"Not longs mah bloods warm!"

"Don git smart now!"

"Yuh git outta mah house!"

"Spose we don go?" the sheriff asked.

They were crowded around her. She had not moved since she had taken her place in the doorway. She was thinking only of Johnny-Boy as she stood there giving and taking words; and she knew that they, too, were thinking of Johnny-Boy. She knew they wanted him, and her heart was daring them to take him from her.

"Spose we don go?" the sheriff asked again.

"Twenty of yuh runnin over one ol woman! Now, ain yuh white men glad yuh so brave?"

The sheriff grabbed her arm.

"C mon, now! Yuh done did ernuff sass fer one night. Wheres tha nigger son of yos?"

"Don yuh wished yuh knowed?"

"Yuh wanna git slapped?"

"Ah ain never seen one of yo kind tha wuznt too low fer . . ."

The sheriff slapped her straight across her face with his open palm. She fell back against a wall and sank to her knees.

"Is tha whut white men do t nigger women?"

She rose slowly and stood again, not even touching the place that ached from his blow, her hands folded over her stomach.

"Ah ain never seen one of yo kind tha wuznt too low fer . . ."

He slapped her again; she reeled backward several feet and fell on her side.

"Is tha whut we too low t do?"

She stood before him again, dry-eyed, as though she had not been struck. Her lips were numb and her chin was wet with blood.

"Aw, let her go! Its the nigger we wan!" said one.

"Wheres that nigger son of yos?" the sheriff asked.

"Find im," she said.

"By Gawd, ef we hafta find im we'll kill im!"

"He wont be the only nigger yuh ever killed," she said.

She was consumed with a bitter pride. There was nothing on this earth, she felt then, that they could not do to her but that she could take. She stood on a narrow plot of ground from which she would die before she was pushed. And then it was, while standing there feeling warm blood seeping down her throat, that she gave up Johnny-Boy, gave him up to the white folks. She gave him up because they had come tramping into her heart demanding him, thinking they could get him by beating her, thinking they could scare her into making her tell where he was. She gave him up because she wanted them to know that they could not get what they wanted by bluffing and killing.

"Wheres this meetin gonna be?" the sheriff asked.

"Don yuh wish yuh knowed?"

"Ain there gonna be a meetin?"

"How come yuh astin me?"

"There *is* gonna be a meetin," said the sheriff.

"Is it?"

"Ah gotta great mind t choke it outta yuh!"

"Yuh so smart," she said.

"We ain playin wid yuh!"

"Did Ah say yuh wuz?"

"Tha nigger son of yos is erroun here somewheres n we aim t find im," said the sheriff. "Ef yuh tell us where he is n ef he talks, mabbe he'll git off easy. But ef we hafta find im, we'll kill im! Ef we hafta find im, then yuh git a sheet t put over im in the mawnin, see? Git yuh a sheet, cause hes gonna be dead!"

"He wont be the only nigger yuh ever killed," she said again.

The sheriff walked past her. The others followed. Yuh didnt git whut yuh wanted! she thought exultingly. N yuh ain gonna *never* git it! Hotly, something ached in her to make them feel the intensity of her pride and freedom; her heart groped to turn the bitter hours of her life into words of a kind that would make them feel that she had taken all they had done to her in her stride and could still take more. Her faith surged so strongly in her she was all but blinded. She walked behind them to the door, knotting and twisting her fingers. She saw them step to the muddy ground. Each whirl of the yellow beacon revealed glimpses of slanting rain. Her lips moved, then she shouted:

"Yuh didnt git whut yuh wanted! N yuh ain gonna nevah git it!"

The sheriff stopped and turned; his voice came low and hard.

"Now, by Gawd, thas ernuff outta yuh!"

"Ah know when Ah done said ernuff!"

"Aw, naw, yuh don!" he said. "Yuh don know when yuh done said ernuff, but Ahma teach yuh ternight!"

He was up the steps and across the porch with one bound. She backed into the hall, her eyes full on his face.

"Tell me when yuh gonna stop talkin!" he said, swinging his fist.

The blow caught her high on the cheek; her eyes went blank; she fell flat on her face. She felt the hard heel of his wet shoes coming into her temple and stomach.

"Lemme hear yuh talk some mo!"

She wanted to, but could not; pain numbed and choked her. She lay still and somewhere out of the grey void of unconsciousness she heard someone say: *aw fer chrissakes leave her erlone its the nigger we wan.* . . .

IV

She never knew how long she had lain huddled in the dark hallway. Her first returning feeling was of a nameless fear crowding the inside of her, then a deep pain spreading from her temple downward over her body. Her ears were filled with the drone of rain and she shuddered from the cold wind blowing through the door. She opened her eyes and at first saw nothing. As if she were imagining it, she knew she was half-lying and half-sitting in a corner against a wall. With difficulty she twisted her neck and what she saw made her hold her breath—a vast white blur was suspended directly above her. For a moment she could not tell if her fear was from the blur or if the blur was from her fear. Gradually the blur resolved itself into a huge white face that slowly filled her vision. She was stone still, conscious really of the effort to breathe, feeling somehow that she existed only by the mercy of that white face. She had seen it before; its fear had gripped her many times; it had for her the fear of all the white faces she had ever seen in her life. *Sue* . . . As from a great distance, she heard her name being called. She was regaining consciousness now, but the fear was coming with her. She looked into the face of a white man, wanting to scream out for him to go; yet accepting his presence because she felt she had to. Though some remote part of her mind was active, her limbs were powerless. It was as if an invisible knife had split her in two, leaving one half of her lying there helpless, while the other half shrank in dread from a forgotten but familiar enemy. *Sue its me Sue its me* . . . Then all at once the voice came clearly.

"Sue, its me! Its Booker!"

And she heard an answering voice speaking inside of her, Yeah, its Booker . . . The one whut jus joined . . . She roused herself, struggling for full consciousness; and as she did so she transferred to the person of Booker the nameless fear she felt. It seemed that Booker towered above her as a challenge to her right to exist upon the earth.

"Yuh awright?"

She did not answer; she started violently to her feet and fell.

"Sue, yuh hurt!"

"Yeah," she breathed.

"Where they hit yuh?"

"Its mah head," she whispered.

She was speaking even though she did not want to; the fear that had hold of her compelled her.

"They beat yuh?"

"Yeah."

"Them bastards! Them Gawddam bastards!"

She heard him saying it over and over; then she felt herself being lifted.

"Naw!" she gasped.

"Ahma take yuh t the kitchen!"

"Put me down!"

"But yuh cant stay here like this!"

She shrank in his arms and pushed her hands against his body; when she was in the kitchen she freed herself, sank into a chair, and held tightly to its back. She looked wonderingly at Booker. There was nothing about him that should frighten her so, but even that did not ease her tension. She saw him go to the water bucket, wet his handkerchief, wring it, and offer it to her. Distrustfully, she stared at the damp cloth.

"Here; put this on yo fohead . . ."

"Naw!"

"C mon; itll make yuh feel bettah!"

She hesitated in confusion. What right had she to be afraid when someone was acting as kindly as this toward her? Reluctantly, she leaned forward and pressed the damp cloth to her head. It helped. With each passing minute she was catching hold of herself, yet wondering why she felt as she did.

"Whut happened?"

"Ah don know."

"Yuh feel bettah?"

"Yeah."

"Who all wuz here?"

"Ah don know," she said again.

"Yo head still hurt?"

"Yeah."

"Gee, Ahm sorry."

"Ahm awright," she sighed and buried her face in her hands.

She felt him touch her shoulder.

"Sue, Ah got some bad news fer yuh . . ."

She knew; she stiffened and grew cold. It had happened; she stared dry-eyed, with compressed lips.

"Its mah Johnny-Boy," she said.

"Yeah; Ahm awful sorry t hafta tell yuh this way. But Ah thought yuh oughta know . . ."

Her tension eased and a vacant place opened up inside of her. A voice whispered, Jesus, hep me!

"W-w-where is he?"

"They got im out t Foleys Woods tryin t make im tell who the others is."

"He ain gonna tell," she said. "They just as waal kill im, cause he ain gonna nevah tell."

"Ah hope he don," said Booker. "But he didnt hava chance t tell the others. They grabbed im jus as he got t the woods."

Then all the horror of it flashed upon her; she saw flung out over the rainy countryside an array of shacks where white and black comrades were sleeping; in the morning they would be rising and going to Lem's; then they would be caught. And that meant terror, prison, and death. The comrades would have to be told; she would have to tell them; she could not entrust Johnny-Boy's work to another, and especially not to Booker as long as she felt toward him as she did. Gripping the bottom of the chair with both hands, she tried to rise; the room blurred and she swayed. She found herself resting in Booker's arms.

"Lemme go!"

"Sue, yuh too weak t walk!"

"Ah gotta tell em!" she said.

"Set down, Sue! Yuh hurt! Yuh sick!"

When seated, she looked at him helplessly.

"Sue, lissen! Johnny-Boys caught. Ahm here. Yuh tell me who they is n Ahll tell em."

She stared at the floor and did not answer. Yes; she was too weak to go. There was no way for her to tramp all those miles through the rain tonight. But should she tell Booker? If only she had somebody like Reva to talk to! She did not want to decide alone; she must make no mistake about this. She felt Booker's fingers pressing on her arm and it was as though the white mountain was pushing her to the edge of a sheer height; she again exclaimed inwardly, Jesus, hep me! Booker's white face was at her side, waiting. Would she be doing right to tell him? Suppose she did not tell and then the comrades were caught? She could not ever forgive herself for doing a thing like that. But maybe she was wrong; maybe her fear was what Johnny-Boy had always called "jus foolishness." She remembered his saying, Ma we cant make the party grow ef we start doubtin everbody. . . .

"Tell me who they is, Sue, n Ahll tell em. Ah jus joined n Ah don know who they is."

"Ah don know who they is," she said.

"Yuh *gotta* tell me who they is, Sue!"

"Ah tol yuh Ah don know!"

"Yuh *do* know! C mon! Set up n talk!"

"Naw!"

"Yuh wan em all t git *killed*?"

She shook her head and swallowed. Lawd, Ah don blieve in this man!

"Lissen, Ahll call the names n yuh tell me which ones is in the party n which ones ain, see?"

"Naw!"

"Please, Sue!"

"Ah don know," she said.

"Sue, yuh ain doin right by em. Johnny-Boy wouldnt wan yuh t be this way. Hes out there holdin up his end. Les hol up ours . . ."

"Lawd, Ah don know . . ."

"Is yuh scareda me cause Ahm *white*? Johnny-Boy ain like tha. Don let all the work we done go fer nothin."

She gave up and bowed her head in her hands.

"Is it Johnson? Tell me, Sue?"

"Yeah," she whispered in horror; a mounting horror of feeling herself being undone.

"Is it Green?"

"Yeah."

"Murphy?"

"Lawd, Ah don know!"

"Yuh gotta tell me, Sue!"

"Mistah Booker, please leave me erlone . . ."

"Is it Murphy?"

She answered yes to the names of Johnny-Boy's comrades; she answered until he asked her no more. Then she thought, How he know the sheriffs men is watchin Lems house? She stood up and held onto her chair, feeling something sure and firm within her.

"How yuh know bout Lem?"

"Why . . . How Ah know?"

"Whut yuh doin here this tima night? How yuh know the sheriff got Johnny-Boy?"

"Sue, don yuh blieve in me?"

She did not, but she could not answer. She stared at him until her lips hung open; she was searching deep within herself for certainty.

"You meet Reva?" she asked.

"Reva?"

"Yeah; Lems gal?"

"Oh, yeah. Sho, Ah met Reva."

"She tell yuh?"

She asked the question more of herself than of him; she longed to believe.

"Yeah," he said softly. "Ah reckon Ah oughta be goin t tell em now."

"Who?" she asked. "Tell *who*?"

The muscles of her body were stiff as she waited for his answer; she felt as though life depended upon it.

"The comrades," he said.

"Yeah," she sighed.

She did not know when he left; she was not looking or listening. She just suddenly saw the room empty and from her the thing that had made her fearful was gone.

V

For a space of time that seemed to her as long as she had been upon the earth, she sat huddled over the cold stove. One minute she would say to herself, They both gone now; Johnny-Boy n Sug . . . Mabbe Ahll never see em ergin. Then a surge of guilt would blot out her longing. "Lawd, Ah shouldna tol!" she mumbled. "But no man kin be so lowdown as t do a thing like tha . . ." Several times she had an impulse to try to tell the comrades herself; she was feeling a little better now. But what good would that do? She had told Booker the names. He jus couldnt be a Judas t po folks like us . . . He *couldnt*!

"An Sue!"

Thas Reva! Her heart leaped with an anxious gladness. She rose without answering and limped down the dark hallway. Through the open door, against the background of rain, she saw Reva's face lit now and then to whiteness by the whirling beams of the beacon. She was about to call, but a thought checked her. Jesus, hep me! Ah gotta tell her bout Johnny-Boy . . . Lawd, Ah cant!

"An Sue, yuh there?"

"C mon in, chile!"

She caught Reva and held her close for a moment without speaking.

"Lawd, Ahm sho glad yuh here," she said at last.

"Ah thought somethin had happened t yuh," said Reva, pulling away. "Ah saw the do open . . . Pa tol me to come back n stay wid yuh tonight . . ." Reva paused and started. "W-w-whuts the mattah?"

She was so full of having Reva with her that she did not understand what the question meant.

"Hunh?"

"Yo neck . . ."

"Aw, it ain nothin, chile. C mon in the kitchen."

"But theres blood on yo neck!"

"The sheriff wuz here . . ."

"Them fools! Whut they wanna bother yuh fer? Ah could kill em! So hep me Gawd, Ah could!"

"It ain nothin," she said.

She was wondering how to tell Reva about Johnny-Boy and Booker. Ahll wait a lil while longer, she thought. Now that Reva was here, her fear did not seem as awful as before.

"C mon, lemme fix yo head, An Sue. Yuh hurt."

They went to the kitchen. She sat silent while Reva dressed her scalp. She was feeling better now; in just a little while she would tell Reva. She felt the girl's finger pressing gently upon her head.

"Tha hurt?"

"A lil, chile."

"Yuh po thing."

"It ain nothin."

"Did Johnny-Boy come?"

She hesitated.

"Yeah."

"He done gone t tell the others?"

Reva's voice sounded so clear and confident that it mocked her. Lawd, Ah cant tell this chile . . .

"Yuh tol im, didnt yuh, An Sue?"

"Y-y-yeah . . ."

"Gee! Thas good! Ah tol pa he didnt hafta worry ef Johnny-Boy got the news. Mabbe thingsll come out awright."

"Ah hope . . ."

She could not go on; she had gone as far as she could. For the first time that night she began to cry.

"Hush, An Sue! Yuh awways been brave. Itll be awright!"

"Ain nothin awright, chile. The worls jus too much fer us, Ah reckon."

"Ef yuh cry that way itll make me cry."

She forced herself to stop. Naw; Ah cant carry on this way in fronta Reva . . . Right now she had a deep need for Reva to believe in her. She watched the girl get pine-knots from behind the stove, rekindle the fire, and put on the coffee pot.

"Yuh wan some cawffee?" Reva asked.

"Naw, honey."

"Aw, c mon, An Sue."

"Jusa lil, honey."

"Thas the way to be. Oh, say, Ah fergot," said Reva, measuring out spoonsful of coffee. "Pa tol me t tell yuh t watch out fer tha Booker man. Hes a stool."

She showed not one sign of outward movement or expression, but as the words fell from Reva's lips she went limp inside.

"Pa tol me soon as Ah got back home. He got word from town . . ."

She stopped listening. She felt as though she had been slapped to the extreme outer edge of life, into a cold darkness. She knew now what she had felt when she had looked up out of her fog of pain and had seen Booker. It was the image of all the white folks, and the fear that went with them, that she had seen and felt during her lifetime. And again, for the second time that night, something she had felt had come true. All she could say to herself was, Ah didnt like im! Gawd knows, Ah didnt! Ah tol Johnny-Boy it wuz some of them white folks . . .

"Here; drink yo cawffee . . ."

She took the cup; her fingers trembled, and the steaming liquid spilt onto her dress and leg.

"Ahm sorry, An Sue!"

Her leg was scalded, but the pain did not bother her.

"Its awright," she said.

"Wait; lemme put some lard on tha burn!"

"It don hurt."

"Yuh worried bout somethin."

"Naw, honey."

"Lemme fix yuh so mo cawffee."

"Ah don wan nothin now, Reva."

"Waal, buck up. Don be tha way . . ."

They were silent. She heard Reva drinking. No; she would not tell Reva; Reva was all she had left. But she had to do something, some way, somehow. She was undone too much as it was; and to tell Reva about Booker or Johnny-Boy was more than she was equal to; it would be too coldly shameful. She wanted to be alone and fight this thing out with herself.

"Go t bed, honey. Yuh tired."

"Naw; Ahm awright, An Sue."

She heard the bottom of Reva's empty cup clank against the top of the stove. Ah *got* t make her go t bed! Yes; Booker would tell the names of the comrades to the sheriff. If she could only stop him some way! That was the answer, the point, the star that grew bright in the morning of new hope. Soon, maybe half an hour from now, Booker would reach Foley's Woods. Hes boun t go the long way, cause he don know no short cut, she thought. Ah could wade the creek n beat im there. . . . But what would she do after that?

"Reva, honey, go t bed. Ahm awright. Yuh need res."

"Ah ain sleepy, An Sue."

"Ah knows whuts bes fer yuh, chile. Yuh tired n wet."

"Ah wanna stay up wid yuh."

She forced a smile and said:

"Ah don think they gonna hurt Johnny-Boy . . ."

"Fer *real*, An Sue?"

"Sho, honey."

"But Ah wanna wait up wid yuh."

"Thas mah job, honey. Thas whut a mas fer, t wait up fer her chullun."

"Good night, An Sue."

"Good night, honey."

She watched Reva pull up and leave the kitchen; presently she heard the shucks in the mattress whispering, and she knew that Reva had gone to bed. She was alone. Through the cracks of the stove she saw the fire dying to grey ashes; the room was growing cold again. The yellow beacon continued to flit past the window and the rain still drummed. Yes; she was alone; she had done this awful thing alone; she must find some way out, alone. Like touching a festering sore, she put her finger upon that moment when she had shouted her defiance to the sheriff, when she had shouted to feel her strength. She had lost Sug to save others; she had let Johnny-Boy go to save others; and then in a moment of weakness that came from too much strength she had lost all. If she had not shouted to the sheriff, she would have been strong enough to have resisted Booker; she would have been able to tell the comrades herself. Something tightened in her as she remembered and understood the fit of fear she had felt on coming to herself in the dark hallway. A part of her life she thought she had done away with forever had had hold of her then. She had thought the soft, warm past was over; she had thought that it did not mean much when now she sang: *"Hes the Lily of the Valley, the Bright n Mawnin Star"* . . . The days when she had sung that song were the days when she had not hoped for anything on this earth, the days when the cold mountain had driven her into the arms of Jesus. She had thought that Sug and Johnny-Boy had taught her to forget Him, to fix her hope upon the fight of black men for freedom. Through the gradual years she had believed and worked with them, had felt strength shed from the grace of their terrible vision. That grace had been upon her when she had let the sheriff slap her down; it had been upon her when she had risen time and again from the floor and faced him. But she had trapped herself with her own hunger; to water the long dry thirst of her faith her pride had made a bargain which her flesh could not keep. Her having told the names of Johnny-Boy's comrades was but an incident in a deeper horror. She stood up and looked at the floor while call and counter-call, loyalty and counter-loyalty struggled in her soul. Mired she was between two abandoned worlds, living, but dying without the strength of the grace that either gave. The clearer she felt it the fuller did something well up from the depths of her for release; the more urgent did she feel the need to fling into her black sky another star, another hope, one more terrible vision to give her the strength to live and act. Softly and restlessly she walked about the kitchen, feeling herself naked against the night, the rain, the world; and shamed whenever the

thought of Reva's love crossed her mind. She lifted her
empty hands and looked at her writhing fingers. Lawd,
whut kin Ah do now? She could still wade the creek and
get to Foley's Woods before Booker. And then what?
How could she manage to see Johnny-Boy or Booker?
Again she heard the sheriff's threatening voice: Git yuh
a sheet, cause hes gonna be dead! The sheet! Thas it, the
sheet! Her whole being leaped with will; the long years
of her life bent toward a moment of focus, a point. Ah
kin go wid mah sheet! Ahll be doin whut he said! Lawd
Gawd in Heaven, Ahma go lika nigger woman wid mah
windin sheet t git mah dead son! But then what? She
stood straight and smiled grimly; she had in her heart
the whole meaning of her life; her entire personality was
poised on the brink of a total act. Ah know! Ah *know*!
She thought of Johnny-Boy's gun in the dresser drawer.
Ahll hide the gun in the sheet n go aftah Johnny-Boys
body. . . . She tiptoed to her room, eased out the
dresser drawer, and got a sheet. Reva was sleeping; the
darkness was filled with her quiet breathing. She groped
in the drawer and found the gun. She wound the gun in
the sheet and held them both under her apron. Then she
stole to the bedside and watched Reva. Lawd, hep her!
But mabbe shes bettah off. This had t happen some-
times . . . She n Johnny-Boy couldna been together in
this here South . . . N Ah couldnt tell her bout Booker.
Itll come out awright n she wont nevah know. Reva's
trust would never be shaken. She caught her breath as
the shucks in the mattress rustled dryly; then all was
quiet and she breathed easily again. She tiptoed to the
door, down the hall, and stood on the porch. Above her
the yellow beacon whirled through the rain. She went
over muddy ground, mounted a slope, stopped and
looked back at her house. The lamp glowed in her win-
dow, and the yellow beacon that swung every few sec-

onds seemed to feed it with light. She turned and started across the fields, holding the gun and sheet tightly, thinking, Po Reva . . . Po critter . . . Shes fas ersleep . . .

VI

For the most part she walked with her eyes half shut, her lips tightly compressed, leaning her body against the wind and the driving rain, feeling the pistol in the sheet sagging cold and heavy in her fingers. Already she was getting wet; it seemed that her feet found every puddle of water that stood between the corn rows.

She came to the edge of the creek and paused, wondering at what point was it low. Taking the sheet from under her apron, she wrapped the gun in it so that her finger could be upon the trigger. Ahll cross here, she thought. At first she did not feel the water; her feet were already wet. But the water grew cold as it came up to her knees; she gasped when it reached her waist. Lawd, this creeks high! When she had passed the middle, she knew that she was out of danger. She came out of the water, climbed a grassy hill, walked on, turned a bend and saw the lights of autos gleaming ahead. Yeah; theys still there! She hurried with her head down. Wondah did Ah beat im here? Lawd, Ah *hope* so! A vivid image of Booker's white face hovered a moment before her eyes and a surging will rose up in her so hard and strong that it vanished. She was among the autos now. From nearby came the hoarse voices of the men.

"Hey, yuh!"

She stopped, nervously clutching the sheet. Two white men with shotguns came toward her.

"Whut in hell yuh doin out here?"

She did not answer.

"Didnt yuh hear somebody speak t yuh?"

"Ahm comin aftah mah son," she said humbly.

"Yo *son*?"

"Yessuh."

"Whut yo son doin out here?"

"The sheriffs got im."

"Holy Scott! Jim, its the niggers ma!"

"Whut yuh got there?" asked one.

"A sheet."

"A *sheet*?"

"Yessuh."

"Fer whut?"

"The sheriff tol me t bring a sheet t git his body."

"Waal, waal . . ."

"Now, ain tha somethin?"

The white men looked at each other.

"These niggers sho love one ernother," said one.

"N tha ain no lie," said the other.

"Take me t the sheriff," she begged.

"Yuh ain givin us *orders*, is yuh?"

"Nawsuh."

"We'll take yuh when wes good n ready."

"Yessuh."

"So yuh wan his body?"

"Yessuh."

"Waal, he ain dead yit."

"They gonna kill im," she said.

"Ef he talks they wont."

"He ain gonna talk," she said.

"How yuh know?"

"Cause he ain."

"We got ways of makin niggers talk."

"Yuh ain got no way fer im."

"Yuh thinka lot of that black Red, don yuh?"

"Hes mah son."

"Why don yuh teach im some sense?"

"Hes mah son," she said again.

"Lissen, ol nigger woman, yuh stand there wid yo hair white. Yuh got bettah sense than t blieve tha niggers kin make a revolution . . ."

"A black republic," said the other one, laughing.

"Take me t the sheriff," she begged.

"Yuh his ma," said one. "Yuh kin make im talk n tell whos in this thing wid im."

"He ain gonna talk," she said.

"Don yuh wan im t live?"

She did not answer.

"C mon, les take her t Bradley."

They grabbed her arms and she clutched hard at the sheet and gun; they led her toward the crowd in the woods. Her feelings were simple; Booker would not tell; she was there with the gun to see to that. The louder became the voices of the men the deeper became her feeling of wanting to right the mistake she had made; of wanting to fight her way back to solid ground. She would stall for time until Booker showed up. Oh, ef theyll only lemme git close t Johnny-Boy! As they led her near the crowd she saw white faces turning and looking at her and heard a rising clamor of voices.

"Whos tha?"

"A nigger woman!"

"Whut she doin out here?"

"This is his ma!" called one of the men.

"Whut she wans?"

"She brought a sheet t cover his body!"

"He ain dead yit!"

"They tryin t make im talk!"

"But he will be dead soon ef he don open up!"

"Say, look! The niggers ma brought a sheet t cover up his body!"

"Now, ain that sweet?"

"Mabbe she wans t hol a prayer meetin!"

"Did she git a preacher?"

"Say, go git Bradley!"

"O.K.!"

The crowd grew quiet. They looked at her curiously; she felt their cold eyes trying to detect some weakness in her. Humbly, she stood with the sheet covering the gun. She had already accepted all that they could do to her.

The sheriff came.

"So yuh brought yo sheet, hunh?"

"Yessuh," she whispered.

"Looks like them slaps we gave yuh learned yuh some sense, didnt they?"

She did not answer.

"Yuh don need tha sheet. Yo son ain dead yit," he said, reaching toward her.

She backed away, her eyes wide.

"Naw!"

"Now, lissen, Anty!" he said. "There ain no use in yuh ackin a fool! Go in there n tell tha nigger son of yos t tell us whos in this wid im, see? Ah promise we wont kill im ef he talks. We'll let im git outta town."

"There ain nothin Ah kin tell im," she said.

"Yuh wan us t kill im?"

She did not answer. She saw someone lean toward the sheriff and whisper.

"Bring her erlong," the sheriff said.

They led her to a muddy clearing. The rain streamed down through the ghostly glare of the flashlights. As the men formed a semi-circle she saw Johnny-Boy lying in a trough of mud. He was tied with rope; he lay hunched and one side of his face rested in a pool of black water. His eyes were staring questioningly at her.

"Speak t im," said the sheriff.

If she could only tell him why she was here! But that was impossible; she was close to what she wanted and she stared straight before her with compressed lips.

"Say, nigger!" called the sheriff, kicking Johnny-Boy. "Heres yo ma!"

Johnny-Boy did not move or speak. The sheriff faced her again.

"Lissen, Anty," he said. "Yuh got mo say wid im than anybody. Tell im t talk n hava chance. Whut he wanna pertect the other niggers n white folks fer?"

She slid her finger about the trigger of the gun and looked stonily at the mud.

"Go t him," said the sheriff.

She did not move. Her heart was crying out to answer the amazed question in Johnny-Boy's eyes. But there was no way now.

"Waal, yuhre astin fer it. By Gawd, we gotta way to *make* yuh talk t im," he said, turning away. "Say, Tim, git one of them logs n turn that nigger upside-down n put his legs on it!"

A murmur of assent ran through the crowd. She bit her lips; she knew what that meant.

"Yuh wan yo nigger son crippled?" she heard the sheriff ask.

She did not answer. She saw them roll the log up; they lifted Johnny-Boy and laid him on his face and stomach, then they pulled his legs over the log. His knee-caps rested on the sheer top of the log's back and the toes of his shoes pointed groundward. So absorbed was she in watching that she felt that it was she who was being lifted and made ready for torture.

"Git a crowbar!" said the sheriff.

A tall, lank man got a crowbar from a nearby auto and stood over the log. His jaws worked slowly on a wad of tobacco.

"Now, its up t yuh, Anty," the sheriff said. "Tell the man whut t do!"

She looked into the rain. The sheriff turned.

"Mabbe she think wes playin. Ef she don say nothin, then break em at the knee-caps!"

"O.K., Sheriff!"

She stood waiting for Booker. Her legs felt weak; she wondered if she would be able to wait much longer. Over and over she said to herself, Ef he came now Ahd kill em both!

"She ain sayin nothin, Sheriff!"

"Waal, Gawddammit, let im have it!"

The crowbar came down and Johnny-Boy's body lunged in the mud and water. There was a scream. She swayed, holding tight to the gun and sheet.

"Hol im! Git the other leg!"

The crowbar fell again. There was another scream.

"Yuh break em?" asked the sheriff.

The tall man lifted Johnny-Boy's legs and let them drop limply again, dropping rearward from the knee-caps. Johnny-Boy's body lay still. His head had rolled to one side and she could not see his face.

"Jus lika broke sparrow wing," said the man, laughing softly.

Then Johnny-Boy's face turned to her; he screamed.

"Go way, ma! Go way!"

It was the first time she had heard his voice since she had come out to the woods; she all but lost control of herself. She started violently forward, but the sheriff's arm checked her.

"Aw, naw! Yuh had yo chance!" He turned to Johnny-Boy. "She kin go ef yuh talk."

"Mistah, he ain gonna talk," she said.

"Go way, ma!" said Johnny-Boy.

"Shoot im! Don make im suffah so," she begged.

"He'll either talk or he'll never hear yuh ergin," the sheriff said. "Theres other things we kin do t im."

She said nothing.

"What yuh come here fer, ma?" Johnny-Boy sobbed.

"Ahm gonna split his eardrums," the sheriff said. "Ef yuh got anythin t say t im yuh bettah say it *now*!"

She closed her eyes. She heard the sheriff's feet sucking in mud. Ah could save im! She opened her eyes; there were shouts of eagerness from the crowd as it pushed in closer.

"Bus em, Sheriff!"

"Fix im so he cant hear!"

"He knows how t do it, too!"

"He busted a Jew boy tha way once!"

She saw the sheriff stoop over Johnny-Boy, place his flat palm over one ear and strike his fist against it with all his might. He placed his palm over the other ear and struck again. Johnny-Boy moaned, his head rolling from side to side, his eyes showing white amazement in a world without sound.

"Yuh wouldnt talk t im when yuh had the chance," said the sheriff. "Try n talk now."

She felt warm tears on her cheeks. She longed to shoot Johnny-Boy and let him go. But if she did that they would take the gun from her, and Booker would tell who the others were. Lawd, hep me! The men were talking loudly now, as though the main business was over. It seemed ages that she stood there watching Johnny-Boy roll and whimper in his world of silence.

"Say, Sheriff, heres somebody lookin fer yuh!"

"Who is it?"

"Ah don know!"

"Bring em in!"

She stiffened and looked around wildly, holding the gun tight. Is tha Booker? Then she held still, feeling that her excitement might betray her. Mabbe Ah kin shoot em both! Mabbe Ah kin shoot *twice*! The sheriff stood in front of her, waiting. The crowd parted and she saw Booker hurrying forward.

"Ah know em all, Sheriff!" he called.

He came full into the muddy clearing where Johnny-Boy lay.

"Yuh mean yuh got the names?"

"Sho! The ol nigger . . ."

She saw his lips hang open and silent when he saw her. She stepped forward and raised the sheet.

"Whut . . ."

She fired, once; then, without pausing, she turned, hearing them yell. She aimed at Johnny-Boy, but they had their arms around her, bearing her to the ground, clawing at the sheet in her hand. She glimpsed Booker lying sprawled in the mud, on his face, his hands stretched out before him; then a cluster of yelling men blotted him out. She lay without struggling, looking upward through the rain at the white faces above her. And she was suddenly at peace; they were not a white mountain now; they were not pushing her any longer to the edge of life. Its awright . . .

"She shot Booker!"

"She hada gun in the sheet!"

"She shot im right thu the head!"

"Whut she shoot im fer?"

"Kill the bitch!"

"Ah *thought* somethin wuz wrong bout her!"

"Ah wuz fer givin it t her from the firs!"

"Thas whut yuh git fer treatin a nigger nice!"

"Say, Bookers dead!"

She stopped looking into the white faces, stopped listening. She waited, giving up her life before they took it from her; she had done what she wanted. Ef only

Johnny-Boy . . . She looked at him; he lay looking at her with tired eyes. Ef she could only tell im! But he lay already buried in a grave of silence.

"Whut yuh kill im fer, hunh?"

It was the sheriff's voice; she did not answer.

"Mabbe she wuz shootin at yuh, Sheriff?"

"Whut yuh kill im fer?"

She felt the sheriff's foot come into her side; she closed her eyes.

"Yuh black bitch!"

"Let her have it!"

"Yuh reckon she foun out bout Booker?"

"She mighta."

"Jesus Chris, whut yuh dummies *waitin* on!"

"Yeah; kill her!"

"Kill em *both*!"

"Let her know her nigger sons dead firs!"

She turned her head toward Johnny-Boy; he lay looking puzzled in a world beyond the reach of voices. At leas he cant hear, she thought.

"C mon, let im have it!"

She listened to hear what Johnny-Boy could not. They came, two of them, one right behind the other; so close together that they sounded like one shot. She did not look at Johnny-Boy now; she looked at the white faces of the men, hard and wet in the glare of the flashlights.

"Yuh hear tha, nigger woman?"

"Did tha surprise im? Hes in hell now wonderin whut hit im!"

"C mon! Give it t her, Sheriff!"

"Lemme shoot her, Sheriff! It wuz mah pal she shot!"

"Awright, Pete! Thas fair ernuff!"

She gave up as much of her life as she could before

they took it from her. But the sound of the shot and the streak of fire that tore its way through her chest forced her to live again, intensely. She had not moved, save for the slight jarring impact of the bullet. She felt the heat of her own blood warming her cold, wet back. She yearned suddenly to talk. "Yuh didnt git whut yuh wanted! N yuh ain gonna nevah git it! Yuh didnt kill me; Ah come here by mahsef . . ." She felt rain falling into her wide-open, dimming eyes and heard faint voices. Her lips moved soundlessly. *Yuh didnt git yuh didnt yuh didnt* . . . Focused and pointed she was, buried in the depths of her star, swallowed in its peace and strength; and not feeling her flesh growing cold, cold as the rain that fell from the invisible sky upon the doomed living and the dead that never dies.

Note on the Text

This volume presents a collection of stories by Richard Wright. All were completed between 1936 and 1940. The texts of the five stories and one essay in *Uncle Tom's Children* are from their first collected appearance, and these texts are the last, or last-known, versions that Wright approved. A great deal of material pertaining to the publication of this work, including typescripts, page proofs, and correspondence between Wright and his publishers, is contained in the James Weldon Johnson Collection of the Beinecke Library at Yale University. Other significant materials are held in the Fales Collection of the New York University Library and the Firestone Library at Princeton University.

Uncle Tom's Children was Wright's first book to be published. Issued by Harper and Brothers in 1938 as a Story Press Book, it contained four stories, two of which had been published previously: "Big Boy Leaves Home" in *The New Caravan* in 1936; and "Fire and Cloud" in the March 1938 *Story Magazine*. The other two stories—"Long Black Song" and "Down by the Riverside"—appeared for the first time in the Harper collection in 1938. Wright had entered the stories in a contest for members of the Federal Writers' Project sponsored by *Story Magazine*, and "Fire and Cloud" won the first prize of $500. Collation of the periodical texts of the two previously published stories with the book publication reveals a number of differences, and the extant typescripts and proofs for *Story Magazine* reveal that the book publication of "Fire and Cloud" follows the typescript rather than the periodical version. In addition, the correspondence between Wright and Edward Aswell, his editor at Harper and Brothers, shows that Wright oversaw the production of the book collection in each of its stages—from assembling the manuscript to reading proofs. Therefore the text of these four stories presented in this volume is that of the first book printing, published by Harper and Brothers in 1938.

Wright sent a fifth story, "Bright and Morning Star," in January 1938 for inclusion in the first edition of *Uncle Tom's Children*, but Harper and Brothers rejected it. The story was first published in a literary supplement to the May 10, 1938, issue of *New Masses* and was later collected in Edward O'Brien's *Best Short Stories of 1939* and in *The Fifty Best American Short Stories 1914–1939*. In 1940 Wright arranged for a second printing of *Uncle Tom's Children* and offered to pay the costs of including "Bright and Morning Star" and his essay "The Ethics of Living Jim Crow," which had first appeared in *American Stuff: WPA Writers' Anthology*, published by Viking in 1937. Harper and Brothers absorbed the costs of including the new pieces, and correspondence between Wright and Aswell shows that Wright read and corrected proofs for the two additions. The second printing of *Uncle Tom's Children* in 1940 used the 1938 plates for the first four stories and new plates for the additional two parts. The texts of "Bright and Morning Star" and "The Ethics of Living Jim Crow" presented in this volume are those published in the expanded second printing of *Uncle Tom's Children*, published by Harper and Brothers in 1940.

This volume presents the texts of the original edition or typescripts chosen for inclusion; it does not attempt to reproduce features of the typographic design, such as the display capitalization of chapter openings. The text is reproduced without change, except for the correction of typographical errors. Spelling, punctuation, and capitalization often are expressive features and they are not altered, even when inconsistent or irregular. The following is a list of the typographical errors corrected, cited by page and line number: 49.35, trou; 90.24, says; 90.24, boys; 109.17, Ahll; 139.26, mantle; 141.31, mantle; 143.28, mantle; 144.12, Eh; 148.24, cried; 180.29, "There; 191.3, gonan; 204.18, days; 218.1, though; 226.23, chile; 231.14, mucha like; 240.17, Gut; 249.17–18, on way; 259.29, sheriffs.

Notes

In the notes below, the reference numbers denote page and line of this volume (the line count includes chapter headings). No note is made for information available in standard desk-reference books such as *Webster's Collegiate* and *Webster's Biographical* dictionaries. Footnotes in the text are Wright's own. For more biographical background than is included in the Chronology, see: Michel Fabre, *The Unfinished Quest of Richard Wright*, translated from the French by Isabel Barzun (New York: William Morrow & Company, Inc., 1973); Addison Gayle, *Richard Wright: Ordeal of a Native Son* (Garden City, New York: Anchor Books/Doubleday, 1980); Constance Webb, *Richard Wright: A Biography* (New York: G. P. Putnam's Sons, 1968). For references to works by Wright and to other studies, see: Charles T. Davis and Michel Fabre, *Richard Wright: a primary bibliography* (Boston: G. K. Hall & Co., 1982); Keneth Kinnamon, *A Richard Wright Bibliography: Fifty Years of Criticism and Commentary, 1933–1982* (Westport, Connecticut: Greenwood Press, 1988); and "Introduction" to *New Essays on Native Son*, edited by Keneth Kinnamon (Cambridge and New York: Cambridge University Press, 1990).

14.31–32   13th . . . Constitution] The Thirteenth Amendment, proposed to the states by Congress and ratified in 1865, prohibited slavery throughout the United States. The Fourteenth Amendment, proposed to the states in 1866 and ratified in 1868, granted national and state citizenship to all persons born or naturalized in the United States. It prohibited states from making or enforcing laws that abridged "the privileges or immunities of citizens of the United States," deprived "any person of life, liberty, or property, without due process of law," or denied "any person . . . the equal protection of the laws." Further clauses made denial of the right to vote grounds for reapportioning the House of Representatives, specified the classes of former Confederates disqualified from holding government office, and protected the validity of the public debt while repudiating all debts incurred by the Confederacy and all claims for the loss or emancipation of slaves. Although the citizenship, due process, and equal protection clauses had been intended to protect newly freed blacks against discriminatory state legislation, a series of Supreme Court decisions culminating in *Plessy* v. *Ferguson* in 1896, which declared "separate but equal" segregation constitutional, made it increasingly difficult to argue civil rights cases on Fourteenth Amendment grounds.

16.1–9   *Is it true* . . . Song.]   Song (1936) composed by Gerald Marks, lyrics by Irving Caesar and Sammy Lerner.

19.7–22   *Dis train* . . . *train* . . .]   "This Train," an African-American spiritual.

54.14   *"We'll* . . . *tree* . . ."]   A parody of "They will hang Jeff Davis from a sour apple tree," a line from "John Brown's Body." The original words were written by Union soldiers in 1861, and the eponymous hero was Sergeant John Brown of the 2nd Battalion, Boston Light Infantry, a member of the battalion choral society that first performed the song, setting it to the tune of a familiar hymn, "Say, Brothers, Will You Meet Us" ("Battle Hymn of the Republic" by Julia Ward Howe, published in 1862, was set to the same music). It became a popular Union marching tune, quickly evolving into a song about the abolitionist John Brown (1800–59).

62.2   *Down* . . . *Riverside*]   In this story, Wright perhaps draws on accounts of the great Mississippi River flood of 1927, when the Mississippi overflowed its banks from Arkansas in the north to the Gulf of Mexico. In spite of often heroic efforts by local authorities, the flood devastated the region and left thousands homeless.

73.1–13   *Ahm gonna* . . . *no mo* . . .]   From the popular hymn "Down by the Riverside."

132.21–133.7   *When* . . . *be there* . . .]   From the hymn "When the Roll Is Called Up Yonder," by J. M. Black.

218.27–31   *"So* . . . *way* . . ."]   From an old hymn. Cf. Exodus 40:38.

222.14–15   *Hes* . . . *soul*]   From "The Lily of the Valley," a Protestant hymn. See Song of Solomon 2:1 and 5:10, and Revelation 22:16.

224.6–7   *He walks* . . . *own* . . . .]   From the hymn "In the Garden," by C. Austin Miles.

About the author

About the book

Read on

Insights,
Interviews
& More . . .

A Chronology of Richard Wright

The Granger Collection, New York

1908

Born Richard Nathaniel Wright, September 4, on
Rucker's Plantation, a farm near Roxie, Mississippi,
22 miles east of Natchez, first child of Nathan Wright,
an illiterate sharecropper, and Ella Wilson Wright, a
schoolteacher. (All four grandparents had been born
in slavery. Father was born shortly before 1880, the
son of Nathaniel Wright, a freed slave who farmed
a plot of land he had been given at the end of the
Civil War. Maternal grandfather, Richard Wilson,
born March 21, 1847, served in the United States
Navy in 1865, then became disillusioned because
of a bureaucratic error that deprived him of his
pension. Maternal grandmother, Margaret Bolton
Wilson, of Irish, Scottish, American Indian, and
African descent, was virtually white in appearance.
A house slave before the Emancipation, she later
became a midwife nurse, a devoted Seventh-Day
Adventist, and the strict head of her Natchez
household, which included eight surviving children.
Mother, born 1883, married Nathan Wright in 1907
despite her parents' disapproval, and then gave up
school teaching to work on the farm.)

1910

Brother Leon Alan, called Alan, born September 24.

1911–12

Unable to care for her children while working on the farm, mother takes Wright and his brother to live with Wilson family in Natchez. Father rejoins family and finds work in a sawmill. Wright accidentally sets fire to grandparents' house.

1913–14

Family moves to Memphis, Tennessee, by steamboat. Father deserts family to live with another woman, leaving them impoverished. Mother finds work as a cook.

1915–16

Wright enters school at Howe Institute, Memphis, in September 1915. Mother falls seriously ill in early 1916. Grandmother comes to care for family. After grandmother returns home, mother puts Wright and his brother in the Settlement House, Methodist orphanage in Memphis, where they stay for over a month. Spends relatively pleasant summer at 1107 Lynch Street in Jackson, Mississippi, where maternal grandparents now live, before going with mother and brother to Elaine, Arkansas, to live with his favorite aunt, Maggie (his mother's younger sister), and her husband, Silas Hoskins, a saloonkeeper.

1917–18

After Hoskins is murdered by whites who want his prosperous liquor business, terrified family flees to West Helena, Arkansas, then returns to Jackson with Aunt Maggie to live with the Wilsons. After several months they go back to West Helena, where mother and aunt find work cooking and cleaning for whites. Aunt Maggie leaves with her lover, "Professor" Matthews, a fugitive from the law (they eventually settle in Detroit).

1918–19

Wright enters local school in fall 1918. Mother's health deteriorates early in 1919 and Wright is forced to leave school to earn money. Delivers wood and laundry and carries lunches to railroad workers. Family moves frequently because of lack of rent money; Wright gathers stray pieces of coal along railroad tracks to heat their home. Mother suffers paralyzing stroke, and grandmother comes to bring the family back to Jackson. Aunt Maggie helps care for mother, then takes Leon Alan back to Detroit with her; other aunts and uncles help pay for mother's treatment. ▶

A Chronology of Richard Wright *(continued)*

1919–20

Wright moves into home of aunt and uncle, Clark and Jody Wilson, in nearby Greenwood, Mississippi, where he is able to attend school. Finds household calm and orderly but his aunt and uncle cold and unsympathetic, and is terrified by episodes of sleepwalking. Returns to grandparents' home in Jackson. Mother begins to show signs of recovery from paralysis, then has relapse caused by a cerebral blood clot that leaves her virtually crippled. Her illness impoverishes the family, already hurt by the rheumatism that makes Grandfather Wilson unable to work.

1920–21

Enters Seventh-Day Adventist school taught by his youngest aunt, Addie. Only nine years older than Wright, she is a rigid disciplinarian often at odds with him. Wright rebels against the rules and practices of the religion, including its diet, which forbids eating pork. Finds himself opposed to his family in general, except for his mother, who is too sick to help him.

1921–22

Enters the fifth grade of the Jim Hill School in Jackson, two years behind his age group. Does well, quickly gains in confidence, and is soon promoted to the sixth grade. Begins friendships, some of them lasting into his adulthood, with a number of other students, including Dick Jordan, Joe Brown, Perry Booker, D. C. Blackburn, Lewis Anderson, Sarah McNeamer, and Essie Lee Ward. Takes job as a newsboy, which gives him the chance to read material forbidden at home because of religious prohibitions. Family life continues to be difficult, although his mother's health improves slightly. Travels briefly during summer in the Mississippi Delta region as "secretary-accountant" to an insurance agent, W. Mance. The trip allows him to know better the rural South, but he is dismayed by the illiteracy and lack of education he encounters among blacks.

1922–23

Enters the seventh grade. Grandfather Wilson dies November 8. After many arguments, grandmother reluctantly lets Wright take jobs after school and on Saturday (the Seventh-Day Adventist sabbath). Runs errands and performs small chores, mainly for whites. For the first time has enough money to buy school books, food to combat his chronic hunger, and clothing. Baptized in the Methodist Church, mainly to please his mother. Avidly reads pulp magazines, dime novels, and books and magazines discarded by others. Uncle Thomas Wilson, his wife, and their two daughters come to live with the family in spring 1923. Mother's health worsens. Wright works during the summer at a brickyard and as a caddy at a golf course.

1923–24

Enters eighth grade at the Smith Robertson Junior High School, Jackson (a former slave, Smith Robertson had become a successful local barber and a community leader; the school, built in 1894, was the first black institution of its kind in Jackson). Until he can afford a bicycle, Wright walks several miles daily to and from the school. Makes new friends at school, including Wade Griffin, Varnie Reed, Arthur Leaner, and Minnie Farish. Begins working for the Walls, a white family he finds kindly (will serve them for two years). Later remembers writing his first short story, "The Voodoo of Hell's Half-Acre," in late winter (story is reported to have been published in the spring as "Hell's Half-Acre" in the Jackson *Southern Register*, a black weekly newspaper; no copies are known to be extant). Brother Leon Alan returns from Detroit. Wright is initially pleased, but their relationship soon disappoints him. Works for the American Optical Company, cleaning workshop and making deliveries.

1924–25

Enters ninth grade at Smith Robertson Junior High School, and graduates on May 29, 1925, as valedictorian. Rejects graduation speech prepared for him by the principal and instead delivers his own, "The Attributes of Life." Works as a delivery boy, sales clerk, hotel hallboy and bellboy, and in a movie theater. Begins classes in fall at newly founded Lanier High School, but quits a few weeks later to earn money. Leaves Jackson for Memphis, Tennessee, where he boards with a family at 570 Beale Street.

1926

Works for low pay as a dishwasher and delivery boy and at the Merry Optical Company. Reads widely in *Harper's*, *Atlantic Monthly*, *The American Mercury*, and other magazines. Moves to 875 Griffith Place. ▶

A Chronology of Richard Wright (*continued*)

1927

Joined by mother, who is still in poor health, and brother; they take an apartment together at 370 Washington Street. After reading an editorial highly critical of H. L. Mencken, long noted as a critic of the white South, Wright seeks out Mencken's *Prejudices* and *A Book of Prefaces* and is particularly impressed by Mencken's iconoclasm and use of "words as weapons." These books serve as guides to further reading, including works by Theodore Dreiser, Sinclair Lewis, Sherwood Anderson, the elder Alexandre Dumas, Frank Harris, and O. Henry. Aunt Maggie, who has been deserted by "Professor" Matthews, joins family in the fall. In December, Wright and Maggie, who hopes to open a beauty salon, move to the South Side of Chicago, while mother and Leon Alan return to Jackson. Sees his aunt Cleopatra ("Sissy"), but is disappointed to find that she lives in a rooming house, not an apartment, and moves into a rooming house with Aunt Maggie.

1928

Works as delivery boy in a delicatessen, then as a dishwasher. Wright finds Chicago stimulating and less racially oppressive than the South, but is often dismayed by the pace and disarray of urban life. Passes written examination for the postal service in the spring, then begins work in the summer as a temporary employee at 65 cents an hour. Rents an apartment with Aunt Maggie and is joined by mother and brother. In the fall Wright fails the postal service medical examination required for a permanent position because of chronic undernourishment and returns to dishwashing. Disputes over money and his reading cause tension with Aunt Maggie. Wright takes another apartment for family and invites his aunt Cleopatra to move in with them.

1929

After undertaking a crash diet to increase his weight, Wright passes the physical examination and is hired by the central post office at Clark Street and Jackson Boulevard as a substitute clerk and mail sorter. Moves with family to four rooms at 4831 Vincennes Avenue, which allows him to read and write in relative comfort. Dislikes the post office bureaucracy, but becomes friendly with many fellow workers, both black and white. Among his friends are schoolmates from the South, including Essie Lee Ward, Arthur

Leaner, and Joe Brown. Writes steadily and attends meetings of a local black literary group, but feels distant from its middle-class members. Attracted by the Universal Negro Improvement Association, a group inspired by Marcus Garvey, but does not join it.

1930

Volume of mail drops in decline following the 1929 Wall Street crash; Wright has his working hours cut back before losing his job altogether. South Side sinks into economic depression. Works temporarily for post office in the summer. Mother suffers a relapse, aunt Cleopatra has a heart attack, and brother develops stomach ulcers. Begins work on *Cesspool*, novel about black life in Chicago. Enrolls in tenth grade at Hyde Park Public School, but soon drops out.

1931

Reads books recommended by friend William Harper (who will later own a bookstore on the South Side). Wright is particularly impressed by Dreiser and Joseph Conrad, and continues to write. Short story "Superstition" is published in April *Abbott's Monthly Magazine*, a black journal (magazine fails before Wright is paid). Through a distant relative, finds job as a funeral insurance agent for several burial societies. Also works as an assistant to a black Republican precinct captain during the mayoral campaign, and at the post office in December. Becomes interested in views of Communist orators and organizers, especially those in the League of Struggle for Negro Rights.

1932

Sells insurance policies door-to-door and works briefly as an assistant to a Democratic precinct captain. Family moves to slum apartment as Wright is increasingly unable to sell policies to blacks impoverished by the Depression. Asks for and receives relief assistance from the Cook County Bureau of Public Welfare, which finds him a temporary job as a street cleaner. Works at the post office during the Christmas season.

1933

Digs ditches in the Cook County Forest Preserves, then works at Michael Reese Hospital, caring for animals used in medical research. Recruited by ▶

A Chronology of Richard Wright *(continued)*

fellow post office worker Abraham Aaron to join the
newly formed Chicago branch of the John Reed Club,
a national literary organization sponsored by the
Communist party. Welcomed and encouraged by
the almost entirely white membership of the club,
Wright begins to read and study *New Masses*
and *International Literature*, the organ of the
International League of Revolutionary Writers.
Writes and submits revolutionary poems ("I Have
Seen Black Hands," "A Red Love Note") to *Left Front*,
the magazine of the midwestern John Reed Clubs.
Elected executive secretary of the Chicago John Reed
Club and organizes a successful lecture series which
allows him to meet a variety of intellectuals. Gives
lecture at open forum on "The Literature of the
Negro."

1934

Hoping to consolidate his position in the John Reed
Club, Wright joins the Communist party; is also
impressed by the party's opposition to racial
discrimination. Publishes poetry in *Left Front*,
Anvil, and *New Masses*. Becomes a member of
the editorial board of *Left Front*. Enjoys literary
and social friendships with Bill Jordan, Abraham
Chapman, Howard Nutt, Laurence Lipton,
Nelson Algren, Joyce Gourfain, and Jane Newton.
Grandmother Wilson comes to Chicago to join the
family; they move to apartment at 4804 St. Lawrence
Avenue, near the railroad tracks. Mother's paralysis
returns after attack of encephalitis. Wright is laid off
by the hospital in the summer, and again works as a
street sweeper and ditch digger before being hired to
supervise a youth club organized to counter juvenile
delinquency among blacks on the South Side. Attends
Middle West Writers' Congress in August and the
national congress of John Reed Clubs in September.
Dismayed by party decision to cease publication of
Left Front and to dissolve the John Reed Clubs in
1935 as part of its Popular Front strategy. Meets Jack
Conroy, editor of *Anvil*. Reading in Chicago by this
time includes Henry James (especially the Prefaces to
the New York Edition), Gertrude Stein (notably her
Three Lives, with its portrait of a black character,
Melanctha Herbert), Faulkner, T. S. Eliot, Sherwood
Anderson, Dos Passos, O'Neill, Stephen Crane,
Dreiser, Whitman, Poe, D. H. Lawrence, Conrad,
Galsworthy, Hardy, Dickens, George Moore, Carlyle,

Swift, Shakespeare, Tolstoy, Dostoevsky, Turgenev, Chekhov, Proust, Dumas, and Balzac. Lectures on the career of Langston Hughes to the Indianapolis John Reed Club in November and contributes fee to new publication *Midland Left*.

1935

Publishes leftist poetry in *Midland Left*, a short-lived journal, *New Masses* ("Red Leaves of Red Books" and "Spread Your Sunshine"), and *International Literature* ("A Red Slogan"). Family moves to 2636 Grove Avenue. Begins submitting novel *Cesspool* to publishers (later retitled *Lawd Today!* by Wright; it is rejected repeatedly over the next two years, then published posthumously as *Lawd Today* in 1963 by Walker and Company). Wright attends the first American Writers' Congress, held in New York in April. Speaks on "The Isolation of the Negro Writer," meets Chicago novelist James T. Farrell, and becomes one of fifty members of the national council of the newly formed League of American Writers. Works on story "Big Boy Leaves Home." Publishes "Between the World and Me," poem about lynching, in July–August *Partisan Review*. Falls seriously ill with attack of pneumonia during the summer. Article "Avant-Garde Writing" wins second prize in contest sponsored by two literary magazines but is never published. First piece of journalism, "Joe Louis Uncovers Dynamite," describing the reaction of Chicago blacks to the Louis-Max Baer fight, published in *New Masses*. Grandmother Wilson dies. Family, with Wright still virtually its sole support, moves to 3743 Indiana Avenue. Wright is hired by the Federal Writers' Project (part of the Works Progress Administration) to help research the history of Illinois and of the Negro in Chicago for the Illinois volume in the American Guide Series. Discusses influence of Hemingway with fellow writers in federal project.

1936

Publishes "Transcontinental," a six-page radical poem influenced by Whitman and Louis Aragon, in January *International Literature*. Becomes a principal organizer of the Communist party–sponsored National Negro Congress (successor to the League of Struggle for Negro Rights), held in Chicago in February, and reports on it for *New Masses*. Transferred in spring to the Federal ▶

A Chronology of Richard Wright *(continued)*

Theatre Project, where he serves as literary adviser and press agent for the Negro Federal Theatre of Chicago and becomes involved in dramatic productions. Finishes two one-act plays based in part on a section of his unpublished novel. In April, Wright takes a leading role in the new South Side Writers' Group (members will include Arna Bontemps, Frank Marshall Davis, Theodore Ward, Fenton Johnson, Horace Cayton, and Margaret Walker). Takes an active role in the Middle West Writers' Congress, held in Chicago June 14–15. Because of what he later describes as a Communist plot against him on the Federal Theatre Project assignment, Wright returns to the Writers' Project, where he becomes a group coordinator. Story "Big Boy Leaves Home" appears in anthology *The New Caravan* in November and receives critical attention and praise in mainstream newspapers and journals.

1937

Publishes poem "We of the Streets" in April *New Masses* and story "Silt" in the August number. Breaks with the Communist party in Chicago, basically over the question of his freedom as a writer. Brother finds job with the Works Progress Administration and assumes some responsibility for support of the family. Wright ranks first in postal service examination in Chicago, but turns down offer in May of permanent position at approximately $2,000 a year in order to move to New York City to pursue career as a writer. Stays briefly with artist acquaintances in Greenwich Village, then moves to Harlem; by mid-June he has a furnished room in the Douglass Hotel at 809 St. Nicholas Avenue. Attends Second American Writers' Congress as a delegate and serves as a session president; stresses the need for writers to think of themselves as writers first and not as laborers. Becomes Harlem editor of the Communist newspaper *Daily Worker* and writes over 200 articles for it during the year, including pieces on blues singer Leadbelly and the continuing Scottsboro Boys controversy. With Dorothy West and Marian Minus, helps launch magazine *New Challenge*, designed to present black life "in relationship to the struggle against war and Fascism." Wright publishes "The Ethics of Living Jim Crow—An Autobiographical Sketch" in *American Stuff: WPA Writers' Anthology* (essay is later included in the second edition of *Uncle Tom's Children* and incorporated into *Black Boy*). In November, publishes influential essay "Blueprint for Negro Writing" in *New Challenge*, criticizing past black literature and urging a Marxist-influenced approach that would transcend nationalism. Lacking party support, *New Challenge* fails after one number. Befriends 23-year-old Ralph Ellison. Wright's second novel, *Tarbaby's Dawn*, about a black adolescent in the South, is rejected by publishers (it remains unpublished). Learns that story "Fire and Cloud" has won first prize ($500) among 600 entries in *Story Magazine* contest. Wright joins the New York Federal Writers' Project (will write the Harlem section for *New York Panorama* and work on "The Harlems" in *The New York City Guide*).

1938

Rents furnished room at 139 West 143rd Street. Engages Paul Reynolds, Jr., as literary agent. Reynolds makes arrangements to place *Uncle Tom's Children: Four Novellas* ("Big Boy Leaves Home," "Down by the Riverside," "Long Black Song," and "Fire and Cloud") with editor Edward Aswell at Harper and Brothers, beginning Wright's long association with Aswell and Harper; book is published in March and is widely praised. Sends Aswell outline of novel about a black youth in Chicago. Announces plans to marry daughter of his Harlem landlady in May, but then cancels wedding, telling friends that a medical examination had revealed that the young woman has congenital syphilis. Moves into home of friends from Chicago, Jane and Herbert Newton, at 175 Carleton Avenue in Brooklyn. Story "Bright and Morning Star" appears in May *New Masses*. Writes about the second Joe Louis–Max Schmeling fight in the June *Daily Worker* and July *New Masses*. In June, replaces Horace Gregory on the editorial board of the literature section of *New Masses*. Works steadily on new novel; often writes in Fort Greene Park in the mornings, and discusses his progress with Jane Newton. Asks Margaret Walker to send him newspaper accounts of the case of Robert Nixon, a young Chicago black man accused of murder (executed in August 1939). Moves in the fall with the Newtons to 522 Gates Avenue. Congressman Martin Dies, chairman of the House Special Committee on Un-American Activities, denounces "The Ethics of ▶

Living Jim Crow" during an investigation of the
Federal Writers' Project. Finishes first draft of novel,
now titled *Native Son*, in October and receives $400
advance from Harper in November. "Fire and Cloud"
wins the O. Henry Memorial Award ($200). Travels to
Chicago in November to research settings and events
used in *Native Son*. Moves with Newtons to 87
Lefferts Place.

1939
Meets Ellen Poplar (b. 1912), daughter of Polish
Jewish immigrants and a Communist party organizer
in Brooklyn. Completes revised version of novel
in February and shows it to Reynolds. Awarded
Guggenheim Fellowship ($2,500) in March and
resigns from the Federal Writers' Project in May.
Discusses black American writing with Langston
Hughes, Alain Locke, Countee Cullen, and Warren
Cochrane during meeting of Harlem Cultural
Congress. After Newtons' landlord evicts them,
Wright moves to Douglass Hotel at 809 St. Nicholas
Avenue in May, renting room next to Theodore Ward,
a friend from Chicago. Becomes close to Ellen Poplar
and considers marrying her, but also sees Dhima Rose
Meadman, a modern-dance teacher of Russian Jewish
ancestry. Plays active role at Third American Writers'
Congress. Finishes *Native Son* on June 10. Ward
dramatizes "Bright and Morning Star." The story is
included in Edward O'Brien's *Best American Short
Stories, 1939* and *Fifty Best American Short Stories
(1914–1939)*. Begins work on new novel, *Little Sister*.
Marries Dhima Rose Meadman in August in
Episcopal church on Convent Avenue, with Ralph
Ellison serving as best man. Lives with his wife, her
two-year-old son by an earlier marriage, and his
mother-in-law in large apartment on fashionable
Hamilton Terrace in Harlem. Attends Festival of
Negro Culture held in Chicago in September. Moves
to Crompond, New York, to work on *Little Sister*
(it is never completed).

1940
Visits Chicago in February and buys house for his
family on Vincennes Avenue. Has lunch in Chicago
with W. E. B. Du Bois, Langston Hughes, and Arna
Bontemps. *Native Son* published by Harper and
Brothers March 1 and is offered by the Book-of-the-
Month Club as one of its two main selections. In
three weeks it sells 215,000 copies. Wright delivers

talk "How 'Bigger' Was Born" at Columbia University on March 12 (later published as a pamphlet by Harper, then added to future printings of *Native Son*). *Native Son* is banned in Birmingham, Alabama, libraries. Takes his first airplane flight when he accompanies *Life* magazine photographers to Chicago for an article on the South Side; tours the area with sociologist Horace Cayton, beginning long friendship (article is later canceled). Sails in April for Veracruz, Mexico, with wife, her son, mother-in-law, and wife's pianist. Rents ten-room villa in the Miraval Colony in Cuernevaca. Takes lessons in Spanish and studies the guitar. Reunited with Herbert Kline, friend from the Chicago John Reed Club, who is filming documentary *The Forgotten Village* with John Steinbeck; Wright travels with them through the countryside and takes an interest in the filming. Signs contract with John Houseman and Orson Welles for stage production of *Native Son*. Marriage becomes strained. Wright leaves Mexico in June and travels through the South alone. Visits his father, a poor and broken farm laborer, in Natchez, but is unable to make anything other than a token reconciliation with him. Goes to Chapel Hill, North Carolina, to begin collaboration with Paul Green on stage adaptation of *Native Son*. Meets producer John Houseman and drives to New York with him. Travels to Chicago to do research for book on black American life featuring photographs selected by Edwin Rosskam. Wright and Langston Hughes are guests of honor at reception given by Jack Conroy and Nelson Algren to launch magazine *New Anvil*. Returns to Chapel Hill in July to continue work with Paul Green. Elected vice-president of the League of American Writers. Harper reissues story collection as *Uncle Tom's Children: Five Long Stories* with "Bright and Morning Star" added and "The Ethics of Living Jim Crow" as an introduction. Starts divorce proceedings. Moves in with the Newtons, now at 343 Grand Avenue in Brooklyn; in the autumn Ellen Poplar moves into the Newton house. In September Wright is elected a vice-president of American Peace Mobilization, a Communist-sponsored group opposed to American involvement in World War II. Works with Houseman on revising stage version of *Native Son* (both Wright and Houseman think that Green has diverged too much from the novel); Houseman agrees that Orson Welles, who is finishing *Citizen Kane*, should direct. Story ▶

A Chronology of Richard Wright *(continued)*

"Almos' a Man" appears in *O. Henry Award Prize Stories of 1940*.

1941

In January the National Association for the Advancement of Colored People awards Wright the Spingarn Medal, given annually to the black American judged to have made the most notable achievement in the preceding year. Rehearsals for *Native Son* begin in February. Marries Ellen Poplar in Coytesville, New Jersey, on March 12. They move to 473 West 140th Street. *Native Son*, starring Canada Lee, opens at St. James Theatre on March 24 after a benefit performance for the NAACP. Reviews are generally favorable, though the play is attacked in the Hearst papers, which are hostile to Welles following *Citizen Kane*. Production runs in New York until June 15. Welles's striking but costly staging causes production to lose some money, but it recovers during successful tour of Pittsburgh, Boston, Chicago, Milwaukee, Detroit, St. Louis, and Baltimore. Wright asks the governor of New Jersey to parole Clinton Brewer, a black man imprisoned since 1923 for murdering a young woman, arguing that Brewer, who had taught himself music composition, has rehabilitated himself (Brewer is released July 8; Wright had previously sent one of his pieces to his friend, record producer and talent scout John Hammond, who arranged for Count Basie to record it). Begins novel *Black Hope* (never completed). Introduces Ellen to his family in Chicago during visit in April. Signs appeal of forty members of the League of American Writers against American intervention in the war that appears in *New Masses* May 27, and publishes "Not My People's War" in *New Masses* June 17. After Germany invades the Soviet Union, June 22, American Peace Mobilization changes its name to American People's Mobilization. Wright travels to Houston with Horace Cayton and John Hammond to accept Spingarn award from NAACP convention on June 27. Delivers enthusiastically received speech, in which his criticism of Roosevelt administration racial policies is muted in response to Communist party pressure. Lectures at Writers' Schools sponsored by the League of American Writers. Wrights move to 11 Revere Place, Brooklyn, in July. At John Hammond's request, Wright writes "Note on Jim Crow Blues" as a preface to the blues singer Josh

White's *Southern Exposure*, an album of three recordings attacking segregation. Hammond then produces recording of Paul Robeson singing Wright's blues song "King Joe," accompanied by the Count Basie orchestra. *12 Million Black Voices: A Folk History of the Negro in the United States*, with photographs selected by Edwin Rosskam (one taken by Wright), published by Viking Press in October to enthusiastic reviews. Wright reads *Dark Legend*, a psychoanalytic study of matricide by psychiatrist Fredric Wertham, then writes to Wertham about Clinton Brewer, who had murdered another young woman within months of his release. Wertham intervenes in the case and helps save Brewer from execution. (Wright and Wertham begin close friendship, and Wright becomes increasingly interested in psychoanalysis). Finishes draft of novel *The Man Who Lived Underground*. Signs petition "Communication to All American Writers" in December 16 *New Masses*, supporting America's entry into the war after the December 7 Japanese attack on Pearl Harbor.

1942

Mother and Aunt Maggie rejoin Addie in Jackson, Mississippi (brother remains in Chicago, though house on Vincennes Avenue is sold two years later). Daughter Julia, Wright's first child, born April 15. Wrights move in summer to 7 Middagh Street, a 19th-century house near the Brooklyn Bridge shared by George Davis, Carson McCullers, and other writers and artists. Excerpts from *The Man Who Lived Underground* appear in *Accent*. As the sole support of his family, Wright is classified 3-A and not drafted. Unsuccessfully tries to secure a special commission in the psychological warfare or propaganda services of the army. *Native Son* returns to Broadway in October (runs until January 1943). Publishes "What You Don't Know Won't Hurt You," article describing some of his experiences as a hospital janitor in Chicago, in December *Harper's Magazine*. Breaks quietly with the Communist party over its unwillingness to confront wartime racial discrimination and its continuing attempts to control his writing.

1943

Accompanied by Horace Cayton, Wright goes to Fisk University, Nashville, in April to deliver talk on his experiences with racism. Strong reaction from the audience leads Wright to begin autobiography ▶

A Chronology of Richard Wright *(continued)*

American Hunger. Neighbors and associates are interviewed by the Federal Bureau of Investigation. (Files obtained under the Freedom of Information Act in the 1970s show that the FBI began an investigation in December 1942 to determine if *12 Million Black Voices* was prosecutable under the sedition statutes. Although the sedition investigation is concluded in 1943, the FBI will continue to monitor Wright's activities, chiefly through the use of informers, for the remainder of his life.) Wrights move in August to 89 Lefferts Place in Brooklyn Heights. Helps organize the Citizens' Emergency Conference for Interracial Unity in response to widespread riots in Harlem following the wounding of a black soldier by white police in August. Finishes *American Hunger* in December.

1944

Writes film scenario "Melody Limited," about group of black singers during Reconstruction (scenario is never produced). Becomes friends with C. L. R. James, a Trinidad-born historian and Trotskyist, with whom he plans a book, *The Negro Speaks*, and a journal, *American Pages* (neither of these projects appear), and James's wife, Constance Webb. Writes series of radio programs on the life of a black family for producer Leston Huntley and is frustrated when Huntley is unable to place the series, in part because of criticism by middle-class blacks. Atter   party held in honor of Theodore Dreiser on June 2, where Wright and Dreiser discuss the influence of life in Chicago on their attitudes. Deepens friendship with Dorothy Norman, New York *Post* editorial writer and editor of *Twice a Year*, who introduces him to existentialist philosophy and literature. Book-of-the-Month Club tells Harper that it will accept only the first section of *American Hunger*, describing Wright's experiences in the South; Wright agrees to this arrangement. Changes title to *Black Boy*. (Second section, telling of Wright's life in Chicago, is published as *American Hunger* by Harper & Row in 1977.) Wrights vacation in August outside Ottawa and in the nearby Gatineau country in Quebec. Excerpts from second section of autobiography appear as "I Tried to Be a Communist" in *Atlantic Monthly*, August–September, making public Wright's break with the Communist party. He is denounced by various party organs, including *New Masses* and the

Daily Worker. Helps the Chicago poet Gwendolyn
Brooks to place her first book, *A Street in Bronzeville*.
Expanded version of *The Man Who Lived
Underground* is published as a novella in
Cross Section.

1945

To circumvent racial discrimination, Wrights form
the "Richelieu Realty Co." and use their lawyer as an
intermediary in buying a house at 13 Charles Street
in Greenwich Village. (Residence is delayed by their
waiting for a Communist tenant hostile to Wright to
leave and by redecorating.) Reviews books for *P.M.*
newspaper; his highly favorable review of Gertrude
Stein's *Wars I Have Seen* leads to correspondence
with her. *Black Boy: A Record of Childhood and Youth*
published by Harper and Brothers in March to
enthusiastic reviews. The book is number one on
the bestseller list from April 29 to June 6 and stirs
controversy when it is denounced as obscene in
the U.S. Senate by Democrat Theodore Bilbo of
Mississippi. Takes part in several radio programs,
including the nationally influential *Town Meeting*,
where he argues the negative on the question "Are
We Solving America's Race Problem?" In the summer,
Wrights vacation on island off Quebec City, and
Wright lectures at the Bread Loaf writers' school in
Middlebury, Vermont. Writes long introduction to
Black Metropolis, a sociological study of black
Chicago by Horace Cayton and St. Clair Drake.
Befriending a number of younger writers, white and
black, Wright helps the 20-year-old James Baldwin
win a Eugene F. Saxton Foundation Fellowship.
Publishes a favorable review of Chester Himes's
first novel, *If He Hollers Let Him Go*, and lends Himes
$1,000. In the fall, Wrights move to an apartment at
82 Washington Place in Greenwich Village to be
closer to a school for Julia. Wright undertakes four-
month lecture tour but stops after six weeks because
of exhaustion.

1946

Serves as honorary pallbearer at funeral on January
12 of poet Countee Cullen, attending service at
Salem Methodist Church in Harlem and burial at
Woodlawn Cemetery in the Bronx. By January 19,
Black Boy has sold 195,000 copies in the Harper trade
edition and 351,000 through the Book-of-the-Month
Club, making it the fourth best-selling nonfiction ▶

title of 1945. Wright, his psychiatrist friend Dr. Fredric Wertham, and others found the Lafargue Clinic, a free psychiatric clinic in Harlem. Meets Jean-Paul Sartre in New York. Receives invitation to visit France, but requests for a passport meet with opposition. Wright goes to Washington for an interview and enlists the aid of Dorothy Norman (who appoints him coeditor of *Twice a Year*), Gertrude Stein, and French cultural attaché, anthropologist Claude Lévi-Strauss, who sends him an official invitation from the French government to visit Paris for a month. Wright leaves New York on May 1. In Paris, welcomed by Gertrude Stein and by almost all the important French literary societies and circles. (Stein dies on July 27 after operation for cancer.) Meets Simone de Beauvoir and André Gide, whose *Travels in the Congo* has impressed Wright, as well as Léopold Sédar Senghor of Senegal, Aimé Césaire of Martinique, and others in the *Négritude* movement. Assists Senghor, Césaire, and Alioune Diop of Senegal in founding the magazine *Présence Africaine* and attends its first board meeting at the Brasserie Lipp. Donates a manuscript to an auction for benefit of experimental dramatist Antonin Artaud. "The Man Who Killed a Shadow" published in French in *Les Lettres Françaises* (first appears in English in 1949 in magazine *Zero*). Leaves Paris in late December and travels to London.

1947

Meets the Trinidad-born intellectual George Padmore and dines with members of the Coloured Writers' Association, including its president, Cedric Dover, author of *Half Caste*, and the colored South African journalist and novelist Peter Abrahams. Returns to New York in January. Moves with family into their Charles Street house in Greenwich Village. Helps to welcome Simone de Beauvoir to New York in the spring. Refuses offer from Hollywood producer to film *Native Son* with character Bigger Thomas changed to a white man. Wright's works are being translated into French, Italian, German, Dutch, and Czech. Decides to return to Europe permanently with his family, partially in response to the racial hostility they are encountering in New York. Sells Greenwich Village house in June. Vacations at a cottage at Wading River, Long Island, owned by a friend. Buys an Oldsmobile sedan to take to Europe. Wright, his wife, and daughter reach Paris in August. They rent rooms from a friend, Odette Lieutier, in her apartment on the rue de Lille, then move into an apartment at 166 avenue de Neuilly. Albin Michel publishes French translation of *Native Son* in autumn.

1948

Begins to read more deeply in existentialism, including Heidegger and Husserl. Sees much of Sartre and Simone de Beauvoir. Wright is particularly impressed by Camus's *The Stranger*, and begins work on an existentialist novel, eventually titled *The Outsider*. Gallimard translation of *Black Boy* wins French Critics' Award. Wright establishes friendships with the Reverend Clayton Williams, pastor of the American Church, and with Harry Goldberg of the American Library. Becomes unofficial spokesman for African-American colony in Paris, which includes James Baldwin. Visits Italy for the publication there of *Native Son*. Meets with Carlo Levi and Ignazio Silone, who later introduces him to Arthur Koestler in Paris. Interviewed by his Italian translator, Fernanda Pivano, Wright says he likes to read *Metamorphosis, Moby-Dick, Ulysses,* and *The Sound and the Fury.* Travels through Belgium to London, where he sees a performance of *Native Son* and renews friendship with George Padmore, who stirs Wright's interest in the question of colonialism in Africa. Moves with family to 14 rue Monsieur le Prince in the Latin Quarter in May. Ellen returns to New York in June to select furniture and other possessions for their new life in France. Wright is beset by recurring sinus problems and influenza. His tonsils are removed. Aids Sartre and Camus in the leadership of the Rassemblement Démocratique Révolutionnaire (RDR), an organization of intellectuals critical of both the Soviet Union and the United States. Wright plays prominent role in its writers' congress, held in Paris on December 13, delivering lengthy speech (translated by Simone de Beauvoir). Spends $6,000 to buy Paul Green's share of film rights to *Native Son* in hopes of making screen version with French director Pierre Chenal.

1949

Daughter Rachel born January 17 at the American Hospital. Wright travels again to Rome and to Switzerland, for the publication of *Black Boy*. In ▶

A Chronology of Richard Wright *(continued)*

April, James T. Farrell and Nelson Algren visit him in Paris. Suspects socialist David Rousset of trying to shift the RDR toward a more pro-American, anti-Soviet stance. Refuses to attend large RDR rally held on April 30 (organization soon splits and dissolves). In May, visits London to consult with Richard Crossman, who is including "I Tried to Be a Communist" with similar essays by Koestler, Gide, Silone, Stephen Spender, and Louis Fischer in collection *The God That Failed* (published later in year, book is widely reviewed). Continues work on his existentialist novel. Assists George Plimpton and others in launching of *Paris Review*. James Baldwin's essay "Everybody's Protest Novel," attacking Stowe's *Uncle Tom's Cabin* but including criticism of *Native Son*, sours relationship between Wright and Baldwin. Wright writes screenplay for *Native Son*, adding several dream sequences to the story, then revises it with Chenal. After Canada Lee withdraws from project because of new commitments and worsening health, Wright undertakes to play the main role of Bigger Thomas. Sails for the United States in August, briefly visiting New York before going to Chicago for filming of exteriors for *Native Son*. Sees old friends Horace Cayton, St. Clair Drake, and others. Leaves New York in September for Argentina, where film is being made (Chenal had worked there during World War II, and political pressure had blocked access to French studios). Makes brief stops in Trinidad, Brazil, and Uruguay before arriving in Buenos Aires in October. Loses 35 pounds in preparation for the role by following strict diet and exercise program. Continues working on screenplay with Chenal.

1950

Production is delayed by financial problems. Wright finds atmosphere of Argentine life under the Perón dictatorship oppressive. Filming ends in June. Wright leaves Buenos Aires in July. Stops briefly in Brazil and Trinidad, spends two weeks in Haiti, then returns to Paris by way of New York, where he visits Fredric Wertham and the Lafargue Clinic. In Paris, begins work on screenplay about Toussaint L'Ouverture of Haiti. Works with Aime Césaire on "Revelation of Negro Art," an exhibition that includes works from the Musée de l'Homme and song and dance performances at the Cité Universitaire. Vacations in the fall in the Swiss and French Alps, visiting Basel,

Zurich, and the Aoste Valley, where he is a jury member with Paul Eluard, Louis Bromfield, and others for international San Vicente literary prize. Founds and becomes president of the Franco-American Fellowship, intended to protest official American policies and oppose racial discrimination by American companies and organizations active in France. Fellowship members take precautions when meeting in anticipation of surveillance by the American government (files released in the 1970s show that the Fellowship was monitored by informers employed by the Central Intelligence Agency and the FBI).

1951

Lectures in Turin, Genoa, and Rome in January. *Sangre Negra* (the film version of *Native Son*) opens to acclaim in Buenos Aires on March 30. American distributor cuts almost 30 minutes from film under pressure from New York state censors (original length was approximately 105 minutes); shortened version opens in New York on June 16 to unfavorable reviews. (Several states ban the film, but it is shown in Beverly Hills and, in spring 1952, in Mississippi, where members of Wright's family see it.) A partially restored print is warmly received at the Venice Film Festival in August. The Milan press praises Wright's acting; in general, his performance is deemed sincere but awkward, especially by American critics who compare it with Canada Lee's stage version. Wright visits the sociologist Gunnar Myrdal in Geneva, beginning a long friendship. With Jean Cocteau, inaugurates the Cercle International du Théâtre et du Cinéma. *New Story Magazine* accepts excerpts from Jean Genet's *Our Lady of the Flowers* on Wright's recommendation. Baldwin's essay "Many Thousands Gone," an explicit attack on Wright in *Partisan Review* (November–December), leads to painful break between the writers. Submits screenplay about refugees forced to choose between sides in the Cold War to the French Association of Film Writers.

1952

Travels to England in February. Spends several months in London and Catford, Surrey, completing the first full version of *The Outsider*. Vacations with his family in Corrèze at the end of August and continues to revise and cut novel. Refuses suggestion by John Fischer, his new Harper editor, ▶

A Chronology of Richard Wright *(continued)*

that he come to the United States for the publication of his book, citing the risk that he would be subpoenaed by an anti-Communist congressional investigating committee. Begins work in December on a novel about a white psychopathic murderer, based in part on his experience with Clinton Brewer.

1953

Begins correspondence with Frantz Fanon. *The Outsider* published by Harper and Brothers in March. Reviews are mixed; sales are initially brisk but eventually disappointing in comparison to *Native Son* and *Black Boy*. Wright composes an introduction to *In the Castle of My Skin*, first novel by the young Barbados writer George Lamming. Friendship with Sartre cools as Sartre moves closer to Communism. Wright's circle of friends remains wide, including Americans such as Chester Himes and William Gardner Smith, but he begins to withdraw from official organizations and to avoid formal gatherings. He is a regular at favorite cafés such as the Monaco and Tournon, where he entertains a steady stream of visitors from America, including Elmer Carter, Dorothy Norman, Nelson Algren, E. Franklin Frazier, and Louis Wirth. Discusses treatment of Algerians in France with Ben Burns, editor of *Ebony* magazine, during his visit. Wright tells Burns that he avoids criticizing French policies for fear of being deported. Ellen Wright begins work as a literary agent with Hélène Bokanowski, a prolific translator of Wright's work. From June to August, Wright travels in the Gold Coast (then a British colony with limited self-government, after 1957 the independent country of Ghana) to collect material for a book on Africa. Boat stops briefly in Freetown, Sierra Leone, en route to Takoradi; from there travels by road 170 miles to Accra, his main stop. Meets Prime Minister Kwame Nkrumah and other members of the pro-independence Convention People's Party, as well as Osei Agyeman Prempeh II, king of the Ashanti, and other traditional leaders. Excursions take him from Accra to Cape Coast, Christianborg, and Prampram; visits slave-trading fortresses and dungeons. Travels almost 3,000 miles in a chauffeur-driven car, touring the interior through Koforidua to Mampong, and the Secondi-Takoradi to Kumasi regions. In general, Wright is fascinated by Africans but is reinforced in

his sense of self as a Western intellectual. Visits
England to discuss his impressions with George
and Dorothy Padmore before returning to Paris in
September to begin work on book about his trip.
Undergoes surgery for hernia.

1954

Revises book on Africa. Decides to write an account
of Spanish life and culture. Drives his Citroen almost
4,000 miles between August 15 and September 9 on
a route that includes Barcelona, Valencia, Saragossa,
Guadalajara, Madrid, Córdoba, Seville, Granada,
and Málaga. On September 16 State Department
and FBI officials interview Wright in Paris about his
relationship to the Communist party when he goes to
renew his passport. *Black Power: A Record of Reactions
in a Land of Pathos*, about his African trip, published
by Harper and Brothers September 22. Receives
mixed reviews in America, but is widely praised in
France. *Savage Holiday*, novel about psychopathic
murderer, is published as a paperback original by
Avon after having been rejected by Harper. Book
attracts little attention in the United States but is
well received as *Le Dieu de Mascarade* in France.
Visits Geneva with Gunnar Myrdal for further
research on Spain at the United Nations library.
Lectures on Africa in Amsterdam in October, where
he meets Margrit de Sablonière, his Dutch translator,
and begins an important friendship with her. Returns
to Spain on November 8. Hires a driver and travels
through Irun and on to Madrid, where he stays before
returning to Paris in mid-December.

1955

An old Chicago friend, the cartoonist Ollie "Bootsie"
Harrington, arrives to live in France. Wright secures
funding for his attendance at forthcoming conference
of non-aligned nations in Bandung, Indonesia, from
the Paris office of the Congress for Cultural Freedom,
an international alliance of anti-Communist
intellectuals. Returns to Spain February 20, and
spends several weeks there, including Holy Week
in Granada and Seville. Leaves Spain on April 10
for Indonesia. At Bandung, Wright shares room
with missionary Winburn T. Thomas. Leaders
attending conference include Nehru (with whom
Wright speaks), Sukarno, Sihanouk, Nasser, and Zhou
Enlai. Remains in Indonesia at home of Thomas until
May 5, working on notes of his impressions, then ▶

A Chronology of Richard Wright *(continued)*

returns to Europe via Ceylon and Kenya. Begins
writing an account of the conference. Spends July
to October with family at their new country home,
a small farm in village of Ailly in eastern Normandy.
Plans series of novels dealing with the conflicts
between individuals and society (including one
set in Aztec Mexico), but abandons the project
on the advice of Reynolds and Aswell (now with
McGraw-Hill). Returns to Paris when daughter
Rachel falls ill with scarlet fever, then goes back to
Ailly when her continued quarantine makes work
at home difficult. *Bandoeng: 1.500.000.000 hommes*.
French translation of book on nonaligned
conference, published in December.

1956

Prepares manuscript of book on Spain in February
and March, often living alone at Ailly, where he enjoys
hours of gardening. Fearing deportation, remains
silent on Algerian war of independence while in
France (will offer guarded criticism of war when
in other European countries). *The Color Curtain:
A Report on the Bandung Conference*, with an
introduction by Gunnar Myrdal, published March 19
by World Publishers in America and receives
favorable reviews. Revises and cuts book on Spain.
Adapts Louis Sapin's play *Papa Bon Dieu* as *Daddy
Goodness* but is unable to have it produced. First
Congress of Negro Artists and Writers, sponsored by
Présence Africaine and which Wright had helped plan,
meets in Paris in September, attended by delegates
from Africa, the United States, and the Caribbean.
Wright speaks on "Tradition and Industrialization:
The Tragic Plight of the African Elites" and
participates in several sessions. Suspects that *Présence
Africaine* is being secretly taken over by the French
government through anti-nationalist Africans and
considers withdrawing from its activities. Lectures
in Hamburg on "The Psychological Reactions of
Oppressed Peoples" and tours the city with Ellen.
Attends a meeting in London of the Congress for
Cultural Freedom, organized by Arthur Koestler.
Travels alone to Stockholm in late November for the
Swedish publication of *The Outsider*; it sells 35,000
copies in four days (*Native Son* had sold 75,000 copies
and *Black Boy* 65,000). Lectures in Sweden, Norway,
and Denmark before returning to Paris in early
December. Agrees to help found the American Society

for African Culture, inspired by the French Société Africaine de Culture. Returning to native material, Wright begins work on novel set in Mississippi.

1957

Aunt Maggie dies January 20 in Jackson, Mississippi, where she had been taking care of Wright's mother (Wright has continued to help support them through the years). Mother moves in with a niece, then goes to Chicago at the end of June to live with Leon Alan. *Pagan Spain* published by Harper in February to good reviews but weak sales. Works at Ailly on new novel. Travels throughout Italy with Ellen during the spring. Visits West Germany in July to interview black American servicemen stationed there. *White Man, Listen!*, a collection of essays drawn from Wright's lectures, published October 15 by Doubleday (where Edward Aswell is now an editor). The book is especially well-received by the black press in the United States.

1958

Finishes *The Long Dream*, Mississippi novel, and begins *Island of Hallucinations*, sequel set in France. Seeking to renew his passport, he is again compelled to report to the American embassy in February and sign a statement admitting his past membership in the Communist party. Becomes increasingly alienated from the black community in Paris, which is torn by suspicion and dissension; finds himself the object of resentment, including rumors that he is an agent of the FBI or the CIA. Depressed and isolated from other blacks, Wright suspects that he is being persecuted by agents of the U.S. government. Takes part in a session of the Congress for Cultural Freedom, and in seminars on American literature sponsored by the American Cultural Center in Paris. Supports Sartre and Simone de Beauvoir in their opposition to the new regime of General de Gaulle. Works on new novel at Ailly during summer. *The Long Dream* published by Doubleday in October to often hostile reviews and flat sales. When Leon Alan telegraphs that their mother is seriously ill, Wright is forced to borrow extra money from Reynolds to send to his brother. Edward Aswell, his long-time editor, dies November 5. Considers moving to England and enlists aid of Labour member of Parliament John Strachey, who obtains assurances from the Home Secretary that Wright's application for residence will be fairly considered. Wright ▶

distances himself from various organizations he had previously supported, including *Présence Africaine* and the Société Africaine de Culture.

1959

Mother dies January 14. Wright sends the manuscript of *Island of Hallucinations* to Reynolds in February. Later in the month, he spends a day with Martin Luther King, Jr., who is passing through Paris en route to India. Timothy Seldes (Aswell's successor at Doubleday) asks for major revisions in *Island of Hallucinations*; Wright puts book aside (it is never completed). Discouraged by financial worries, weak reviews, poor health, and frustrating state of his novel, Wright continues to curtail his public activities. Declines to attend the second Congress of Black Writers and Artists in Rome. Plans a study of French Africa. After Doubleday promises a $2,500 advance, Wright asks the American Society for African Culture for an additional $7,500, but is turned down; believes CIA infiltration of the organization is responsible for his rejection. Tired of what he considers to be growing American political and cultural influence in French life and in the wake of increased attacks by other expatriate black writers, Wright prepares to leave France and live in England. Sells farm at Ailly. His play *Daddy Goodness* is produced in Paris in the spring. Wright falls ill in June with attack of amoebic dysentery, probably picked up in Africa. Illness persists despite treatment at American Hospital. Vacations at the Moulin d'Andé near Saint-Pierre du Vauvray in Normandy. With daughter Julia now at the University of Cambridge, his wife Ellen and daughter Rachel establish themselves in London. Ellen works there as a literary agent and looks for a permanent home for the family. Wright begins writing haiku (eventually completes some 4,000 pieces). Harassed by British passport officials during visit to England in September. Sees George Padmore, who dies not long after Wright's visit. Wright returns to England for the funeral. Tries to obtain resident visa from the Home Office, but is denied one without explanation. Alone in Paris, he sells home on rue Monsieur le Prince and moves to a two-room apartment on rue Régis. Recovers from dysentery but continues to have intestinal problems. Among his close friends at this time are Michel and Hélène Bokanowski, Colette and Rémi Dreyfus, Simone de

Beauvoir, Ollie Harrington, and the Reverend Clayton Williams. "Big Black Good Man" is included in *Best American Stories of 1958*.

1960

The Long Dream, adapted by Ketti Frings, opens on Broadway February 17 to poor reviews and closes within a week. Translation of *The Long Dream* well-received in France, but earnings are not enough to quell Wright's deepening anxiety about money. In April, driving his own Peugeot, Wright accompanies his gastroenterologist, Victor Schwartzmann, and Dr. Schwartzmann's father to medical conference in Leiden, Holland, where he visits Margrit de Sablonière. Selects and arranges 811 haiku for possible publication. Declines offers from Congress for Cultural Freedom to attend conferences on Tolstoy in Venice and New Delhi, believing that the organization is controlled by the American government (the Congress is later shown to have received substantial covert funding from the CIA). Records series of interviews concerning his work in June for French radio. Spends much of summer at Moulin d'Andé, where he begins new novel, *A Father's Law*. Falls ill on return to Paris in September. Julia Wright decides to study at the Sorbonne and visits her father before returning to England to pack her belongings. In September, Dorothy Padmore comes to visit. Later, old Chicago friend Arna Bontemps makes his first visit to Paris. Wright delivers lecture on November 8 at the American Church on the situation of black artists and intellectuals. Accuses the American government of creating and manipulating dissension among them through spies and provocateurs. Continues to suffer from intestinal difficulties and dizzy spells. Finishes complete proofreading of collection of stories, *Eight Men* (published by World Publishers in 1961). Welcomes Langston Hughes to his home for a brief but enjoyable visit on the morning of November 26, then enters the Eugene Gibez Clinic for diagnostic examinations and convalescence. Dies there of a heart attack shortly before 11:00 P.M., November 28. Cremated, along with a copy of *Black Boy*, at the Père Lachaise cemetery December 3, where his ashes are interred. ✧

Title Page and
Early Draft
Two Facsimiles

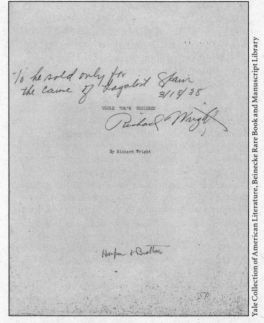

Title leaf of draft. "To be sold only for the cause of Loyalist Spain."

JOHN J. TROUNSTINE
24 WEST 55th STREET
NEW YORK

Richard Wright
3742 Indiana Avenue
Apartment #1
Chicago
Illinois

DOWN BY THE RIVERSIDE

Each step he took made the old house creak, as though the earth beneath the foundations was soggy. He wondered how long the logs which supported the house could stand against the water. But what worried him were the steps. They might wash away at any moment, then they would be trapped. He had spent all that morning trying to tie them with ropes, but he did not leave much faith. He walked to the window and glanced under his feet. He had never realized they were that rickety. He pulled back a tattered curtain, wishing the dull ache would leave his head. He had been feverish all day. Feels like Ah got the flu. Through a dirty pane he saw yellow water swirling around a corner of the barn. A steady hiss filled his ears. In the morning the water was brown. In the afternoon it was yellow. At night it was black, like a tide of restless tar. It was about six feet deep and still rising. It had risen two feet that day. There was a tiny ridge of white foam where the water struck a side of the barn and veered sharply. The seeds for spring planting were wet now. Gone gonna rot, he thought with despair. The morning before he had seen his only cow lowing and pushing through three feet of water for the hills. It was then that Mister Jeff had said that a man who would not follow a cow was a fool. Well, he had not figured it that way. This was his home. But now he would have to leave, for the water was rising, and there

Page one, draft of "Down By the Riverside"; typescript, corrected.

was no telling when or where it would stop. Two days ago he had told Bob to take the old mule to Bowman's plantation and sell it, or swap it for a boat, any kind of a boat. N non ain back here yit. Ef it ain one thing its anothaw. When it rains it pos. Shh, Lawd, ef only tha levee don break. Ef only the levee don break ...

He turned away, rubbing his forehead. A good dose of quinine would kill that fever. But he had no quinine. Lawd, have mercy!

And there was Lulu flat on her back these four days, sick with a child she could not deliver. His lips parted in silent agony. It just did not seem fair that one man should be hit so hard and so many sides at once. He shifted his body, listening for sounds from the front room, wondering how Lulu was. Ef something don happen soon Anna haveta git her outta here, some way. He leaned against a damp wall, knots keepin bobn so long? Well, in a way it was all his own fault. He had had a chance to get away and he had acted like a fool and would not take it. He had figured the water would soon go down. He had thought if he stayed he would be the first to get back to his fields and start spring plowing. But now even the mule was gone. Yes, he should have cleared-out when the Government had offered the boat. Now he had no money for a boat, and Bob had said he could not even get near that Red Cross.

He took a gourd from the wall and dipped some muddy water from a bucket. He could not swallow it. It tasted thick and bitter. He hung the gourd back and spat the water into a corner. He leaned his head, listening. It seemed he had heard the sound of a shot. There it was again. Something happenin in town, he thought. Over yellow water he heard another shot, thin, dry, far away. Mbe be trouble, mbe be trouble somewhere. It was said that white folks were threatening to conscript all Negroes they could find to pile sand- and cement-bags

Page two, draft of "Down By the Riverside"; typescript, corrected.

Have You Read?
More by Richard Wright

Other classic works by Richard Wright available from Harper Perennial:

A FATHER'S LAW

Richard Wright wrote *A Father's Law* in a six-week period near the end of his life. He never finished the novel and never managed to correct the typescript.

But his daughter Julia Wright, now his literary executor, was with him while he wrote in a remote farmhouse in the French countryside. She has written an introduction that explains how the book came to be written and why she believes it is an important addition to the Wright corpus.

"It comes from his guts and ends at the hero's 'breaking point.' It explores many themes favored by my father like guilt, the difficult relationship between the generations, the difficulty of being a black policeman and father, the difficulty of being both those things and suspecting that your own son is the murderer. It intertwines astonishingly modern themes for a novel written in 1960."

—Julia Wright

BLACK BOY

Black Boy is a classic of American autobiography, a subtly crafted narrative of Richard Wright's journey from innocence to experience in the Jim Crow South that remains a seminal work in our history about what it means to be a man, black, and Southern in America.

"Richard Wright uses vigorous and straightforward English; often there is real beauty in his words even when they are mingled with sadism."
—W. E. B. DuBois, *New York Herald Tribune*

"A major event in American literary history."
—*The New Republic*

NATIVE SON

Right from the start, Bigger Thomas had been headed
for jail. It could have been for assault or petty larceny;
by chance, it was for murder and rape. *Native Son*
tells the story of this young black man caught in a
downward spiral after he kills a young white woman in
a brief moment of panic. Set in Chicago in the 1930s,
Wright's powerful novel is an unsparing reflection on
the poverty and feelings of hopelessness experienced
by people in inner cities across the country and of
what it means to be black in America.

"Certainly, *Native Son* declares Richard Wright's
importance . . . as an American author as distinctive
as any of those now writing."
—*New York Times Book Review*

THE OUTSIDER

The Outsider, a complex tale of crime and politics,
shows the influence of French existentialist
philosophical theory as filtered through
Wright's unmistakable prose.

"It is in the description of action, especially violent
action, that Mr. Wright excels, not merely because he
can make the reader see but because he compels him
to participate. There is not a murder in the book that
the reader, at the moment of reading about it, does
not feel that he would have committed under the
same circumstances."
—Granville Hicks, *New York Times*

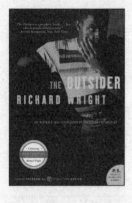

EIGHT MEN

Each of the eight stories in *Eight Men* focuses
on a black man at violent odds with a white world,
reflecting Wright's views about racism in our society
and his fascination with what he called "the struggle
of the individual in America." These poignant,
gripping stories will captivate all those who love
Wright's better-known novels.

"There is not a touch of phoniness or fakery in the
book. All eight men and all eight stories stand as
beautifully, pitifully, terribly true. . . . All the way
through this is fine, sound, good, honorable writing,
rich with insight and understanding, even when
occasionally twisted by sorrow."
—*New York Times Book Review*

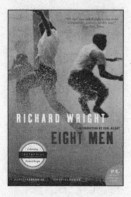

PAGAN SPAIN

Richard Wright chronicles his trip to Spain in 1954, capturing the beauty and tragedy of the country under the rigid rule of Francisco Franco.

"*Pagan Spain* is a book which required courage to write—and even greater courage to publish. For it is a volume which seems certain to call down upon another author and publisher a tempest of bitter, resentful, and frightened criticism."
　　　—Joseph G. Harrison, *Christian Science Monitor*

BLACK POWER: THREE BOOKS FROM EXILE: BLACK POWER; THE COLOR CURTAIN; AND WHITE MAN, LISTEN!

Three late books by Richard Wright—*The Color Curtain; Black Power; White Man, Listen!*—are here gathered in one volume for the first time, with a new introduction by Cornel West. The title book is one of Wright's most persuasive works of nonfiction. First published in 1954, it is his impassioned chronicle of the conditions he found on his trip to Africa's Gold Coast, then in the process of becoming the free nation of Ghana.

"The reader of *Black Power* will be grateful . . . for many fascinating and even illuminating glimpses of primitive tribal life in a country marked out for precocious political development."
　　　—*New York Times*

Don't miss the next book by your favorite author. Sign up now for AuthorTracker by visiting www.AuthorTracker.com.